ROUGH **BEAST**

ALSO BY ANTHONY OLCOTT

MURDER AT THE RED OCTOBER
MAY DAY IN MAGADAN

ROUGH **BEAST**

· ·
AN IVAN DUVAKIN NOVEL
· ·

ANTHONY OLCOTT

CHARLES SCRIBNER'S SONS • NEW YORK

MAXWELL MACMILLAN CANADA • TORONTO

MAXWELL MACMILLAN INTERNATIONAL • NEW YORK • OXFORD • SINGAPORE • SYDNEY

Charles Scribner's Sons   Maxwell Macmillan Canada, Inc.
Macmillan Publishing Company 1200 Eglinton Avenue East,
866 Third Avenue   Suite 200
New York, NY 10022   Don Mills, Ontario M3C 3N1

Macmillan Publishing Company is part of the Maxwell Communication Group of Companies.

Library of Congress Cataloging-in-Publication Data
Olcott, Anthony.
     Rough beast: an Ivan Duvakin novel / Anthony Olcott.
      p. cm.
     ISBN 0-684-19406-6
     I. Title.
     PS3565.L28R68 1992
     813'.54—dc20   91-37406

10 9 8 7 6 5 4 3 2

Printed in the United States of America

For Ali, Andy, and now Hillie,
but most of all for Martha

ROUGH **BEAST**

I
t's damn hard work to get born in Moscow, and it's damn hard work to live there; little surprise, then, that dying in Moscow should prove such a nightmare. It was after four in the morning, and Duvakin had been reporting the murder of his wife for over two hours.

The man in the next chair kept lolling onto him, a smeary blob of drunken drool and coagulating blood oozing from his swollen purple lower lip, dampening Duvakin's suit each time he shoved the man back. The drunk was burbling out an account of some fight, which a young female officer, grown too stout for her inspector's uniform, black roots showing through her straw-blond (and straw-stiff) hair, was slowly two-fingering into a typewriter, one key of which stuck every time she struck it. Never looking up, she would raise a hand to halt the drunk's slobbering account of being assaulted or assaulting someone (Duvakin couldn't make out which), free the key, pause for a drag on her Belomorkanal cigarette, then return to her patient tapping, her gnawed nails yellow from the cheap tobacco.

Duvakin's own inspector came back into the room, from a fifteen-minute errand he didn't bother to explain. "So, Ivan Petrovich, what you're saying is that the lock seemed normal?" Duvakin stared wearily up at him, a broad-faced Ukrainian with the mud of the village still on his boots, ears like the handles on a breakfast mug, a gap between his front teeth wide enough to hold his cigarette, and little brown-yellow eyes that looked like the windows in a building undergoing renovation—dull, empty, and without light.

"Pavlovich," Duvakin corrected him wearily, then ran his hand over his head, which felt remote and wooden. "Ivan Pavlovich. . . . No sign of a forced entry, if that's what you mean."

When he had returned to the flat late that evening there had been no sign of anything, in fact, except the hoarse hammering of the Finnish and normally silent refrigerator. A worried glance into the kitchen told Duvakin that the stout-hearted compressor was doing its brave best to cool the entire kitchen down to plus two degrees, because the door had been left wide open, its innards ravished. Jars were opened and strewn about; a slab of sausage was bitten into; a kefir container lay on its side, the gooey contents in a puddle on the bottom.

Galya would *never* have left her beloved machine like that, he knew, his heart seconding the compressor.

The light was out in the next room, too, but his echoing footsteps told him all he needed to know. The rug was gone, a real Afghan oriental that Galya had treated like a baby. And the Yugoslav living room suite, and the television too. The JVC. The room sounded hollow.

Even though Galya had paid several thousands for it—she had never dared tell him exactly how much—Duvakin wasn't surprised to find Galya's *antikvariat* still in the next room. No apartment burglars would bother with an enormous table and eight massive chairs of some dark wood as heavy as pig iron, or with the matching cabinet, carved all over with deer heads and flying birds and fat naked babies, which had been squeezed into the flat only by knocking off the top two angels and the biggest deer head.

The burglars hadn't ignored the *antikvariat*'s contents, though. The chairs had been gutted, their stuffing flung about, and every drawer and cupboard of the vast breakfront had been ripped out, the contents scattered over what little floor the huge *antikvariat* didn't already occupy. Quite a pile, which is why it had taken Duvakin some moments to understand that among the heaps of sheets, towels, and tablecloths were Galya's feet, bare but for nylons, extending, toes down.

"How about the balcony?" The inspector had found whatever he had been looking for between his back molars, and was now pressing on with his investigation. His posture and voice made plain that whatever Duvakin had to say, it was all the same to him; he would tap into this typewriter the size of an accordion whatever words left Duvakin's mouth, have Duvakin sign the bottom of every page, and then sew the whole thing into a brown folder, to be filed and forgotten.

"Christ, man, we're on the fifth floor!"

The inspector shrugged. "Regular monkeys, some of these break-and-enter boys. Had one last summer, fellow found him swinging his leg over the balcony on the seventeenth floor, hit him with the broom before he thought too much about it. When they finally scraped him together, turned out the lad was about twelve. Then again"—the inspector straightened his shoulders, then cracked his knuckles luxuriantly—"the kid already had two convictions. So, maybe whoever this was, they got in by the balcony?"

"I didn't look at the balcony," Duvakin said sullenly, too weary even to blink. He wondered for a moment about the trees; Fotieva Street was just one block from the mad traffic of Leninski Prospekt, but might have been in the country: a narrow lane overhung with lilacs and honeysuckle and cottonwoods, from which ravens squawked beside their windows. Then he shrugged; climbed, flew, appeared in a puff of smoke—what did it matter?

There had been more than an hour between his call to 02 and the arrival of the inspector, leaving him lots of time to contemplate the huddle on the floor that had once been his wife, to whom he could now give no aid other than the decent cover of a blanket. He couldn't even close her eyelids one last time, because there was nothing left of her face.

"Looks like she happened to come home as they were stripping the flat," the militia inspector had said when he finally arrived. With his ballpoint he poked gingerly at the pulp that had been Galya's head. "Bad luck, really, matter of minutes. Place like this"— he had stood up and looked around with the rapid indifference of the professional—"they can clean out in ten minutes, leave you as naked as baby Jesus . . . but still better than getting your face done with *that*."

He meant the chair leg, an iron-black spindle carved with a spiral below, topped by a fluted ball the size of a grapefruit. The one loose leg, which Duvakin had promised to fix "one day." Too late now, because whoever it was that Galya had surprised in the apartment had ripped that wobbly leg free and then battered her until her face was unrecognizable, black crusts of blood shot with splinters of bone. She had not had time even to remove her new fur hat, which now looked like some forest creature run over on the highway.

Beyond the inspector's hunched shoulders the first thin red edge of dawn could be seen oozing under the far clouds, highlighting the dust rings on the windowsill among the reptilian succulents that someone was cultivating in emtpy tins of Hungarian peas. The office was no more than a warren of underpaid, overtired, and not very bright militiamen, who were all but drowning in a flood of whores and currency speculators and drug users and thieves and drunks and black marketeers.

The inspector pulled his form-plus-four-carbons from the type-writer, fussed with assembling a new wad of paper and carbons to insert. "Now, what property is missing?"

Numb, as if after a long painful session with an unfamiliar dentist, Duvakin began to enumerate.

"A color television, you say? A JVC?" The inspector made an appreciative face. "And a rug, room size, from Afghanistan? . . . tape recorder, Panasonic? Finnish coat? . . . French boots?" The man repeated each item, pecking the list laboriously into the machine, each item making it clearer that the militia would do nothing. Plums like that in your apartment, chum? You goddamn *asked* for it! And anyway, like they say, dirty hands don't wash dirty hands clean. Come right down to it, it's almost like your wife killed herself, isn't it?

Duvakin cradled his head in hands still smelling faintly of Galya's blood. The unspoken allegation hung in the air like stale smoke, because the same thought had flitted, unwanted, through Duvakin's brain, too. Not surprisingly, since that was what he and Galya had been fighting about, earlier that evening, why he had stormed out, fearful that he might punch his wife if he did not.

Possessions, curse them. Objects. Bloody, goddamned *things*.

When Galya had forced her way into his life, back there in Magadan, she hadn't come alone; all sorts of *things* had tumbled in after her, like dead autumn leaves in the wake of a speeding truck. At first he had liked it, liked having someone to cook proper meals for him, and choose his clothes, and find oranges when there were none to be had anywhere. More or less an orphan, then in the army, then a country militiaman brought to Moscow to work night watch at the down-at-heels Red October Hotel (boarded up now, supposedly being converted into an office building, for foreign businessmen to rent, for hard currency), Duvakin had lived most of his life as a bachelor. A single room, clothes bought off the rack in dusty, empty stores, shoes that melted in the rain . . . living on bread, groats, boiled potatoes, and maybe a cold, underfed pullet to gnaw at the hotel buffet, when the girls there thought to save him one. But what began as a blessing—Galya's energy and ambition— had turned inexorably into a curse. Where did all these *things* come from? Duvakin didn't even know. There was nothing in the stores, and the prices for what little there was were like a cruel joke. A kilo of grubby little carrots now cost more than what Duvakin used to make in a month, when he first joined the militia. True, the chaotic price rises, the growing inflation, had caused so much concern at his ministry that salaries had been raised. He now made almost 350 a month. Or three dollars, if you could find someone fool enough to part with them. Galya though, the last time he had asked, admitted her salary was "around eleven." Thousand? Hundred? Per month, per year? Duvakin could only guess, gaping at the flow of goods into their life. The *antikvariat*, the almost Italian suit he was still wearing, the Finnish refrigerator, the Yugoslav divan and two armchairs that clogged their bedroom, their color television, a real JVC . . .

Making Duvakin feel turgid with possessions he neither needed nor wanted, but of which he could be now be robbed.

Like the solid mound of his belly, which pouched before him now, a stranger in his lap. He had been thin before Galya. Well, not *thin*, but his thighs hadn't been like stuffed peppers, and his *fingers* . . . He looked with distaste at his fingers. *Thick* now, like a bureaucrat's.

As he had sat waiting for the militia, Duvakin studied the

hillock which had once been his wife, horrified at his own numb mixture of grief and—he was appalled to recognize—a certain relief. They had fought that evening, as they fought most evenings. Moscow had been kinder to her than to him, after the return from the Far East. With the *aerobiki* and the weight loss, you'd think Galya was thirty, maybe less. At a distance anyway. Which was precisely where Duvakin had generally felt himself to be lately—at a distance.

Left behind, even.

Plucked from far eastern Magadan as mysteriously as he had been exiled there in the first place, back in Moscow Duvakin had traced an erratic and slow, but still relentless descent. Flunked out of the Higher Party School, he had been moved to the Ministry of Oil and Gas, where he settled toward the bottom of the *nomenklatura* jobs like a dead leaf in a pond, finally coming to rest in the muck of the cadre division; he had very little idea what the papers he and the others moved about meant, but they seemed to concern ideological education of the workers.

As might be expected of a woman and a doctor who had appointed herself his wife in order to get herself out of Magadan, Galya had flourished with Moscow registration. Within two days of arrival she found work, in a birthing hospital. Later, a women's clinic, and then, about the same time they moved to their present apartment on Fotieva Street, a cooperative, also doing women's complaints. Duvakin never asked about her work; it embarrassed him. And she never volunteered, after the first time, when she exulted that the Japanese tape recorder the size of a suitcase she had just pulled out of its box cost "only" seven hundred rubles.

"*Seven hundred rubles!*" Duvakin had choked. "I make *two hundred and sixty-three* rubles a month, and you make one eighty-six! Where are we going to get *seven hundred* from?"

Galya had smiled, superior, a little distant, then looked at her lap. "From down there—all of us lady Muscovites have one, you know, and those of us who can, they pay to take care of it. . . ."

Now she was a blanketed mound, her hands poking out the sides, hands that had kneaded so much dough for him, sliced so many onions, making the delicious meals that had made him stout.

Her legs too, poking from the blanket's bottom as they might on a hot summer morning . . .

Because of a video-recording machine.

Duvakin had returned from work that afternoon, early and angry. Galya, just going out, had cut off his explanations curtly. Stepping into her costly French boots and belting up her electric-blue, iridescent Finnish winter coat, she had said tersely, "Dasha just called. Somebody at her office has a cousin who came back from America this afternoon, and she's pretty sure that if we go right away, they'll sell her the video recorder."

Dasha was also a doctor in Galya's medical cooperative, who had invited Galya and him to her flat to watch cassettes a few times, where they had perched uncomfortably on ottomans, peering around the bottoms of the more favored guests, who had rated chairs. The visits reminded Duvakin of how it had been when people first started to get televisions, except for what they were now crowding into the proud owner's apartment to watch—one time it was some film about America that included several almost nude women fighting in a pool of mud, another time it was a James Bond, which had been so poorly overdubbed that Duvakin was never certain whose automobile had just blown up, and why.

"Video recorder? What does Dasha want with another video recorder?" Duvakin had asked, furious at Galya's indifference to the news he was trying to tell her, that they wanted to reassign him to new work.

"That's just it, woodenhead." Galya had grabbed the door handle, refusing to listen. "They're cousins, so they'll sell to the cousin, and the cousin will sell it to Dasha, and Dasha will sell it to *us*. Don't you see, we'll have a video of our own!"

"Video! Video! For a *year* I've heard nothing but that cursed video! We can't go to the kino hall like everyone else, if you want to watch movies?" Duvakin had blazed, disgusted, and fearing the inevitable consequences—an endless search for black-market installers and repairmen, the nerve-wrenching wrangling to scrounge cassettes.

Galya in turn had been so angry she spat as she shouted. "I'm *not* everybody else, damn it! And I'm tired of *waiting*! Waiting,

waiting, all my life they tell me I can't have a nice dress, or boots that the zipper doesn't rip, or a machine so I can watch films in my own house. In America *everybody* has videos, Rivka's cousin was there, visiting his son that emigrated, he says the *Negroes* even have them. Remember, the American Negroes that we were always supposed to be outraged about, for getting lynched and put in jail with Angela Davis? Well, *they've* got videos and I *don't!* Well, *not anymore!*"

Prophetic words, Duvakin thought bitterly, fatigue and pain and worry gnawing like wood ants at his heart. He had to ask the inspector to repeat his question.

"I said, who else would have a key, then? Apart from you, I mean?" The inspector rubbed his hands on his pants, plainly thinking things would be easier if Duvakin would just confess.

Who would have a key? Anya, of course.

Anya, Annechka, long-legged, busty, sometimes blond, sometimes brunette Anna.

"Your daughter?" The inspector's head went up, his eyes showing the first glint of alertness.

"*Her* daughter, my wife's. By an earlier marriage, I guess."

"But the last name is yours?"

"God knows what name she uses, but it isn't mine. Berezkina maybe, like her mother."

"Know where she is?"

No, no more than he knew where she had come from. The first Duvakin knew of her existence was when Galya had announced they were moving, again.

Why? he had barked, having already endured three moves in five years, and liking the apartment they now had.

Because my daughter is coming to live with us, Galya had explained, irrefutable.

Soon afterward Duvakin became a parent for the first time, the father of a nineteen-year old girl. She was a full head taller than her mother, and half a head taller than him. She called him Papenka and mussed up the edges of his bald spot when she wanted money from him, and called him old gob when she didn't. She filled the bathroom with stockings and bright underwear and cans of strange imported chemicals and long strands of hair, and she writhed and wriggled her way through dreams which Duvakin was too embarrassed even to remember he had had.

In fact, she wasn't even Anya anymore. "Susi is what you're to call me," she had waltzed in to announce, three nights after failing to come home from a New Year's party, an absence which she didn't deign to explain, but during which she had lopped her hair short, dyed it platinum blond with green at the temples, and acquired one earring made from an enameled red star that should have been pinning back the visor of a soldier's fur cap. She had informed them of her new name as she sat at the kitchen table, wolfing down the chopped-meat cutlets that Galya was forking from the pan, and ignoring the advice and imprecations that came with them. Duvakin's angry attempt to toss in some scolding of his own had ended in red-faced retreat when he discovered Anya-Susi was wearing only a faded Levi's shirt so short it would have been immodest even if she hadn't been sitting with her legs tucked up beneath her.

"You see what happens because you won't adopt her!" Galya had raged afterward, thoroughly confusing Duvakin. *Adopt* her? You don't adopt full-grown girls, with big long legs, and a scattering of freckles over the cheeks and nose, even in winter, and two laughs, the more common one high-pitched and faintly derisive, but the other one, though infrequent, a wonderful low chuckle that seemed to burst from deep beneath the girl's large . . .

But what *do* you do with her?

Not turn her over to this beagle-eyed inspector as a prime suspect, anyway. That much Duvakin knew.

It was some measure of how much Duvakin tried not to think about the girl that it was about a half hour after he found his wife's body before he thought to look in the girl's room as well. His stomach had tightened; would he find *her* dead too? Duvakin could not have said what he expected when he swung open the girl's door, but it was not the hotellike cleanliness he found. The single daybed made precisely, the coverlet pulled taut, the blanket showing through the cover linen in an exact diamond of wool, the square pillow plump above it. The desk, which Duvakin didn't remember ever having seen, was empty save for three pencils, lined up accurately, like a militiaman's rank stripes. He opened the wardrobe. Two empty hangers, and, far back in the shadows of a shelf, one of Anya-Susi's red star earrings, apparently forgotten when she moved out.

"She just moved out?" The inspector cocked an eyebrow in dim-witted skepticism. "Coincidentally? On the same day her mother was murdered?"

Duvakin didn't need the innuendo, because he had wondered the same thing himself, in spite of his best efforts not to. Anya was petulant, Anya was wild, but to *kill* her mother? He shrugged.

"We had a fight. Earlier."

"You seem to fight a lot. Your wife, your daughter . . ."

"A disagreement, then, and she isn't my daughter. I told you that. She has this tutor, for English—her mother wants her to sit for the university entrance exams again. Wanted her to. Except the tutor is more . . . well, I suspect . . ."

He remembered the blat of the doorbell, Anya's shriek of "I've got it!" as she flung open the door, leaping into the arms of the grinning young man who had stepped across the threshold, fur cap pushed back on curly blond hair. In the flurry of limbs Duvakin had noted that the girl was considerably more stocking than skirt, and wondered, not for the first time, precisely what kind of lessons Galya was paying for.

"Ciao, pops," the cretin mumbled, waving as they passed along to the girl's room, intertwined like laundry in a washtub.

Then came the faint, rhythmic clatter of Anya-Susi's bed. God, Duvakin had flared, the girl snogging away in the bedroom, his wife out heaven only knew where, scouring Moscow for *things* . . .

"I wanted to talk to somebody . . . I had just been told about something at work. About a transfer."

The inspector wasn't typing. He was methodically loosening the tobacco in his cigarette, studying Duvakin with an expression that Duvakin was almost certain had come from an inspector's handbook. How to Look Skeptical.

"A transfer?"

"Well, a new assignment . . . and they wouldn't have wanted to go. My wife and her daughter. I wanted to talk about it, but . . ."

But but but. What happened was what seemed always to happen. His wife walked out, the girl laughed in his face, he erupted and flung the tutor down the stairwell in a clatter of limbs and coat and book and shaggy fur hat. Followed, two minutes later, by red-faced, furious Anya. He should apologize, Duvakin thought vaguely, before remembering that he now had something more pressing to tell the girl.

That she was an orphan.

The inspector tapped at his space bar, bringing Duvakin back to the station. "So you have no idea where she would have gone?"

Unless, Duvakin wondered still about Anya, she already knew?

His reply was surly with fatigue and hopelessness. "She wasn't under the *antikvariat*, and she wasn't in her room. Beyond that, your guess is as good as mine." Whatever his suspicions, Duvakin was damned if he was to give this bone-idle investigator so easy a solution as Anya-Susi.

"Well, we'll have to be asking around, I suppose . . ." the inspector said with weary indifference when he at last understood Duvakin would say no more. He pushed the last few pages of the protocol across the desk for Duvakin's ink-blotchy signature, then tapped the pages together, stretched. He made ready to stand, but paused, hands braced on the edge of the flimsy pinewood desk.

"I suppose I should have asked, but . . . you said you were reassigned. Where to?"

Duvakin looked over the inspector's plump shoulder, where morning was turning the sky the color of a rusted-through bucket. It was Moscow, almost February, almost morning. Not yet spring, no longer winter. Overcast, as it had been since October, low gray clouds spilling round gray snowflakes, like dirty saucers from a waiter's tray.

"Novii Uzen. In western Kazakhstan."

For the first time that day, someone looked at Duvakin with genuine sympathy.

Duvakin had seen death; what he had never had to deal with before was the housekeeping that follows, after the militia's questions were finally over. What ought he to put in the space on the bookshelf where the JVC used to sit? Should he sell Galya's clothes, the ones the thieves hadn't taken, or save them for Anya? Anya was slimmer and taller than her mother. What about the apartment registration? Would he lose their flat on Fotieva, now that he was entitled to fewer cubic meters? And the burial, what of the burial? How do you bury someone in Moscow? He would have to find out, but his knees ached just antici-pating the lines at the registry offices, at the cemeteries scattered all over Moscow, the harried, surly secretaries at the bureaus where they took orders for coffins, and for trucks to cart them with.

And Kazakhstan? What now of Kazakhstan?

Duvakin had refused the assignment of Novii Uzen, of course, even before he discovered his wife had been murdered. Lord, to be stuck out on a peninsula on the east side of the Caspian, the desert side, without even the grapes and sturgeon that would console him if it were the western, Azerbaijani shore. Nearly as far from Alma-Ata, the republic capital, as it was from Moscow, Novii Uzen was the very definition of nowhere.

More precisely, he had *tried* to refuse the assignment, but the man who had sent for him hadn't exactly asked.

Ministers don't, as a rule. They order.

Especially Igor Aleksandrovich Chistoplotskii, minister of energy for the entire Russian Republic.

Christ Model II, Duvakin's fellow workers had dubbed their boss, and the Ayatollah of Oil, and, most often, the Bloody American.

Life hadn't gotten so bizarre—yet, anyway—that the first minister of energy of the newly sovereign Russia was really an American, and the blood was metaphoric, but during that long drive out Leninski Prospekt and over to Profsoiuznaya neither fact consoled Duvakin, who sat in the middle of the Volga's backseat nearly rigid with fear. What had begun as a drearily normal morning at work had suddenly come unglued when Kostenko, head of personnel, secretively summoned Duvakin to his office, then plopped a thickish cardboard file onto the desk between them, smoothing his broad, tobacco-stained Cossack mustache with a tobacco-stained finger as he peered thoughtfully at Duvakin.

"You're a deep one and no mistake, Ivan Palych. A person would never think to look at you that you'd been in the MVD."

A purge, Duvakin had thought in panic, part of the post-coup witch-hunt that still smoldered on. "Dmitri Ivanich, believe me, I was thrown out of the militia years ago—Brezhnev was still alive, even! And as for the Party membership, they made me join! And I never paid dues after 1986!"

Kostenko had waved the explanation away. "They've been reading your file, Ivan Palych. Your *whole* file." He glanced up at the ceiling, to make clear who "they" were. "The minister thinks you're just the man he needs."

All his objections and protestations were waved away and Duvakin was packed into a Volga idling outside, which drove him out to an ordinary one-room apartment in an ordinary high-rise in an ordinary new region, almost at the Moscow city limits.

Where with a slither in his bowels, which might have been dysentery save that it was cold as slush, Duvakin found himself face-to-face with the wire-thin, leather-complexioned, icicle-eyed minister. Duvakin knew at once why panic had raged through the new ministry all fall and winter, heads tumbling like frost-softened apples. Chistoplotskii had taken over the revamped ministry the September before, part of the dust settling after the August explosion. He was the perfect choice for the newly sovereign Russia—a field geologist, trained in part abroad, who had been nowhere near Moscow during the coup, because he was out beyond Tiumen, slapping mosquitoes and searching for oil.

Soviet ministers once had been as solid as the ministry buildings over which they presided, men made bulky and dense by the food and drink and authority to which simpler mortals had no access. Like the Ministry of Foreign Affairs building—vast, impressive, its top in the clouds, its flanks so broad you could get around it only with difficulty.

Not so Chistoplotskii. Tall—a meter ninety or ninety-three and slender. Not thin—slender. The gray at the temples of his well-cut hair suggested he was perhaps older than he looked, which was maybe early forties. There was something about him, though, that made it hard to guess his age, as if he were a foreigner. His complexion was so tan he might have been a football star or a tennis player. All this was sinister, in a man who controlled thousands of jobs and millions of rubles.

Even this "office" to which Duvakin was driven. The room maybe three meters across and five long, with tiles poorly laid over a rough-poured concrete-slab floor, so that many of the tiles were cracked and some missing. Instead of the furniture Duvakin would have expected if this had been an apartment—the divan that folds down into Mama's and Papa's bed, the armchair that folds out to become a child's bed, the footstool that opens to disgorge bedding, the table that serves as table and desk and work surface, the combination china cupboard–wardrobe–bookcase–pantry—he saw only a desk, with a table behind. Not even a good desk and table, but simple pine, as if made in Vladimir or someplace. The only item on the desk that was remotely personal was a small calendar picturing the elongated heart shape of some leggy blonde's bare rear end, still beaded from a bath, her left breast cradled in the thick yellow towel like some costly, plump fruit. The computer on top of the table was foreign, of course, as was the telephone. Only one telephone, but with a lot of buttons down one side, like the kind Duvakin had seen in foreign films. The closest thing to apartment furniture was the divan, but instead of the rug that would have hung behind it in an apartment there was a huge map, marked with stylized oil derricks of various sizes. Big ones along both sides of the Caspian, smaller ones in Moldova, big ones again in the Far East.

The room was austere and businesslike and totally confusing, because anyone important enough to have a whole apartment to use just as an office was far too important to have such ratty furniture. "My hideaway," Chistoplotskii had explained as he sat. "The only place I can get work done, without all those damn stupid meetings. Let's dispense with the Russian obsequies, shall we, and be like Americans instead, just get down to *efishent biznes?*"

Which he had done, explaining that he wanted Duvakin to go to Novii Uzen, on Kazakhstan's Mangyshlak peninsula.

To help steal an election.

That wasn't exactly what Chistoplotskii said, of course, but that's what the job amounted to. The Mangyshlak oil fields, in extreme western Kazakhstan, were seriously underproducing, which in turn was threatening Chistoplotskii's production schedules, and denying the newborn Russian Republic fuel—and what was more important, cash—just at the moment it needed both most desperately.

"The director down there is a fellow named Ibragimov, Mogammed Alievich, or Alioglu, as they insist. Doesn't matter though, because everybody calls him Momish. Apparently it's a respectful nickname, one of those Asian kind of things," Chistoplotskii had grimaced with distaste. "He only became director a couple of years ago, after the riots, but he's been in Novii Uzen for, God, I don't know, twenty-something years. Replaced the last director. All the reports speak of Ibragimov as a model manager. Ibragimov did this, and Ibragimov did that. . . . The man has built houses, schools, clinics. . . . After the riots he built a youth club, and he has organized a soccer league."

"So what's the problem, Comrade Minister?" Duvakin had finally asked, puzzlement grown larger than his fear.

"We're none of us comrades anymore, remember?" Chistoplotskii grinned, without humor. Then, eyes like blue marbles, he said, "Only one problem, really—the man can't seem to get oil out of the ground, and up here to us. Which is why we have to get rid of Momish, Ivan Palych."

The two words "we" and "rid" had careened around in Duvakin's fear-stiff brain like loose barrels in an empty boxcar, until finally he ventured a tremulous "Couldn't you just fire him?"

Chistoplotskii had sighed, stood, gone to the window, his shoulder blades standing out against the fabric of his shirt. Addressing the glass, he said, "To tell you the truth, things are such a *kasha* now, I don't even know. A year ago, sure. . . . Now? I'm a Russian minister, and he's in Kazakhstan. But he's an Azerbaijani by nationality, so the Kazakhs don't want him, either. The man Momish forced out was a Kazakh, and the people in the Alma-Ata ministry want the directorship back, for one of theirs. Momish though, all those years in Novii Uzen, before he was director and after he became head even more so, he's been stuffing the place with his own. Azerbaijanis, Lezgins, Avars . . . Dagestani types," Chistoplotskii said wearily. "So even if I can figure out who has the right to fire him and get it done, what then? Momish's people will walk out, and then the Mangyshlak fields will go down, completely down, for six weeks, two months *minimum*. Longer, probably, since the Kazakhs would insist on the jobs going to Kazakhs, and there's more French whores in Moscow than there are Kazakh roughnecks and roustabouts. You know what that would do to us, to lose Mangyshlak, pumps, drills, loading facilities, *everything*, completely shut it down, when stocks were already drawn down to tank-bottom last winter? You think you were cold and hungry *last* winter? We lose Mangyshlak now, and you'll want to think about moving maybe to Romania!"

Then the minister had sat next to Duvakin on the divan, his hand on Duvakin's arm. Stiff with apprehension and surprise, Duvakin smelled French soap and foreign toothpaste. "See, this isn't a question of just replacing a director, if his chair is going to be taken by someone as corrupt as the old one. It's a new world we have to live in now, Ivan Palych, a hungry, pushing world. We can't just sit back and wait while some papa bird in Moscow drops worms in our mouths. The workers have to understand that it is *they* who hold the future of the country in their hands, *they* who determine whether Russia lives or just becomes history, like Rome or Byzantium, some place little Japs and Yankees and Fritzes have to memorize to get their school-attendance certificates!"

The idea so agitated Chistoplotskii that he stood again, pacing almost manically. "In our oil towns it always used to be that the sector chief also ran the local government. It made sense; the only reason there *were* towns in most of those places was because there was the oil. They were always appointed, of course, until this business with elections started. In fact, that's how Momish took over in the first place. They had an election after the first riots; he won, then appointed a commission and forced his own boss to 'retire.' "

Which was precisely the script that Duvakin was now being sent to Novii Uzen to repeat. Now that Kazakhstan had become a sovereign republic in a stillborn commonwealth, the president had mandated new elections.

"You want me to go take part in the Novii Uzen elections?" Duvakin was too astonished even to feel horrified. "What, am I to *run?*"

Chistoplotskii had laughed a sharp vulpine bark. "No, Ivan Palych, I want you to go down there and help do whatever you can to persuade those workers to throw Momish out. We've got a man down there already, Ermolov, Boris Nikolaevich, a good man, who's been working to make the people of Novii Uzen understand that *they* are the owners, *they* are the bosses. But it's a bigger job than we anticipated. You're the man we need, to help the workers of Novii Uzen understand that it isn't whether you're Lezgin or Kazakh, or whether or not some 'they' is sending down soap or cheese, it's how *you* work, and what *you* do for your country, that is going to determine what your country can do for you. Teach them democracy, in other words." Chistoplotskii had bared his teeth in what probably was meant to be a smile. "I want you to go help Ermolov, Ivan Palych. But you better understand something, keep it in mind. Up here in Moscow, maybe people think democracy is just a market economy and publishing *Dr. Zhivago* and having bare tits in the movies. Out in places like Novii Uzen, though, they understand what democracy is really about."

Here the minister had looked Duvakin full in the face, his expression illuminated, as if he were speaking from on top of a tank. "It's about power. Who's in charge. And you know what they call it, don't you, when people fight for power?"

"War" was the answer the minister had given when he answered himself, but "senseless" was the word that stayed on Duvakin's tongue, as he did his best to stammer refusal through the minister's self-absorbed oration. Call it fighting for power or call it grabbing for spoils; Duvakin's experience had convinced him that life moved in one direction only, no matter who was in charge. Life begins bad, and it gets worse. Russia had been one enormous prison camp, but at least people ate; now there was freedom, and damn little else. Freedom for people to trample each other into the mud, clawing to be first at what little swill was thrown into the trough.

Like Galya, killed for a television, a coat, and some boots.

Her body was already on the way to the morgue before Duvakin had thought to look for his wife's shiny nylon winter coat and spike-heeled French boots. They weren't behind the door, weren't in the kitchen, hadn't been on the body. And suddenly, with a nausea that had driven him to heave in the toilet, Duvakin understood. Someone had battered her head to a pulp, taken her coat and boots, then fixed himself a snack from the refrigerator.

Exhausted but sleepless, Duvakin passed the next days wandering the apartment, stabbing feebly at the dull tidying required after a death. His sleep and waking came unpinned from day and night, so events floated about in his brain like the fat in soup, glistening bright clear circles, but each entire in itself, not linking up with any other. For reasons Duvakin didn't understand, Anya-Susi's daybed was the only place he could occasionally find sleep. Maybe because the room was empty and the bed anonymous. No odors lingered, no stray hairs from the now bare mattress stuck to his shirts. Everything in Anya's room was different from how it had been in the room he shared with Galya—the sounds from traffic outside, the cracks in the plaster overhead, the way the street lights shone through the curtain. The mother was dead, and the girl had moved out. . . .

Galya's friends learned of her death by telepathy, as far as Duvakin could understand. Most of them were women like her—strong, brisk, and capable. It was they who found the burial space in the Vaganov cemetery, they who arranged the funeral service in the brightly painted little church just down from Oktiabr Square, opposite the French embassy.

Duvakin had never buried anyone before Galya. His father had died in the war, in some birch swamp near Gomel. Not that Duvakin's mother would have been likely to give Pavel Duvakin much of a funeral even if he had died in his bed; fearing for his own skin, Duvakin's father had walked out on his wife and three-year-old Vanya, because his wife's second cousin, a pig farmer, had just been unmasked as a Trotskyist agent of British imperialism. Worn out by raising a boy through the war alone, Duvakin's mother had been carried off quietly by grippe while Duvakin was in the army; on his return he found her fresh mound in the densely packed graveyard that once had surrounded the village church but now stood alone, the church dynamited and the bricks used as landfill. Duvakin remembered standing by the roughly fenced plot, staring at the vertical plank at its head, fixed with a photograph of his mother, younger than he remembered her, Orthodox crosses burned into the wood on either side of it. Those crosses had nearly cost Duvakin the village militiaman's post, until objections from the village atheist were overcome by general sympathy for an orphan, and the fact that Duvakins had *always* been policemen in the village, even under the czars.

He left his wife's burial unconsoled and aching, his soul a scorching wound that only vodka seemed to cool, a bit. Duvakin had never really believed in the atheism he had once preached for a living, back in Magadan, but his life in Russia had accustomed him to regarding the moaning long-haired priests, the fervent women demonstratively crossing themselves, and the smell of burning bees-wax and incense as dark superstition and ignorance. Fortunately there was no shortage of vodka at the memorial dinner Galya's girl-friends had also organized, to follow the burial. The *antikvariat* groaned beneath glass and china, all of the traditional memorial dishes conjured up, inexplicably, out of the universal deficits. Fish, for mourning, and beetroot salad, to remind the guests of our common end, and bread, for rising, and vodka, to dampen the earth, and drown the tears, and sweeten the memory. . . .

Duvakin sat numbly at the head of the *antikvariat*, studying the echoing new bareness of the burgled apartment the way an amputee studies his stump when the anesthetic first wears off. There were about fifteen people, all Galya's colleagues or friends. Constrained a little by death, they also vibrated with the suppressed liveliness of people jubilant that disaster has struck another, and not them. Duvakin sat among them like a leper, aching with fatigue, incomprehension, uncertainty. Opposite him, leaned against the window, the women had put a portrait of Galya, garlanded in black ribbon. An old photo, which one of these iron-willed women had stolen from the Red Roll of Honored Workers at the clinic where Galya had worked when they first moved to Moscow; Duvakin, even to his own surprise, had proved to have no photos of his wife. Now Galya glowered at him, a black-and-white, steely-eyed trench soldier in the war on disease, hair under her conical doctor's cap crimped into a home permanent that would have stopped shrapnel, lips pomaded with something that looked like a bruise in the photo, neck heavy and jowls solid. Her face seemed to scold him—Like *this* you let my friends see me? Fifteen kilos heavier than I was when I died, with that horrible Magadan hair and the first real Moscow lipstick that I had ever come across, that now I wouldn't put on a cow?

Duvakin averted his eyes, certain now that his only future, and the quickest path to his own grave, lay down the neck of a bottle. Not waiting for a toast, not even looking for someone with whom to click glasses, Duvakin drained his vodka, then poured himself another and downed that too, savoring the corroding fire of the liquor as it scorched its way along his gullet. Lord God, he thought, feeling the energy drain from him like juice from a rusted-through tin, what am I to do now?

"Ivan Palych?" someone suddenly whispered in his ear, breaking his reverie. "Ivan Palych . . . what about the *antikvariat?*" The words hit his ear like warm spittle.

He turned, to focus on a raven-haired woman of considerable handsomeness, in spite of her obvious middle age and even more obvious iron character. Tatiana something, Duvakin dimly recalled, the administrator of the elite English-language school two blocks up Fotieva. "A proper bitch," he remembered Galya saying of her, "but she's always got theater tickets. The theaters always put some aside for school groups."

" 'Scuse me?" he mumbed, surprised that his lips were so rubbery.

"The *antikvariat* . . . will you be selling it? It's big—and, well . . . has all those memories. Ten thousand?"

Duvakin turned his head around to look her full in the face. He had understood every word, but comprehended nothing. She was still squatting, holding on to the arm of his chair, but the haughty, slightly amused tilt of her head, the glint in her eyes, made it seem somehow that she was standing, arms crossed and ruler tapping impatiently, while tardy little Vanya dragged himself guiltily to his bench in the third-year room. Addled, he said nothing.

"Fifteen, then, but no more," this Tatiana said with a pinch of her lips, then stood, smoothing the precise folds in her pleaded skirt. "After all, we'd also have to pay to get it out to the dacha."

Duvakin nodded absently, then realized from the woman's smile that he had probably just sold his furniture.

"Ivan Palych? Ivan Palych?" Duvakin felt a hand on his thigh. He looked down, then over: Frida, with the lined thin face and fat pear-shaped bottom, whose hair was cut in hedgehoggy tufts and who wore black-rimmed eyeglasses with one cracked and taped lens. She was a nurse, and she was registered to live only in Klin, an impossibly long trip from their clinic. She had been among the first to come with food and advice and, before long, an offer to take over as many of Galya's functions—including those in the bed, if Duvakin desired—on the sole condition that he help her obtain Moscow registration.

"It's the telephone, Ivan Palych," Frida said in a voice dripping with so much concern and understanding that Duvakin jerked himself upright, away from her. "I wouldn't disturb you, but . . . they said it was official."

Duvakin blinked, looked at his watch, then found it wasn't on his wrist. Where had he left it? What time was it? The guests were still at the table—nobody had left and nobody had passed out—so it couldn't be terribly late. Grunting with the effort, Duvakin got up and went out into the hall, expecting some militiaman, with the news perhaps that Galya's boots had been found.

"Duvakin," he mumbled into the receiver, his lips still thick.

"Ivan Palych! Chistoplotskii here. They told me about your tragedy, and I wanted to express my condolences."

With a jerk like that of a wildly skidding car whose wheels have just touched bare pavement, Duvakin's life returned to where it had been just before he had opened his apartment door to find his wife dead.

"Jesus! Kazakhstan!" he blurted, nearly dropping the phone.

The energy minister snapped icily, "You have guests. I would remind you that your assignment and your destination are secret."

"Assignment?" Duvakin repeated in a whisper, glancing to see whether anyone at the table had heard. "But I refuse the assignment! I told you already, I refuse."

The voice was smooth. "What has Moscow to offer you now, except memories and red tape? Work, Ivan Palych, that's what you need. Pour yourself into it, rise above your sorrow. Do something for your poor wife, too, roll back some of this tide of, well, excuse me for saying so, but shit that's about to drown us. Your people need you, Ivan Palych. . . . Russia needs you."

"Me?" Duvakin squeaked. "Me? Look, I *told* you—"

Hearing the distress in his voice, Frida sidled back again, to put a dry and turgid forearm on his shoulder, wobbly like a hot-water bottle. Angry, he jerked himself away.

"This is the world you want your stepdaughter to inherit, Ivan Palych?" the minister was asking, with scorn. "How will you explain to her that you did nothing to make Russia better when your country was in need?"

Duvakin was hard put not to snort. Explain it to Anya? He couldn't even *find* her.

Though, heaven as witness, he had tried. Since the murder, time no longer seemed to flow but to writhe, leaping hours ahead, then standing still, even seeming—when he caught himself planning to put this question or that to Galya—to loop backward. Through all this tangle, though, had stretched the trembling thread of that question: What had become of the girl?

The first time he went looking he had found the local kids where he expected to, in the next stairwell over, on the second-floor landing. About twelve of them, sexes impossible to make out, with their identical nylon jackets and their lanky hair and their knit caps that said "SKI." They had a tape recorder and two guitars, a candle stuck onto the radiator, which the house committee had turned off in an attempt to get them to congregate elsewhere, and a clutch of wine bottles, some the light green of empty, others the darker green of full. They were howling some song in English, yapping up the stairwell like homeless dogs baying at the moon.

They paid Duvakin no attention as he approached, until he grabbed the bigger of the two guitar players by his lapels, dragged him from his stair, and, grunting, shoved him against the wall, hard enough to force a wheeze from the youth's shocked face.

"*Scum!*" Duvakin shouted, banging the boy for emphasis. "When you open your mouth, I want to hear just one thing come out of it, understand? Berezkina, Anya. Where is she?" Another bang, to make sure he was listening.

The boy's face had gone from the ash of blank shock to the crimson of anger and confusion.

"You damn old shit, your brains freeze up?" the kid growled, white spots blossoming like frostbite on his furious cheeks. "Get your fucking paws off me!"

Duvakin had held him up higher and shook him, too angry even to be astonished that he had this strength. "Susi, she called herself. Blonde. Height of one of your whores over there behind me, lived in the next stairwell over, but moved out, not long ago. Where is she?"

"Susi? Don't know no Susi," the kid mumbled, but his eyes, shifting as he looked over Duvakin's shoulder, said that was a lie.

"Different crowd, old man," someone said behind him. Duvakin turned, to look at another long-haired, wispy-mustached punk, little different from the one in whose throat Duvakin still kept his fist. "Older . . ."

"Susi? She runs with the Steelheads, down at the Institute?" one of the girls asked the stairwell in general. "Remember, last summer, that disco?"

"Steelheads?"

"The Metallurgical Institute, down behind the metro. . . ."

"Oktiabr Square," someone else said.

"Next to the park, there's a club, for students . . . A disco . . . They hang out there . . . Call themselves Steelheads," disjointed, half-fearful, half-disrespectful voices answered from around the darkened stairwell. "She never spoke to us, in fact." Then, plaintive: "She's older than us . . . she called us kids. . . ."

No other news of Anya in their courtyard, or on their street. And frequent nightmares provided other explanations, which left Duvakin wide awake and caked in sweat, shivering on the daybed. Anya battering her mother, Anya cowering as the mother is battered, Anya who looked like her mother . . .

Just then Tatiana the school principal came by, carrying plates to the kitchen. She paused to whisper in Duvakin's free ear, a warm wet tickle. "Seventeen thousand, but it's robbery, and I can't do a kopek more."

Revulsion rose like a rictus; suddenly Moscow, his life, his past, all this seemed like the hemorrhoids on the backside of hell. Moscow was huge, and got bigger every year, more people on the buses, more lines, more dirt. Nobody gave a damn about anything anymore, everybody at everyone else like rats in a bucket. Nothing worked, no one cared. Even the goddamn weather! All summer the smog hung in the air like brown galantine, and all winter . . . Christ, the past few years, "Russian winter" was becoming as much of a joke as "Soviet might," seven long dirty months of ankle-deep slush on the sidewalks, muddy lakes between curb and bus large enough to raise bream in, endless clouds the color and texture of the cotton wadding in an old beggar woman's winter underwear.

So what would it be like, to look out a window and see sun? To just go where you wanted, when you wanted? To wear what *you* wanted? Think what you wanted?

What would it be like to feel worth something again?

Am I going to do this? Duvakin suddenly wondered. Am I actually going to go to Novii Uzen?

To his own astonishment, the first shoots of life he had felt since Galya's murder began to push their pallid way through the dead thatch at the bottom of his soul.

But the girl? What of the girl?

Duvakin remembered another night, when he had gone to look for her at the Metallurgical Institute. Even at the bus stop out on Leninski Prospekt you could hear the music, or feel it, really: vibrations tickling across your diaphragm. He had sprinted past the shuttered ice-cream, newspaper, and tobacco kiosks, up the long, low stairs, past the pillars three stories tall, and under a display clock that was meant to give time and temperature, but now lacked so many bulbs that the alternating patterns suggested the clock was playing dominoes against itself, to kill time. Duvakin remembered his breath, a blue fog against the courtyard lights, and glittering ice shimmering in the air around the indistinct groups of milling people who huddled in the shadows, their occasional guffaws punctuating their muttering. The moon rode low behind the dark and silent carnival attractions of Gorki Park, beyond the institute's back fence.

Coming into the bulging heat of the disco, Duvakin was aware of the young men, who eyed him as dogs do a rabbit. One was in baggy pants held up by suspenders, with no shirt to cover his slab-like chest and pumpkin-sized arms; another was thin as a razor, in a sleeveless black undershirt with a grinning death's-head painted across it. Girls, too, their apron-sized skirts cupping their bottoms as tightly as did the young men against whom they rubbed and purred, their hair gnarled and knotted and dyed and bleached, their eyes slathered with color and knowing things of which Duvakin had never dared even dream. Writhing, all of them, so many eels in a bait bucket, to the sounds that crashed from the edge of the stage like bits of bombed-out building being bulldozed into a crater, the rising-falling-rising shriek of some creature neither man nor woman who, if he/she had not been visible gyrating spasmodically in the smoky red and yellow stage lights, might have been thought to be pinned in the rubble.

No Susi there either, or perhaps a hundred Susis, a thousand, multiplying in that dim red caterwauling with the amorphic speed of a nightmare.

This is the future, Duvakin had thought, nauseated. This is what they all want. This is freedom. . . .

"I'll go," Duvakin decided suddenly, surprising even himself. "I'll do it . . . I'll go."

"Good, I knew you would, I knew Russia could count on you. A man will bring the documents and money in the morning, he'll have your instructions." Chistoplotskii was brisk again. "Well done, Duvakin . . . you're a fellow your Anya can be proud of!"

Sensing the minister was about to hang up, Duvakin was convulsed with panic. "But wait! I need more than that! What am I doing? That other man will be in charge? The one you told me about? Boris something? Ermolaev?"

The minister suddenly sounded mournful. "That's a problem, I'm afraid. You're a clever lad, so you'll be able to get your feet under you down there. Unfortunately though, you'll have to work out what needs to be done on your own now."

"But what about that What's-His-Name, Ermolaev, Ermolov? You said he was down there?" Duvakin was already wishing he could retract his impulsive agreement.

"A terrible tragedy, just terrible. Two days ago Ermolov was conducting an inspection, apparently, in an old building, and there was a gas explosion. The building came down on top of him."

"Dead?" Duvakin squeaked, feeling the word had become too familiar.

"Fellow left a four-year-old son. See, like I told you, Pavel Ivanych, democracy is a dangerous game, so you be careful. I'd wish you luck, but I know that's the one thing you'll have by the bucket, so let's just say 'see you later,' all right?"

"Ivan Pavlovich," Duvakin corrected the minister, when he finally got his breath back, but the line was already dead.

E xcuse me, please, sir. You are bound to Novii Uzen?"

Startled, Duvakin stumbled off the end of the gangplank, almost pitching himself into the arms of the man who had asked him the unexpected question. The fellow was a local of some sort, dark and hairy, but his Russian was all right, apart from a Caucasian accent and an odd choice of words.

"What?" He hastily straightened himself, then bent down for his dropped diplomat's briefcase, nearly butting heads with the other man, who had ducked even faster, and was now cradling the case, smiling a broad white-and-gold smile.

"I am asking, sir, you are going to Novii Uzen?" His inky black eyes twinkled as he nodded vaguely in the direction of a white Niva, the only car standing on the dock. Across the corroded dock and beyond the rusting crane gantries stood stacks of the same concrete-slab apartments as might be seen in every city from Kaliningrad to Vladivostok, from Ashkhabad to Arkhangelsk, irregular veins of tarring daubing over the stress cracks in the walls, which the sun here had bleached the color of old bone. Duvakin offered no reply, instead looking wearily out over the crowd that milled about the dock under a blinding sun.

So this is Shevchenko, eh? he thought, with dull surprise, just beginning to understand that this person had come to pick him up at the dock, which was impossible, because no one knew he was coming, and even if they had, Duvakin had been supposed to fly to this, the city closest to Novii Uzen. If a cast-concrete rusting excrescence of Soviet-era slums a thousand miles south of Moscow could presume to be called a city. Duvakin, scratched at his unshaven stubble and looked south, wondering how far it was to Iran.

The driver's "instructions" had proved to be four thousand rubles, bound into two neat packets, an official letter from Chistoplotskii, I. A., to Ibragimov, M. A., naming Duvakin, I. P., a "temporary interministerial liaison," and two airplane tickets, both of them Moscow–Shevchenko.

"Where's the girl?" the driver had asked in the freezing pre-dawn. "Supposed to be two of you."

"Where's the return ticket?" Duvakin had countered. "And what the hell am I suppose to do when I get there?"

"Beats the devil out of me, friend, I just drive. Here, sign the receipt. And hop it—the plane leaves at oh-seven-fifty."

Actually, takeoff had been around noon, but that was close enough, these days. When his airplane had finally grunted its way into the sky and wheeled over the sulfur and dun of late-winter Moscow, Duvakin had sighed, feeling like a man slipping off shoes which were a half size too tight.

Why had he agreed to go to Novii Uzen, especially after the news about Ermolov? God knew it wasn't out of patriotism or duty; the ministry was simply where he worked, and if Moscow, and Russia beyond it, were something deeper and more complicated than simply the names of the places where he lived, that tangled sense of patriotic responsibility most definitely did not extend to Novii Uzen. Even if the old Union had not collapsed, and Kazakhstan were still part of *his* country, Novii Uzen would have meant nothing to him; it might have been on the backside of the moon, for all it connected with Duvakin's sense of his citizenship. He didn't want to suppose he had agreed just for the chance to leave Moscow, to escape from Galya's girlfriends, from the memories. Or maybe to put the girl, Anya-Susi, behind thirty-nine horizons, and with them his gnawing suspicions about her, alternating with washes of guilt and impotent pity?

It must have been *something* like that though; by the time the plane broke through to bright cold sunshine, Duvakin was whistling softly to himself, serene with anticipation.

All right, so maybe he *had* felt caged, by Moscow, and the life he had had with Galya, and his dust-dull paper-twitching at the ministry, and the complexities of that girl; maybe he *was* running away . . .

But running away, that was also starting over, right?

Duvakin had entered the militia right out of the army, back under Khrushchev, posted to his native village. Apart from his uniform all he owned in the world then was a pair of Chinese basketball shoes, a white shirt that he saved for New Year's parties, and a pair of linen pants cut so high they had to be buttoned across the ribs, and even then they fell down, because he had no belt, or belly either. The village store was closed more days than it was open, the peasants were bound like serfs to the land because they had no passports, and a year could go by before you'd see a wheeled vehicle other than a truck or a tractor. No televisions or tape recorders then; the only music in the village came from homemade records, scratched into discarded X rays at traveling booths that set up during the infrequent fairs. But by God, June evenings, the swallows darting against the milk-white and violet sky of a northern summer, they'd wind up the village's only gramophone and dance until it got so dark that all you could see was the glowing dots of cigarette ends and the dull glimmer of the girls' white sweaters as the couples wandered wearily homeward through the dew-scented tendrils of mist.

It seemed a big world then, a good world, where he and everybody else was finally able to get on with building a decent life. The people at the top told everyone "We're building communism!" so the next guy down said, "Build communism!" and the guys on the bottom, whatever the devil they were doing, why it must be communism they were building, mustn't it? So we could leave America in the dustbin of history, become the envy of the rest of the world.

Then, about the time Duvakin had moved to Moscow, one by one, people were starting to wonder just what the devil it was they *were* building. A persistent wondering whisper in the inner ear— suppose it isn't communism we're all laboring for, but just a good life for those fat old farts up there on the reviewing stand?

Later, somewhere around the time that Duvakin's foolish curiosity had gotten him kicked down the long tube to Magadan, suddenly *everybody* understood that nobody was building *anything*, and never had been.

Stunned by that discovery, everybody had kept it to himself for a while, while also taking care to fork as much onto his own plate as he could, whenever the platter was passed around. Came a time, though, when nobody could pretend any longer. The ships ran into the bridges, the trains ran into each other, the atomic power stations melted down, and some pimple-faced teenager from Germany—from the home of the Reich, for God's sake!—was able to lark an airplane the size of an ice-cream booth through all the eagle-eyed, hawk-winged guardians of the Motherland, and land it in the middle of Red Square.

After that people said it out loud—Soviet designers can't design, Soviet planners can't plan, Soviet drivers can't drive, Soviet teachers can't teach, Soviet farmers can't farm, Soviet doctors can't heal, and most of all, Soviet leaders can't lead. Brezhnev was incompetent; his family and friends were crooks. Khrushchev had been incompetent, too, and Lenin was a power-blind maniac. The only competent leader the country had ever had was Stalin, who was only competent at killing.

It cripples a man, to learn day by day, piece by piece, that everything he had ever been taught, everything he had ever believed that the country stood for, all that was a lie. And the people in charge had known it was a lie.

Little wonder, then, that the place had finally all caved in, like the nose on a syphilitic whore.

Christ, in Moscow *everything* felt like a lie. Duvakin possessed more than he had ever had in his life, and felt poor. Food and clothes had disappeared from the shops, and he was putting on weight, going from plump to fat, growing out of the suits Galya had somebody sew for him, using Bulgarian cloth but following Italian patterns. No one trusted the politicians or the administrators or the television or the newspapers or anything, and yet everyone clamored for them to do something. About the Jews or the Masons or Stalin or the economy or the Uzbeks or crime and corruption or the environment or the schools or the buses or the empty shops.

Those who might do good did nothing but talk, while those who could do evil worked round the clock, with the energy of spotted demons.

So whatever might be waiting for him in this Novii Uzen, he thought as he attacked the tray of boiled chicken that the stewardess had plopped in front of him, it was at least a blank page, which would give him an opportunity to fill it with a better, braver, and more useful Duvakin.

Soon after that the pilot announced that Kazakh officials were now demanding payment for landing permission in hard currency, and so they would be putting down in Astrakhan instead.

Astrakhan, on the mouth of the Volga, is an ancient and ugly city, all dust, heat, and flies dancing in a hypnotic shimmer. The pack of panicky, outraged passengers had rushed into the airport to lay siege to the Air Russia office, waving bona fides from places of employ, wads of money, and wailing airsick infants, but the only administrator unlucky enough to have been on duty resolutely shook off all the threats and offers; she was a Cossack with red-gold teeth and dyed blond hair, who was so stuffed into her uniform that the buttons restraining her milkmaid's bosom threatened to explode across the waiting hall. Her refusals to help weren't even especially rude; they were just adamant.

"I didn't make them slant-eyed monkeys decide to leave Russia, so you can't hardly expect me to get 'em to come back in. Where are you to sleep? Please, here is the entire hall, sleep where you wish. And there is food as well. The buffet usually opens around three, and sometimes there is kielbasa. And if the Kazakhs want you there so bad, maybe they'll send their own plane, eh?"

The waiting area was a glass hangar which the sun, even in late February, warmed like an oven, cooking up a rich stink of baby and sweaty wool and soured cheese. People milled without hope, jackets over arms, fanning their faces, or sat, knees spread, chests heaving in the airless, baking room, into which people were packed as tightly as sweet peppers into a jar. Sweating stickily in his Moscow overcoat, Duvakin had milled with them, endlessly circling in vain search for an empty seat.

Then, suddenly, Duvakin realized: Why am I standing around this shithole, waiting for someone *else* to do something?

Now whistling jauntily, he set off to find some way of getting to Shevchenko. Or Ak Tau, as it was now apparently redubbed.

Of which there proved to be two. Intercity bus two hundred kilometers across the sunbaked salt flats and sand dunes of the Caspian Depression, to Gurev, and from there go by rail to Shevchenko–Ak Tau.

Or directly, by overnight boat.

Duvakin had never before been on a body of water large enough to let him lose sight of land, and the bloated red sun dissolving into an undulating horizon had immediately convinced his knees and stomach that the boat was about to sink. Unable to endure the coffinlike bunk below decks (for which he had paid seven hundred rubles), Duvakin passed the night clinging to the railing, dozing between fits of retching.

"I might be going to Novii Uzen," Duvakin finally replied to the anxiously waiting young man; his voice was harsh with salt and surly with sleeplessness. "But what business is that of yours?"

Now this young man with a mustache like a horse's mane and a smile more gold than tooth studied Duvakin's face intently, as if verifying the sleepless, stubbled face against some other photo or description. "No, I am not mistaken!" he shouted, dark brown eyes gleaming. "You *are* Ivan Pavlovich, from Moscow!" Then he shifted the briefcase to one hand and reached with the other to take Duvakin's bag.

Not pausing to answer Duvakin's "And who the devil are you?" the slender young man threaded his way through the throngs still spilling down the gangway.

Then Duvakin remembered that all his money and his passport were in the briefcase.

"*Wait*, damn it!"

The wharf was chaos, crowds of mostly dark little people overburdened with bulging, rope-tied suitcases and flimsy cardboard cartons from which bits of bicycles and pedal cars wrapped in greased tissue paper had burst; gold-toothed women in bright floral dresses and fringed head scarves giving suck to children the color of shoes as they sat guard on piles of boxed-up vacuum cleaners; gold-toothed men in cheap cloth caps like the ones statues of Lenin use to wave at their invisible crowds, gesticulating angrily with the private-car owners who were bargaining ferociously for fares; little boys chasing each other wildly through the crowd and around the legs of the two militiamen who stood, hats back on their heads, gossiping and impassively studying the crowd before them.

The fellow was already in the Niva, windows up and the engine running. It began to creep forward, and a bolt of panic jabbed through Duvakin. "Hey!" he shouted, jogging over to pound on the miniature truck. "Hey, where are you going with my bags?"

"It is all right, Ivan Pavlovich, I take care of it, you don't have to show them to customs."

"Customs?" Duvakin looked back at what he had thought were militiamen; indeed, instead of proper insignia, they had green-and-white armbands, and were poking fastidiously at someone's bundle.

The car door hit Duvakin's knee, spilling chill air down his leg as well. "Feel the cool?" The driver leaned across, patting the seat, which was covered with a fleece. "This is Momish's own car, sir. There are only two other cars with conditioning on the whole peninsula."

Duvakin froze, right hand on the door handle.

Momish, the boss of Mangyshlak, the man whom Duvakin had been sent here to find cause to vote out of office? Like what's-his-name, Ermolov, had? Who was now dead?

"I am sorry!" the driver bleated as he leaped from behind the wheel and came around, misunderstanding Duvakin's hesitation. "Of course you are not to open your own door—forgive me! I was trying to bring the car closer, that's all! We are provincials here, excuse me!"

Of course, Duvakin thought with relief, I am a Boss. A bigshot, from Moscow. Fear wasn't much, as protection went, but it was all he had, and Duvakin was going to have to use it while he got his bearings. Especially if his enemy was a man who had just had him picked up from a boat no one could have known he was on.

"Does Momish have flunkies waiting at the airport and the train station too?" he asked, dry and Bosslike, after the young man had jumped back behind the wheel and pulled expertly away from the dock, escaping the crush of cars on the outside of the protective fence by driving over a concrete island, then speeding away on the wrong side of the road.

"Oh my, no!" The fellow laughed off the insult as if he had never heard a funnier joke.

Novii Uzen was only 140 kilometers from Ak Tau, but within a few minutes Duvakin was intensely grateful that he had been met, and so spared a bus or something even worse. The road was a ribbon of asphalt, crumbled at the edges to about the width of a lane and a half; at first it followed a tangle of leaking pipes over brackish pools of some iridescent fluids, then abandoned them, to strike off through a flat, rocky country of widely spaced low shrubs and ground covered with dry brown and white flakes, like the bottom of a stale rye bread. With the conditioning blowing small Arctics up his leg Duvakin could not judge the temperature, but the sun sat high in the milky-white sky, obscured just enough to make its disc visible. The only relief in the undulating plain was the power line, which looped long arcs from pylon to pylon, marching off across the desert from no apparent place to no apparent place; the only break from the monotony was an infrequent tanker truck, the front of the ovoid tank so much higher than the back that it looked like an animal with its hind legs broken, and the even more infrequent cows, wandering alone through the scrub in an apparently vain search for something with which to put flesh between fly-bitten hide and hard bony ribs.

"Well," Duvakin said after a time, "I suppose someone telephoned from Moscow then?"

Again that sidesplitting laugh, which was beginning to get on Duvakin's nerves. "Oh my, that would not have been possible, alas." Again that formal, slightly rusty touch to the driver's Russian, even though it was grammatically perfect. "You see, Novii Uzen isn't quite on the telephone yet."

"What do you mean, isn't *quite* on the telephone?"

No laugh now. "The Kazakhs have promised next year they will join the city to the commonwealth network, or the year after that at the latest, but . . ."

"But what?"

With the look of the flunky who tells you his opinion but takes no responsibility for it, the driver stared grimly over the steeing wheel and said, "The Kazakhs lie to us now. It was better when we had our own district, Mangyshlak district. But those cowardly sheep-followers are afraid of us Lezgins, so they made Mangyshlak part of Gurev district."

"Lezgin?"

"I am Lezgin." The driver smiled. "My name is Abdulla. My people are very ancient, with many historical achievements. When people in France still lived in caves, my people were making buildings four, five, even seven stories tall!"

Instead of pursuing this dubious history, Duvakin asked, "But what if there's an accident or something? How do you get the word out?"

Abdulla's smile dimmed. He looked ahead again, answered stiffly. "Momish has a radio linkup with the army in Ak Tau; they can contact the authorities."

Duvakin watched the empty landscape slide by and wondered where the boundary of Momish's influence lay. No buildings, no trees, almost no vehicles, and now, he learned, no telephone.

Christ, it was like being on another planet. He crossed his legs, trying to force himself to concentrate, because the planet, it seemed, belonged to Momish.

They were already in the town when Duvakin woke up, his eyes sticky with rheum.

"What . . . what time is it?" He rubbed his eyes, peering at the twilight beyond the windshield, where the oncoming cars had their headlights on.

"About two." Abdulla was hunched forward to see through the murk. "Anticyclone—it brings down sand from the Aral." A traffic light shone dull crimson through the gloom, and Abdulla relaxed; the car stopped. "This was Lenin Prospekt. It has no name now, but over there is the Café Dustball, straight ahead our famous fountain, the city administration building down there to the right, on Auezov Square . . ." Abdulla waved his hands, pointing out vague shapes in the shimmering, shifting light. "Unfortunately, the sand makes it difficult to see."

"This is all because of the Aral?" Duvakin had heard about how the Aral Sea was almost dried up, leaving vast flats of salt and mud exposed to battering sun and blowing winds, but up in Moscow he had paid it no attention; nowadays, everybody was crying doom and gloom about everything—Lake Baikal is polluted, the northern peoples are dying, the Uzbeks are stealing Russian water, Leningrad's water was too poisoned to drink, the fruits and vegetables had so many fertilizer salts in them that you'd die if you ate them, and the mothers were so degenerate they were having pinheaded children that they couldn't nurse anyway, because the milk in their breasts was saltier than seawater. Plus AIDS, plus riots, plus train wrecks, plus inflation—so who could care about some pond out in Central Asia?

What he now saw from the windows of the Niva was considerably less abstract: an undulating curtain of grit through which the sun glowered like a dim ember, a few townspeople stumbling about with their faces covered and their heads bowed, like victims of some terrible war.

Duvakin knew that nothing in this dismal town was more than twenty years old, and yet all of it looked two hundred; the buildings were three- and four-story blocks of cut limestone, their stucco façades peeling away or mottled black with mildew, sand-scoured to irregular blotches of paint and bare cement, more windows than not covered with wood or missing.

"What's wrong with all those buildings? They're abandoned?" Duvakin pointed at the apartments on either side.

Abdulla shook his head, not laughing. "Sand-reapers, that's what we call them. It's the Armenian architects up in Alma-Ata do this to us, they think it's just a joke that we call this place the City of the Seven Winds. They make our windows some way so that the wind pops them right out, like caps off a beer bottle." The young man studied the building to their left for a moment, then said more darkly, "I use to think they were just stupid. Now I know they do it on purpose, trying to choke us on their dust." Abdulla's brief frown was like the toothy slash of a huge pike, snatching a duckling from the surface of a placid pond.

Along the sidewalks and between some of the buildings anemic cottonwoods wilted, leafless and dust-covered, their trunks scrawled with initials, their limbs broken as high as the children could reach. There were few people on the streets, presumably because of the sandstorm, but there was no shortage of sheep, which the people of Novii Uzen seemed to keep the way people in other towns kept dogs. Duvakin saw sheep tethered in playgrounds, penned in courtyards, wandering loose and apparently unsupervised, cropping at ground so bare Duvakin wondered whether they ate gravel. They even passed one sheep which sat patiently in the back of a faded green Zhiguli, mechanically chewing as it watched the world with dull yellow eyes.

Then, as suddenly as they had entered the town, they were beyond it, on a narrow ribbon of asphalt attended by massive oil pumps on both sides, dipping endlessly up and down, like huge iron birds ripping tirelessly at some carrion.

"Where are we going?" Duvakin tried to sound uninterested, not panicked. "Shouldn't I present myself to this Ibragimov?"

"He must meet today with voters," Abdulla said gravely. "The capital has ordered a new municipal election, so I take you to the ministry rest houses." Abdulla gestured at the road ahead, which disappeared in the shimmering sandy air. "You must wash, eat, refresh yourself." Then, as if apologizing, he added, "And shave."

About ten kilometers beyond the town they slowed, turned onto a sand-strewn asphalted road that led arrow-straight to a high green gate made of a tin sheet welded over bars; Abdulla got out, fiddled with a padlock, then swung the gate open, to reveal a cluster of one-story cottages, freshly whitewashed, their roofs painted the same green as the gate. Shrubs that had no leaves but that Duvakin knew to be rosebushes lined some of the paths, and high shrubs—already with leaves, like knives—lined the others. Oleanders? Was that what they were called? Most of the sternly pruned trees were still leafless and thus anonymous, but some of them were already heavy with buds.

"Almonds," Abdulla explained, reverentially touching a branch that hung close to the front door of the cottage he was showing Duvakin into. "They should be blossoming soon."

"There's snow up to here back in Moscow." Duvakin waved vaguely, stunned by the comfort of the cabin. Just two rooms, plus a little kitchen, but the floor was tiled and the walls whitewashed. A sofa and two chairs like their Yugoslav suite at home, except that this was orange plush, and much higher-backed. A desk, a bookcase, a television . . .

"A video player?" Duvakin gaped at the rectangle, which blinked with a glowing blue: 12:00, 12:00, 12:00.

Abdulla smiled apologetically, then switched on the television, which Duvakin saw was a JVC like the one they had lost, but much bigger. Something that looked like a colored version of the sand-storm came on. "Novii Uzen doesn't receive any transmissions yet. Before the coup there were plans to build relays in Mangyshlak to send in Moscow programs, but now Alma-Ata won't pay for Russian broadcasts, and we don't want their damn Kazakh. Anyway, that's the big house." Abdulla pointed at a larger building that could just be seen through the shrubs, beneath a low palm. "Your meals are prepared there, but they will serve them in here for you. For your privacy. And anything else you might want, too"—he pointed at the desk, where there was a modern-looking brown telephone—"just phone."

"You said there isn't any telephone service." Duvakin rubbed his neck, the sand gritting painfully.

"That'll connect you to the main house, and they'll put you through to town. To Momish, or me, or anybody else you might want. All the officials are on this network."

Everybody I'm supposed to try to get fired, Duvakin thought nervously, then remembered Ermolov; which cottage had *he* lived in, before the building fell on him?

Abdulla showed him the bedroom, then went into the bath-room, where serious, almost grim, he said, "I am afraid that I must warn you, Ivan Palych, there is very great danger here . . ."

The journey, the exhaustion, the knowledge that he was on this peninsula a thousand kilometers from anywhere with all travel, all communication controlled by the man whose career he had been sent to destroy, and who might well have destroyed Ermolov—all this was suddenly too much for Duvakin, who sat, light-headed and dizzy, feeling miserably like a sheep put in the care of a wolf.

Abdulla twisted a faucet, which emitted a shuddering gasp, coughed twice, and then spat a yellow-brown trickle. "You must never drink this water ever, Ivan Pavlovich, not even a drop! It is piped from the Amu Darya, and is too poisoned for life."

Friendship!" the driver barked, jerking the bus to a stop on the windy outskirts of the city, throwing the doors open before a view of two blocks of apartments, sun-pounded bare hummocks of rock-hard dirt, and, quivering in the distance, the tireless oil pumps. Curious and somehow hostile, the driver watched him; three-day beard over a receding chin, big swollen belly, arms like lesser men's legs, eyebrows that were fierce black slashes across a face the color of a beer bottle, the driver made the hairs on Duvakin's neck stand up. The front window was hung with miniature soccer pennants, and a sun-faded photo of some fierce-looking man in a turban was taped to the dash.

Duvakin finally heaved himself out of the bus, the only person to do so. The driver watched him a moment longer, then shrugged and slammed the doors. The bus was already pulling away before Duvakin saw that nothing marked the place as a bus stop.

Wondering how he was going to find his way back to the compound, or even into the town, Duvakin understood that he was going to have to get used to the idea that this wasn't Moscow, where a man on foot blended into the crowd. There didn't seem to *be* a crowd in Novii Uzen. In fact, looking around now, he was the only human he saw. A clutch of sheep over there, cropping at the weeds on a mound, and a filthy cat dozing on top of a garbage bin. A snatch of song blown from a distant open window, and the mournful

sound of windblown sand scouring the weeds. Still, for all the soli-
tude, his spine itched with the sensation of being watched.

"FRIENDSHIP OF PEOPLES IS THE BULWARK OF SOCIALISM!" a
concrete embankment announced, and, farther along, in precast
concrete letters seven feet high, "TO MAKE THE XXI CENTURY A
NUCLEAR-FREE AGE!" There were a lot of Lenins, too, most partial
but some still complete. A faded portrait was painted the full five
stories down the side of the apartment building behind Duvakin,
and across the street, in the road divider, a bust the size of a refrigerator, now with the nose chipped off and red paint poured bloodlike
over the original gold.

Straight ahead of Duvakin were two and a half floors of a building's skeleton, surrounded by gaping gouges and hummocks of rubble, roughcast concrete spars halfheartedly fencing other holes that
seemed scratched at random into the rocky soil; a rusting crane, its
unsecured hook swinging in the wind, clanging against its own gan-
try; rust-red coils of wire and loops of reinforcing rods lying about
as if scattered by an enormous and ill-tempered child.

The warm wind scratched irritatingly at Duvakin's neck as he
stood, trying to figure out which of these buildings were still going
up, and which was the one which had recently come down, crushing
Ermolov beneath it.

Duvakin had been jolted from a dreamless sleep when a woman
pushed a cart loaded with covered dishes into his cottage and introduced herself as "Rosa, any problems, anything you want, just call
for Rosa!" Then she had set about tidying his few possessions, hum-
ming as she folded and wiped and dusted. The sun was pouring
through the windows, and birds nattered in the shrubs outside.
Duvakin had washed, shaved, and accepted a cup of the woman's
excellent—and real!—coffee, before lifting the stainless steel lid
from the largest covered dish, to reveal a steaming plate of eggs fried
with sausage and onion.

Eggs! Christ, there hadn't been an egg in Moscow for over a
year!

Rubbing his hands together, Duvakin had realized he felt better
than he had in months. Ready, even, to take on this shadowy
Momish.

Still, confidence was one thing, foolhardiness another. It

seemed a prudent first step to learn what he could of how his predecessor had died. Mumbling greedily around a forkful of eggs, Duvakin
asked, offhandedly, "How would a person get from out here into
town?"

"Abdulla will take you, Ivan Palych," the woman said, arranging the silverware around another covered dish. A large-bosomed,
middle-aged woman, Rosa was handsome in her way, dark brown
skin making her gold front teeth gleam, the red-and-gold threads of
a flowered scarf she had knotted about her head catching the few
white strands in her otherwise coal-black hair. She was some kind
of local, of course, with that soup-plate flat face, but her Russian
was fine, even if it did have a foreign, musical little twist, a hint
of throaty harshness. "He is coming at ten."

"Without Abdulla."

"Oh, Ivan Pavlovich"—Rosa had turned around, her eyes
bright with alarm—"that wouldn't be right. He's your driver."

"I never have a driver," Duvakin said, with perfect honestly.

"But you have not yet met Mogammed Alioglu." Her alarm
was obviously rising. "You must—"

"I will, but it is a pleasure I fear I must postpone." Duvakin
had pushed the plates away, feeling confident, even cocky, after
sleep and food. For a moment he wished he had a cigarette; then
he arranged himself more comfortably on the divan. "There are tasks
that are more pressing."

"Oh, I just don't know what to say, Ivan Pavlovich," Rosa
finally murmured, after spending a long silence gathering Duvakin's
silverware, scraping his plate, tidying his tray. "Abdulla is picking
you up at ten," she repeated. "And Momish hasn't given—"

"His permission?" Duvakin had guessed gleefully. "Surely
Mogammed Alioglu can't mean to keep me a *prisoner* out here, can
he? Besides . . . I want to pay my respects to a comrade."

The woman had opened her mouth to object, then shut it again
and nodded. Looking flush and disturbed, she had stacked all the
dishes again in silence, then wiped nonexistent dust from the
low table at which he had breakfasted. "Abdulla is meant to
drive you," she repeated, not looking at him. "Everywhere you
go . . ." Then, whispered, "But he would not show you where
Borya died, I think . . ."

Ants ran down Duvakin's spine, as he realized Rosa knew precisely who his "comrade" was.

Swiftly, still whispering, she told him where Ermolov had died, and where he could flag down a bus, out where the road to the compound met the main road.

Then, as he had set off through the shimmering heat, she shouted at his back, "Be careful, Ivan Palych . . . it is very dangerous!"

Duvakin had waited nearly an hour for a bus to arrive, wondering about Ermolov and how he had become "Borya" to this Rosa. What he had hoped ever since the phone call from Chistoplotskii— that his predecessor's death had been some sort of accident—seemed more unlikely than ever.

But where had death come from, and why? The landscape was as flat and empty as the bottom of a box, the only living things other than himself withered stalks of what looked like nettles, to which bits of paper and plastic bags adhered, rattling in the constantly moaning wind. When the white Niva shimmered and later came into focus through the sun devils on the blacktop, Duvakin lay facedown in the drainage ditch, so Abdulla would not see him.

The bus had pulled up, though, before Abdulla had headed back for town, sparing Duvakin a second stretch in the dust, and, after a ride for which the driver charged him four rubles, delivering him here.

Duvakin circled the site, then noticed another possibility about a hundred meters farther on. He picked his way through the rubble and sheep dung of the uneven, weed-covered ground, over to a small mound of powdery white, dry soil. On top of it, the warm wind pushed his pants tight around his legs, annoying, like an overly affectionate cat. There were two more apartment buildings to the left, about seventy meters off; to the right, farther, maybe three or four hundred meters, across a double roadway, there was a line of buildings, shops below, plywood-shielded apartments above.

And here, in front of him, concrete slabs collapsed into one another like the folds of a concertina, or a biscuit torte dropped on the floor. The edges of the broken slabs looked raw, and the ground showed signs of recently departed trucks, excavators, and other equipment.

Duvakin shivered in that scratching wind, wondering what could have brought down so much concrete.

"Hey, Ivan! What are you looking for, eh?"

Duvakin whirled, startled, heart pounding, wondering who knew his name. A man was walking through the lot toward him, holding a hat in his hand. Duvakin glanced around, but there was no one else whom the fellow might want, and nowhere for him to go. The man had come from a car, left at the curb, between Duvakin and the sun. Glare made it difficult to see anything, but the car might at one time have been painted the yellow and blue of a militia vehicle. Duvakin was unsure whether he hoped it was or not.

"You want something from me?" he asked rudely, as if the man had burst unannounced into Duvakin's office.

"Passport, for a start, then maybe some explanations," the fellow said, when he came close. He was a captain in the militia, a local, about seven or so centimeters shorter than Duvakin. Solidly built, though, with a squarish head, the hair cropped so close it might almost have been unshaved beard, the face smooth and impenetrable. A light sweat glinted in the furrow between his dark, almost bushy eyebrows, but otherwise the man seemed unaffected by his quick walk across the ragged lot. His uniform was as crisp as if it still hung in his closet.

"What do you need my passport for"—Duvakin was just the acceptable side of insolent—"since you already know my name?" Still, he had extended his identity booklet.

"Ivan of Moscow, eh? You're a long way from home," the captain cocked his head at Duvakin after a quick glance, tapping the passport on his thumb. "Touring our little peninsula on pleasure, are you?"

"That's a laugh, my friend," Duvakin replied with deliberate offhandedness. It had been his experience that people who assumed they should be deferred to generally were, and he had no intention of submitting to the scrutiny of this local in pigeon-gray serge. "I'm from the Ministry of Energy."

"That doesn't tell me much, does it?" The captain smoothed his almost nonexistent hair with his hand, then placed his service cap precisely in position. That done, he pointed left and right, with open arms and upturned palms. "You look around, tell me if you think this is Russia, all right? No? But your passport says you're from in Moscow, so I know you're not from *our* ministry. Times have changed, but even so, I'm kind of used to figuring, any Russians we find wandering around where they shouldn't be, either they escaped from the labor camp or they got sent to Novii Uzen by the Ministry of Gas and Oil. So I'll repeat my question: What are you looking for?"

This one's face was even flatter than the housekeeper's, and his eyes were squinted up against the glare, which made him impossible to read. There was a sinking feeling in Duvakin's gut; the man was not going to be easy to impress or cow.

On the other hand, it didn't hurt to try, did it?

"Listen, Captain . . . sorry, you didn't give me your name, so . . ."

"Tansybekov."

"Captain Tansybekov, being as we're in the same line of work, more or less, you can appreciate that Moscow . . ."

"So you've been sent down to snoop around after our latest dead Ivan, have you?" The captain swept Duvakin's condescension aside as a bull does a horsefly.

"Meaning Ermolov *was* killed," Duvakin half said, half asked.

The captain looked exasperated, his first change of expression. "That happens when a building falls on you."

"Killed by somebody," Duvakin corrected himself, as though it were a point of grammar, not law.

The Kazakh looked amused. "That's what your 'special assignment' is, to find out whether that guy was murdered?"

"No, no," Duvakin lied immediately, then straightened his back, twisted the other way. "Or yes, I suppose so, in a way. You see, it's a question of . . . depending on how he died, what . . . what we have to pay the widow."

The captain's eyebrows furrowed together, almost locked. "What do you mean?"

Trying not to smile at his own cleverness, Duvakin lied glibly now. "See, it's a question of whether his death was work-related or not, because if it was, then the widow gets a full pension, but if it wasn't, then she doesn't. Unless the death was somebody else's fault—then other circumstances apply."

The captain's face was noncommittal. "We sent a full report to Mogammed Alioglu, and one to Alma-Ata. If Moscow wanted one, they should have requested it, officially. Through the proper channels."

"Oh, of course, I quite agree. And I'm really shocked that no one did," Duvakin said hastily. Nothing to be gained by antagonizing the captain immediately. "But you know how it is, old habits and all that. People can't get used to . . . well, the new ways. But I'm from a different department anyway, so . . ." Then he made his face grave and—he hoped—officially bureaucratic. "This looks to have been a terrible tragedy, Captain. An entire *building*. There must have been a lot of other casualties?"

Tansybekov didn't quite smile, but whatever his face did, it was the first unofficial expression the man had made. He twisted his neck a little, then said, "At least you ask . . . But no, as it happens, there weren't. As far as we know, the Ivan was the only person in the building."

The building had been a typical five-stacker, six entrances and thirty flats, but none of them were inhabited. That would have been a crime even without Novii Uzen's acute housing shortage, but "due to a construction oversight" the building had been sited too far from existing sewage mains, and after the building was completed, the decision had been made that it was cheaper to abandon it than to dig new drains. The other services—gas and power and even incoming water—were in the building, so people had tried to move in anyway, using the windows to dispose of waste water. The authorities tried to force them out by turning off the incoming water, but families were so desperate for housing that they tried to cope by carrying water from the neighboring complexes. Then the authorities turned off the water for the entire region. That had been in July, when temperatures reached into the forties; within two days the residents of the neighboring blocks of flats had driven the squatters out.

Then the building had sat sealed five or six years, while Mangyshlak winds and sun reduced it to total dereliction, one more monument to the Soviet genius for transforming raw materials into wreckage, at great cost.

"Oh, it wasn't a *dead* loss." Tansybekov shrugged. "The kids around here used the basement at least as a kind of club, a place to smoke cigarettes or take their girls, and it gave the drunks somewhere shady to guzzle and pass out. Now?" Tansybekov pursed his lips, raised his narrow eyebrows. "The only thing it's good for is stray cats."

Duvakin could hear cats bawling and scrapping somewhere in the rubble.

"What . . . what took it down?"

"Well, some of the people who were up here right after, they said that the wonder was it hadn't come down before. Most of the support columns had almost no steel reinforcing in them, I guess because the rods were stolen during construction. The concrete too, that they were supposed to be reinforcing, that was mostly sand. Cement is even easier to steal than steel rod. But what seems to have done it was a gas leak."

"A gas leak?"

"The lines were never shut off. There must have been a leak somewhere, then a spark, or something, and . . ." Tansybekov's hands sketched a weary upward fountain, more eloquent than any sound.

Shivering slightly in spite of the warm milky sun, Duvakin realized that this building had been carefully chosen. Well away from other structures, a building with no people in it . . .

And then a gas leak, just when Ermolov had the incredible bad luck to be there?

"Well . . ." was all he managed to say. "Well . . ."

Tansybekov seemed to understand Duvakin's confusion. He grinned, front teeth large and white. "Does that answer your question about whether this was a work-related accident, Mr. Ivan of Moscow?"

"So what you're saying . . ."

"I'm not saying anything!" Tansybekov put up his hands, fending something off. "I'm militia, I do facts, numbers, times, and those are all in the report. You want a copy, I might even find you one, but that's all."

"Come off it." Duvakin felt his own irritation rising. "I was militia myself once, I know facts are *this* much of any case!" He measured off the last joint of his little finger with his thumb. "You have any hunches, any guesses?"

However, his appeal to collegiality fell flat. The captain cleared his throat dryly, then said, "Rumors, lies, and whispers, you mean." Then he pointed back at his car, which was still at the curb. "The man you want for those, that's your Momish. Better you ask him . . . God knows he's been asking about you!"

"That's why you're out here? Mogammed Alioglu sent you to pick me up?" Duvakin suddenly felt claustrophobic, for all that he stood in the middle of a weed lot, on a treeless, empty plain.

Tansybekov seemed to understand Duvakin's sudden paleness; he snorted, and smiled a little. "Momish can be a little bit overwhelming as a host, especially when he feels insulted. You should at least have seen him, before . . ." A wave of the hand took the place of the end of the sentence.

Duvakin shrugged, trying not to look as foolish as he felt.

Then the captain's face was serious again. "You want my advice, though? You listen to Momish and stay close to him. He may be a little overbearing, but he'll keep you healthy."

"Everyone seems worried about my health here."

"Accidents happen in towns like this." The captain smiled, without humor, then waved his hand at the wreckage in front of them. "Come on, I'll give you a ride over to Momish's office."

"Why? I can't stay here? This is maybe a closed military strategic point?" Duvakin stood his ground, frustration at how this Momish seemed to hem him in turning his voice sarcastic and shrill.

The captain was already moving toward the car. He stopped, shook his head as one might at a child, then turned around, hands on his hips. "Look, this is Victory of Communism District. Only Kazakhs, Aral Kazakhs, and Karakalpaks live here. Oh, and a couple of Uzbeks, but they're wives. No Caucasians, and certainly no Russians. The last Russians anybody saw out here, that was during the riots. They were soldiers." He grinned that dry smile again. "Wellarmed soldiers."

"Wait a minute, you're telling me that Ermolov got killed because he happened to go into the wrong neighborhood? That he had a building dropped on his head just for being Russian?"

The captain looked to be near the end of his patience. "As it happens, it's illegal to kill people even if they're not the same nationality as you. Now, if you have official questions in connection with this 'special assignment' of yours, and you've got papers to prove I should be answering you, then we'll go to my office and you can ask. Otherwise, do both of us a favor and let me take you over to Momish, so him and his Azeris can cart you around, keep you out of trouble. Don't forget you're a foreigner now, all right? You know how much paperwork it is, somebody from another republic gets killed in your patch? We're just finishing up one Ivan, and I don't need another."

Duvakin had had enough of being called Ivan. "Listen here, they kill a Russian for coming into their neighborhood and you deal with it by keeping *me* out? Damn it, Tansybekov, that's condoning racial violence! And you're MVD, it's supposed to be your job to *stop*—"

He couldn't finish because the captain was suddenly right beneath his chin, shouting. *"One dead Russian is not racial violence!"* Then, after a deep breath, he stepped back. "Racial violence, racial violence—every time we insist on what's ours, you damned Russians turn us all into fanatical damned Muslims, sharpening our knives so we can rape your creamy fat blondes!"

"Captain, I never implied—"

"You Russians talk a lot. You want to try listening for a minute?" The captain's voice offered Duvakin no choice. "Who lived on this peninsula twenty-five years ago? Kazakhs and Karakalpaks, and a few Turkmens, who scraped along by herding a few skinny sheep and the occasional camel. Then along come the Russians, to put in the oil wells. First the wells, then the pumps, then the new town. Who was asked whether we wanted this? Nobody. Who gets the jobs? Who gets paid for all this? Russians at first, but pretty soon it's Dagestanis and Azerbaijanis and Lezgins and God knows what else that Moscow sends down here. Who lives in the new apartments? Not the Kazakhs. Who drives the cars? Not the Kazakhs. And then they made the damn cooperatives legal. . . . You want to buy bread in Novii Uzen? One of your Russian economic geniuses decided it was more efficient to close our bakeries and have the bread trucked in from Ak Tau. Meaning that bread just disappeared, of course. And so who moved in? Couple of Lezgin cooperatives, that's who. God knows where they got the flour, but they had flatbreads, rolls, sour loaves, sweet loaves, whatever you want. Even *nan*, the bread that Kazakhs have eaten for four hundred years. Only problem is, it costs twenty times more than state bread. So they got rich, and when the sovereignty came, they bought the bakeries. Now, even if we wanted to, we couldn't make our own bread. Clothes? Same thing, the department store in the middle of town is entirely owned by cooperatives now. Jeans? No problem, six hundred rubles. A shirt? Three ninety, and it'll have 'ADIDAS' in red right across the front, courtesy of an Azeri cooperative. You hungry when you come out of the store? Buy yourself a couple of shish kebabs, eight rubles a skewer, from another Azeri cooperative. You know what, Duvakin? The toilets, the goddamned fucking public toilets behind the bus station, you want to go put right the demands of nature, you have to hand a ruble to the old Balkhar who sits there and pretends to swamp out the toilets. *Balkhars* that Stalin moved out to Uzbekistan during the war, even goddamned Balkhars own businesses now. And what about the Kazakhs, who have lived here for a thousand years? Most of us have no jobs, and the ones that do, they make one fifty, one seventy a month. Not money you buy blue jeans and cross-country shoes on, is it? Or Zhigulis either. So who do you think gets all the girls?" He smiled sadly. "Novii Uzen isn't about race, Ivan-from-Moscow, it's about money and sex. What happened to this Ermolov of yours, we're doing what we can to investigate. He was in the building, there was a gas explosion, the building fell down. That's all for sure. What he was doing out there, and whether someone caused the explosion, that we're trying to find out. But if you really were in the militia, then you can understand why one or two dead Russians aren't the only things that I have on my plate. Anyway, did you know Ermolov?" The captain's tone changed suddenly.

Duvakin was still thinking about those "one or two" Russians. "I don't see what that has—"

"Answer my question. Did you know Ermolov personally? Do you know anything about him?"

Damn it, Duvakin thought, the fellow never blinks! There was no clue on Tansybekov's pan-flat face as to what he was driving at. Slowly Duvakin shook his head.

The captain studied him a moment longer, then seemed to make a decision. He took Duvakin's arm.

"Come on."

"Where to?" Duvakin jerked back.

"The morgue."

"The morgue? What in the devil . . . I don't want to see the body!"

"Just come on," the captain insisted, then made his way back to the car. After a moment, Duvakin followed, looking about for the unseen eyes that had let Tansybekov know he was here in the first place.

There was a brief conversation on the crackly radio, in a language Duvakin couldn't understand, and then they set off with the jerk of a failing clutch. Tansybekov was silent the whole short trip to the morgue, which proved to be down a back entrance, in the basement of Novii Uzen's only hospital and polyclinic.

"I hate this place," the captain remarked, as they went down into the comparative cool of the basement.

"It is the lights, I think, Comrade Captain," answered the doctor who was standing at the bottom of the rickety stairs, waiting for them. He was a very young man, Duvakin thought. "All the tiles make it too bright in here. I myself find I have headaches, especially when I work late hours . . . and the smells of the chemicals too, of course."

"It's the dead people," the captain contradicted flatly. "When I have to come see dead people here, it means we didn't do our job properly. Anyway, come on, show Moscow-man here what you've got."

Fighting a nauseous panic, Duvakin held up his hands. "No, really, it's all right, I mean I'm not an expert, so it wouldn't mean anything to see it . . . him . . ."

The doctor smiled. "We don't still have your Russian, we shipped him back." How was this young man even old enough to be a doctor? Duvakin wondered. His coppery skin looked as if it had no idea what a razor was, and the way he clumsily adjusted his conical paper hat, then patted the pockets of his stained whitish laboratory coat, as if looking for something, made the man seem more a schoolboy than a doctor. "Anyway, we don't even have our own cooler, you know. I mean, look at the space we have here— this was never built to be a morgue. It wasn't even supposed to be a *hospital*. The building was going to be a school, until the oil ministry took the new hospital for offices. They gave us this, but . . ." He shrugged, not feeling a need to explain why a school made a bad hospital. "They didn't give us much equipment either, so the morgue has to use the freezer down at the produce storage *kombinat*. But they don't like us to have more than three or four corpses at a time down there, and as of this morning there's six."

"You keep the bodies with the *food?*"

"Not *with* it, of course." The doctor laughed. "It's—"

Tansybekov interrupted, face flinty. "Six? I know about four. They brought in more this morning?"

The doctor looked serious. "One was just another drunk, drowned in his own vomit. Found in the railyard by the hide-processing plant, age unknown, but somewhere between thirty-five and forty-five, tattoos on both hands and left arm, half the teeth gone, and when we finally open him up, I'll be surprised to find a liver . . ." He touched the captain's arm lightly, then pointed down the corridor, which was cluttered with wooden crates, pieces of office furniture, bits of medical equipment too dilapidated to use but not so far gone as to justify being thrown out.

"Nationality?" Tansybekov asked.

"My office," the doctor said brightly, indicating a partitioned-off cubicle with no door; it was scarcely bigger than the kitchen table, its one drawer fitted with a lock, that served as the desk. "No passport, but he looks Slavic. Russian, most likely, probably a wild goose."

"A bum, he means," Tansybekov translated for Duvakin. "They come down south to avoid the winter, then drop dead drinking brake fluid or something. Damned headache, and the border guards can't seem to keep them out." Then, to the doctor, "There was another?"

The answer was in Kazakh this time, and the doctor's face was grim.

After his unsettling morning Duvakin didn't need this reminder that he was so far from home territory, and Tansybekov's translation didn't make him feel any more comfortable.

"They found a first-grader this morning, under some rubbish in the bushes in the park, not far from the main fountain. A little girl, beaten to death with something heavy and blunt—a rock, most likely. Raped first, the doctor says."

Duvakin felt his gorge rise, but said nothing, uncertain why he had been brought, and why the captain was making him hear all this. He shook his head, unable to think of another response.

The doctor said something else, which this time Tansybekov didn't translate, but instead answered, also in Kazakh. The doctor agreed.

Captain Tansybekov switched back to Russian. "She was a kind of relative of my wife's people."

"I . . . I . . ." Duvakin stammered, thoroughly rattled now. He had no idea what to say, or even what to think. Tansybekov, though, cut him off with a flat chopping gesture.

"Enough. Doctor"—he gestured—"tell him about his comrade from the center—"

"He's not exactly my comrade," Duvakin began, but then stopped, uncertain whether to claim Ermolov or not.

The doctor frowned as he fussed with the tapes holding the case file closed, and when he finally began to speak, his tone was very formal. "As per your instructions, respected Captain, routine investigation of the body in file 1427-Zh was supplemented with extraordinary analyses of selected tissues and body fluids—"

"That's your Ermolov," the captain translated, then spun his right hand, telling the doctor to get on with it. The doctor blinked. "The upper bronchial surfaces and eustachian tube show tarry residues, but analysis is consistent with regular tobacco use only, and the liver and kidney damage revealed, while reasonably extensive, are typical of sustained alcohol use. The tissue samples selected showed no reaction to reagents indicative of other substance abuse," the doctor continued in official tones. Then he laughed unexpectedly. "Not that you could trust it if they *had*! Those testing kits were already past their expiration date when Gurev bought them from the MVD down in Ashkhabad, and it was another two years after that before they sent them up here to us . . . assuming it wasn't just camel piss the Turkmens put in the bottles in the first place."

Duvakin grabbed at the only glimmer of sense he could make from all this. "Substance abuse?" he asked the doctor, then turned to the captain. "You had Ermolov's body tested for narcotics?"

For the first time that day the captain looked wholly happy, now that Duvakin was beginning to understand. He laughed, and pointed at the doctor. "Yes, but it was the tests I *didn't* order . . ."

"I did scrapings under his fingernails," the doctor explained, his suppressed excitement making plain that he had taken some gamble and won, "and microscopic examination of the skin of the deceased's hands and of his hair."

"And?" Duvakin knew he wasn't going to like what they were about to tell him.

"There is a very high probability that the deceased had been in sustained contact with hemp resins," the doctor said severely.

"Hemp resins?" The information meant nothing to Duvakin.

"Hemp is *anasha*, marijuana," Tansybekov explained, almost happily. "It grows wild all over the peninsula. The plant is fibrous, and characteristically leaves minute cuts on the surface of the skin, which get impregnated with resin, and pollen too . . . that's very sticky, and also has the highest concentration of narcotic. People who handle a lot of wild marijuana often have hands like your colleague Ermolov's."

Duvakin was silent, blinking in astonishment at this wholly unexpected news. The captain could be forgiven for driving his point in a little bit further.

"A stranger to Novii Uzen, someone who handles *anasha* but doesn't smoke it, and then a building happens to fall on him, in the middle of the night at that? So tell me, now that you know all that, you think your colleague was killed just because he was *Russian?*"

"Ah, Ivan Palych, at long last we have the pleasure of meeting!" The stocky, large-eyed man, his head the color of a walnut and the size of a watermelon, rose from his restaurant seat slowly, extending a hand that seemed to inflate as Duvakin approached; when they shook hands, the other man's felt as large and thick as a loaf of bread. "Welcome to our steppes! You traveled well, and now you have rested, that you may enjoy this modest welcome to our town!"

"It is a long way." Duvakin smiled faintly, looking over the spread of delicacies, and acceding to the fiction that he had slept late, which explained his absence of the morning.

Stunned by the revelation about Ermolov, Duvakin had actually wanted to go directly from the morgue to the Energy Ministry offices; the morning had left him disoriented, convinced that it would be unwise to continue to flail along on the basis of his own assumptions, at least until he could better sort out which way was up in this demented town. Until he had heard about the hemp resin embedded in Ermolov's hands Duvakin had thought of him simply as a man, a colleague much like himself, someone with a wife and child, a victim of bad luck. Like Duvakin himself, tumbled around in the cement mixer of Soviet life.

Hemp resin, though—that meant Ermolov was no victim.

It was narcotics that had first knocked Duvakin's life out of its fated furrow. Heroin, which he had found hidden in a souvenir stacking doll, in the room of a murdered tourist. What followed came closer to killing him than Duvakin ever cared to get again, and even without killing him, that heroin, and the long, lonely freezing years of Magadan it had brought him, had taught him more about the ugliness of life than a man ought to know.

Duvakin had no sympathy for anything that touched on narcotics. But then, hemp isn't narcotics. Heroin *is* narcotics, like in that stacking doll, and opium and morphine. Hemp is just like vodka or something, recreation. At least that's what Susi-Anya always insisted, when she overheard Duvakin cursing the kids who infested the stairwell, calling them narcomaniacs. Susi would say that it was nothing, that Ermolov had just been handling hemp.

"Just," as if it were the difference between jaywalking and armed robbery. "Just," as if Ermolov hadn't ended up beneath tons of rubble. And didn't hemp make young people take dangerous, bizarre risks? Not to mention that it was expensive, so that kids had to do terrible things to pay for it, like steal bottle-return kopeks from frail old widows. Become prostitutes.

Break into apartments. Steal things.

And then not care about the consequences, if someone happened to walk in on them.

He had asked Tansybekov to drop him off at Momish's headquarters; instead the captain had insisted on driving him all the way back to the compound.

"Abdulla lost you, so you better let him find you. Question of face, you see, one of the mysteries of the East . . ." The militia captain had grinned, with the air of a man who has won an argument. "Besides, I doubt you will want to explain to Momish why it is the militia is delivering you to his door."

It had not been hard for Duvakin to recognize the wisdom of that, especially later, when Abdulla reappeared at the compound, radiant with joy that Duvakin had slept so long and so well, and so would now be well rested for the modest welcoming meal that Mogammed Alioglu had arranged.

Duvakin had caught Rosa's eye and nodded, in what he hoped she understood was thanks.

The main room of the Tumbleweed Restaurant was painted

black, the tables set behind wooden screens that looked like the dividers in a maze. The full-length mirrors on some of the walls multiplied the maze, and cigarette smoke hung above the dividers, pulsating and swirling to the hammering music. The table to which a fawning waiter in a spotty red coat had led Abdulla, and Abdulla Duvakin, was in a separate room, behind the band. In the low-ceilinged, smoky outer room, conversation would have been impossible and pointless; in this side room, the noise was low enough to permit a discreet conversation, yet loud enough to assure it would remain discreet.

Plus, Duvakin noted as he came up to shake his host's hand, the glass partition allowed you to keep an eye on the noisy outer room. An arrangement that had its uses, no doubt.

Momish, the man Duvakin had been sent to Novii Uzen to fire, grinned, his eyes becoming narrow slits above his high, slab-shaped cheekbones. "Ahh, I regret the new times, esteemed Ivan Pavlovich! This is not hospitality, alas, this is merely eating! The way it once was, in the East, the guest was washed by pretty maidens, then offered bread, meat, *kumys*, *shubat*. Work stopped and everyone feasted." He shrugged, arms flung wide. "You Russians have become so severe now, you see corruption under every bunch of grapes. You take our hospitality amiss!"

Out in the restaurant everyone seemed to know one another; people wandered from table to table, shaking hands, clicking glasses in toasts and drinking, grabbing girls to dance with or to sit on laps. There were a lot of girls, moving from table to table in tight-skirted, teased-hair, scooped-top, cosmetic-painted gaggles, shimmying with laughter. The men in the café were mostly Asians, and mostly older, but the girls were mostly Russians, or Ukrainians. Germans maybe. There were a lot of Volga Germans in Kazakhstan, exiled there by Stalin during the war.

They reminded Duvakin of the young people back in Moscow, their hellish music and their shaggy hair, the randy way the girls dressed, and the arrogance of the boys, who fondled the girls with an ease that Duvakin had not even dreamed was possible when he was a boy.

"You gave us a bit of a fright this morning, Ivan Palych," the Azerbaijani said with cumbersome humor, when the cringing waiter had helped them be seated, then poured them mineral water, which trembled to the beat of the band next door.

"Sleeping so late?" Duvakin smiled.

Momish held Duvakin's gaze. "Going sightseeing so early."

Duvakin must have gone pale, for the Azeri smiled. "It is unusual that our guests show so much . . . mmm, *interest* in our city."

Duvakin straightened his silverware, toyed with a piece of flatbread. Then, rather than try to resurrect a lie that had not been his, he shrugged. "This is a new place for me. I wanted to look around."

"I understand." His host smiled reassuringly, then, with no change of tone, but with a look now considerably shrewder and more attentive, he said: "What I am wondering though, Ivan Palych, is what you are looking around for?"

Duvakin's mouth had gone dry; he could not have answered even if he had thought of something to say.

The director straightened one shoulder, aware his sneak punch had landed. "I'm a direct man, Ivan Palych, and in these times we can't permit ourselves the luxury of drawing-room manners. When I first came to this peninsula, we lived in tents. We drank distilled seawater carted in from Shevchenko in drums that had gotten too rusty to be used for crude oil." He laughed, pointed at the mineral water in front of them. "You think this stuff tastes bad? It's from the fountains of paradise, next to the stuff we drank then! But we drank it! Twelve, fifteen hours a day working on the rigs, under that sun, hoisting drill pipe until your bones hummed, you'd drink your own urine, if your body could make some. When I got out here things were in a pitiful way, just a handful of geologists trying to show a flock of unlettered sheep-chasers how to drill for oil. Oil! Which the country needed like a wounded soldier needs blood! So I rolled up my sleeves . . ." Momish mimed it, then stopped, waved a hand dismissively. "Just like an old man, eh? Boasting about his youth." He held both hands out, palms up. "Let's just say that I worked hard enough I *still* can't scrub all the oil out." Indeed, the hands looked hard and rough, the cuticles outlined by something dark. The man fell silent for a moment, studying Duvakin with an intensity that made Duvakin look away, around the restaurant.

"Ivan Palych"—the man's voice was a complex mix of assertion and question when at last he spoke again—"everything in Novii Uzen, I built. These houses, the schools, this restaurant. It was me who put in three-quarters of those pumps out there! Pumps that pumped out three hundred million rubles' worth of oil last year! But that's not the main thing . . . you walk down former Lenin Prospekt, Dzhanibekov Street, Auezov Square, Trutny Street, *any* street in this city, and what do you see? Trees! You see *trees!*" Agitated, he began waving his large arms. "This whole town, this whole peninsula is solid limestone—you want to plant even a tree, even a post to hang a stop sign on, you have to *blast* yourself a hole! With dynamite, man!" He leaned over the table, his tie looping down to rest on the bread. "I dynamited a hole for *every tree in this city!*" He straightened, disgust plain in his face. "I have been twenty-two years on the Mangyshlak Peninsula! Building *socialism*, damn it, while you all sat up in your Moscow whining about how there's no Japanese tape recorders to buy, or French stockings. What do you think we pay for those foreign trinkets *with*? Oil, that's what! And I pumped nine million tons of the stuff last year!"

Duvakin sat rigid, his head up, what felt like ants crawling up and down his spine. Mouth dry, heart pounding with tension so that he thought his temples must be visibly pulsating, Duvakin did his best to speak gently. "Dear Momish, we seem to be beginning our work together on the wrong note. No one in the center holds any prejudices against you." Duvakin was faintly surprised, and very glad, that the lie came so easily to his lips. "Your services are well known and highly appreciated."

"Then why have they sent you to spy on me, and fabricate some reason to let those cursed Kazakhs get me?" Momish cut in, in a voice that made Duvakin's guts churn. He glared, then sat back, smoothed his tie, and looked at Duvakin as teachers used to, waiting for answers they knew he wouldn't have in his brain.

Duvakin was silent for a moment, staring at the man upon whom he depended for life in Novii Uzen as certainly as a fetus does on its mother. Desperation brought a memory to his tongue, like the beads of sweat on his brow. "You're right, Mogammed Alioglu," he croaked, then took a sip of the water, which had a slick, oily taste, "that my presence here is not wholly what it seems." He spoke slowly, voice still creaking with strain. "But you have matters stood heels-up and head-down. I have come not to blacken your name, but, well, to help."

Now it was the Azerbaijani who was puzzled. He sat back in the chair, bracing his barrellike body with his thick arms. "Help *me*? With what?" His tone was not quite incredulous, not quite scornful.

Stalling, to avoid saying it aloud and so learning whether his lie would be a brilliant stroke or a fatal one, Duvakin looked about. His eye was caught by a girl outside, leaning far across the table for a bottle. Lifting her leg high to balance herself, she thrust out a smoky-black stocking, with a black rib that ran up the back of her leg into darkness, just at the edge of which was a small puncture through which popped a round little mound of flesh, like a button upholstered in pale rose. Duvakin swallowed, pushed away from the table.

"You forget . . . we all forget . . . The Central Ministry is gone, dead. We may be colleagues by profession, but . . ."

"I know that." Momish brushed the words away with an angry sweep of his hand. "This is Kazakhstan, you are from Russia."

"All the more reason then, that we are . . . well, *concerned*. That our relationship, umm . . . continues. The election . . . you have the election"—he gulped—"and Moscow is worried . . . that local government here . . . might become less friendly."

While they were sitting, staring at each other, a balding waiter in a misbuttoned, grease-spotted scarlet coat darted nervously in, then, with the distracted air of a busy man who is startled to find his hands are full of food, plonked steaming skewers of shish kebab and rice before them. Duvakin looked up, grateful for the distraction as much as for the food, and noticed a plump blonde at another table, just beyond the glass. Her hair teased up into something like baked meringue, with dark roots, she had plunged forward to spear a piece of something on her fork, and from the scooped neck of her striped jersey out popped her left breast, which was large, bare, and tattooed with the word "Kolya."

She noticed him and, laughing, blew him a kiss. Cheeks flaming, Duvakin snatched his eyes back to the Azerbaijani.

" 'Alternative elections' on a 'multiparty basis,' " Momish was saying, twisting his skewer of meat over and back, as if examining it for defects. Then he waved the back of his hand. "Games. This is all something to entertain children. Cities, and countries even more so, these cannot be run in the way that children play soldiers, deciding themselves who will command, who will follow. Last summer, even our soldiers were as children, deciding for themselves what they would do. Look around, the results are everywhere." Momish snorted, pushed the shish kebab away, looked about for a waiter.

In a minute the headwaiter was at his side, bobbing, grinning, wringing his hands.

"Something is not right, Momish? You are dissatisfied?"

The Azerbaijani pointed his cucumber-size finger at his plate. "This is not meat."

The waiter's head seemed to shrink back into his collar, shoulders rising to protect the neck. The man's large wet eyes seemed almost to slide down his face in despair. "This we were brought, there is no other. You are quite right, this is not meat . . ."

"This man is my guest!" Momish pointed sternly at Duvakin, then repeated, "A guest in our city!"

"I apologize a thousand times, Momish! Ten thousand times! But . . . ah! I know! Kidneys on rice!" He sped away, bearing the two offending plates, leaving Duvakin no place to spit out his gob of half-chewed gristle.

"You see?" Momish turned sideways in his chair, which creaked in complaint beneath the solid Boss. His manner was more confidential now, as if some point had been demonstrated. "That is your democracy, isn't it? Don't we already have complete *democracy* in this country?" He spoke the word as if it were smeared with something foul. "Government of the rabble, by the rabble? Putting a piece of filth like that in front of a man and calling it food? But why not? The waiter cannot be fired, the cook cannot be fired. I can refuse to pay the bill, I can refuse ever to come to this café again, but this café will not close, because there are only three in the entire city. It is only I who will suffer, because the other two places are even worse. So why not serve us garbage, eh? And charge us as if it were gold!" He leaned forward, drawing Duvakin nearer with a crook of his finger. "Listen, in my village, when I was a small boy, there were no rats, no mice." Momish spoke with ardor, his glance like a campfire deep in a cave. "We had nothing to eat, so what could vermin survive on? After the war, I went off to Baku for the Oil Institute, and then to Siberia, to the fields. It was many years before I was able to return to my village. Do you know what I found when I did finally return? My village, the village of my father, and of his father before him, this village was overrun with vermin, grown fat on what my villagers were now rich enough to throw away."

Uncertain what this Eastern allegory was about, Duvakin nodded, a sage look on his face. Then he placed the gnawed gristle on the table's edge and shrugged.

"But the thing of it is, Mogammed Alioglu, that's how it's done now. I don't know about rabble and all that, but democracy is what, well, that's what it is. The union is gone, the Party is dead. Elections, that is how our governments are to be chosen now."

"Ivan Palych"—the Azerbaijani looked offended—"last summer, when your Yeltsin dissolved the old government, did he *elect* the new one? No! He and his Russians appointed the new deputies. Appointed them! And why? Because they needed men who could do the job. I have been first secretary of the municipal Executive Committee since 1981, and I've lived in Novii Uzen since even before there was a city here. Why should there be any question of who is best fit to govern this city?"

"Ah, my dear Momish," Duvakin said urgently, "that's just what concerns your friends in Moscow! Elections are the new tyranny, the new Terror! Where there are elections, who is it the voters throw out? The man already in office! No matter if he is the best man, no matter if he never took a kopek in bribes, if he lived like some saint of communism! Believe me, Mogammed Alioglu, people nowadays choose their leaders the way housewives buy apples at the market. 'Don't give us the old rotten ones from the top of the pile, give us the fresh young ones you've hidden on the bottom!' "

"Young men? Let me tell you something about young men," Momish said, after a reflective pause long enough to make Duvakin fidgety. He pointed through the glass, to a knot of people who were flailing about on the dance floor. "Do you know what happens when a young man decides he is his own master, answering to no one?

We did not do this, Ivan Palych. When we were young, our fathers told us how to live, just as their fathers had once told them. That is how nature intends. A father has lived longer than his son, and knows more, isn't that so?"

Duvakin didn't think it worth explaining that he had never known his own father, and that he was the father of no one, so he made noises of agreement and encouragement. One day here had been enough to make plain that Novii Uzen was not a good place to make an enemy of the Boss.

Fortunately Momish was still reflective. "Two years ago, our young men first took it upon themselves to settle their own disputes. We, the elders, tried to intercede, but . . . they wouldn't listen." Momish shrugged at the hopelessness. "We had a riot, our first ever. Almost a week, many stores looted, the private farmers' market burned down . . . and fourteen young men dead. Last summer we imposed military curfew in June, and managed to hold the town together. Summer is coming again, Ivan Palych, and I wonder. I watch our young men eye each other, I hear them mutter through their teeth. I know there are knives in the apartments, and some guns. Homemade things, from pipes and nails, and maybe a service revolver or two. But the army has collapsed, and who knows where the pieces will go? Once it was not hard to buy a brand-new Kalashnikov, right at the factory gate. Six bottles of vodka, that was the last price I knew. Now it is harder for individuals to buy such weapons. You know why, Ivan Palych? Because dealers would rather sell a hundred guns, a thousand. Ten thousand! And there are armies that buy them, armies of *young men*." Momish waved his arms extravagantly, then pointed a plump forefinger at Duvakin's chest. "Actually, I lie. These are not young men, Ivan Palych, these are wolves. Wolves!" He smashed his fist against the tabletop, rattling the glasses and knocking the spoons to the floor. "And now, like wolves, they will throw themselves upon each other, rip out each other's throats, and die."

The waiter must have feared the fist was for him, because suddenly he reappeared, to put down before them plates of rice with something gray and lumpy oozing over it.

Not hungry, but alarmed by the conversation, Duvakin tried a forkful of the dinner, then put it back down, his throat clenching. The stew may once have been kidneys, but not recently. "You are right, Mogammed Alioglu, you are right. The republics must have men with experience, men such as yourself. That's why my . . . um, Ministry is so concerned that . . ." He stumbled on, with almost no idea of what he was saying, or thinking. Christ, from Moscow everything had seemed clear—Ermolov was a dead hero, so Momish must be the live villain. But Ermolov proved to be no hero, and much of what this Momish was saying Duvakin felt too.

Momish interrupted, shaking his head slowly from side to side, like a bull tormented by flies he has learned he can never gore. "Nonsense. Ermolov was a scheming little bastard who was concerned only with his own pocket!"

Duvakin squirmed, unspoken accusation thunking into his forehead like an arrow. Struggling not to blink as he returned Momish's glare, Duvakin said simply, "I didn't know Ermolov, so I can't answer for what he was."

Momish smiled like a bear that has just seen lunch. "Is that right? Then how is it that Ermolov's accident is the first place in Novii Uzen you went to, eh?"

Surprised at how angry the word "accident" had made him, Duvakin spat back, "Accident? That explosion was no more an accident than what they did to my wife!"

The Azerbaijani blinked in surprise, head tucked back to make thick rolls at his collar.

"Your wife?"

Duvakin felt as though he had taken out some intimate part of his person and laid it on the table. He grunted and turned away.

"Your wife?" Momish repeated. "Something has happened to your wife?"

Stiffly and painfully, as if he were removing mustard plasters from his soul, Duvakin gave as brief an explanation as he could, hating himself for having opened his mouth, and daring the Azeri to show sympathy.

Instead Momish raised one eyebrow, then straightened in his chair, knit his thick fingers together. "If your wife is dead, then you have been insulted, Ivan Pavlovich."

Even for Duvakin's determined indifference, that was too much. "Insulted? That was my wife they killed, not my foot somebody stepped on!" he snapped.

Momish nodded gravely, the flesh of his thick neck making sausage rolls. "This is what I mean. Your home has been defiled, they have spat in your face. You must restore your honor, Ivan Palych."

When Momish said it, Duvakin realized that dishonored was precisely how he felt, even if the word did reek of Caucasian campfires and swarthy men with fierce mustaches, blood oaths sworn in guttural languages. He would not, however, be lectured to. "My *honor*, Momish? What has my honor to do with this? Vipers of some sort broke into my home—vermin, as you imply—my wife discovered them, and she is dead. That is all. I can't bring her back, and I don't know who killed her. I can't even attempt to find out, because my duties have brought me here." No need to explain to Momish that he had snatched at this job as at a life preserver thrown from a riverbank; he couldn't explain his flight from Moscow even to himself.

The Azeri's eyes were chocolate now, melting with commiseration. "The militia have at least identified the person who broke into your flat?"

Duvakin shrugged, wanting no sympathy from a man whom he feared, and to whom he must lie.

"That week, they tell me, there were seventeen killings in Moscow, and three hundred forty-seven reported apartment break-ins. Fifty-nine autos were stolen, and persons unknown dumped three truckloads of half-rotten frozen Dutch chickens onto the railroad tracks opposite the Molodezhnaya Hotel . . ." He paused, remembering the indifference at militia headquarters, whenever he had called to inquire. "Besides, my wife had recently purchased a Japanese television."

"In Moscow it is now a reason to kill someone, that she has a foreign television?" Momish looked genuinely appalled; a small worm of gratitude stirred at the bottom of Duvakin's heart. He said nothing, though, simply shrugging.

Momish spooned a bit of the gelatinous stew into his mouth, studying Duvakin thoughtfully. Something sly kindled slowly in his eyes, until he pushed his plate away and smiled. "You say you've come down here to help me, Ivan Palych—"

"As I can, with my meager resources and humble self," Duvakin interrupted, trying to sound both flowery and noncommittal.

Momish accepted the point with a nod, then went on. "But perhaps first I should help you, eh?"

"Help me?" Duvakin couldn't help repeating. "How?"

Momish smiled modestly. "You know how I rid my village of rats? I cleaned up the rubbish, and then the vermin had nothing to eat! Shall I do that for you, Ivan Palych? Shall I find the ones who killed your wife, Ivan Palych, and together we punish them? Shall we gain back your honor?"

Taken aback, Duvakin managed only to stammer, "But . . . you are here, and . . ."

Momish grinned, gold teeth flashing ruddily through the black of his mustache. "Abdulla found *you*, didn't he?"

Surprised that it had been there at all, and saddened to have to snuff it, Duvakin killed the spark of hope that the Azeri had momentarily struck. "All right, then, from a thousand kilometers away you will do what the militia of Moscow cannot do. We won't ask how, we will just say you do it. But what then? Bring this man down here perhaps? Jail him? Kill him?" Duvakin waved his arms in exasperation, before putting them angrily back into his lap. He felt cheap and foolish as he said, "My wife will still be dead."

"The rabble are defiling our common home, Ivan Palych, spitting in the face of every man who is worthy of calling himself a man! These are stern times, my friend"—Momish's eyes glowed with enthusiasm—"and they demand stern measures."

Just then there was a sudden frantic rapping, metal striking the glass partition. Two waiters and an administrator were holding the door shut, and a young woman was struggling to get around them, hitting the glass with a spoon and urgently beckoning toward the door.

"*Momish!*" Duvakin could hear the woman shout. "Momish sweetie, it's me, tell them . . ."

The Azerbaijani's face went opaque with anger.

"Just a second, Ivan Palych," he said politely, then stalked over to the entrance. Duvakin followed, wanting no more of this restaurant, of Momish, of himself. But he couldn't squeeze through, because of the scrum. The waiters were still holding the door shut, and Momish and the young woman were arguing nastily through the crack, in some local language. The girl was Asian, not Caucasian, but her hair was bleached blond, and the lids of her slanted, narrow eyes were painted with brilliant blue. Her dress of broad horizontal stripes barely stretched from her rear end to her breasts, but the effect was more comical than erotic.

Duvakin understood nothing of their argument, but the girl's face was wheedling, then flirtatious, then angry, her eyes opening wide for a moment, glittering. Then, suddenly, Momish barked something and her face went ashen. She pulled herself up with dignity and stalked away from the door.

Momish was ashen, too, and trembling, his lips thin and blood-less. After a moment of indecision, he followed her through the restau-rant and out to the coat area. Suddenly repelled by the noise, the smoke, the shouting, the day, Duvakin followed, wanting to leave.

"An old girlfriend?" he asked, because something had to be said.

Momish paled further, glared at Duvakin, nearly said some-thing, but instead nodded and patted Duvakin's arm.

Feeling he had committed some sort of error he did not under-stand, Duvakin tried to make amends. "You must have chosen some good words though, to make her look like that?"

The Boss took a deep breath, then smiled brilliantly, even the-atrically. "I told her that she didn't belong here, that this is no place for her."

They reached the partly opened front door, where Duvakin could sense chill night air, smelling of dust and oil and sheep. Un-able to bear the restaurant any longer, he pushed past the doorman and out into the street, where a dusty wind snatched urgently at his clothes, like an urchin wanting coins.

"Oh, what does it matter, Momish, one *putana* more or less, in a place like this?" he said, gulping at the cooler air gratefully. "For me, though, I regret, it is true. This is no place for me—not tonight, at any rate."

Momish's paleness had passed, replaced by a large but insincere smile. "You are going? But we were talking. Ah well, if you must. . . . Come, I will call Abdulla."

But Duvakin wanted no more tonight, not of Abdulla, not of Momish, not of the city. He pulled his arm away. "No, no . . . please, you go back, enjoy yourself. It is . . . the unfamilar food, and the trip and . . . the music, the pleasure, so close to the death of my wife . . ."

"Good for you, Ivan Pavlovich." Momish pulled himself up, almost at atttention. His eyes, his lips, and even his mustache seemed to droop toward the ground. "Mourning is a heavy burden, but a true man carries it worthily." Then, with a smile: "But if I stay here, how are you going to get back out to the compound?"

Beyond the bright pool of light in front of the restaurant a desert blackness had clamped over the city. The boarded-over windows and the thin distant stars only made the few unboarded windows and irregularly spaced wind-tossed tin street lamps look even darker and more lonely.

"I'll take a taxi."

"In Novii Uzen? There are no taxis in Novii Uzen."

Just then a fluttering ribbon of flame streaked through the sky, slashing this way and that until the motion became a smooth downward arc, fading to ruby sparks before disappearing entirely.

"Mother of God!" Duvakin stepped back, nearer to Momish, who didn't seem to have noticed. "What in the devil was that?"

"What?"

"That thing, the flame. In the sky. A rocket? A spaceship?"

Puzzled, Momish looked where Duvakin pointed. For a moment, long enough to make Duvakin's extended arm ache, there was only blackness, but then, just as he was about to decide it had been an apparition, the same whirling mad zigzag streaked across the horizon, ending in the stone-dead arc toward earth.

"That?" The Azeri smiled, waved a hand dismissively. "Boys, having fun."

"Boys?"

"They're catching bats."

"Bats?" Duvakin knew he sounded like a stupid echo, but couldn't stop himself.

"Sure." Momish smiled. "Didn't you do that when you were a kid? Catch a bat, tie a rag to his leg, soak it in gasoline, set it on fire, then let it go? For fun, like fireworks. . . ."

CHAPTER SIX

It was hot. Green flies buzzed torpidly, heavy from feeding. There was no air, just a thick smell of stale salami. Duvakin sat in a chair, people talking around him, paying no attention to the hammer he held in his hand. Something sticky and warm ran down his sleeve, down the hammer's handle, onto the floor. Anya was sitting on his lap. She was nude. Licking her finger, she was sticking it in his ear. *Don't,* Duvakin said, *your mother's in the other room. She's dead.* He held up the hammer. Now it was her tongue Anya was putting in his ear, straddling him, breathing heavily. *She's with Borya, ignore her, it's okay. . . .* Duvakin raised the hammer and hit Anya, with a noise like breaking glass.

Breaking glass . . . Duvakin was wide awake, panting, sweat a hard crust on his body. Heart thumping, he moved, and heard the tinkle of glass shards. Gingerly, still confused by the abrupt transition from dream to sunlit bedroom, he sat up. More glass shards, sliding down the coverlet, and the moist breath of a morning breeze.

The window was broken.

Trembling, Duvakin put his feet out of the bed, to find more glass on the floor. Next to his shoes, though, alongside the bed, there was a stone the size of a fist, a piece of paper tied clumsily around it with cheap string. A puff of gritty air stirred the curtain, prompting Duvakin to get out of bed. Tiptoeing carefully, he put on pants and shirt, socks and shoes. Only then did he feel able to pick up the rock.

It was coarse lined paper, apparently torn from a child's copybook.

"IVANS OFF KAZAKH LAND!" the note read, block-printed with a blotchy ballpoint. "KAZAKH OIL FOR KAZAKH PEOPLE! DEATH TO RUSSIAN COLONIALISM!"

It was signed "ALASH."

"Ivan Palych! Ivan Palych!" Rosa was rapping urgently at the front door now. "Are you all right? We heard . . ."

Duvakin let the caretaker in, held up the rock, and pointed at the broken window above his bed. "I'll be needing some of that Novii Uzen plywood, I guess, Rosa," he tried to joke. "Terrible stiff wind you get on this peninsula, blowing pebbles like these around."

Rosa fussed around the room like a large, gold-toothed hen. She was still in a bathrobe or housecoat, slippers over bare feet, but she worked like a fury, sweeping the shards up, making up the bed, and examining Duvakin as closely as he would permit.

"Who do you suppose I've offended, Rosa?" he asked, when the frenzy of cleaning had abated a bit, and he had collected his wits.

She straightened up, holding the broom under one arm, tucking a stray curl, coal interwoven just here and there with white, back under her purple floral head scarf. The look of real distress she gave him made him regret he had ever asked. "Oh, it's not you personally, Ivan Palych, it's just a name, it's what those people call Russians. . . ." She reached out for the note, but Duvakin, pretending not to notice, folded it and put it in his breast pocket. "They're hooligans, that's all they are." She gave him a cryptic look, then tried a little cheer. "Well, since you're up so early, would you like some breakfast? I could make you a nice bowl of buckwheat kasha and milk."

Even when he was a half-starved little boy, during the war, warm milk had made Duvakin's stomach want to turn itself inside out like a shopping bag. Swallowing to suppress his gorge now, Duvakin said, "No, no . . . some tea perhaps. You said 'they.' Why?"

"'Tea, of course, and perhaps an egg, maybe with sausage again? Green onions, fresh, only the freshest . . ." Rosa was grinning wildly, tucking her bathrobe tighter about her.

"Rosa, you said 'they,' " Duvakin repeated, reaching out for her arm. "The note is signed, 'Alash,' but you said 'they.' "

Rosa shook her head, like an animal tormented by flies. "Hooligans, Ivan Palych, I told you that. It's a terrible thing, but . . . it's not serious, they're just youths, young men. . . . You know how things are with young men, Ivan Palych, there's nothing to do, they listen to that music, and then the devil himself doesn't know what they'll get up to. Just wait until I show Momish that paper, he'll be furious!" She actually reached toward his breast pocket, but Duvakin clapped his hand on his chest.

"Well, furious might be extreme"—Duvakin spoke dryly—"but it wouldn't hurt to have somebody look at the wall around this place."

"Oh, it's not the wall," Rosa said hastily, her eyes wide. "What I mean is, the wall is fine, but the problem is the guards, there aren't enough guards. . . . I don't know what we're coming to, Ivan Palych, I really don't. It used to be that people *respected* this place, you know how it is, we see a high green fence, you and I, and we go to the other way, isn't that right? A government place, the state . . . Well, why should an important visitor like you be distracted from his work? But nobody seems to care anymore, the little boys pry holes in the fence to come steal our apricots, and sometimes the young men bring their bottles or their girls. . . ."

As she talked, Duvakin realized that she had pocketed the rock, which surely had not been thrown by a pilfering boy. It was too big; any boy would have had to be standing right under the window in order to break it. That warned him that perhaps it was better not to insist on getting the rock from her, or on any more answers either, since the ones he had gotten so far weren't adding up.

Duvakin agreed to breakfast, to let her escape, because he wanted to think. The sick sense of dread and guilt that his dream had brought had not entirely dissipated, but the rock and Rosa's obvious evasiveness helped change that sense into a morbid clearheadedness, which Duvakin, to his surprise, rather enjoyed. That there were worse dangers in Novii Uzen than the water he had no doubt, but rather than being paralyzed by it, Duvakin found himself beginning to understand it.

No, he said to himself sternly, understanding is too certain a word. What he was beginning to see, though, were the ripples on the surface that warned that jagged rocks lurked below.

Momish, for example, who in Moscow Duvakin had assumed would be just an old Boss, clinging to a power he no longer had. And so he was, but what Duvakin had learned last night was that it wasn't just power the Azerbaijani loved, it was the city, and he didn't think he was losing it, he thought it was being stolen from him by a bunch of upstart local ingrates. And Momish was a Caucasian, mad about honor. Or worse, mad about dishonor, capable of extraordinary cruelties if he felt slighted as a man.

And then this rock, evidence more tangible than Duvakin needed to be convinced of the truth of what Captain Tansybekov had been saying, that the local Kazakhs felt robbed, victimized and insulted by the Azerbaijanis, Lezgins, and other Caucasians who had taken their land.

But why the note about Russians? "Ivans." How many times had he been called that already here, in tones that made the word sound like a synonym for "shithead"? And what was this "Russian colonialism"? Colonialism was in Africa, or used to be, before it turned out that America was to be emulated and admired, instead of cursed.

There weren't any Russians in Novii Uzen, at least not that he had seen so far. Just him, all pink and glowing, among all these Asians, like an egg in a basket of blackberries. And of course Ermolov.

God, Ermolov . . .

Momish had boasted of his familiarity with dynamite last night; could it be he whom Ermolov had been buying hemp from? But why then bring the building down on him? And besides, if Momish controlled the whole city, what need would he have to trade in illegal narcotics? Or put it another way, if Momish *was* trading in illegal narcotics, why would he depend upon a Russian sent down from Moscow to buy them? Especially since it was the minister who had sent Ermolov, not Momish who had asked that he be sent. So perhaps Momish had wished to punish Ermolov, when he discovered what the Russian was doing? Surely, though, it would have made more sense to have Tansybekov arrest this criminal Russian; it would have made Momish a hero while at the same time discrediting the minister, Moscow, and any further attempts to oust him, Momish.

Unless, of course, Momish was *also* dealing in hemp, and Ermolov was trying to cut into his territory—

"Hello? Are you receiving yet?"

Duvakin whirled, heart flown up his throat like a startled pigeon.

"Who in the devil are *you*?"

"I'm sorry, I knocked, but I don't think you heard me, so . . ."

It was a young man who had let himself in the front door of the cottage, thirty perhaps, certainly no more, in jeans and cross-country shoes, a sweater tied carelessly across his shoulders, glasses pushed up to the top of his head, where they nestled in a mat of curly red hair. Seeming to understand Duvakin's alarm, he held up his open hands and smiled. "Ivan Palych?"

"I know who I am, young man! Who the devil are *you*, and what in God's name are you doing in my cottage?"

Instead of answering, the fellow closed the door and came the rest of the way into the room. "Look, I'm sorry to startle you, but—"

"Apologizing is for after you go back outside." Duvakin did his best to sound forceful, but the combination of dream, rock, and now this was against him.

As the visitor seemed to understand. Smiling, he came closer, close enough that Duvakin was struck by the stranger's odd complexion; his cheeks and nose were liberally scattered with freckles, but so closely matched in color to the man's skin that they were almost invisible. He said softly but very precisely, "If you think about it, you'll probably figure out that there might be a good reason why I'd sneak into your cottage."

"I can't think of *any* reason why—" Duvakin began glacially, but then stopped. If nothing else, this redheaded stranger was the first non-Asian he had seen since arriving. "All right." Duvakin nodded abruptly. "I can give you a few minutes. What did you say your name is?"

"I didn't, but it's Mordachkin, Eduard Andreich. Everybody

calls me Edik." The fellow grinned as he held out a hand, which Duvakin automatically shook. "Mind if I sit?" He waved at the divan. "You know where that comes from, incidentally?"

Duvakin shook his head silently as the young man folded himself, catlike, onto the orange plush. "Israel."

"What?"

The young man laughed, rotating his hand in circles. "By a roundabout way, naturally. And the tiles are from Syria"—he tapped his toe on the ceramic floor—"and the bathroom fixtures from Italy, via Jordan, and did they tell you that that little Korean refrigerator back there is kept full of Czech beer?"

"You know a lot about how this Momish operates," Duvakin finally replied, keeping his voice neutral, because he was uncertain whether these were boasts or accusations.

"Everybody in Novii Uzen knows Momish." The other refused to be led, instead gesturing that Duvakin should sit too. "And everybody knows that he takes good care of himself. But only a few of us know *how* he takes care of himself."

Damn it, Duvakin thought, it's *my* cottage, and so continued to stand.

"How did you get in?"

"You aren't going to offer me any refreshment? This is the East, Ivan Palych; it isn't done to have serious conversation without refreshment. Like one of those Czech beers, for example."

"Early for me," Duvakin grunted, but shrugged, waved his hand at the little kitchen area in the rear of the cottage. "If you're so thirsty for foreign beer . . ."

Lithely this curious Edik uncoiled himself, fished out two caramel-colored bottles, and returned, glass clinking, to the divan.

"I said I didn't want one." Duvakin was stern.

"I don't either. I want two." Edik laughed, prying the cap off the first beer with a bread knife he had apparently found in the kitchen. "How did I get in? It's an old story, Ivan Palych, the gate's in the front, so that's where the guard is. To our meeting!" The young man took a hearty swig, then put the bottle down with a grimace. "Damn it! This is Russian beer!" Wiping his lips with the back of his hand, he said, abashed, "See what things have come to?

Those uppity Czech bastards refuse to sell beer to us now, so even Momish has to drink Zhiguli." He took another sip, then shrugged. "Oh well, it's wet."

"Count yourself lucky that *Russia* will still sell to you," Duvakin sneered with as much Muscovite bureaucratic chill as he could manage. "Well, you're in my cottage, and you're drinking my beer. Now what have you come to tell me?"

"Tell you?" Edik looked away from his bottle, a little surprised. "Who said I've anything to tell you? Perhaps I just wanted to—"

"Make my acquaintance? I don't think so." Duvakin smiled in what was meant to be a withering way. "Very pleasant, I'm sure, but . . . for beers we could have met at the Tumbleweed Restaurant."

Edik laughed again, shook his head. "They showed you our little local Savoy, did they? Wonderful place, but even *this* you couldn't buy there, because the manager sells everything decent out the back." Edik held up his bottle, grinning, then leaned forward and looked up, his face more serious. "Look, do you have any idea at all what's going on here in Novii Uzen?"

Suppressing a galvanizing surge of excitement, Duvakin shrugged, said nothing, stared expectantly at his visitor.

"That's what you've been sent here for, isn't it?" Edik sounded anxious, peering into Duvakin's face more closely. "To replace Ermolov?"

"You knew Ermolov?" Duvakin was having more trouble keeping his voice flat.

Edik smiled, pushed his mirrored sunglasses farther back in his tangled curls. "How many Russians do you think there are here on the peninsula? Of course I knew Borya."

"And you know how he died?" It was now Duvakin who peered intently.

Instead of answering, Edik looked down, playing nervously with his bottle for a second before looking about the little room. He spoke not quite in a whisper, but he wouldn't have been heard in the bedroom. "Twenty years ago this town was planned for forty thousand people, and there's fifty-six thousand of us living here, with a city heating plant that just barely copes with half the town. There's *forty-five hundred* families waiting for apartments. And what apartments? Most of the people who live here aren't like Russians, you know, who count themselves kings if they have two or three rooms. Most of the people here, they're Kazakhs, Lezgins, Avars, Azeris. *Asians*, Ivan Palych, who don't send Grandma to the old people's home when she can't take care of herself anymore, who don't even consider a woman fertile until she's had four or five children. Ivan Palych, there's apartments out there I can show you, they've got *fifteen people* sharing three rooms."

Wondering what this had to do with his question, Duvakin held up his hands, both calming and quieting. "What you're telling me is not unknown to the competent authorities." He hoped he wasn't lying. "Nor are such problems unique, alas. These are difficult times, Eduard Andreich, there are many demands. . . ."

"Did they teach you to say that kind of drivel, or do you get hired because you already can do it?" Considering the rudeness of what he said, Edik sounded remarkably friendly, grinning at Duvakin and toying with his sunglasses. "Look, call me Edik, all right? And you'll forgive me, Ivan Palych, but let's agree that we already did this part, where you tell me that there's lots of other problems and while you applaud my concern and initiative we've also got to take other factors into account, all right?"

Damn him, Duvakin scowled, the boy had come within about two syllables of saying precisely the phrases that Duvakin had already clunked together in his mind, ready to spit them out in precast chunks, like drainpipe. And besides, there was still the question about Ermolov to be answered. "Very well"—he looked up—"suppose we do. What then?"

"Ivan Palych, the young people of this town have nothing. *Nothing.* There's a big fountain, down in Dzhangeldin Park, where the kids used to hang around. The fountain made it cooler, and people played the guitar and sang. Well, the authorities shut the water off last year, when the town got switched over to water piped down from the Volga. That made water too expensive to waste on fountains, they said." After a moment's silence, Edik folded over a finger, went on. "Eight movie theaters"—he clicked off another of his slender fingers—"that by the time we get the films they're all scratched and the soundtrack is half missing, not that it matters, since mostly we get foreign films—"

"Foreign movies? They show foreign movies here?"

"Sure, almost nothing but. *Russian* movies." Edik smiled slyly.

Duvakin was puzzled. "Russian movies? You mean émigré Russian?"

Edik laughed. "No, I mean Russian, from Russia. You're in Kazakhstan now, remember?"

"The young people don't know Russian?" Duvakin peered at Edik, surprised. "They don't teach it in the schools?"

Edik waved his hand dismissively, readjusted his glasses on top of his head, and leaned comfortably back into the divan. "In fact, Alma-Ata can make all the noises it wants about Kazakh being the state language now, but noise doesn't make teachers. What few we've got here, the only language they know how to teach in is Russian. Which would probably be all right, since the only textbooks there are, those are Russian too. Lenin, Motherland, the Party, all the words are there, just like the good old days. But maybe you won't be surprised that nobody *learns* Russian, or much of anything else." Edik resumed his lecture, calmly ticking the points off on his fingers, folding down each digit. "We're trying to fit twelve thousand kids into schools built to hold a maximum of eight thousand. Not that many of those kids care, since they know that anywhere from a third to two-thirds of our graduates can't find work. There's *fifteen hundred* unemployed young people in this town *right now*, Ivan Palych!" Edik took a deep swig of his beer, with a passion that suggested his calm was more apparent than real. He chewed for a moment, then cocked his head. "Anybody tell you about Tenga?"

Duvakin shook his head, wondering why Edik was pouring all this out to him.

"A place, a village . . . just over there." Edik pointed over his shoulder, back in the direction of the town. "About three kilometers the other side of Uzen, right on top of the gas fields, and you know what? Sitting on top of one of the biggest natural-gas fields in the *world*, these people are not hooked up to the central gas pipelines. *They have to buy kerosene!*" In his agitation Edik knocked off his own sunglasses, just catching them before they hit the floor. "But that's not the story. Tenga is a tuberculosis center, because the other tuberculosis center they built, out there"—he gestured toward his right—"*that* one the MVD took over at the last minute, for a labor colony, and when the Health Ministry complained, the MVD gave them Tenga. The place is terrible for a TB clinic—there's just one kitchen, and everything in the same building, so you can't isolate anyone. But that's not the worst. You know what the worst is? All the sewage, everything from Tenga, everything from the hospital, it gets pumped out about half a kilometer, and dumped into settling ponds. God knows how they got there, but there's *fish* in there . . . and the little boys try to catch them."

Duvakin blanched, remembering an old fisherman he had seen on the bus yesterday, a wind-dried old man with canvas-wrapped fishing pole, bait bucket at his feet. Preoccupied with what he was about to do, Duvakin had not thought even to wonder where someone might fish, amid that brown and sun-blasted landscape.

Edik, apparently pleased to have had some effect, smiled slyly. "And when it gets *really* hot, forty-two, forty-three degrees, then the little boys swim in there too . . . so a third of the children in Tenga have tuberculosis, Ivan Palych."

Fighting his urge to shrug, Duvakin crossed over to the chair across from Edik, wondering at his own numbness. It was repetition, perhaps, that made such stories slide off the skin like so much summer rain. How many of these stories had there been? Twenty-seven children get AIDS because the nurses can't be bothered even to wipe the blood off the needles, let alone disinfect them. A hundred and fifty children die on their way back from summer camp when their train is caught in a gas-pipe explosion. Eight hundred thousand Belorussian children, exposed to high radiation from Chernobyl, will probably die of leukemia or cancer.

And four million people died during collectivization, twenty-five million died during the war.

So maybe it was the size of the numbers that made you numb? One person dead, he could understand. Galya, say, her toes stretched out, soles still wrinkled beneath the stockings . . .

But a hundred, a million? It was all words.

"I'm from the Ministry of Energy, not the Ministry of Health," Duvakin said, after a short, silent wait. "Oil is my concern, not health."

Edik convulsed forward, laughing loudly. "What a slogan!" he
hooted. "Couldn't you just see *that* on banners, if they ever do May
Day again? 'OIL, NOT HEALTH!' "

Duvakin smiled his bureaucrat's smile. "What I mean is, the
comrades are concerned about production, not—"

"And if my child is dying in a Tenga TB ward, how productive
do you think I'm going to be?" Edik shot back. "Or I'm out on the
pumps wondering whether the kid's down fishing in the shithole
again?" Edik's anger was quickly replaced by weariness, and the
young man seemed to shrivel a bit, pulling his arms tight about him
as he sank back into the couch. "But you're quite right, Ivan Palych,
that's the Moscow line, and Alma-Ata's, too." Edik made a show
of relaxing, crossing one leg over the other and putting his hands
behind his neck as he sank into the tweedy orange fabric. "That's
the thinking that got us our last project from Moscow. Kind of a
monument now, if you think about it. One last gift from the old
whore, before she dropped dead. The food supply got just terrible
after they merged Mangyshlak into Gurev, which any fool could
have predicted, but . . . well, anyway, the geniuses in Moscow decided the solution was to make Novii Uzen self-sufficient in meat,
so they put twelve million rubles into setting up a pig farm and
slaughterhouse, just up the road near old Uzen. That's the Kazakh
aul that's been here as long as anyone can remember."

Duvakin crossed his legs, knit his fingers together in his lap,
and waited for the end of the story.

"A *pig* farm, Ivan Palych, a *pig* farm! For Kazakhs and Azeris
and Dagestanis—"

"And Russians," Duvakin interjected.

Edik waved the point away, then accepted it with a nod.
"That's right, and Russians, which in fact only made the insult
worse."

"Which made *what* insult worse?" Duvakin asked impatiently.

Edik laughed and shook his head, marveling. "See what I mean?
Ivan Palych, except for the Russians, everybody on this peninsula
is Muslim, and Muslims think pork is unclean."

Duvakin twisted his foot around, trying to draw some sort of
connection between himself, a pig farm, Ermolov, and that note.

Finally, curious to get this young man's reaction, Duvakin asked, "Is that why we're Ivans?"

Edik laughed.

"But why Ivans?" Duvakin insisted.

"Why not? What do you call them up in Moscow? Slant-eyed camel-fuckers, black-butts, slopes . . ."

Duvakin was beginning to get annoyed with this intruder, and wished that Rosa would reappear with coffee. He had come home hungry last night, and now that the nausea of his dream and alarm was passing, he was hungry again. "All right, then, how about Alash? Does that mean anything?"

Edik did not laugh this time. "Alash was the first leader of the Kazakhs."

"I thought Kunaev was."

Edik looked annoyed. "In the fifteen hundreds, when the people began. What do you think, Khrushchev invented the Kazakhs in 1958, so he'd have a name for the people he was forcing off their land, so he could plant his stupid corn?"

"So how is it this Alash threw a rock through my window this morning?"

"Ah, *that* Alash!" Edik nodded, smiling again, then leaned forward to pop the cap off the second beer. "The stuff is dreadful, but the second bottle is always better than the first, you know?" He saluted with the bottle, swigged, shuddered, then answered. "It was the name of the first newspaper in Kazakh, and the group of people who published it."

"Hundreds of years ago the Kazakhs had a newspaper?"

Edik grimaced. "At the time of the revolution, just before. They were nationalists, romantic fools who thought that the Bolsheviks would let them set up a Kazakh republic and have their own country. Then the revolution came, and they all died in Stalin's camps, for being 'bourgeois nationalists.' "

"Still not very likely suspects for having thrown the rock this morning, are they? So what you're saying is that this is some new sort of nationalist group that's taking the name of the earlier one, or of the founder?"

"Actually"—Edik's smile was starting to look a little beery—"I couldn't say, because this is the first time I've heard of any Alash in Novii Uzen. Who would be throwing rocks, I mean."

"Wasn't that a terrible thing? And where are we going to find glass? You know where there's any glass, Edik?" Duvakin heard a woman's voice on his right, where Rosa was appearing, back first, through the door. She turned, a tray before her. She was dressed now, and scrubbed, her dark brown skin seeming to radiate, along with the gold front teeth in her beaming smile and the red and gold threads of the flowered scarf she had now knotted about her head. "You should have told me you were here, Edik, I would have brought for you too!"

"Morning, Rosa!" Edik jumped up, gave the woman a quick kiss on the cheek, which made her giggle, nearly toppling the tray. Edik caught one edge, then lifted the stainless steel dome over the plate, releasing a tendril of steam. He examined the tray, then laughed. "Still no pastries!" he said to Rosa, turning to Duvakin and indicating with a flick of his fingers that the tray should be served. "You know why? Because last year some genius at Aeroflot decided that since yeast is an animal, it comes under the rules for livestock, which isn't allowed to fly, so yeast has to come up here by truck, which means it's always dead by the time we get it. They should have told you that up in Moscow; a suitcase full of yeast would have made you just about the richest fellow in Novii Uzen!" He looked back at the woman. "And you want *glass*?" He snorted, as if she had asked for strawberries in December.

"Well, none of that fixes the hole in poor Ivan Palych's window, does it?" She bent to put the tray down in front of a badly puzzled Duvakin.

This Edik sneaks into his cottage, intimates they should whisper for fear of being overheard, and then when Momish's own housekeeper comes in, he behaves like they're old friends? Duvakin watched them, joking and pinching almost like mother and darling son, until Rosa turned, flustered, to say, "Well, look at me, chattering on about those hooligans like an old woman, and you wanting to eat your breakfast. It's not as if there's nothing for me to be doing, either."

"You two know each other, then?" Duvakin said the obvious, for want of anything else to say.

"How could I not know him, when we worked together? He was recreation director here," Rosa said, looking fondly at Edik, then, more sternly, at Duvakin. "Before Momish took Nurlikhan Bekbosynov's job. Before the riots." Again she gathered herself, and said loudly, "Besides, Edik is one of our town heroes, aren't you, Edik? Did his duty like a man in that Afghanistan."

Edik looked embarrassed, and when his eye caught Duvakin's sharp glance, he turned away entirely, throwing his hands in the air. "Ah, ah—hero! The hero who sneaks in to steal beers, eh? Some hero."

"Well, you *are* a hero." Rosa patted him on the back; then, after a nervous glance around, she whispered, "And after we all vote for you, you won't have to steal any more beers." Then, blushing and nervous, she left the cottage, pausing at the door to add, "And there won't be any broken windows, either!"

Duvakin spread soft cheese thoughtfully on a piece of hard bread the color and texture of plyboard. He looked across at the young man, who had sat again. Rosa's words had pulled several pieces of the puzzle into place.

"Vote? You're running for something?"

"Hsst!" Edik jerked a thumb at the ceiling, then nodded.

"For the city Executive Committee?" Duvakin mouthed this more than said it, but didn't need an answer. Edik was challenging Momish's control of the city. And how much chance that challenge had was suggested pretty plainly by this young man's fear of his opponent, even when Momish was God knew how far away from here. But then on the other hand, perhaps it was Momish who should be worrying, if Rosa was supporting Edik.

All this rather made Duvakin's head spin, so he asked, in a normal voice, "And you really are a hero?"

Edik shrugged, face closed. "I got some medals."

"For what?"

"For killing the people they told us to kill. For keeping alive the people they told us shouldn't get killed."

"But all these problems you're telling me about . . . you'd be able to do something about them?"

The man shrugged again, stretched back along the couch, still saying nothing, but grinning like a cat.

Duvakin laughed. "Going to fire Momish just like he fired you, eh?"

Surprised, Edik sat up and pushed the sunglasses back up into his curls. "I never said that."

"Well, you told me all that about the pork and the yeast and the TB and the, I don't know, the fountain. And Borya Ermolov, you never answered my question about him, either. Momish is in charge of the only industry this whole town has, and he's the first secretary of the city Executive Committee too, so if all those problems aren't his fault, then whose fault are they?"

Edik seemed to pale. "The issue isn't *fault*, Ivan Palych, the issue is . . . sovereignty. This is Kazakhstan. Ibragimov is an Azeri, from Azerbaijan."

The answer not only made no sense, it also reminded Duvakin of the rock that had greeted him at dawn. He waved away the objection irritably. "What difference does that make? Momish is in charge, isn't he? That's the main issue, isn't it, that he's the one who should be fixing these things, shouldn't he? What the devil does it have to do with whether he's an Azeri or a Kazakh or, God, I don't know, a Chukchi?" And then Duvakin remembered one more thing. "Besides, you're Russian—what do you care what kind of Asian he is?"

Edik drew himself up with chilly dignity. "I was born here, I am a citizen of Kazakhstan, and I have a right to care about this land."

Amused, Duvakin took a sip of tea to conceal his grin. Election talk. That rock through the window this morning suggested that at least a part of the Novii Uzen electorate took a stricter view of nationality than Edik did. Putting the tea down, and grimacing slightly from the strong metallic taste, Duvakin assumed a solemn air.

"You asked me not to spin you all the usual Ministry stories, so I can also ask you not to spin me election stories, all right? You are in my cottage, you are keeping me from my breakfast. Just tell me, what is it you want?"

Edik was still sprawled across the divan, spinning his dark glasses by the ear pieces. "Why? You going to give it to me?"

"I didn't say that, did I?"

Edik looked up at the ceiling, this time not to warn for listening devices, but rather to temper a bit the sting of what he was saying.

"You have come from Moscow to help Momish win the election. Fine. The new rules say nothing to prevent that. Maybe you will even be *buying* the election, giving out deficit goods to those who vote for Momish, or making sure there are bananas in the stores the week before the election, so that Momish can claim he has taken care of the food problem. Is this fair?" Edik sat up, raised his hands in a stagy shrug. "Who knows? After seventy years of one party, one candidate, and no way to vote no, an election like this at least *feels* like democracy, even if Momish is as secure in his seat this way as he was the other. . . ." Then, less facetiously, he added, "At least voting this way the people have a chance to ask the questions we have muttered to each other these seventy years."

Duvakin listened with half an ear, because suddenly his thoughts were spurting ahead. Edik had hold of the rabbit all right, but what he thought was the ear was really the back foot. Duvakin *had* been sent down here to help with the election, but to make Momish lose, not win.

As Chistoplotskii had warned, though, Duvakin couldn't guarantee that Momish would lose, but if he tried, and the Azeri won, he sure as the devil could guarantee that the Boss would be impossible to work with in the future.

And now that he had seen the peninsula, Duvakin knew one thing more: that even before the election, before Momish could either win or lose, Duvakin only needed to come out openly against the man, and he would be out sleeping on the sand, trying to make a breakfast of rocks, sand, and bugs.

Now, listening to this angry young hero, Duvakin saw the glimmer of a way out of the dilemma.

Incompetence.

"Help" that you wouldn't wish on your worst enemy.

Making his face so stiff that none of his thoughts could surface, Duvakin waved the gnarled aluminum fork. "Enough, just tell me what you want."

"Will you meet some of the voters, Ivan Palych, and answer some questions, about what the Russian ministry wants from us, and what you can offer us in return?"

Duvakin could have cheered, had he not been holding himself so tightly that his teeth ached. Instead, he frowned, then made a show of reaching into his briefcase for a piece of paper and a pocket calendar.

"I suppose it would be the fair thing to do," Duvakin allowed, reluctantly. "But you'll have to give me advance warning—I'm a very busy man."

Surprised by Duvakin's acceptance, the young man put the sunglasses back on his head, sat up, looked thoughful. "Monday?"

Duvakin spent a long time looking at his pocket calendar, apparently thinking deeply. "Monday? Well, perhaps I can be free . . ." he finally said sternly, his lips aching with the effort not to laugh, as he wrote the date on his slip of paper.

Such "help" I'm going to give Momish, he thought gleefully, the man will be lucky not to go to jail!

F or a war hero, political activist,
and former social director, Edik proved to be a remarkably indecisive
conspirator.

"Edik says he will take you to the meeting himself," Rosa had
whispered when she brought dinner. Apparently she was now Edik's
go-between. "It's in the afternoon, so be ready right after dinner."

"Won't that give the wrong impression?" Duvakin had asked,
surprised. "Make people think that . . . well, what we don't want
them to think?"

The answer came two days later, in a note under the steam
cover of Rosa's pilaf, which was tasty in spite of having no meat.
Shaking grains of rice from a scrap of paper that grease had made
as luminous as old parchment, Duvakin read: "The meeting is in
the Oilmen's Club; see if you can get there yourself."

To which Duvakin had replied, again through Rosa, "Shouldn't
I have some *reason* to go there? I mean, I can't just tell Abdulla
I've taken a sudden whim to drop in at this club."

This point must have been a good one, for no answer came,
but that only fed Duvakin's swelling sense of pleasure with himself.
Have to think of everything, do I? he chortled to his face as he
shaved. Have to do all the arranging myself?

In fact, this ever-increasing sense that he had both understood,
at last, what he was to do in Novii Uzen and, more important, had

seen the proper way to do it, gave him a gently throbbing pleasure that was almost physical, like the relief of finally undoing your belt late in a banquet. Damn it, that wasn't what life was meant to be, a daily wrapping around and around of obligations, injunctions, habits, and customs that cinch tighter and tighter, like some kind of python, until a man's tongue hangs out and his eyeballs bulge! A real man does what's right and necessary, and leaves the devil to sweep up behind!

Now that he was to become Momish's apparent supporter, Duvakin had turned into a model visitor, letting Abdulla pick him up every morning at ten, to take him now to a kindergarten, now to a youth club, now to a neighborhood center. The sites blurred together, all two-story concrete-block structures so alike that they might have been discarded shells from some kind of giant, nightmarish sea creatures, square rooms right and left, corridor down the center, badly tiled with ceramic squares that crackled as they walked, Duvakin mewing approval deep in his throat. Sometimes when he returned to the cottage at night, Duvakin had the sensation that he had even seen the same people in each place.

Each visit also confirmed Duvakin's conviction that, even if it was an arbitrary twist of fate that he should ever have been asked to take sides in the internal affairs of this God-forgotten speck on a bone-dry rib of land that looked more like an architect's mock-up of a world than like any world Duvakin ever had known and loved, at least he was taking the *right* side. Novii Uzen was a poor and nasty city, dusty and diseased, filled with people who glowered at one another from the corners of their eyes, who seemed to slink away or sidle past. Had Mogammed Alioglu caused this? Duvakin didn't know. But Momish certainly hadn't fixed it, which seemed reason enough to help Edik get his chance to attempt to put right a city he appeared to love, for no reason that Duvakin could understand.

Besides, there was an exhilarating rush of events now, as if Duvakin, who had spent so much of his life staggering upstream against the flood of fate, had now suddenly brought his boat about, and was rushing down toward what was meant to be.

One proof of which was that Momish himself solved the problem of how to get to the Oilmen's Club.

"The new election rules are very strict, Ivan Palych." Momish furrowed his forehead anxiously, fingering the bumps with one hand, reading from a newspaper he held in the other. "They set the size of the picture a candidate can have on his posters, how big the posters can be, and what color. . . ."

They were in Momish's office, which was about double normal size, with a red carpet leading up to a T-shaped desk made of two conference tables set together. The wood was too smooth to be domestic. Scandinavian, maybe? The table facing him was covered in green felt, set with glasses, water carafes, and pencils, as if for a conference. The crosspiece was absolutely empty, save for eight telephones and Momish, who was looking troubled. Behind him was a large map of western Kazakhstan, and a rectangle of slightly darker wood where Lenin had once hung.

"Listen, Momish, what are you worried about?" Duvakin leaned back expansively, even crossing his legs. "That's how the rules are everywhere now, and what happens? It means that everybody looks alike, nobody can tell one candidate from the next, so who do people vote for, when they actually get to the box? They vote for the name they remember, that's who they vote for. And whose name do people remember in Novii Uzen?"

Momish had looked a little relieved, before another thought slid across his face. "But the meetings with the candidates are the same thing, we're only allowed to speak for ten minutes each, and nobody else is allowed to make speeches for us. . . ."

"Do the rules say anything about having someone answer questions?"

"Answer questions?"

"Sure, like about Novii Uzen's place in the integrated federative economic structure, and your new relationship to Moscow."

The cave fire had kindled again in Momish's dark eyes, and Monday afternoon, just before four, Duvakin was at the Oilmen's Club, a sheet-metal barn that looked as if it should have been a pumping station, the sides whanging and whining in the wind, the air stale and hot both from the sun beating down outside and the crush of oil-blackened, sweat-stained men inside.

"Today is such an important meeting," Momish had explained as Abdulla drove them to the hall—Duvakin had had to scrunch

into a backseat that had been designed for people without knees—
"that we asked the men to be here early, so that no one could pack
the hall."

No one else, you mean, Duvakin thought, when they entered,
to deafening chants of "Momish! Momish! Momish!"

It was difficult to imagine how the space could serve as a club.
A cement floor, sheltered by sheet metal that was pocked here and
there with holes through which shafts of sunlight descended, in
swirls of dust motes and smoke. A platform had been erected near
one end, with a table and several chairs, and, as a backdrop, an
anachronistic banner in red, slightly drooping because the left stan-
dard was crooked; the gold letters still urged "ALL POWER TO THE
SOVIETS!" The club could have held half Novii Uzen, but still the
men crushed themselves up against the platform, like piglets straining for a teat. It was a sweaty group; the air was rich with oil and
tobacco and hair pomade. The din reminded Duvakin of beer
halls, but there was nothing of the beer hall's urine stink, the
stickiness of beer slosh, and the thick-lipped incoherent mumble
of drinkers. Young, most of them were, and with that typical
southern swagger, shirts rolled up over arm muscles, mouths a
mass of gold teeth. They were excited, punching each other in the
arm, shouting and shoving. Momish's chanters, a good majority of
the crowd, held most of the half circle nearest the stage, waving
their placards and elbowing aside interlopers; some of their signs
were in Russian, but most were in some kind of modified Cyrillic,
the words readable but nonsense.

Beyond these men the crowd whistled, not cheered; the signs
were fewer, and more brandished than waved. Those signs, too,
were in a language Duvakin did not understand, and most were
handmade. Several weren't even in an alphabet that Duvakin understood, but instead seemed to be the wormy scrawls of Arabic or
Persian. Duvakin's stomach twisted nervously when he noticed the
word "Alash" on some of the signs.

If any of this disturbed Momish, the man certainly gave no
sign. Smiling so broadly that two dimples Duvakin had not yet seen
appeared on either side of his broad white teeth, the Azerbaijani
climbed onto the stage and raised his hands in greeting; improbably,
the noise in the building grew, to become physically painful, almost

an assault. Duvakin let Abdulla guide him to the edge of the stage, his confidence draining away.

He had imagined this as a Moscow meeting, in a dusty hall somewhere in the administration building of a factory. There would still be a quote from Lenin on the walls, with letters missing where the glue had given out, and hard wooden seats, which would groan as people shifted about to pass forward their scraps of paper scrawled with questions; Duvakin would open them, and calmly, dispassionately, would recite some stern fictions about rising prices and the need for increased productivity, so that people would come to know that a vote for Momish was a vote for longer hours, less pay, and the threat of being fired.

Christ, he thought now as he was jostled and pushed, it wasn't even clear that this crowd would understand Russian, and even if they did . . .

They didn't look calm or rational.

"Comrades! Friends!" Mogammed Alioglu held his right hand high, like the statue he probably dreamed of becoming one day. Keeping his eyes on the crowd, he greeted the two other men who were already on the platform; both were Asians, but Duvakin was already beginning to grow used to the physical differences between the Caucasians and the Central Asians, and so guessed that they were one of each. Certainly the round-faced and narrow-eyed one, with hair stiff and black as a horse's tail, kept aloof, greeting Momish with a simple, unsmiling nod. The other, with luxuriant black curls, and eyes like pools of ink, rushed over to Momish, to whisper nervously in his ear. The message was long, and the man hopped from foot to foot like a child, but Momish nodded gravely, seriously, imperturbably.

Another candidate and the moderator, Duvakin decided, wondering where Edik was and who his supporters might be. The man speaking to Momish finished, looked expectantly at Momish, who spoke a few words, then turned to the crowd.

"I am informed . . . please, please, I am touched by your friendship, but let me speak. . . ." The cacophony of shouts, claps, and jeering whistles subsided slightly. "I am told that one of the candidates has not been able to come, but that someone wishes to speak on his behalf! The rules forbid this. . . ."

The noise swelled up instantly, like a shriek of pain, and the signs thrashed about like grass in the wind rush before a bad thunderstorm. Momish simply waited, both hands raised. Finally he was able to ride down the dying wave of noise with his voice. "*But . . . but I move that we let the man speak! This is a candidates' meeting, the people are entitled to hear . . .*" The end of the sentence was lost in another uproar; Momish smiled majestically and withdrew to take a seat beside the other candidate, who looked decidedly pale and dim next to the beaming Boss. The rough edge of the plywood stage was cutting into Duvakin's middle, but even with that preoccupation he felt the first shivers of doubt that it would be so easy to unseat Momish, no matter what his administrative sins.

In a crowd, at least in this crowd, the man *looked* like a leader. Especially when, with considerable strain, a small knot of men squeezed through the crowd, to emerge, flushed and crumpled, on the floor below the elevated Momish, who gave a courtly nod and extended his hand, with the distinct air of a man generously sharing a taste of his dinner.

The knot loosened, to disgorge one of the oddest-looking people Duvakin had ever seen. An elderly Asian so slight and short that he might have been carved from some wind-twisted root, the man wore his wispy graying beard to the middle of his chest, and his hair down to his shoulders, like an Orthodox priest. Instead of the priest's black cassock, though, this man's clothes were white, save where they were embroidered (or painted?) with intricate spiderwebby designs. When the man was first handed up to the stage Duvakin assumed the thigh-length shirt was cloth, like the one Tolstoy always wears in pictures, but as the man moved to his seat, smiling as though feeble-minded, Duvakin realized it was primitive leather, as if from a museum exhibit. Well, it went with the fellow's necklace of bones or perhaps stones, the white felt cap shaped like an Easter cake, and the horsetail flywhisk.

Duvakin snorted; say what you would about this new democracy business, it certainly has made life more amusing!

It was then that he realized he was the only person who had laughed. The men in the crowd, even the other men on the podium, seemed suddenly edgier, and the shouting and whistling had ceased. Even Momish rose to offer the man a seat, and did not sit again until this character had sat and beamed his weak-eyed thanks out at the audience.

"We are here"—the man who was moderator stepped to the front of the stage to begin in a nervous voice, speaking Russian even though, as far as Duvakin could make out, he was the only Russian in the room—"we are here to listen to the candidates for the post of executive secretary for the city soviet, to become acquainted with their programs and to ask them the necessary questions, before voting for comrade Ibragimov, Mogammed Alioglu . . ."

There was an angry bark from the crowd, quickly drowned by a roar and more foot-stomping. One of the men who had helped pass the medicine man up leaped onto someone's shoulders, clutching his friend's head with one hand, haranguing the crowd, face crimson, and gesturing with the other, until someone else grabbed him and he sank back into the mob. The uproar continued for a moment; then Momish motioned the speaker to come nearer. The plump and sweaty announcer bent quickly, listened, then came back to the microphone, where, over the squeak of the apparatus, he corrected himself. "Before the balloting, which takes place next month. There are three candidates. Each of them will have ten minutes, and five minutes for questions."

There was another huddle on the stage: the moderator speaking with Momish, who leaned back to invite the other two men to participate. The man who had been there first leaned over, but the medicine man just blinked and smiled, like a pensioner enjoying the sun as he licks the last of his gruel from his toothless gums.

"In the interests of fairness," the moderator announced, with an uncertain glance back, "Mogammed Alioglu has agreed that the order of speakers should be alphabetical, so first to address you will be . . ."

The man's name was something like Baimukhametov, and he introduced himself, in accent-free Russian, as an engineer at the natural-gas pumping station. He held up a sheaf of papers, put on a pair of glasses, and began to read his speech in a voice that quickly became difficult to distinguish from the hum of the wind-shaken sheet metal.

"The entire weight of the complex problems that are pinning us to the ground, dear friends, is a direct result of the administrative-command system of the past, which long ago outlived its usefulness. Now we are moving toward the world-standard practices of the market economy, and neither Alma-Ata nor Moscow can dictate to us where and how we are to live, to whom we will sell what is ours and at what price . . ."

Knowing that in his own remarks he might have to refer in some way to what the man was saying, Duvakin did his best to listen, but the combination of the flat, metallic voice and the phrases, as familiar and as empty as the shelves of any shop, immediately induced a drowsy inattention, so that even though he listened to every word, Duvakin could not have repeated a single thing the engineer said.

The effect on the crowd was much the same, save for a thin scattering of people near the back, who tried with their shouts and clapping to stimulate some vivacity. As nearly as Duvakin could make out, the man recommended that instead of letting politicians in Alma-Ata and Moscow control their lives, they should elect him and thereby pass the city over wholly to the control of technicians, who would run the city on a rational economic basis.

Enthusiasm was measured, and there were no questions.

Momish's turn was less a speech than a celebration. No recitation of accomplishments past, nor promise of what was to come, was completed; each time the Azerbaijani managed a word or two, the front half of the crowd would erupt in chants of "Momish! Momish! Momish!," the back half in equally loud whistles and jeers. The edge of the crowd surged and seethed, and here and there, at the frontier between the two groups, were flurries of fists, subdued by the dense crush of the crowd. Duvakin was swallowing compulsively, dreading the moment when the Azeri would turn to him, and ask him to the stage. He had no idea what he would say.

Momish's time ended, and Duvakin tensed his hands on the edge of the stage, wondering nervously whether he would be able to haul his bulk up onto the platform without seeming foolish. To his surprise, though, he wasn't called.

Instead, Momish withdrew and the third speaker came forward, with an energy that had seemed impossible seconds before. The raucous hall grew still, and an excitement began to crackle round the building like summer lightning, making Duvakin's neck hairs stand on end.

The man took a position on the edge of the platform, raised both hands high, palms up, and proclaimed in a ringing voice, "Allah akhbar!"

To Duvakin's amazement, the crowd, or most of it, repeated the chant, and did so two more times, led by the old man, who faced right, then left, for this prayer.

Duvakin wriggled sideways away from center stage, to whisper in Abdulla's ear. "Who *is* this person?" Disturbingly, the young driver was as rapt as the other men in the hall, and when the fellow on the stage brought his hands down over his face, like a cat grooming, Abdulla did the same.

After an impossibly long breath, the man began speaking, in Russian that sounded like someone shaking a box full of broken dinner plates. "Air good, friends. *Breathe* good." His voice was high and nearly singsong. "Allakh make air for man to breathe, man make air no good breath. Man poison own air. Man poison soil, man poison water. . . ." Well-muscled, sunburned leathernecks and roustabouts, oil black around their fingernails and ground into their horn-tough hands, they were now rapt on the speaker, who seemed to grow taller and younger as he spoke. "Land no belong one man, Allakh make land for all man. Land belong man who live on land, who make living from land. When we break word with land, life break too. . . ."

Duvakin could have hooted with relief and amusement. All his nervousness and incomprehension slid away, because he immediately understood who the man was and what he was doing.

He was mesmerizing the crowd, like any Moscow television charlatan. For all his buckskin shirt and "Allah akhbar," this singsong old man was no more than a Novii Uzen version of Anatolii Kashpirovskii.

Duvakin shook his head in amused disgust, and continued to push his way sideways along the stage through the dense, sweaty crowd like a stone through tar. He had come to take for granted the disorder, the street demonstrations, the strikes, the dirt and the rudeness and the corruption, everything that "new thinking" had brought to Russia. The only thing he could never quite get over was these charlatans, like Kashpirovskii. People abandoned everything to these faith healers and hypnotists, lolling their heads and waving their arms and letting spittle run down their chins. People spent hundreds, thousands of rubles for "cures"—water "energized" by Sasha Chumak's brain waves, crystals "imbued" with Dzhunna Datashvili's special powers. Most of all, though, they *believed*. The Party had failed them, perestroika had failed them, communism had failed them, capitalism had failed them, and now people were prepared to kill rather than let Kashpirovskii and the other shamans fail them. If one of these miracle men said that their blood pressure was going to go down, it did. If he said their hair would grow back, it did.

Duvakin did his best to laugh at these new Rasputins, but in fact the healers worried him. People believed so fully; what would happen if they were told to attack the militia or kill the Jews or quit their jobs, burn their clothes, and walk naked into the sea?

And in *this* crowd of half-civilized Asian roughnecks?

As if having read his mind, the speaker suddenly chanted something, flung his hands high. The men in the audience did the same, the chant a roar in the tin building. The chant was repeated—if anything, louder. Duvakin glanced at Abdulla, at the other young men around him.

Kashpirovskii's hypnotic method was to have you relax, but these men were anything but relaxed. There was a glint in their eyes, nervous energy rippling across their skins. Muscles were taut, and the crowd pressed ever tighter, straining. Christ, Duvakin could feel the air coming shallower, as his ribs had no place to expand. Fighting a rising panic, he grunted and shoved his way along, trying to fight free of the crowd.

Finally, blessedly, Duvakin found himself on the edge of the tangled mass and with a final jerk got himself free. His clothes were twisted and crumpled, he was wringing wet with sweat, but he was free.

He stood panting like a man pulled from a quagmire. It was several minutes before he was collected enough again to wonder what Momish was making of this. Good God, the man couldn't *hope* that Duvakin would be able to hold this crowd's attention, not now, after the shaman here got through. It would be a lucky thing if the crowd didn't go out looking for virgins to sacrifice or something, Duvakin thought, as he did what he might to put his clothes straight.

See, even Momish! he thought, as if he had won an argument. The Azerbaijani was sitting rotated leftward, resting his left elbow on the chair's arm, and he was holding his head at a slight angle, listening intently to this singsong priest-who-wasn't-a-priest. Being at the edge of the stage, Duvakin couldn't see Momish's face, but everything about the man's body said he was as caught up by Comrade Deerbones as the rest of the hall.

Ugh, he thought, the devil take them all, this whole crazy peninsula of sand, oil, and flies!

The shaman was talking now, his voice soaring and dipping like some sort of desert bird. He was almost singing, and somehow the pinging of the sheet metal, the moan of the wind, the rustle of the crowd, all seemed only to make the crowd's silence more profound. The voice went up and down Duvakin's spine like bedbugs, and he decided to go outside to wait.

It was hot there, but even so the breeze knifing through the door felt cool compared to the damp oven of the crowd. Duvakin stood in the shade of the doorway, trying to adjust his eyes to the painful glare of the midafternoon sun, bounding off the chalky dust like bullets off a tank.

Duvakin sighed, melancholy replacing his earlier panic. Melancholy for the country, really. What was that saying? "In Russian, all roads lead to disaster"? The Momishes had taken the country to the absolute lip of the abyss, and who was there left to stop the whole damn contraption from toppling over into bloody chaos? A handful of children, who had the intentions of saints and the perseverance of butterflies. Where was Edik, anyway? The whole reason Duvakin had come to this crazy club was to "meet the voters" for him, and then he doesn't show up. Not that there was much Edik could have done here this afternoon anyway, once the shaman began his chant, but still, the young man might at least have *been* here. . . .

The medicine man seemed to be finishing up, his amplified voice louder here than it had been inside.

". . . know several things. We know we are men, we know we are Muslims, we know we are Turks. I am Kazakh, you are Azeri, you are Lezgin, and Allakh gives each of us our proper land, to live among our own people. We are one umma, one community, whom the Ivans keep shake together like scorpions in a box, make us fight and kill each other. No more, I say, no more blood, no more hate. We are Muslims, we are brothers. Each of us must take up our own land once more, take back our own history, make our own people great again! It was our Alash who made us Kazakhs, and so we name ourselves for him. Know, though, that this not politics, this not democracy, this *life*, this the way of Allakh! That is why I call upon all Muslim, you maybe Kazakh, you maybe Azeri, you maybe Lezgin, no matter, you vote for the chosen of Allakh, Eduard Mordach. . . ."

Was this a mistake? Duvakin's fist, poised to knock at the dried and splintery boards of the unpainted, sun-warped gate, froze in midair. He looked down the narrow, dusty alley, empty save for a slat-ribbed dog snoozing in the cooler air of the shadow cast by the opposite wall. The mud-brick walls caught the sun and held it, baking the air close and hot. Duvakin had never been in an Eastern town before, and was deeply uneasy at the narrow alleys meandering aimlessly past doors fitted tightly into blind walls higher than a man is tall. Empty, and yet he had the spine-shivering certainty he was not alone. Of course you're not alone, he thought; that's why you've come, to find Edik. The two metal eyes where a padlock would hang were empty, so somebody had to be home. He shook himself, scowled, and hammered imperiously at the door, scattering flecks of dried green paint. The devil take it, he told himself firmly, if with a certain bravado. Watched or not, it wasn't like this visit was going to be any surprise to Edik, not in *this* town.

People in Novii Uzen looked out for Edik, Duvakin was certain of that now.

Shocked and angered by what he could only understand as treachery, Duvakin had had the greatest difficulty containing his fury until they got back to town and he could look for the young man to demand an explanation. As Duvakin expected, the meeting broke up after the shaman finished, and he offered some clumsy pretext on which to be taken to town, rather than back to the compound. Had he been less preoccupied, he might have worried about the thinness of his lie, but there would have been no need to worry; both Momish and Abdulla were as quiet and thoughtful as he while they drove back past the rusty, blackened pumps, which gnawed tirelessly away at the rainbow-hued, greasy ground.

The first likely-seeming group of youths that Duvakin approached, a surly knot of swarthy louts sprawled about a sand-filled fountain in the town's center, affected to know no Russian, muttering answers that made their pals guffaw, covering their wispy mustaches with their hands. Their eyes, though, glittering like damp coals, said they understood and knew where Edik could be found. The old women scuttling in and out of a sour-smelling grocery story didn't even pause when he tried to ask, whisking past before he could spit out the question. Cutting through a courtyard, he came on a group of brightly dressed young mothers hanging out wash and gossiping in the milky sunshine, almost Gypsy-looking with their swarthy faces and squads of bawling infants, but when he came up to them, they immediately pulled the corners of their head scarves across their faces and glared daggers at him, making a noise like clacking knives. Duvakin knew he wouldn't approach young women again.

But he was there already, so he asked anyway. "Edik? Eduard Mordachkin?" Like the louts, like the old women, they replied nothing, but they knew.

Why in the blue-bellied devil had Edik asked him to go to that meeting? And just what kind of game was he playing anyway? "Eduard Mordach." That had to be Edik, didn't it? Who did he think he was going to fool? And why? What on earth was that young man going to gain by pretending to be a Turk of some sort? Even if he *won* this election, how could he possibly run the cursed town, once people understood he was no Turk?

And as for that rock through Duvakin's window . . .

Duvakin returned to the compound as the sun dropped below the horizon, his fury long since usurped by a queasy loneliness. As soon as the sun set, bone-rattling chill closed over the compound as swiftly as if the gas had been turned off. The only heat in the

cottage was an electric spiral with a resistance coil that glowed in-
tense, furious red but radiated almost no warmth; Duvakin had to
put his feet nearly against the aluminum dish before he felt anything.

Edik, Momish, Rosa . . . He huddled against the meager
warmth, wondering who among them was real, who was dangerous?
There was a great deal of night just beyond his cottage door, and
not much else, save for restless, unknown creatures that chuffed and
grunted and, infrequently, barked. The night noises around his cottage made no sense, just as Novii Uzen made no sense. Conjectures,
worries, possibilities wheeled and flitted about Duvakin like bats,
never quite seen, always at the corner of vision, making the heart
pump, the stomach sluice with adrenaline.

After another night restless and sticky with nightmares,
Duvakin awoke, clinging like a shipwreck victim to the one firm
fact he knew. Games were games, and intrigues intrigues, but Borya
Ermolov had died. Whatever Ermolov might have been as a man,
for the moment it didn't matter; what mattered was that he was
dead, and Duvakin was damned if he would let himself end up in
the same position.

Novii Uzen had no shortage of people who seemed capable of
dropping a building on a man's head. Duvakin felt he was collecting
candidates as meat does flies. Until yesterday, though, Duvakin had
been pretty sure Edik wasn't among them. Since that crazy shaman's
speech, though, he was a lot less sure.

Which made it seem very smart to find young Edik, today.

Even Rosa, happy as she was to sing the praises of Edik himself,
was reluctant to speak of Edik's whereabouts when Duvakin raised
the question over his breakfast.

"He's ever so busy, Ivan Pavlovich, doing things for other people. He trains the young men, did you know that? In the prison, so
that they have a trade when they get out."

"His address, Rosa. I have to have his address."

"I'll get him for you, Ivan Palych! He's very difficult to reach,
hardly ever at his home! He does so much for so many people that—"

"Rosa, I need his address."

"Oh, I don't know it precisely, Ivan Palych, it's someplace in
Uzen, and . . . Really, it would be better if you just let me pass the
word along, he'll see you as soon as he knows. . . ."

And there Duvakin had dropped his questions, with an airy "Oh, that's all right, it was just to have a chat with, Rosa. Nothing pressing."

All this reticence, all this coyness, convinced him that he had touched a nerve. Edik was the key to *something*; Duvakin just didn't know what yet.

Coming out to Uzen alone had been a gamble, but it had paid off. Uzen was as Duvakin had guessed it would be, a sprawl of low-roofed mud-brick houses and walls that had been hunched against the Mangyshlak winds long before the coming of the derricks and the pumps. Duvakin had guessed that the population would be small; in fact, the place was almost deserted.

"Edik! Open up! It's me, Duvakin!" he shouted, frustrated by the noises he distinctly heard coming through the boards. He banged again, rattling the door in its frame.

The only response he got was that the dog raised its head, which it now let fall slowly back, as if certain there would be no excitement. The dust his knocking had raised filtered slowly back down to the ground.

The bus had dumped him out where the asphalt ended; the only other sign that this was the twentieth century, not the twelfth, was a scrawny pole helping two brittle black electrical wires safely across the last few meters to a huge antediluvian glass insulator on the wall of the first house. Duvakin peered uncertainly into the inky shadows of the mazelike alleys and thought sympathetically of the unlucky tree that had been brought so far to make that sun-desiccated pole.

A handful of dogs, too skinny and hot to bother him, a few chickens, uncomfortable and grumpy in their feathers, and three old men, sitting cross-legged under some reeds that had been bound together into a table-sized mat. They were as brown and impassive as the mud walls, scarcely turning their heads even to watch him approach, sweating and red-faced.

"Edik? Eduard Mordachkin?"

They were flaying some sort of animal, Duvakin saw with a flip-flop of his stomach. The carcass was too small for a cow and too large for a lamb, and it had a thick tail. God, could it be a donkey? Duvakin would have gagged had his throat not been so dry.

"There." The one with the skinner waved his bloody knife, sending unhappy squadrons of flies off to glint green in the sun. "There . . ."

"Six gate," the man holding the farther pair of legs had added, his face speckled with blood. "Six gate . . ."

Duvakin looked back down the serpentine alley, mentally recounting gates. Five, six . . . no, this was it.

"God *damn* it!" Duvakin barked in disgust, and kicked petulantly at the door. With a shrieking crack something gave, either the sun-dried ancient wood or the wind-flaked dried mud of the walls, and the top of the door tipped dizzily toward Duvakin.

Two slab-cheeked Asians peered out, eyes like chunks of roofing tar.

Duvakin stepped backward, embarrassed. "I was . . . I'm sorry, I . . ." He reached around for his wallet. "I'll pay, of course, it was . . ."

One of the pair gave Duvakin a dull, indifferent glance, looked the door up and down, and then, with a screeching yank, jerked the doorway the rest of the way out. In spite of the heat, the man was wearing a leather jacket, which bulged with what Duvakin doubted were sweaters.

The other man, also in leather, looked the gate over, looked at Duvakin. "Hey, Ivan." He grinned, looking so much like the bus driver from the other day that they could have been brothers, except that this one's nose had once been broken, making his Asiatic face even flatter. "You want make bet so bad Russian boy?"

The leer offended Duvakin. "Bet? I don't want to bet, I want to talk. . . . They told me this is where—"

Except he never got to say anything, because the two men each took an arm, and almost carried him over the remnants of the gate.

Any illusions Duvakin might have nourished about the hidden splendors that lay beyond Oriental gates were destroyed by the tiny sun-baked square he was dropped, stumbling, into. A desultory drip from a cheap plaid shirt flapping on a line hung corner to corner had carved a miniature ravine across the yard, and some chickens had retreated to an inverted oil drum in another corner, from where they examined him disapprovingly. A faded blue plastic washtub hung on the wall opposite him, among other tatters and bits of domestic life.

And in the middle of the courtyard another Asian sat hunched over a table, surrounded by a crush of young men, most of whom were muttering with barely contained excitement and waving money, bound packets of bills. Never looking up, the Asian would extend his left hand from the scrum; a packet or two of bills would be put in it, and would disappear, while the man jotted something with the stubby pencil clutched in his right.

Duvakin marveled; there must have been twenty or thirty men there, who were so silent in their intensity that he had not heard them outside the gate. That intensity was unnerving, even as he understood it: the bills were hundreds, twenty to a bundle.

"Brick, Ivan, two thousand ruble." The broken-nosed man to his left grinned again, showing teeth of ruddy gold. "That how bet we make. How many brick Ivan bet?"

Duvakin made 350 rubles a month, and had been given four thousand rubles for the expenses of this trip. Two bricks, he thought numbly; this Ivan would not be betting many bricks.

"Bet on what?" he said instead of answering.

The two gate watchers exchanged glances; then one indicated with a thick brown finger that Duvakin should step through a doorway on the other side of the sun-baked yard.

Hesitant, Duvakin knew he had no choice, and did so.

In the moment it took his eyes to adjust to the change between brilliant sun and the dark of the room, Duvakin was aware only of the crush and heat of a crowd, jostling and breathing tensely, broken by an infrequent shrill giggle.

Good mother of God, Duvakin thought nervously, it's like being between anvil and hammer here. Go farther into this room, or stay out here with the Asian with a head like a watermelon dropped from a shelf, who wanted him to bet a few "bricks." At least the room must have a back door, Duvakin thought, or a window, or something he could squeeze himself out. Duvakin began to sidle into the crowd, working around to the right.

The crowd was a crush of young men, packed together tighter than seeds in a sunflower. As his eyes adjusted Duvakin could make out that the room was good-sized, maybe ten or twelve meters square, and furnished with crude bleachers—planks set across inverted buckets—so that the men in the back could see. Through their knees Duvakin caught glimpses of a clear floor, the crowd kept back by what looked like hockey boards, save that the rink would have been not much bigger than the table from the *antikvariat*, back home. His vision kept improving, but it only suggested his situation was getting worse. There were no windows; what light and air there were seemed to come in through holes in the tops of small domes that dimpled the roof. He eyed the one nearest him, trying to convince himself that if really necessary he might be able to pull himself up one and through, and so get away. For a man who some mornings had even to elaborate a strategy to manage reaching his shoelaces, the plan would have been unlikely even if it had also provided a way to get up *to* the domes, but still Duvakin let himself be reassured, because he had no choice.

In the depths of the room Duvakin found a space almost wide enough for him at the end of a plank. He legged up, shoving at the men already there, who shoved back, muttering. It was an ugly crowd, which Duvakin was glad to have preoccupied with whatever it was had brought them all here. He perched precariously on the narrow board, wondering whether the old butchers out in the square had misunderstood him, or whether this indeed had something to do with Edik.

He was still trying to jostle a more secure footing for himself when two men came up to the ring and stepped awkwardly over the waist-high boards. One of the men was Asian, but the other was Russian, to Duvakin's surprise. They were carrying sacks, which flopped and wiggled of their own accord. The room began to hum, like a hive when little boys come too near, bearing sticks. Right in front of Duvakin one of the men began to punch another on the arm, convulsing with excitement.

Another Asian stepped from the murk into the shaft of sunlight that stabbed the center of the sand-strewn ring, shouting like a circus master. Duvakin didn't know what language the man was speaking, but whatever his words, they hit the crowd like cut potatoes dropping into heated fat. As the man pointed first at the Russian, then at the Asian, the room exploded in deafening cheers, jeers, catcalls, whistles, and the flurry of men making side bets, fives and tens changing hands not in packets now, but singly.

Then, eyeing each other with the wariness of boxers, the two men set their bags down gently and stepped hastily back. For a moment nothing happened; then the bags shook and slithered down, and first one, then the other bird poked out, then shook their heads, radiating offended dignity.

Roosters, Duvakin saw, admiring the way the sun glinted on the coppery neck feathers, and the delicate, almost dancing way the birds moved, stepping gingerly free of the sacking.

The man who had been doing the announcing reached for the sacking with a long stick, then climbed clumsily over the guard rail. The room was a rising din now, in which the birds stepped slowly, like ballerinas.

Then, with a squawk and a flurry of feathers too fast for Duvakin's eye to follow, the two birds engaged; the crowd surged forward, nearly knocking Duvakin from his bucket top, but also clearing him a little breathing room. If he had been smart, he would have seized that moment, to try to push on around to where he supposed the inner door might be, but like everyone else in the room, he couldn't take his eyes away from the birds.

At first it was impossible to make out anything, beyond a whirling ball of dust and coppery feathers. Then the cocks disengaged and, their first blood rush satisfied, began to stalk one another, circling around with their necks low, feathers fluffed up, wings extended.

How did people decide which chicken to drop their "bricks" on? There seemed to be nothing distinguishing the two birds. Both were about the same size, and were clearly of the same breed, with ruddy necks, coppery chest feathers, and greenish rumps and tail feathers. One might have been slightly younger, though, and maybe less experienced; he seemed nervous, feinting toward the other bird, then leaping, fluttering, back, in what must be a prodigious waste of energy. The crowd shouted at each lunge, shouted louder when the birds were apart. Embarrassed, the two owners began to climb into the ring, but then suddenly there was that rolling ball of dust and feathers, which broke with a squawk.

Duvakin was sickened to see that the younger bird now had

one wing that would not flare open, and when it shook its head, blood splattered the sand.

The crowd's shouts became a howl.

If roosters could smile, the older one would have, just then. The bird hopped forward, head snaked to one side so he could see his opponent, then leaped, feetfirst, his spurs glinting in a sudden flash, as if made of metal. Then the birds turned again, and Duvakin could see that the flash *was* metal: bits of razor blade taped to their spurs, which even without the razors were long and cruel.

The other bird was no quitter; it met the attack coming in, rolling in under the aggressor and extending its claws in the air, but the attacker was even quicker. When the birds disengaged again, the wounded bird had no right eye, but just an ooze of black blood, from which dangled strips of flesh.

The crowd was almost faint with shouting, waving money, screaming. The men on Duvakin's board bounced and beat one another on the shoulders, the head; surely it couldn't be long before the board gave way.

The damaged bird now could only circle away from its blind eye, because the other bird kept leaping to that side, trying to approach from where its victim could not see it. Neck feathers puffed up and yellow beak opened in warning, the losing bird was doing its best to look fierce, but the broken wing, the dangling eye, and the shattered feathers made the effort pathetic, as if he were half in the stewpot already.

In fact, when the bird tottered a few more steps to the right, then lay down, neck stretched out in the dust, the men around Duvakin began to relax, straightening up, laughing, slapping one another on the arm or shoulder, or clutching their heads in despair that seemed more mock than real, holding out hands for bets they had won, looking grim and disconsolate if they were digging into pockets for bets they had lost.

The winning bird strutted about the sand of the ring, studying his opponent now with one eye, now the other, as if flaunting his health to make his victory the sweeter. The bird even puffed out his chest and crowed, before leaping forward in a blinding blur, to hammer his yellow bill into the top of the other's skull, in a coup de grace.

However, as unexpectedly for the crowd as for the bird, the

apparent loser convulsed in the final effort of a hero, to slash out at the cock as it descended. The spurs, their shards of razor blade attached, caught the bigger bird in the base of the gullet, to expose a windpipe that looked like gray radiator hose.

Startled, the cut bird leaped back and began thrashing around, trying to see its own neck. The slashed windpipe whistled above the suddenly silent crowd, spraying blood everywhere as the chicken thrashed, until, with a last bubbling gasp, it toppled sideways into the sand and lay still.

Exultant, the Russian threw a beefy leg over the boards, came into the ring to reclaim his bird, which was a huddled mass of feathers in the bloody sand. He held it aloft, grinning wildly and waving it at the crowd, almost as if taunting them.

"The big money's on the other bird," a familiar voice said below him. Duvakin pirouetted awkwardly, looked down at Edik's lazy grin.

"Edik!" Duvakin's feeling of surprise was quickly washed away in relief. He tried to disguise it, gesturing at the crowd. "Just taking in a little local color. . . ."

Not bothering with explanations, either to offer or to accept, Edik simply held up a hand, to touch Duvakin's elbow. "It's going to get a little busy here, Palych"—he was still smiling, but the meaning of the extended hand was obvious—"so maybe you'll be wanting . . ."

The Russian had picked up his bird and was accepting the crowd's jeers, whistles, and shouts as if they were adulation. Holding the bird aloft and grinning, he circled the sand pit. The rooster bled indifferently, limp, with beak open and tongue hanging out, motionless even when the owner examined the eye, then extended and refolded the broken wing. With a shrug, the Russian took the cock by the head and swung it in a short sharp circle, breaking its neck. With a final swing he chucked the dead bird into the crowd and shouted, "You can all kiss my ass, you goat-fucking greasers!"

"I really think it would be a good time to come on around here, Ivan Palych." Edik now pulled on Duvakin's sleeve, nearly dumping him from the makeshift bench. •

"I don't think I can," Duvakin grunted, seeing no place to put his feet.

"I think you better." Edik jerked again, even harder. This time Duvakin came over, landing on Edik and several strangers.

Fortunately, the strangers seemed preoccupied, for the moment anyway. Some of the men in the crowd must have had enough Russian to understand the insult, or perhaps the dead chicken made words superfluous. One young man, rippling with health, after gesticulating extravagantly about a glob of blood that had spattered across his plaid shirt, had now leaped into the ring, flashing a homemade blade in his right hand.

"I think we had better do some slithering, Palych," Edik grunted, hauling at Duvakin like a sack of guts.

Letting himself be tugged through the surging crowd, Duvakin saw that the Russian had vanished, and that the man with the knife, his blade flicking like a tiger's tail, was now crouching, facing the large man with the shaved head who had been accepting bets. The bet taker was watching carefully but impassively, weight on his toes, legs spread, arms swinging from slightly hunched shoulders. He looked ready to eat this young hoodlum and then have two more for breakfast. Of course, some of his confidence might have come from the two men in leather coats who had just jumped into the ring behind the kid with the knife.

The crowd's yelling warned the boy, for he suddenly leaped, crouching, first left, then right, his eyes now those of the stalked, not the stalker. After a few backward steps he barked something, and a good ten young men much like him leaped over the barrier, tattooed arms flailing, gold teeth flashing in their shouting mouths.

The passions were spreading to the crowd. Duvakin half pushed, half was yanked through the crowd; someone punched him hard, in the right shoulder blade, and another hand grabbed at his jacket.

"God damn it, Palych, God damn it . . ." Edik was repeating now, almost panting, "God damn it . . ."

Then, blessedly, they were free of the crowd and squeezing through a doorway, past more of the bulky Asians who had met him at the front door.

"You can get out this way?" Duvakin puffed.

"You better hope to Christ you can," Edik muttered, intent on the way ahead. He nodded to one or two of the people who were in the darkened room, murmured something to one. Then, suddenly, brilliant sun.

Blinking and wincing, Duvakin stumbled out, tripped over something, banging his shin badly.

"Damn!" he exploded, sitting up in the dust.

"Yeah, damn you say." Edik's voice was that of someone trying to joke, but not yet able to. " 'Thank you' would be nice, but no, he has to kick over my motorcycle instead."

Duvakin's pupils had contracted enough that he could see: He had knocked against a faded red-and-silver Jawa, which was now leaking gasoline sideways into the sand.

"Bloody silly place to leave it," Duvakin grumped, hauling himself to his feet; he was struggling to suppress an absurd buoyancy, as if he had been saved from drowning.

Edik heaved the small motorcycle upright, set it on its slender brace again, then crouched to examine whether there had been damage. From that position he looked up. "Bloody silly place to find you, come to that." He was in canvas trousers, such as workmen wear, and an ancient cotton T-shirt, worn and sweat-stained under the arms. Duvakin noted that he was well muscled, but slight, and boyish somehow, with his pale, heavily freckled skin exposed, pale shoulder hairs glinting in the sun.

"You're here." Duvakin preferred the obvious to an explanation, in the hopes of getting one himself.

Instead, though, Edik went back to examining the machine, which appeared to have had a rubber tube knocked loose. Without his foreign clothes and his mirrored sunglasses, Edik seemed much younger and less commanding than he had in Momish's cottage, but his manner was as assured as ever.

"Meaning, why do I live out here?" he grunted as he twisted the tubing back into place. Then he grinned, unpleasantly feline.

Duvakin shrugged. The answer to that question would do as well as any for a starter.

Edik stood up, slapped dust from his hands and pants, then gestured at the courtyard, which was much like the other, save that they were alone. "Why do I live here? No electricity, no water, most of the village abandoned now, no repairs done for twenty years . . ." He looked Duvakin in the eye, as if trying to decide whether to say something. Then he smiled, as if deciding he wouldn't. "Because I'm crazy, right? Anyway, I don't really live in Uzen, I mostly work here." He pointed down at his clothes. "Reconstruction. Fixing the place up, trying to save the old buildings. Replacing bricks, shoring up, plastering, reroofing, that sort of thing. Roof, that's the crucial thing with these mud-brick buildings. Keep the water off them, they'll last forever, but let the roof go, in two winters the house is gone."

Duvakin shook his head, puzzled by Edik and by his own reaction to the young man. Rosa clearly considered him a hero, while making it awfully plain that it was better not even to mention his name to Momish. The way the people of town had protected Edik against Duvakin's questions, suggested other people revered him, too, and yet here Duvakin had found him at this cockfight. Duvakin could feel himself wanting to trust the young man, to be liked by him, when so much about the fellow should put Duvakin on guard.

"I went to the election meeting, like you asked me." He decided to keep a chilly distance between them yet. "I thought you were going to come."

"Ah, the meeting, of course." Edik smiled as he swung a leg over the Jawa and settled himself on the torn padding. "And Qayip Ali? He spoke?"

"The old man? He spoke."

"You want to meet him, close up? He's one of the natural wonders here, a genuine Kazakh *aksakal*, a 'white beard.' You know something? All it takes is for him to hold your hands for about a minute, lightly, just the fingertips and a little bit of your palm, and then he can tell you every illness you ever had, and what you've got right now. There's cases where he's caught things the Botkin Institute missed, after weeks of tests. And a lot of the illnesses he can cure, too, with roots and grasses. . . ."

"Chrissake, Edik, you're running as part of that Alash? Some kind of Kazakh nationalist bunch of crazy separatists, that threw a rock through my window?" Duvakin cut in, exasperated. "How in the name of the devil's black teeth do you expect to beat Ibragimov that way?"

"Edik! They're coming!"

They both jerked around at the interruption. A young woman,

almost a girl, leaned through the cheap lace covering another door-way. She had the long hair and flat face of a local, but the hair was bleached the color of last summer's nettles. There was something familiar about the girl, which it took Duvakin a moment to understand.

He had seen her before. At the Tumbleweed Restaurant. Talking with Momish.

The Edik to whom he turned back looked very different from any Edik he had seen so far. Smaller and younger, somehow.

"Thanks, Zemfira," he said warmly, then looked at Duvakin. "You feel like a motorcycle ride?"

"Motorcycle? Me?" Duvakin repeated dumbly, tempted even to laugh. He could just about imagine himself as a *roker*, buzzing about with the packs of teens on their blue-belching machines, whining like electric razors.

"You prefer maybe going down to the militia station in a Black Maria?" Then, to the girl, "Hey, Zemfira, bring my jacket!"

"Get it yourself!" the girl shouted from somewhere inside the house. "It's hanging in the front room!"

Edik's face mottled along the jaw, but he climbed from the machine and went into the house. When he returned, he was wearing a leather jacket.

"Come on," he said with a jerk of his now-helmeted head, "otherwise there's going to be some awkward questions." Then he swung his leg back over, and began furiously kicking the reluctant Jawa.

Duvakin watched with the disjointed feeling that usually marks a dream. Every question he had asked seemed to generate two more, until now he felt as though he understood nothing. The girl: Was she Edik's wife? His girlfriend? And what had she been doing at that café? And the cockfight, which seemed to have been held in her house? And who in the devil were the *they* who were coming?

After enough kicks to have made even a dead mule jump, Edik's motorcycle finally fired, with a column of pigeon-blue smoke and a noise like a saw hitting a nail. Edik braced his legs wide, adjusted the helmet, and then pointed, to indicate that Duvakin should sit behind him.

Duvakin shook his head. He had never ridden a motorcycle.

The devil knew, it had been almost forty years since he had ridden a *bicycle*.

Edik kicked the machine off its stand, and then walked it around, toward a gate. Now Duvakin could hear the din from the next courtyard even above the racket of the motorcycle, stabbed through suddenly by a militia whistle.

Edik gestured that Duvakin should open the gate; after another moment's indecision he sprang forward to do so, jerking at the splintery wood. More shouts and whistles, before Duvakin looked carefully enough to note the hook he had to undo; he pushed back the latch, opened the door.

The young man revved the Jawa's motor, pushed out into the alleyway, then looked inquiringly at Duvakin.

Still undecided, and badly mystified, Duvakin went to the gateway to look. The alley was no more than two meters across, curved so that he could see nothing at either end. There were pops, as of explosions, and a white smoke drifted upward behind a wall, down to the right.

The first stinging tendrils reached Duvakin's nose at the same moment that he caught sight of a string of men in uniform running down the alley, their faces covered by gas masks.

Duvakin threw his leg over the vibrating machine and squeamishly held Edik by the waist.

"Better hold tighter!" the young man shouted, accelerating sharply.

Duvakin nearly somersaulted over the Jawa's rear when the machine lurched forward; then he clung to Edik tighter than any lover.

Why is it that what makes sense at five A.M. always seems crazy by the time the offices open?

Duvakin wiped a thin film of sweat from his forehead, wishing that he had bathed instead of leaping up at first light to catch the first bus into Novii Uzen.

But that would supppose he had not spent a sleepless night, panic clawing for him like a blind badger, stray questions chasing each other around like sparrows and crows.

There had been too many unanswered questions these past two days, too many things that did not make sense.

Too many things about Edik.

How he had come to be at that cockfight, and why he was not at the meeting, and what his connection with this Alash was. Up until now it had been sensible and easy to assume that Momish was Duvakin's adversary; not only was it he whom Duvakin had been sent to Novii Uzen to unseat, but Momish was also an old-fashioned Boss, no better than the men who had double-crossed Duvakin before, to rip him away from Moscow, almost to kill him in Magadan.

But is the opponent of my opponent my ally?

If so, then Edik must be Duvakin's ally, and indeed, had Edik not rescued him yesterday, bearing him away on that Jawa and fetching him safely back to the cottage? Plus which, he was a Russian, and someone who appeared to know the ins and outs of Novii Uzen. Whom else could Duvakin trust in this pesthole, if not Edik?

And if he didn't trust Edik, then Duvakin was even more cut off than he had thought.

Still, something deep in the base of Duvakin's brain rejected Edik as an ally, the way a fish that's been snagged once refuses even the tastiest-looking lure. Which was why, as the sleepless night ground on, this telephone call to Chistoplotskii in Moscow had grown from important to vital.

And now that it looked impossible to make, the call seemed a matter of life or death.

"Damn it, how many times do I have to say it, I *have* no direct telephone line to the mainland! And even if I did, why should I let you use it?" Captain Tansybekov had not been especially pleased to discover badly shaven, pale, and baggy-eyed Duvakin waiting itchily outside his office, and nothing since had made him like Duvakin more. The man was plainly irritated.

Exasperated and frustrated, Duvakin ran his hand over his scalp, then shook off the hairs that had come loose. Tansybekov scowled, so Duvakin kicked at the hairs, trying to get them out of sight under the desk. His sole made a high-pitched squeak.

"For the love of God, you're telling me that . . . What if you had a terribly sensitive case? What if . . . what if it was, I don't know, some important local official that you had to report? What if somebody like, say . . . Mogammed Alioglu was breaking the law?" Duvakin chuckled, to suggest that his example was deliberately absurd. "You would still have to ask his permission to phone outside the city?"

"What case could I possibly have against Momish?" The militia captain sat with fingertips touching, his pens aligned to make a precise triangle with the flip-over calendar and a molded three-color plastic relief of the cruiser Aurora firing on the Winter Palace. Tansybekov's head looked freshly shaved, the hairline a bluish gloss on his coppery skin, his eyes black dabs above the massive cheekbones.

"What would it matter, if you'd have to ask his permission to pursue such a case?" Duvakin said testily, shoving himself away from the desk. Had he slept, Duvakin might not have felt as trapped as he did at that moment, but he hadn't, and he was thousands of kilometers from home, dependent upon Momish or Edik or both of them for food, shelter, information. For *telephones*, for God's sake.

There was no one in Novii Uzen he could talk to. Duvakin had understood that over and over as the night wore on. Rosa, who worked for Momish but seemed to love Edik? Momish? Abdulla? Duvakin was at the bottom of a well, at the end of the earth. He was alone.

Just as the sky had grown light enough to let him tell walls from furniture, he had decided that perhaps he could trust no man, but he might still trust a uniform. The familiar dove-gray of the militia captain's uniform.

Tansybekov studied him with livelier interest now, fingertips still together, but eyes brighter. "That means you have made progress with your . . . assignment?"

"Perhaps." Duvakin did his best to sound noncommittal, trying to remember what exactly he had told the captain his "assignment" was. Unconvincing coolness, for a man who had waited the better part of two hours for Tansybekov to come in, shifting miserably from buttock to buttock on a backless, splintery bench in the main corridor of the Novii Uzen militia station. "Nothing concrete, you understand," Duvakin added, so as not to have to tell Tansybekov more, and risk tangling himself up in his own stories, which he had forgotten. "Some ideas I want to test . . . with my superiors. . . ."

Those had been a long two hours, but strangely comforting, too. The station house was welcome and familiar after Duvakin's long nights among the crumpled, sour sheets, hands itching for a cigarette as he groped to think his way out of this maze. Although he had not been a militiaman for ten years, and had been posted to a hotel, not a precinct, for almost ten years before that, Duvakin still felt at home in Tansybekov's domain—the familiar cigarette burns blackening the curling linoleum all around the sand bucket in the corner, the bulletin board invisible beneath sheafs of "SEARCHING FOR . . ." flyers, each poorly photographed robber or murderer or thug looking more terrible than the next, the especially dangerous ones marked by a red diagonal stripe across the yellow, pulpy paper; the familiar parade of arrested and arresters in the too-narrow corridors, with their familiar exaggerated wails of protest or stony stares of indifferent manhood.

There were a lot of arrests in Novii Uzen. Youths mostly, some bleeding, some with swollen eyes, disheveled. Some were drunk, swearing wildly and flailing like hammer mills; others were glassy-eyed, limp as drowned puppies. Prostitutes, too, a brawling busload of them, haughty as alley cats as they stalked by, tails in the air.

Tansybekov studied Duvakin a bit longer, considering something in silence, then reached over decisively, to pluck a red telephone from among the eight or ten receivers that stood in ranks on the windowsill behind him. Carefully guiding the cord with his free hand, Tansybekov put the apparatus on the desk, the dial turned politely toward Duvakin. "Please . . . with this you can raise Gurev, to order your call. They will connect within the hour."

"No, Comrade Tansybekov, I'm afraid you don't understand." Duvakin did his best to sound cool and in control, despite the sweaty bind of his armpits in yesterday's shirt. "I have calls, of a . . . well, a private nature."

What Duvakin really meant was that he didn't want witnesses, for what he knew for certain would be a stupid phone call; after all, what he was going to do, in effect, was call Chistoplotskii, Russia's Minister of Energy, to ask, "Why is it *really* that you sent me to Novii Uzen?"

That was the dark and grasping question that had guaranteed Duvakin would not sleep, that had curled around his arms and legs, sucking him back into doubt, each time he managed, for a moment, to hack his mind free of the winding tendrils of his own suspicions.

Why had he been sent to Novii Uzen?

"Everything in Russia happens by chance, unless it happens to be planned. The difference between a man and a fool, my friend, is knowing the one from the other."

Those words had staggered up from some tomb in Duvakin's memory, in the wolf hour of the night, when his whole body was stale with insomnia. General Polkovnikov's words, all those years ago in Magadan.

Polkovnikov, playing Duvakin for a fool.

Playing him like a chess *grossmeister*, in fact, since it was the *second* time that grinning devil had made Duvakin believe himself to be a free agent, in the interest of making a better pawn of him. Duvakin had lost his job, his apartment in Moscow, and a girl he thought he loved, and had damn near lost his life, because of that cursed General Polkovnikov. What made Duvakin burn brightest with shame, though, was his stupidity, was that he had believed himself to be free when in fact Polkovnikov had a finger firmly in each of Duvakin's ears, hopping him about the board like the lowliest of expendable chess pieces.

In fact, Duvakin had not even understood his own smoldering resentment at this humiliation until two or three winters ago, when he had been riding a suburban *elektrichka*, at evening. A partially crippled old man, his left shoe with a carved wooden sole almost half a meter thick, had slung his gunnysack in next to Duvakin, squeezed up against it with a garlicky sigh, and begun, without preamble or permission, to explain predestination. He was a Christian, and insane. Bored by the journey through the wastelands and backlots of suburban Moscow, unable to read because the car lights were broken, and rather enjoying the soft voice, which reminded him of the sound of a stroll through dry oak leaves, Duvakin had listened. Predestination, the man said, was so artfully arranged that God permits us to imagine we are free, even as He leads us.

"What if I kill myself?" Duvakin had argued with the old man, whose eyes were as clear and steady as a child's, or a dog's. "Or just get off at this next stop, which I don't even know the name of? Or, I don't know, smash my umbrella over your head? Do something that even *I* don't know I'm going to do? Wouldn't that prove I have freedom?"

"You would certainly *believe* that was the case, wouldn't you?" The old man had cackled with huge pleasure, as if he had made Duvakin the butt of a particularly clever joke.

Duvakin had descended from that train exactly where he had meant to all along, but considerably more thoughtful than he had expected. Because about God Duvakin didn't know one way or the other, but about Polkovnikov, what the man said was dead true.

And it had been his own fault!

Duvakin had been a pawn because he behaved like a pawn, reacted like a pawn. Abysmally, horribly *predictably*. The perfect tool.

Which, somewhere in the thick underbrush of last night's questions and doubts, Duvakin had begun to suspect he once again was. The questions he could not answer, the circumstances he could not explain—about all this was an increasingly familiar sensation, of someone's damp and greasy fingers, hopping Duvakin about the board of some game he was not elevated enough to see.

Well, Duvakin had promised himself, not a third time. Even a fool learns eventually.

Now Tansybekov studied Duvakin closely, made an indifferent face, then put the telephone back, pushed himself away from his desk, and went to the window, where he ran a finger along the glass, almost as if tracing something.

"Would your telephone call have anything to do with the cockfight yesterday?" the captain finally asked, one eyebrow raised in question.

Duvakin snapped his head up in surprise, then recovered, to pick at something on his knee. Damn it, how had the man known he'd been there? he wondered, at the same time wondering why the unexpected question made him feel so guilty.

"I was out walking, I saw all the people, I was curious." Duvakin did his best to make his explanation seem unimportant, and then wondered why it was he felt he had to explain himself.

"Uzen is an odd place to walk." Tansybekov seemed to be wondering, too.

"*Every* place on this peninsula is an odd place to walk." Duvakin laughed artificially, then realized he was fidgeting in his chair, like a man caught at something. Damn it, he thought, what's all this about?

"Does it matter why I was there?" He finally met the captain's inquiring stare.

Instead of answering, Tansybekov asked another question. "What did you think of Uzen?"

In the way it will after a sleepless night, fatigue was creeping back, like ground damp sapping the foundations of a building. Duvakin's lips felt numb, too thick to speak with, his thoughts like a collection of birds' eggs, rancid in wads of cotton wool. Duvakin shrugged. "Poor. Old-fashioned."

Now it was Tansybekov's turn to laugh. He turned his back to the window, leaned against it. "The very word! It's your typical Kazakh *aul*, not much to look at, mud bricks and dirt streets, but at least we had the sense to build out of the wind. All falling down now. When Moscow built the new city, they closed all the shops, quit repairing the houses. The only problem was, Moscow never got around to moving the people."

Remembering the empty alleys, the three old men, Duvakin was surprised. "A lot of people live out there?"

Again Tansybekov didn't reply, but put another question, as if this were an interrogation. "All right, you were at the cockfight. Do you have any idea who else was there?"

"Slant-eyes, mostly," Duvakin said, stupid with his own fatigue, then understood he had put his foot in it. "I mean, locals, young men, I don't know . . ."

The captain's face might have been harder, but he made no comment on Duvakin's gaffe, instead strolling around to Duvakin's side of the room. "This cockfighting, it's a new game," Tansybekov said thoughtfully, rolling a wad of paper between finger and thumb, "something we never used to have here on the peninsula. Thimble-and-pea, sure, and car theft and pickpockets and home brewing and the whores, we've had all that as long as I remember. We're an oil town, after all. But this cockfighting, it's much bigger money, and it takes organization, brains. . . ."

Duvakin's fog rolled back a bit, Tansybekov's implication glimmering through it like dawn.

"From the outside, you mean?" Duvakin felt a spasm of excitement; perhaps this was the answer to the question—Chance or Design?—that had gnawed him through the rest of the night. "You think criminal elements are moving into Novii Uzen?"

Tansybekov, indifferent, made no answer, intent on his own thoughts. He was at Duvakin's back now, arms clasped behind him like those of a soldier at rest. "The ringmaster and the two arm squeezers we caught, they're Lezgins, and the guy taking the bets, he's an Uzbek. The bettors, yes, you're right, they are mostly local. Kazakhs, Karakalpaks. Boys whose parents were here before the oil people came in, boys who can't get into the local institutes, and can't get jobs when they get out, boys who can't afford the rubles they throw away on those damn chickens. . . ."

Duvakin twisted about to stare at the captain, wondering just what fairy tales those boys had been spinning for him. Come on, those "poor Kazakh boys" had been betting *bricks*, thousands of rubles at a time!

Tansybekov strolled from the door back toward the window, rolling a paper scrap into a ball between his thick fingers. "There are ugly clouds gathering, Ivan Pavlovich," the captain finally said, in a new tone of voice, then threw the wad at the window.

For one confused second Duvakin thought the man meant real weather, but then Tansybekov crossed his arms and grabbed his own biceps, kneading them hard. "*Evil* clouds," he added, gaze focused somewhere inside himself. After a moment more of thought, he asked another question, his tone light. "Tell me, Ivan Palych, who are the real internationalists, eh?"

The term was as dead as "comrade" or "brother socialist countries," or any of the other comfortable lies of the past. Duvakin simply stared, waiting.

"Who doesn't give a hoot whether you're Uzbek or Russian or Avar or Svan, as long as you've got pockets, and something to keep inside them?" Tansybekov rubbed thumb and finger together contemplatively. "The criminals, of course. It used to be that Russians mostly were sent to Russian prisons, Kazakhs went to Kazakh prisons, and the media kept quiet about them both. Now, precious damn glasnost; television tells the Moscow bandits about the Kazan bandits, the Uzbek bandits read about the Georgian bandits. They travel around, see what each other is up to. Did you know they're linking up, even going abroad? Poland, Hungary, Israel . . . America even. Robbers and con men and shakedown artists and dope peddlers and car thieves, not a one of them gives a goddamn about anything but what's in your wallet and mine. . . ."

"So you think that cockfight is a sign that big crime is moving into Novii Uzen?" Duvakin tried to imagine what big criminals might be like, and what the sun-blasted wastes of Novii Uzen could offer them.

Tansybekov, though, was pursuing his own worries. "And now

the communists cover themselves in shit, like nasty little clowns? The Party is dead, the market is king? Everything we fought against, everything we suffered to prevent—capitalism—this is now good? And what we lived for, all that we *bled* for . . . Gorbachev, Nazarbaev, Yeltsin, all those communists get up and say, 'Sorry, it was a big mistake'?" The captain's voice was hushed, almost as if Duvakin were intruding on a private dialogue. Then, louder and more conversationally: "You know something, Ivan Palych? The oil we send to Moscow, you know Moscow pays us rubles for it? And then they ship us that oil back, and charge us in dollars. Not rubles. Rubles they won't even accept for 'surplus goods,' meaning goods that are so ugly and so bad that even Russians won't buy them. *Them* we have to pay dollars for! So the hospital, we don't even have bandages now, because Uzbeks want dollars for their cotton. I won't even talk about medicines, Ivan Palych, or equipment. The East Germans used to make that for us, and the Balts. The former East Germans, and former Balts, I mean. And I'm not talking about fancy equipment, like computers or radiation machines, I mean things like autoclaves. Do you know that there isn't a single auto-clave in all of Novii Uzen? Anything that has to be sterilized, the only way to do it is boil it. If there's water. And if the natural gas is hooked up."

Tansybekov faded into silence, looking out the window. Fatigue folded around Duvakin like his sweaty and soiled bed linen, as he tried to make out what connection the captain intended, leaping from the cockfight to autoclaves.

"Well, I know there have been problems, but . . ." Duvakin mumbled vaguely.

"Can't even use alcohol to sterilize, you know?" Tansybekov pulled himself back from some reverie with a jerk. "We never get any, anymore. It all gets drunk before it reaches the peninsula. . . . How many dumb blind bastards have you *got* up there in Russia, from drinking rubbing alcohol?"

Duvakin's anger, his suspicions and fear combined; he slapped the desk hard, scattering Tansybekov's few papers. "God *damn* it! The Russians, always the Russians! Who says it's the Russians who drink your damn alcohol? Maybe it's your own people up in Gurev, eh? Or Alma-Ata, you ever consider that? Or are all the Kazakhs pure as snow, and just us Russians are the split-hooved demons?"

The captain had stiffened with surprise, then bent to pick up the stray pages. When he straightened again, he asked, with great dignity, "That's not really the question, is it, Ivan Pavlovich? The question isn't who drinks the alcohol and why there aren't any bandages. The question is, what are we working for? Why do we do what we do? I have spent my entire career in the militia, more than three decades now . . . and I always thought it was for the common cause, the common good. What was good for the militia was good for my town, what was good for my town was good for my country, what was good for my country was good for me. Now?" He shrugged. Perhaps it was the light, perhaps it was Duvakin's imagination, but suddenly the captain looked worn, even old.

"That's the question we all face, isn't it?" Duvakin said, in part because something had to be said, but also because Tansybekov's words were close to ones that echoed at times through his own soul. "There's no more ideology, no religion, no manna in heaven, and no matter whether your heaven is red with hammers and sickles or blue with clouds and winged babies. So what do we work for? We work . . . well, to live better. To give ourselves a better life. Is there any other answer?" For our families, Duvakin would have added, but he had no children, no wife.

"Simply to make ourselves rich, in other words?" Tansybekov shot around, as if catching Duvakin in a telling error. "Each of us to pocket what we can, and the nation can go beg? Isn't that what we had before, with the results there on every empty store shelf for us to see? And isn't that why, whenever you ask somebody what they want to see in the shops, it's never bread or meat or medicine? It's video recorders the people want, or French perfume, or blue jeans with the legs so tight the only work they're good for, you peel the pants off and spread the knees to do it?" Tansybekov's face suddenly looked like glare ice on the highway, rock-hard and dangerous. "Ivan Palych, even monkeys don't live like we do now. Monkeys are smart enough to understand that the health of one depends upon the health of the whole group, and so they work for the group, work together. But we are supposed to work for self-interest now, for our personal 'sense of ownership,' isn't that what they tell us now? Meaning everybody should be like those damned Uzbeks with their chicken fights, taking the money out of the mouths of those boys' families. That's 'sense of ownership,' isn't it? Except I've got another word for it. . . ."

Duvakin waited, unable to guess, unable even to understand what had brought on this tirade and how to stop it. What was particularly confusing was that he agreed with so much of what Tansybekov was saying, which only made him doubt his own feelings, since he and the captain were so different.

Finally the captain heaved himself from the windowsill where he had been leaning. "Chaos, Ivan Palych, that's what I'd call it." Duvakin saw that the back of Tansybekov's uniform was dark with sweat, and that he had left smudges of sweat on the glass; the sun through the glass must have been baking, but Tansybekov hadn't noticed. Now the Kazakh militia officer rose and went to his paper cupboard, which stood, closed, against the wall. He opened it with a tinny clank, revealing shelves of forms, a box of pencils, two rolls of toilet paper, a bottle of glue. And a strongbox in the center, with a combination dial, which the militia chief began to spin.

" 'Chaos' is a bit strong, isn't it?" Duvakin's muzziness was returning, and with it the growing suspicion that he had made a mistake in coming here. Better simply to have stayed at the cottage, or even to have gone back to Moscow. The thought conjured up a swirl of memories—Moscow, the crush of crowds, *Russian* crowds, car-choked streets, green grass, trees. . . . My God, to see *trees* again, pines and firs and maples and limes, just swelling to bud about now, and oaks, for another month or more just inky skeletons against the sky!

Such as he could watch from his chair against the radiator, behind the *antikvariat.* In his apartment . . .

Then the memory curdled with clots of Susi, and the militia, and Galya.

"All right then"—Tansybekov addressed himself to the safe, brow corrugated with concentration—"call it anarchy, or disorder, or civil breakdown . . ." He twirled the dial one way, the other, back. Then he swore, gave the dial a hard spin, and stood up.

"*Anarchy,*" Duvakin repeated sarcastically, tired of the man's complaining. "Look, you think a chicken fight makes *anarchy*? A few stolen automobiles, armed robberies at a couple of newspaper kiosks?"

"And a riot, with fourteen dead, and two hundred in the hospital, and the central market burned to the ground, and four of my vehicles burned out?" Tansybekov shot back. "That's just games? That's nothing to worry about?"

"Oh, for Christ's sake." Duvakin felt packed in weariness, as if in mud at some spa, too tired to lift his limbs, too tired even to breathe. "Even that. There's that many deaths a *week* in Moscow, and ten times that many cars get wrecked in road accidents, get stolen. . . . It's terrible, the way crime has grown, but it's not anarchy. I've got . . . I mean, my own *wife* was a victim . . . was killed, but I don't . . ." Duvakin was startled to feel the sting of tears on his inner lids, and a clot of phlegm in his throat. He coughed, sat up, rubbed his nose. "I mean, even though I lost my own wife, I wouldn't call it anarchy."

Tansybekov had stopped whatever he had been doing to the safe and was studying Duvakin minutely, lips pursed. "You lost your wife?"

Angry with himself for having brought Galya up, and feeling doubly cheap that he had done so simply to win an argument about politics, Duvakin sketched a quick description—Galya, the apartment, the stolen items—all with a surliness that was meant to warn off any sympathy. Then, summoning up his chilliest bureaucrat's manner, he squared his shoulders and said, "Any rate, I'm sure we've both enjoyed this little collegial chat, but I still have my business. Which requires a telephone. A *private* telephone," he stressed again. "I'm sure it's none of your doing that there isn't such a thing in Novii Uzen, but it isn't mine either, so . . . I am afraid, then, I will have to ask you to order one of your men to take me to Shevchenko, or Gurev, or wherever I have to go, to get such a telephone line. Ak Tau, I mean."

"Very well." The captain came over to his desk, hand out. "If you'll just let me see your document, of course . . ."

"What document?" Duvakin knew exactly what the captain meant, but he feigned frosty incomprehension.

Tansybekov still had his hand outstretched and was grinning, though not sarcastically. "Your orders, or bona fides, or anything that says you have the authority to 'order one of my men to drive you to Gurev.' " The imitation of Duvakin's tone wasn't close, but it didn't matter, since Duvakin had no such paper. "You know what they say, Ivan Palych: 'Got no papers, gone like vapors; with your papers, you're a man.' "

Duvakin tried to be airy. He waved a hand. "Well, sometimes it can happen that papers are dangerous. . . ." Duvakin let the words hang in the air, hoping that their mystery, and the grim glare with which he tried to hold the captain's eye, would prove more convincing than explanation.

But Tansybekov didn't stay to let himself be stared down. Instead, he bent back to the combination on the safe, spun the dial, and this time managed to open the sheet-metal door. With a satisfied grunt, he got something out, then turned around.

"You know, in a way, I'd have to agree with you. About the anarchy, not about papers!" he said hastily, shutting the locked door, then the outer door: "Papers, documents—why, without them, I wouldn't have a job, would I!" He laughed, once, waving what looked like a tear-off from a teletype. Then, serious again: "What I mean is, I'm not so worried about that . . . kind of crime . . . like with your wife." He waved his hand, rather than specify, then went on: "But what does worry me is when crime moves into the government, into the institutions and the executive committees. And the ministries. Maybe especially the ministries."

This last was pronounced with such obvious portentousness that, after a moment, Duvakin got the hint.

"Ermolov?"

Tansybekov looked mysterious. "You mean am I accusing the ministry of being consciously involved in criminal activity?" he asked with a gravity that Duvakin understood belatedly was mocking.

The thought jolted him. *Could* the ministry be engaged in criminal activity?

Chistoplotskii?

Duvakin remembered the man's wiry thinness, like a monk's almost. A man who had no excesses, no appetites, save for work.

But all men are mortal, so why exempt the minister? Duvakin reprimanded himself. Why assume he's different? Sweet Christ, it wasn't even two years ago that the prime minister had to have a heart attack, to stop his indictment as part of a plan to sell brand-new Soviet tanks abroad, as scrap metal.

But even if Chistoplotskii wasn't different, wasn't better, there would still have to be a *reason* for his corruption, wouldn't there? No minister would endanger his perks, his position, for what profit was to be made at a cockfight or in selling *anasha*. Even rubles by the thousand were nothing next to the power a minister would enjoy, and the minister of oil even more so!

"Good heavens, who would say such a thing? But I *am* wondering, a little bit," Tansybekov said with exaggerated nonchalance, "about some of the people your ministry sends us now."

"Look," Duvakin snapped, "Ermolov may have had a ministry stamp in his passport, but that doesn't mean that the ministry sent him to buy hemp, any more than that building got dropped on him because he's *from* the ministry!"

"Oh, I don't mean just Ermolov," Tansybekov said in a pregnant voice.

When, after a moment, Duvakin looked up, round-eyed with surprise, the captain gently laid the paper he had been holding on the desk before Duvakin.

Hand trembling, Duvakin picked up the cheap, gray-yellow paper with the ragged bottom. He looked questioningly at the captain, then at the paper, no wider than his palm. Meaningless numbers and letters across the top, a code of some sort, printed by a ribbon that had long ago needed changing. Then, below:

URGENT REQUEST DETAIN QUESTIONS DU-
VAKIN IP RUSSIAN AGE 52 SUSPECT DEATH
WIFE . . . AGENT EN ROUTE . . . MOSCOW
CRIMINAL INVESTIGATION

Mouth open, heart hammering, Duvakin looked up at Tansybekov again, who smiled, clicked his cheek against his molars, shook his head.

"Just what you were saying, isn't it, Ivan Palych? Papers can be so dangerous sometimes. . . ."

I van Palych?"

Duvakin sat up with a start, eyes wild and heart thumping.

"Ivan Palych? Are you all right?"

"Edik?" Duvakin's brain was still trying to separate reality from a dream in which hands clutched at him, and empty rooms echoed with names. "Edik, you're back again? What time is it?"

The white sweater with blue-and-red edges was still draped over the young man's shoulders, and the mirrored sunglasses were clipped to the V of his partially buttoned shirt. He settled familiarly onto the foot of Duvakin's bed, crossed his legs.

"About eight." Edik smiled.

"Mother of God"—Duvakin not-quite-kicked at the unwelcome bottom—"you ever think about knocking? And Sunday morning besides."

"Letter for you." The young man held out a red-and-blue-edged envelope, a preprinted stamp of Lenin in the corner.

"You're a postman now?" Duvakin sat up in the bed, crossed his legs, but didn't reach for the letter.

"Rosa saw me, asked me to bring it in." Then, seeing that Duvakin was making no move toward the envelope, he tossed it into the valley behind Duvakin's crossed ankles. "Go on, it's probably from one of your lady friends."

Trying not to show the tremor in his hand, Duvakin picked up the envelope, turned it over. "Republic of Kazakhstan, Novii Uzen, General Delivery, Duvakin, I. P." was scrawled in an untidy, unfamiliar hand, with no return address.

Well, at least it couldn't be from the procurator, could it? In an envelope like that?

Duvakin had been expecting . . . well, *something*, ever since that moment in Tansybekov's office.

"You're arresting me?" he had finally managed, in a squeak a good octave above his normal voice, after the militia captain had gently removed the teletype sheet from Duvakin's grip.

"Why should I arrest you? You're here in Novii Uzen, aren't you?" The captain had laughed. "Where you going to go from here? You can't even *telephone*, remember?"

But at least jail would have been definite, concrete, with bars he could rattle his cup along, shouting his innocence, with stone walls he could scratch his name into, or mark off the days.

Instead, though, with no accuser to confront and no one who cared whether or not he was innocent, Duvakin had simply to go back to the cottage and wait. Numbly he retraced that ordinary walk down the crumbling concrete steps of the militia station, the dazed shamble to the bus stop, the ride back to Momish's cottages. The sun shining, the wind whipping the laundry, the faded flags, the sheep butting each other hungrily to get at the sparse tufts of grass, all life going on exactly as it had when he marched up the stairs to try to assuage a nagging suspicion that he might be in danger.

Now he *knew* he was in danger, with a rope about his neck and the trap about to open.

"Afraid of bad news, Palych?" The young man nudged his foot, then added, "Come on, read it, there's someplace I want to take you."

Duvakin ran his thumb under the glued flap, then pulled out a square of blue-lined, coarse paper, ragged on the edge where it had been ripped from a school copybook.

"Take me?" The words had a sinister ring, but since his visit to Tansybekov's office, most things did.

"Show you, then," Edik said impatiently. "Come on, put some life in it, will you? I told Rosa to bring your breakfast along, so we can miss the heat." He stood, and went out into the other room.

Not at all certain he wanted to go anywhere with Edik, Duvakin unfolded the piece of paper and read the letter. About ten lines, just going over onto the back. Three misspellings, and a misplaced comma, written in a fourth-grader's round scrawl. "Dearest Papulia," the letter began, "I'm frightened alone, why did you leave me an orphan here?"

Duvakin flipped the paper over. Signed "Anya."

He read the letter four times, five, as if one more reading might blow away the numb confusion that swathed him like fog. She was utterly alone in the world, the letter said, and needed his protection. Tatiana Ivanovna had come for the *antikvariat*, six thousand just like he had agreed, was that right? And she hoped it was all right, she was using the money.

To come to Novii Uzen.

"So, you getting dressed?" Edik stuck his head back in to ask. "Rosa's coming up the path with your breakfast now."

"It's my . . . Anya," Duvakin choked, answering the question that wasn't asked. "Coming to see me here."

Edik smiled, almost leered. "Local talent won't do, eh? Importing a girlfriend, are you, Palych?"

"Damn it, quit calling me Palych," Duvakin said tartly, "I'm not so much older than you . . . and anyway, she's my . . . daughter."

Edik caught the slight hesitation before the noun, and winked. "Sure she is, and a pretty one, too, I'll bet!" He went back out to help Rosa get the tray up the stairs and in the door.

Duvakin listened to them chattering in the outer room, and wondered why Anya was coming. But then irritation overcame him—at Edik, at the fact that he was still in Novii Uzen, at this someone who was coming to . . . QUESTION SUSPECT DEATH WIFE.

Let the girl come, let her stay in Moscow, let her take the six thousand and fly to the devil's seven mothers, it's all one to me, he thought, savagely flinging the bedclothes aside.

Bathed, shaved, dressed, fingering the gash he had given his chin, Duvakin walked into the outer room, to find Edik munching heartily away on a piece of roll, while Rosa watched with an expression somewhere between love and awe.

"This better be worth waking me for, whatever you're showing me," he growled, reaching for the cup of coffee Rosa was extending with a smile.

"Oh, I guess it'll be worth the time, Palych," Edik spoke through his roll, then swallowed it. "I'm taking you to prison."

The coffee cup slipped to the floor, exploded into shards on the stone.

"Welcome to Corrective Labor Colony Number 1642," Edik said when he finally cut the whining engine and crawled stiffly from the motorcycle. They were at a gate in front of a square defined by a double row of two-meter-high cement posts festooned with rusty wire, the clusters of barbs like spiky red flowers quivering in the keening wind. "They begin yet?" Edik asked the guard, an Asian in a Kazakh MVD uniform, a rifle slung on his shoulder, who was opening the outer of the two gates.

"Not yet, but they've arrived." He waved them through.

Duvakin had not helped clean up the cup he had broken; rather, he had sat, hand over his heart like a child calming a bird stunned after flying into a window. Edik had laughed hugely at the success of his joke before finally explaining, "You were so worried about me and the elections, about Alash, that I thought maybe it was time you learned a thing or two about the candidates."

Which gave Duvakin no choice but to swing his leg over the odious Jawa, to perch trepidatiously on the back as they struggled against a brisk headwind, out to this cluster of buildings, laid out in a precise square in the middle of an empty, pebble-strewn plain. Twenty buildings made of pressed gray panels were set, ten to a side, in precise military rows. A basketball court, the hoops without nets, and a volleyball net that was more tears than mesh were to the left, and a two-story cement building was to the right. Shaven-headed prisoners in gray uniforms were strolling in twos and threes in that direction; they looked over curiously as the motorcycle wheeled in, then popped to a halt next to a yellow-and-blue militia truck.

" 'Our Motherland extends her arms, Her riches to behold.' " Edik quoted some poem that Duvakin did not recognize. "You know what they made the barracks out of?" He waved at the nearest file of buildings. "Pressed asbestos panels." When Duvakin didn't react,

Edik added, "Hot in the summer, cold in the winter, and they'll give you cancer whatever the temperature. But that's all right; most of these boys won't live long enough to die of cancer."

Boys? Duvakin thought, stumbling on tingling legs, following Edik into a narrow auditorium that ran most of the length of the cement-block building. Several hundred prisoners were tightly packed on benches facing a small elevated stage overhung with a banner that said in bright red-and-gold, "TO CHANGE LABOR FROM A HEAVY BURDEN INTO A MATTER OF HONOR!"; the men's faded gray canvas uniforms were almost the same color as their closely shaved heads. Despite the glowering surveillance of about ten guards, whose hat brims were pushed almost to the nose and whose arms were crossed so as to make their muscles bulge, scores of the prisoners turned around to goggle.

Christ, they *were* boys, Duvakin realized once he got over the shock of the shaven heads and the hard looks.

"Most of these boys started getting their heads shaved before their chins needed it," Edik remarked to Duvakin in a voice they could all hear. "They're hard ones, Ivan Palych, cut you as soon as look at you." Many of the boys seemed to smirk with pleasure, grinning at Edik and surreptitiously greeting him with little waves or nods. "Actually, this is only a medium-regime camp," Edik said as they took a spot against the rear wall. "For narcotics, breaking and entering, hooliganism, drunkenness. The little fish, here at state expense to improve their skills."

There was a stir as four men entered the room and went up to the stage. The first, plainly the commander of the camp, was Duvakin's age, perhaps a little older, a man whose strength was now overlaid with fat, which he seemed to be lying to himself about. The uniform was pulled into tight cat's whiskers at each button, and his neck rolled over his collar; but his eyes, set deep into a ruddy, puffy face, made plain that he would as soon throw you against the wall as shake your hand.

"Bogdan Tsybulko," Edik whispered. "A dinosaur. Too young to pension off, and the Ukrainians refuse to have him back. Said he was born in Kazakhstan, so he's ours. He hates it, because they don't let him hit people anymore."

"Young men," Tsybulko boomed, in a tone that suggested he'd

really rather describe his charges more colorfully, "you know the rules. This is a lecture, not a church. No praying, all questions from the audience, no coming up individually. All violations will be punished." He let those words hang for a moment, reinforced by a fierce glower—which, Duvakin sensed from the fidgeting and jostling on the benches, wasn't much feared. Then Tsybulko nodded and waved his hand, "They're yours, Father." Tsybulko spat the last word as though he had just bitten an apple and found half a worm.

"Father?" Duvakin hissed in astonishment, at which Edik laughed soundlessly and nodded, then tapped Duvakin's arm, directing his attention back to the stage.

The man was not in the black robes of a priest, nor were his hair and beard flowing tangles; rather, he had the snow-white fluff and close-cropped beard of any semi-intellectual pensioner. He had the apple cheeks and broad smile of good health, with a little cross pinned to his lapel.

"My unhappy children," he began in a gentle voice, eyes glittering blue, like a spider's in a lantern, "once again it is Sunday, Resurrection Day in Russian, the day when Jesus, God's Son, returned from the dead. Jesus was a poor man, you know, and an outcast, too. He was hated by the authorities, and put to death by the state, and yet here we are, nearly two thousand years later, naming this day in his honor. Why do we do so? Because his death and resurrection are what make it possible for each of us, lost, bewildered, and broken though we may be, also to return to life, also to resurrect ourselves, and come back to the life he gave us to live."

The "lecture" wound on for a while, an account of the life of Jesus that made Jesus sound like someone who might also have ended up in a special labor colony if not for being the Son of God, and then the priest dribbled to a halt so questions could begin. The boys seemed used to the priest; their attitude wobbled on an uneasy border between real interest and genial contempt, tempered, no doubt, by the knowledge that this hour of religious instruction was the best of bad choices.

"Father! Father! Father!" Voices rang around the room, until the priest smiled at some particular boy, who stood to ask his question. One or two of them even seemed to have their boy's voices still.

"Father, you say everybody is, what do you call it, precious in the eyes of God? But what about what Fenka, my bitch, gave me? It had no *head* almost, Father, just great big ears and this tiny little face, like on a water demon. . . . How could something like that be a person? How could it be wrong that she threw it in the garbage bucket and we went on drinking?"

"Father, this heaven of yours, nobody's ever seen it. The cosmonauts, they said they didn't see any God. Fur coats, though, I see lots of people have those, and drink champagne in restaurants, while other people have to fight for a place to stand in the buses. Why should I believe in this God of yours, and not in fur coats?"

"Father, this 'other cheek' business, how can you do that when the guys from the next block beat on you with chains and hammers if they catch you? Turn the other cheek and I'm in the morgue, not this here spa!"

The priest replied to each as he could, but he was not an imaginative man, and the answers tended to get tangled in points of dogma. Duvakin listened with a growing dreariness; even *this*, even religion, could somehow become a state function.

Oh, it wasn't just because he had once worked as a paid atheist, although sometimes when he saw the priests on television, or listened to the Sunday morning religious broadcasts, it still made him angry to think how many millions of rubles, *billions* maybe, had been wasted on atheism, only to have the state now forcing religion down people's throats with almost as much zeal as it once had stuffed atheism. It wasn't even because that calculation was so cynical: to encourage religion because it gave people some of the moral gristle that seven decades of utopia had eaten away. No, what made Duvakin want to spit, curse the place, and go back out in the steadily moaning wind was that *even* religion, to which people had once slunk in secret, at risk of their jobs, even religion should become dull and incompetent and tedious when it became part of the all-absorbing state. The room recalled an obligatory lecture in patriotism, which no one in the room was listening to, including the fellow giving the speech.

No, Duvakin realized, there was *one* person listening: Tsybulko, glaring and flushing every time he heard the words "God" and "Christ," checked his wristwatch so often Duvakin wondered that his wrist wasn't sore. For the final few moments the commander simply stared at the numerals, like a nurse taking a temperature.

"*Time!*" The commander stood up, roared triumphantly. "That's an hour! *Stand!*"

The scrape of wood benches on raw concrete did not quite disguise the mutterings of "Fat old fart" and "Whose mother fucks dogs?" that rose from the boys as they got reluctantly to their feet, then dressed toward center and filed out, every muscle of their bodies devoted to being as unmilitary as they could without actually provoking punishment while they slouched sullenly out into the raw morning. The priest followed, giving Edik a nod of greeting that was diluted by a tight-lipped, not wholly genuine smile. That was positively warm, though, compared to the glower Tsybulko gave them.

"You clear this one through the office, Mordachkin?" The commander pointed a finger the size of a flashlight at Duvakin, who found he remembered the old days well enough to shrivel inside, while a sheepish, almost imbecilic grin crept across his face.

Unperturbed, Edik pushed himself away from the whitewashed wall with a flap of the shoulders, then zipped his coat, grinning. "Lovely service this morning, don't you agree, Bogdan Emelianovich? You know, I really think Father Vladimir is beginning to reach some of the lads. . . ."

The commander's face clotted, white splotches appearing along the collar.

"Mordachkin, I asked you a question, damn your insolent—"

Edik's face suddenly froze rock-hard, his eyes glittering. "The contract specifies assistants, Tsybulko, and it has six months to run, so if you have anything you want to complain about, then I suggest you call the Ministry. In the meantime, cork it." Then the ice left his face again, and was replaced by a clearly false friendliness. "Now shouldn't you run along and make some lunch for your lads?" Duvakin could see the commander was doing all he could not to swing one of his meaty paws backhand across Edik's face, but he succeeded, leaving with his underlings after jamming his dress uniform hat onto his head.

"Contract?" Duvakin asked. "What contract?"

Instead of answering, Edik made a face at Tsybulko's back,

grinned at Duvakin. "Like that? That's what we've been breeding, this past seventy years. Triumph of Soviet eugenics, really. We've produced a beast with plenty of muscle. Runs on potatoes and has nothing between the ears except a hole to pour vodka down. The only light in the cave he calls his soul is the hope that one day soon they'll dig Papa Joe back out of the ground. That motto above the stage—those are Stalin's words, you know." He jerked a thumb at the stage. "Up there. Come on"—he touched Duvakin's arm—"I really brought you out here to see my workshop."

Once again out into the wind, but only a few meters, until they came to a neatly assembled brick building that was strikingly unlike the others. Edik opened the door, and Duvakin stepped inside. Out of the wind, the contrast made the room seem almost hot. It was a workshop, an ordinary workshop, except . . . it took a moment to put his finger on what distinguished this place from any he had seen.

It was clean.

Edik had unzipped his jacket and was sauntering across the large, open room, his hands out wide. "Nice, eh?" He smiled with evident pride. "Carpentry over here . . ." He pointed to a row of benches, the tools hung neatly above them on racks, red lines outlining where each tool should go. A big band saw stood against the wall. "And masonry over here . . ." No benches, but the same neatness, the piles of bricks and cement blocks stacked with mathematical precision, the mortar-mixing troughs clean enough to eat from, the trowels glistening as if new. "Plumbing and electricity back there." He waved at the far end. "We even built the building, you know that?"

" 'We'?"

"The boys and I . . . That's what the contract is for."

"The boys built this?" Duvakin looked around, surprised. In fact, the room *was* nice, radiating care, pride.

Edik nodded. "Those boys, they've been wild since they were maybe eight, nothing in their lives but gangs and narcotics and taking turns beating each other's heads in. Mixed-race kids, a lot of them, and the rest of them are from Kazan, or Baku, or Kyzyl-Orda, so what in the devil the government's doing giving them an Orthodox priest, your guess is as good as mine." As he spoke, Edik was rummaging in a cupboard for a teakettle, filling it with a dipper from a small cistern, setting the kettle on a stove. "If I didn't know he was too stupid to think of it, I'd say it was Tsybulko's little joke. The state says they have to have religion now, so he feeds all those little Muslims a weekly slice of Jesus."

"Opium of the people, you mean?" Duvakin essayed a joke.

Edik simply shrugged. "Depends which people, I suppose. But the point is, religion's not the first thing these kids need. . . . Religion won't get your daily bread, you know?"

"That's what this is for?" Duvakin guessed, hands indicating the workshop.

"I got out of the army, after I did my 'internationalist duty' in Afghanistan, and I came back here. Worked for the Oil Ministry, for a while." He pointed out where Duvakin could sit, while he leaned against the neat but clearly handmade counter. "I forgot, you know about that. It was a good job—salary only ninety rubles, but lots of fat to skim off, videocassettes and whiskey, and important visitors from Moscow who would pay lots of *volodyas* for an evening of 'cultural exchange' with the local girls. . . . But I kept wondering—for this I fought in Afghanistan? Is this how a man should live?"

Duvakin listened to the thrum of the wind trying to tear up the corners of the roof, finding himself liking the young man more. "Anyway," Edik went on, after a thoughtful pause, "it ate at me, the guys I had seen die out there, or get their legs blown off, just so some tub of lard from Moscow could guzzle down vodka, tucking a couple of our girls under his fat sweaty belly." Edik fiddled with the enameled cups he had set on the oilcloth table. "Then the labor laws started to change, and I got to thinking. I read in the papers about initiative, and about how, especially things the state used to do poorly, they were turning over to cooperatives. So, I got the idea, why not do something useful, put some of the things I learned in Afghanistan to work." He held out his hands, indicating the workshop. "And here it is, the Alash Experimental Vocational Training Center."

"*This* is Alash?" Duvakin swiveled around, astonished. "These are the people who threw—"

"The rock through your window?" Edik laughed. "I doubt it. I told you, there's a lot of different Alashes, and anyway, what I teach the boys here, it's how to *fix* windows, not break them." Then, more somberly: "Besides, it couldn't have been one of my boys, because so far none of them have been released."

The kettle was steaming, so Edik turned away to fuss with the tea. When he brought the mugs to the table, he also plonked a black bottle down. "*Balzam*," he indicated, "from Latvia. Try some, it puts a little spine in the tea. With that wind, we're going to need it."

Still uncertain what Edik was trying to demonstrate, and mistrusting his own growing sense of admiration for the young veteran, Duvakin hesitated, until Edik poured a healthy dollop of the resiny syrup into his own tea. Embarrassed by his own timidity, Duvakin said, "Very impressive, all this . . . What, the state pays you so much for each boy you train?"

"Pay us?" Edik looked rueful. "The only way I could get anybody to agree to this was to guarantee it wouldn't cost the government a kopek, unless you count the land and the bricks. And there's no shortage of land, plus they get to keep the building, no matter how this turns out."

"Well, then, how do you get paid?"

Here Edik laughed. "I don't, so far. One of the perils of capitalism, I'm learning as we go along. The idea was, I'd train the boys and then hire them for a repair-and-construction business. You've seen the houses back there in Novii Uzen, right? Well, we could put up plywood, enclose balconies, repair plumbing, help people when they move into new apartments—you know what kind of shape new apartments are always in, nothing hooked up and everything broken. My original plan was maybe I could train the boys on the job, work out there in the day and come back here at night, but"—he took a swig of his resinous tea—"you can imagine what the Ministry thought of *that*. So then I figured, all right, teach them the skills the last year they're behind the wire, in return for a guarantee they'll work a year for us. Help the boys get used to civilian life again, and maybe make some money besides. The housing shortage is so bad, why not take an empty block in old Uzen, renovate the whole thing, fix up the old buildings, and then sell them to the people? They'll have a place to live, the boys will have jobs, and we can make some of the money we've lost on this already!"

"So what's the problem? The boys won't give you the guarantee?"

"Come on, try your *balzam*," Edik urged. "No, the boys are delighted to give us the guarantee."

"So?" Duvakin prompted him, then put his lips to the cup. The tea leaves must have been stale to begin with, and Duvakin had waited until the tin cup was cool enough to hold, so the tea was icy, and the *balzam* tasted of turpentine. Oddly, the bitterness washed away Duvakin's final resistance to the young man: Only an honest man could drink such trash!

But what was Edik? Duvakin could think of no word. "Patriot" meant the same as "Stalinist"; the coup committee last summer had all been "patriots." "Citizen" is what the policeman yells at the drunk who is urinating in a bus stop. And the phrase "good Soviet man" was long gone, but all it had ever meant was somebody quick to agree, no matter what nonsense his boss was spouting.

Edik finished his mug, grimaced, shrugged. "It's the Executive Committee; it denies the boys residence registration after they are released, so they have to move away from Novii Uzen."

Duvakin pushed his mug away, anger letting him finish Edik's story. "And that's why you want to get elected?"

Edik smiled bashfully, nodded, then said, "Now would you like to see why my 'honored opponent' wants to get elected?"

The wind and the keening whine of the Jawa's engine made conversation impossible, to say nothing of the concentration required to keep Duvakin on his narrow, unstable perch behind the younger and much lighter man. The road—a dirt track really—had run about ten kilometers from the prison before reaching a heavily eroded ravine, the flanks of which bristled with oil pumps.

"Short cut!" Edik shouted as they bounced around an abandoned, rusty steel barrel and over a pipe that was half buried in the dirt. "Hang on!"

All around them the huge pumps dipped their beaks and raised them again, powered by the enormous counterweights at the other end, up, down, up down, each bob bringing another surge of oil sludge to the surface, where it flowed into pipes, and then bigger pipes, heading ultimately for the refinery at Shevchenko. An invisible wind made a low moaning sound, stinging with unseen crystals of sand. There wasn't a soul in sight.

"This used to be winter pasture. There's a spring up there that washed this out." Edik shouted, taking his right hand from the motorcycle to wave to a spot farther up the ravine. "So this was all grass. . . ."

It was hard to believe that anything could ever have grown on the oil-soaked soil, littered with cast-off scraps of rusted metal, bits of bulldozers and stretched-out springs, through which ran the collecting pipes, all of them oozing black-green, sticky crude oil.

"This is what you want me to see?"

"No, this is!" he shouted, pointing up the ravine. With a bump they crested the hill, to find themselves on a rocky tableland that was probably no more than ten meters higher than the plain to the southeast but seemed to tower above it because the plain was so flat, stretched out in all directions like a piece of discarded, crumpled wrapping paper. Novii Uzen was a smudged sketch where the horizon dissolved in the bromide haze. Still, the rise and the rock lip were enough to make the wind moan like a small animal with a broken spine, and claw at their clothing as if in death throes. The bones under Duvakin's bottom felt rubbed raw. Trying to walk some of the vibration out of his thighs and rear end, he strolled aimlessly, until a needle of pain stabbed into his left big toe.

"Ow!" he shrieked, and hopped on one foot, then sat, heavily, on the lichen-covered, dusty brown rocks. Grunting, he used his trouser cuff to pull the foot up to where he could see it. A short needle protruded from the front of his shoe.

"Cactus, Palych." Edik smiled, twisting around to look back from whatever he was admiring. "This is the desert, remember?"

Now Duvakin examined the ground about him; sure enough, ground-hugging dusty green lobes of some kind lurked among the stones, bristling with spikes, translucent as cod bones.

Duvakin eased himself upright, out of sorts. The long ride on the little motorcycle had jiggled away a good deal of his admiration for Edik. "You brought me out here to look for cactus?"

Edik shrugged, smiling, then faced back to the south, extending his hands upward, letting his jacket billow in the seven winds. They were on the lip of a ravine similar to the one they had ridden up, save that this was perhaps a bit steeper and was utterly empty. In fact, had it not been for the smudge that was Novii Uzen and the sagging crescents of what must be power lines glinting in the sun, they might have been standing on Mars.

Edik had a dreamy, almost transcendent look on his face. "Imagine springtime, Palych: This is all green, the grass up to here." He held his palm out just above his knee. "Over there"—he indi- cated the west—"two, maybe three flocks. Sheep and goats, white and gray, ambling along like the clouds overhead. Up here, closer to the headland, there would be yurts, little felt tents, round like bread rolls, the women hanging out clothes, children playing. Over there"—he indicated the east—"heading for Urgench and Bukhara, a caravan, sixty, eighty camels, straight as an arrow through the steppe."

"Yes, well . . ." Duvakin could think of few sights which would attract him less. "Very lovely. This is what you want to show me?"

Edik blinked, puzzled, then looked around, the spell broken. "Yes, it is. I wanted to show you Momish's farm." He pointed, and headed down the ravine, not waiting for Duvakin. Gingerly watch- ing for cactus and loose stones, Duvakin followed, wondering what kind of farm, if *grass* wouldn't grow here.

Duvakin caught up with Edik below the shoulder of the hill, in a kind of cleft between two ridges.

"Momish is renting land, Edik?" he panted, nearly falling on the slithering stones.

Edik caught him, steadied him, then pointed down at the ra- vine, choked with greasewood and thorn apple. "Look, there's water here, and the hill shelters the area from everything but southeast winds. That's a problem, of course, because in the summer, when the winds come off the Kara Kum, they can dry the plants out like *that*"—he snapped his fingers—"but on the whole . . ." He shrugged, smiled. "Trust Momish to find himself the land he needs."

Duvakin could see nothing save the thin thread of vegetation, which marbled the sere landscape like a rotting vein in a piece of spoiling meat. "What plants?" he finally asked.

Edik pointed with his chin. "Hemp."

Duvakin spun to look, slipped, nearly fell. He clutched Edik's front for support, then pushed him away.

"Momish is raising hemp?" Blobs of thoughts came to him like pulsing blood—Ermolov, the boys on the stairs, Susi-Anya, the distance back to the compound, the distance back to Russia. A quick look around told him the landscape was as empty as it had seemed before, but now he wanted to crouch, to hug the ground and be invisible.

Edik, calm as before, was looking about, hands in his back pockets. "Well, it isn't really hemp yet. It's only spring, so the plants wouldn't be more than, oh, about this high." He separated thumb and forefinger of his right hand about as far as they could go. "They were only set out last week. They won't flower for, mmm, another couple of months maybe." He picked up a stone, turned it over and over in his hand, then, with a sudden contortion, flung it sidearm down into the thicket. With a screech of protest a pigeon-sized bird burst from the brush and sailed down the ravine on round, down-curving wings. The sudden noise made both of them start. Edik turned around and laughed.

"Up in Moscow, do people ever talk about what comes next?"

"Next?"

"Sure, after all this, the union dissolves, and everybody is sovereign, and the economy collapses. What then?"

Moscow might have been on another planet, for all this exposed, windblown knob of bare ground reminded Duvakin of it. He remembered the complaining, the rumors, the worry.

"I don't know," he admitted cautiously. "You kind of concentrate on the days . . . I mean, down here it's easier, but up in Moscow . . . Well, if you don't slip on the ice and no ice falls on you from the roof and nobody picks your pocket and they don't run out of sausage before you can get up to the counter with your coupon and it isn't already spoiled before you take it home, and nobody shoots you on the way there, then maybe people will worry about tomorrow, but—"

Edik pointed out at the empty landscape again. "I think about it all the time, Palych. This hill isn't going anywhere, and neither are you and I, or most of us, anyway. The Party is dead, and chunks keep falling off the syphilitic old whore of an empire, and every time you turn on the radio, it seems there's riots and strikes someplace new. . . . But still, even after the worst night, the sun's going to come up the next day again. That wind will blow. This rock will be here." He turned around now, to face Duvakin. "So, what happens after a world collapses? Do the factories fall down? Do people stop having to eat? What I'm saying, Palych . . . *somebody* is going to be in charge, *somebody* is going to, well . . . get that oil over there." He pointed back the way they had come.

Duvakin understood that what Edik said was true, but failed to see why it mattered. "That's why you're running to be city representative?"

"In a way." Edik began walking back up the hill, angling along the contours, climbing slowly. "Politics is one way, Palych, and I'm going to do what I can. To make life better."

Even at so small an angle, the climb was winding Duvakin a little. He could feel his pulse hammer at his ribs. "You said that's *one* way?" he asked, after a short silence filled only with the tug of the wind and the low moan of the desiccated shrubs, punctuated by a "Chkk! Chkk!" from some sort of bird. On the crushed-paper landscape far below, a vehicle of some sort was speeding along, trailing a rising plume of dust.

Edik strode on a pace or two more, then stopped, turned around. "Well, *if* I get elected, and *if* the legislature up in Alma-Ata doesn't dissolve the city committee again, and *if* I can make whoever else gets elected listen to my arguments . . . and *if* the rest of the council agrees and votes with me."

The way Edik spoke put Duvakin in mind of someone moving a huge rock uphill, each "if" a clunk of the ratchet, achieved at huge labor and immediately to be repeated.

"Then yes, maybe the people of Novii Uzen can keep control of the oil that is under their land." Then Edik laughed sadly. "If nobody buys them first."

"Buy the oil fields? How do you buy an oil field?"

Edik grinned enigmatically. "There's different ways. . . . How about shares, for one? Create shares in government enterprises, sell them to the workers of those enterprises."

"Shares," "stocks," "stock market": The words were lumps in

the huge porridge of new parliamentary and financial and sexual and criminal terms that had been ladled over the country since 1985, under the name of "new thinking." Duvakin had only the haziest idea of what most of them meant, including this one.

"So? The workers own the factory, they have to work harder because it's for them. What's the problem?"

"What happens if one or two people buy up all the shares?"

"How could that happen? That would be capitalism again. The government will offer these share things to all the workers, like in Sweden!"

Edik nodded, deeply. "Well, you've done your reading, anyway, Palych. The Swedish model, workers' capitalism . . . and two or three of the biggest industrial combines in the world, Palych. Let me ask you this: They can make workers buy these shares, the same way they forced them to volunteer to buy bonds during the war. But how are they going to make people keep them?"

"But if shares are such a good deal, then why would people get rid of them?"

"What if they don't have a choice?"

Duvakin had lived in Russia too long to have to ask how a man might be forced to give up his shares. And out here in the east even more so, now that the U.S.S.R. was gone. This was the Orient. A few years ago people had joked that perestroika was like sausage: The farther you got from Moscow, the rarer it was. Of course, that was before sausage had vanished from Moscow, too.

"But surely Momish can't just *steal* the shares?"

"What do you think? Of course not. Maybe just a 'suggestion' that everybody contribute them to some fund, the same way they make all those Miss Something-or-Other contestants donate their prizes to an AIDS fund. But I kind of doubt they'll be that crude. No, you know what I think they're going to do, Palych?" Edik peered out into that expanse of nothing, savoring the winds as if for the last time.

Duvakin waited, following the gaze. The vehicle he had noticed before had stopped, but the dust was still hovering, ending at the glitter of sun on windshield.

"I think he's going to just plain buy the shares."

"But aren't there thousands and thousands of shares? Wouldn't that take—"

"A lot of money?" Edik smiled in feline triumph, purring like a cat in the sun. "Now where, I wonder," he went on with delicate sarcasm, "could a man make a lot of money? Narcotics, perhaps?"

Duvakin sat slowly, as though the wind had been kicked from him. Something sharp stung his ankle, making him start. He rubbed the place absently, wondering about insects.

Edik was still staring, not answering.

There was a rolling *crack!* Duvakin looked up. Thunder? But there were no clouds.

The next time he heard the bullet ricochet, again stinging him with stone chips, followed by the thunder of the slower-moving report.

"Mother of God, Edik! They're shooting at us!" Duvakin whispered, frozen like a rabbit in headlights.

Days passed like a book read on the train—paragraphs reread four times, or skipped, familiar words suddenly looking as odd as if Duvakin had never seen the alphabet before, characters whose names he forgot.

When, despite his distractions, Duvakin had thought to inform Momish that his . . . daughter . . . was coming to visit, the Azerbaijani had blinked in surprise at hearing that Duvakin *had* a daughter, which Duvakin distantly understood meant his personnel file had gotten a careful looking over. Then Momish did some grumbling about regulations and whether this might not reduce Duvakin's effectiveness and ability to work. The real objection, Duvakin eventually understood, was to what Anya might eat.

"The girl's twenty," Duvakin had reassured Momish. "You know what they're like at that age. What she puts in her mouth wouldn't keep a bird alive! Besides, I don't expect that she would be on government food—"

"Ah, it's not the money!" Momish had waved dismissively.

There at least Duvakin could agree; it wasn't the money. And it wasn't even that Duvakin walked around peering into every passing face . . . well, European face . . . wondering whether *this* was the one who had been sent to QUESTION SUSPECT DEATH WIFE. Although the words from the teletype were a constant and dreary clickety-clack underneath his everyday life, it was other words that kept Duvakin awake at night, that knotted his throat with tension so he couldn't eat, that left him so sunk in thought that he bumped into people on the street.

Two words, to be precise.

When the second shot rang out, Edik, too, had been like a toad nailed to a table. Somewhere in the eternity between the second shot and the third, though, Duvakin convulsed into a galvanic scrabble to his left, grabbing the younger man, forcing him to run. Flailing arms and legs, Duvakin had lunged up the loose slide of rocks and dirt, slipping backward with every frantic thrashing lunge upward. There was nothing to get behind, just sky and ground; they might as well have had bull's-eyes painted on them.

And yet, miraculously, they had made it, scrambling over the lip of the upland, panting, the air squeezed from them like paint from a tube. Duvakin still could taste the sharp chalky dust he'd inhaled, the stab of the cactus, which he then rejoiced at, alive still to feel pain.

Then the scuttle to the motorcycle, and one, two, three more infinities of agony before the Jawa finally belched blue, and they were off and away, bouncing down through the ruts of the oil field like acorns down a drainpipe.

The exhilaration of escape came over them as the distance between them and the tableland grew. Duvakin's wrenching around, to see whether they were pursued, nearly unseated them both, but theirs was the only plume of dust in the milky air. Duvakin had laughed, hugged Edik's waist; embarrassed, he had then pounded a quick tattoo on Edik's back.

He was alive!

Hemp, Momish, Ermolov, and those shots. Somehow, somehow it all fit together, and Momish would leave the stage, as a criminal or as an honored pensioner, but he would leave. But most of all . . .

Duvakin was alive!

"Sweet Christ, I can't go back to the cottages, not now!" His euphoria had turned to panic when he realized Edik was slowing at the familiar turnoff. "What, he shoots at me at ten and gives me lunch at two?"

"You have to go back, Palych." Edik was iron-jawed. "They

couldn't know it was us, the distance is too great. But if you were to disappear right now, it wouldn't take a genius to figure out who was standing up there, looking over the Boss's crop. And remember, Novii Uzen isn't Moscow, Palych, where a Russian can just wander off and disappear. There's a lot more rocks than water out there." He indicated the desert with a wave of his hand. "Don't you fear, Palych, we'll stop the son of a bitch. . . . But one hasty move, and—" He drew an eloquent finger across his throat, grinned.

Duvakin had liked that "we." Whatever Chistoplotskii might think, Duvakin had not come *to* Novii Uzen, he had run away *from* Moscow, imagining as he did so that he would also be leaving himself, and his years, and his corpulence, and, above all, his sense of being buried, day after day, year after year, in the endless sifting dust of other people's vanities and greeds. And not just Galya's forthright acquisitiveness, although there had been pangs of pleasure at her absence, which he instantly, shamefully, concealed from himself. All of Moscow! A people condemned to a hell of endless shopping, a people who bought up all the matches out of fear that all the matches would disappear, a people reduced to hoarding socks. Muscovites glared with hatred at every other person, because each wore clothes the other might wear, ate food the other might eat.

Standing there that morning, in the simplicity of an empty landscape scoured by wind, with no witness save the shimmering heat dervishes on the crumbling tarmac, Duvakin thought he glimpsed the truth of good and evil. On the one hand, a man who had fought in an ugly, stupid war and brought home lessons that would improve tens of lives, perhaps hundreds. Self-effacing, jesting, young and energetic, Edik would call his motive self-interest and enterprise, but the winner would be Novii Uzen. Apartments properly rebuilt. Young criminals given a trade.

And on the other hand, a man who in words claimed to work for the People, to represent the will of the People, but who in deeds had saddled the city and ridden it into the ground, and who was now planning to buy it at fire-sale prices. And then, when it was his, he would do properly all the things he had done poorly when the responsibility was his but the profit was the state's, and he would grow rich.

Then Edik had revved the motorcycle, dropped the pedal into

gear. Still holding back the clutch, he cautioned gravely, "Just keep your tongue in your head about today, though, all right? This isn't a game of hide-and-seek we're playing with those people. I mean, if the army issued better rifles, you and I would have been having lunch with Borya Ermolov today!"

Army rifle.

Those were the two words that clawed at Duvakin's throat like a badger.

Sure, Edik had been in the army—*that's* how he knew it was an army rifle. The man had been shot at in Afghanistan; he'd know what it was that was shooting at them. And anyway, it had to have been a rifle, if whoever was shooting was so far away they could just barely see them.

The problem was, though, that there was another, and simpler, explanation. That Edik knew because Edik *knew*.

And if that was true, then the world was stood on its head, as completely if two and two suddenly made five.

Which was why Duvakin couldn't manage more than a numbed confusion, when, one evening, the white Niva roared into the compound, and Abdulla leaped out, bellowing, "She's here, Ivan Pavlovich, your daughter!"

Eyes bright as a ground squirrel's, and mustache quivering, Abdulla dashed to the door of the cottage, then back to the Niva, letting the cottage door close in Duvakin's face.

White stockings under a denim skirt cut a hand's width above the knee. Black shoes laced over the ankle, old-fashioned somehow, but . . .

"Papulia! Papenka!" A ball of leather jacket over fluffy sweater, blond hair cut short so that it stood out like a bristle, exploded from the automobile to hug him, an embrace that Duvakin, surprised, automatically returned, before going limp in embarrassment.

Abdulla watched, looking as though he had just swallowed his tongue.

"Susi," Duvakin managed halfheartedly, confused because he had not been immune himself to the sponge-firm swells of breast and hip in that embrace, nor to the kiss the size and color of a Pioneer's scarf that she punctuated the embrace with before stepping around him to look over the compound.

"Ah, no more of that 'Susi' stuff, Papasha." She was brisk. "It's Anya, always was, just like Mama named me. What is this place we've landed in, anyway?"

"This? It's . . . Belongs to the state . . . ministry . . ." Duvakin flapped his hands weakly; then, like a father with his child at the botanical gardens: "This is an almond tree."

"The bags in here, I guess." Anya glanced neither at the tree nor at Abdulla, but marched into the cottage, where Duvakin heard her ask, "And the bath . . . I suppose there's water in this palace? Good God, Papasha, getting here, it's Moses and the children of Israel, forty days and nights to the top of Ararat! A *video*!" The voice became a squeal, and she reappeared at the door. "My God, Papa, but you're a man!"

"Bring the bags in, put them in the . . . bedroom." Duvakin went from gruff to squeaky again, then explained loudly, to everyone, including himself, "I'll sleep out on the couch is plenty big enough not really meant for guests. . . ."

Already the room had the faint tang of her smell, part flower, part earth, and Duvakin was ashamed that he had not changed his shirt in two days nor his trousers in four. Abdulla did as told, grinning, then came back, to stand by the front door, grinning.

Grinning wider when Anya stretched voluptuously, then stamped and shivered, like a horse coming out of the barn in spring. "What a nightmare! The air conditioner in the auto is broken, it's like from a freezer or something, so it turned our butts to ice, and to get any warm air at all we had to roll the windows down, so I'm all *dust*."

"Very cold," Abdulla agreed happily, "windows down . . ."

The realization that the driver might stay forever to gape at Anya got Duvakin moving. He pushed Abdulla out the door and banished the girl to the tub, while he paced the front room and tried not to think about the splashing, the snatches of song she gurgled to herself, the little shriek when she slipped into the tub.

"Don't drink any of the water!" he remembered to yell—out of sorts, because, he only now realized, he had come to think of this cottage as his. Now, her coat on his chair, her things on his bed, her body in his tub, he wandered about—touching the edge of the couch, tracing his initials in the whitish dust on the screen of the

TV he had never turned on, checking the miniature refrigerator three or four times to see what he could offer her.

Anya, and Moscow, and their apartment, and Galya . . .

Stockings dripping into the tub, and hairs on the sink, and . . .

She emerged, rosy and steamed, hair turbaned in a bath towel, body zipped into a gray training suit tight enough to show the nipples at the end of her obviously unfettered breasts.

"Oooh, what a relief!" She rubbed vigorously at her right ear. "The plane to Baku was delayed *eighteen hours*, and then—"

"Why have you come?" Duvakin, scowling, plumped down onto the orange divan, like a child claiming a toy.

She stopped rubbing. "I'm not welcome?" Her eyes narrowed ever so slightly, as her mother's used to.

Duvakin plucked that arrow from his heart and shrugged, hands out, palms up. "Welcome, not welcome . . . This isn't a rest home on the Black Sea, to welcome people to. Where were you? You had moved out. Taken your things."

Anya took a couple of steps toward the chair across from Duvakin, head high, back straight. Suddenly, startling Duvakin, she ground at her eyes with the heel of her right palm, left eye first, then the right. When she glared at him, her eyes were round and wet.

She's crying? Duvakin thought. He had never seen her cry before.

"That was . . . a mistake."

"What was a mistake?"

"Moving out."

Duvakin watched her cry, not sure what to do, not even sure what he thought. She wasn't really crying; it was more as if the few tears had sneaked past an elaborate system of watchtowers, guard dogs, and fences.

After a few moments, she said, almost calmly, "See, Dzhimi and I, we had been, well . . ." The girl's hands waved in search of words. "We had been together for a while, and so when he said he had this friend who was going to sea—"

"Dzhimi?" Duvakin broke in sharply. Christ, they can't even have proper *names*!

Like a largish bird landing, Anya suddenly swooped on the other end of the divan, tucked her feet beneath her, and made an impatient face.

"Dzhimi's the tutor, for English. Or that's what he said he was." She looked at her knee, worrying a loose thread. Duvakin studied the top of her head, brown roots just showing through the blond, the pale scalp exposed where her damp hair was tufted, the line of her neck, where a pulse was faintly throbbing. She was, he realized, watching him out of the corner of her eye.

Duvakin blushed. "Well, I suspected he wasn't . . . I mean, the walls in the flat aren't so thick . . ."

She jerked her head upright. "I didn't mean *that*. Well, I mean, that, too, but . . . his English *is* beautiful, you know."

The sun was low, throwing reddish beams directly into the cottage, missing Anya's face, but hitting her hands. They were broad and short-fingered, with well-tended nails that were meant to make the fingers seem longer. Not pretty hands, for so pretty a girl. But almost precisely her mother's hands.

"Why have you come?" he repeated, but now in a different voice. "It's— This isn't a good place. And you and I . . . aren't . . . You have a father. . . ."

Anya snorted, but without particular spirit. "My father . . . You know, I actually met him once? I was eleven, and Mother . . ." She paused, inhaled, went on. "Mother had just gotten the post at her clinic. In Magadan. It came with an apartment . . . not the one she had when you met her, she had already traded about four times. . . . Anyway, to get *any* sort of apartment in that mudhole, that was something, with people living inside construction pipes and railroad cars and old shipping boxes. It was March eighth, I remember, Women's Day, because at the door here's this half-shaved, mumbling specimen, holding these three wilting carnations he'd probably stolen from the Lenin downtown, and a plastic dump truck under his arm. That was for *me*, the 'beloved child,' but he couldn't even remember I'm a girl!" In her indignation she had risen to her knees. "Ha! When Mama got home, didn't she send *him* flying down the stairs!" She stayed that way for a second, then sagged, to sit on her haunches. "But I had to spend an hour or so listening to him mumble. *Smelling* him." She shook, as after a nasty taste.

"But if he was such a . . . poor example, then how did your mother . . ." Duvakin felt oddly jealous, even insulted. She was dead now, for heaven's sake, and this was years ago!

Anya shrugged. "He had been something big, before the wine got him. Also a doctor, I think, but exiled there. After a sentence. At least that's what Mama said." She looked at him in silence a moment, then hung her head, almost whispering. "So you see, if I ever had a father . . . it's you."

Frightened by these last words, Duvakin almost shouted, "That's why you came all this way? You got yourself into a mess and now you want Papasha to pull you out of it?"

The girl looked up, face pinched. "They think I did it!"

"The murder." It wasn't a question, because Duvakin remembered his own reaction. The empty bedroom, the girl gone, his wife lying dead in the other room . . . "Well, you were gone, weren't you? I tried to find you."

"Don't you see? That's just it!" She was back up on her knees, and closer to him. "We knew she was going to be out, that's why we planned it for that night. I told them!"

"Told who? What 'them'? And anyway, what would it matter whether your mother was out? She never stopped you . . . from staying out. I mean, I didn't even know you *existed* until . . ."

" 'Them' is Dzhimi, and Wolf, his pal, and Kostya . . . the guys, his friends, the group we hung out with."

"What are they, students? Workers?"

"Swindlers and hoodlums," she said, her bitter spareness again like her mother's. "Dzhimi's tutoring at least was real . . . after a fashion. The rest of them . . ." She shook her head. "Money changing, peddling bogus Adidas, speculating in cassette tapes. All small-time things. They are trash."

"That you ran away from your mother to live with."

Blood flushed across her cheeks as if Duvakin's slap had been physical, not verbal, but there were no tears. Anya stiffened her chin, spoke with the disembodied remoteness that people use in talking to the militia. "Dzhimi told me it was a friend's dacha, he's in the merchant marine, and he would be gone for four months, at least. Dzhimi and I would live there. Like husband and wife. It would be like our own apartment, and then, after the four months, we'd see. About registering for real. It was lovely, at first, two big rooms, in this house made of logs. The walls gave the most wonderful smell when we lit the stove. Except that Dzhimi would only let me light it at night—during the day I had to use electric spirals—and the place never got properly warm. Idiot that I am, I never even wondered that I wasn't allowed to light the stove during the day!" She slapped herself lightly on the forehead.

Duvakin stated the obvious. "It wasn't a friend's dacha."

"God knows, it could have been, even. But for sure whoever it was didn't know we were there."

"And nobody bothered you? They just let you live there?"

"Well, you know how it is, winter, and nobody was around, really. Plus this dacha is pretty far back, set kind of apart from most of the others, in a pine stand. Those trees made it plenty cold and dark, let me tell you! And it was just me alone there all day. Dzhimi'd come at night. By train. It was a pretty long walk from the station, but the weather wasn't bad. . . . And he'd bring food, so we didn't need the shops, not that I suppose there was much in them."

"So what happened? The militia discovered you there? This Dzhimi's 'friend' came back?" Duvakin asked—still irritated, but now because help seemed to be what she wanted, and he didn't know what help, or how to give it. When they had shared the apartment on Fotieva, she had been like something better kept in a zoo, raging at a chance kind word or staring glass-eyed at Galya's sternest order, now structuring whole battles, almost wars, out of issues that Duvakin had not even understood were issues, now disappearing for days on end, leaving her mother to fret and to gnaw at him. Always the best solution had seemed to him to go sit behind the *antikvariat* until mother and daughter left.

And now the daughter had come here.

Anya still had her chin raised nobly, her face somber, so it was the more striking that she suddenly smiled, childish dimples creasing alongside her mouth. "We fought, Dzhimi and me. I was bored sitting there all day, doing nothing but sewing, while he got to go into the city . . ."

"Sewing?"

"Sure." Anya seemed a little surprised. "You didn't know?

Mama taught me how to sew, back in Magadan. You get me the labels and the cloth, and I can make you name brands you can't tell from what you buy in New York."

"What you mean is you were making counterfeit goods for the black market?"

She giggled, eyes merry. "Sure sounds grim when you put it that way, doesn't it?" She straightened up, tossed her short hair. Drops landed on Duvakin. She reached out, wiped them off. "Sorry . . . Anyway, we were just making clothes, that's all. Rags, for the kids. Ten rubles' worth of material, fifty for the labels . . . that's the real expensive part, there's only a couple of factories in the whole country that have the equipment to fake labels, Dzhimi says, so the prices . . . pffft!" She jabbed her thumb at the ceiling a couple of times. "And then kids beg you to sell them for three fifty, four. Cheaper than the real thing, and who can tell the difference? So they're happy, and we're happy. Class, eh?"

There was less than a meter between them, and Duvakin's face still burned with the trace of those fingers. What was she to him, this daughter–not daughter, woman–not woman? He stood up abruptly, cleared his throat. "Well, yes . . . Dinner, I should see about dinner. . . . So you fought, you say?"

The girl gave him an odd look before nodding. "Like cats in a bag, but I didn't walk out until the next day. Put my things together while he was gone, then wrote 'Ciao' on the mirror with my lipstick, just like in a movie he took me to once . . ." Suddenly the story trailed off, as the girl went back to tugging at the thread. "Do you ever believe in, like, fate?"

Duvakin, who found it easier to breathe with his back to her, was squatting to rummage through the little refrigerator. "Fate?" he repeated over his shoulder.

"Or, you know, luck. See . . . they were coming for me."

"Who was?"

"The militia . . . I'd gone out the back door anyway, because I had to throw the trash out—I was mad at Dzhimi, but that was no reason to leave garbage lying around—and so I was going along this alley that heads toward the train platform. On the other side of the fences I saw these two little *gaziks*, humping and bumping through the mud toward the dacha."

The sun had gone below the horizon, and the ground released its pent-up heat in a puff, as if exhaling. Now the chill of night would come slithering in. He should plug in the electric spirals, Duvakin knew, but instead he asked: "So the militia was there. Why does that mean they were coming for you?" He wondered whether the girl could hear what he *really* wanted to know, that rhythmic tap at the back of his brain, "QUESTION SUSPECT DEATH WIFE, QUESTION SUSPECT DEATH WIFE, QUESTION SUSPECT . . ."

"Because they stopped in front of our dacha, and because when I got back to Fotieva Street, the apartment was sealed—"

"Sealed? Our apartment was sealed?"

"Big paper seal, with two rubber stamps and lots of signatures, 'CLOSED BY ORDER OF MOSCOW CRIMINAL INVESTIGATION.' " Then she laughed. "Not that it was difficult to scrape off one end so I could get in. The hardest part was finding more flour, to make the paste to glue it back."

"Well, but still . . ." Duvakin protested weakly after a moment's thought. "A normal precaution, wouldn't you think? Sealing the apartment."

"Look, I told you, they think I did it! They think I killed my mother! Can't you understand that? I was so scared when I got there, I couldn't figure out why the apartment was sealed, I didn't know where you and Mama were, I didn't know about . . ." With a mighty sniff, she forestalled the tears rising in her voice. "About Mama, and I was sure that Dzhimi and Kostya and Wolf would be after me, so I did the only thing I could think of, which was call Tatiana Ivanovna."

"Who's Tatiana Ivanovna?"

"The school director who was Mama's best friend, remember? She was helping pull strings to get me into university or something in Moscow. The one you sold the *antikvariat* to."

Now Duvakin remembered the hard black hair, the eyes that weighed you as if knowing to within four kopeks how much was in your pocket, the voice, honey spread thin over a saber. "I didn't sell her the *antikvariat*," Duvakin snapped, then added, "and besides, it was seventeen thousand I refused."

Anya readjusted herself, put her feet primly on the floor, zipped the neck of her *dzhogging* all the way up, so that her chin was partly buried. "Well, she thought you had sold it to her, and it's a good thing she thought so, because it was she who told me about Mama, and she let me stay with her for a while, too."

"That was decent of her, but . . ." Duvakin couldn't think of what else to say.

Anya laughed, but with no pleasure. "Not really. It was only until she could find a truck driver honest enough for her to rely on, but not so honest he wouldn't mind standing by while I took the seal off the apartment. It was just lucky that that took her ten days. . . ."

Then, suddenly, the girl collapsed, burying head in hands, fingers run deep into hair; she was curled nearly double on the sofa, her back quivering.

After painful indecision Duvakin tentatively crossed the three, four steps to her, hesitated before patting her gingerly on the back, trying to avoid the hummocks of spine, the bands of ribs beneath the warm, bath-scented flesh . . .

"Don't cry," he said, his voice husky with strain, "it's probably just routine, it'll clear up, I mean, if you—"

—really didn't do it. He caught himself before he said it. Confused, he pulled his hand back again, wondering whether she had understood.

"It's not the *militia* that scares me." She looked up, tears carving runnels down her blotchy red cheeks, one of them tufted with fluff from the pants of the *dzhogging*. "It's Kostya and Dzhimi . . . and Wolf."

Her eyes indeed had a haunted look, of genuine terror.

Duvakin was grateful to hear of a problem that he could deal with.

"Because you ran out? Moscow's full of girls; your Dzhimi will forget you, if he hasn't already found somebody to share his dacha with."

"Not *that*," Anya said scornfully. "They're going to kill me if they can."

"Kill you?" Duvakin echoed blankly, watching her rise from the divan and disappear into the bedroom, then stalk immediately back with something in her hand. "Because you left?"

"Because when I left, these left with me!" The girl chucked

the object in her hand at him; it fell on the couch, proved to be a loosely wound ribbon, the width of a thumb. White, with foreign words woven into it somehow.

Not picking it up, he looked at the girl. "For that somebody would kill you?"

"A thousand labels, at fifty rubles apiece? You figure it out." Sharp and scornful, now she sounded like the Anya he knew from the apartment in Moscow again, and he was surprised to feel a certain sorrow; it had been good to talk, even for a moment, to someone he did not fear.

"Well, not to worry, nobody would ever find you here." He handed back the roll, giving it the reverence ten years' salary deserved.

"I found *you*, didn't I?" the girl growled.

For the space of a second Duvakin wondered how, but then decided he didn't care. The Moscow militia seemed to have found him, too, and that was going to cause him infinitely more trouble, Duvakin thought but didn't say out loud.

Who had known he was in Novii Uzen?

Just the Ministry people, and not many of them. Kostenko. Chistoplotskii, of course. Some secretaries, assistants, that sort of thing . . .

So it must have been the Ministry that had told the criminal-investigation people where he was?

But if so, why wouldn't the Ministry have informed him about the inquiry?

Worse, he was beginning to realize what a pretty package this would make for that Moscow detective, if he ever were to arrive. The mother is killed, the same day the daughter disappears, and the husband leaves a few days later, "transferred."

And now the daughter shows up at the husband's, with a bagful of rubles that she got from selling the wife's furniture.

Hard on the heels of that picture came another one, even more chilling.

"These pals of yours"—he panted with sudden tension—"Dzhimi and Kostya and . . . Wolf? You think they had anything to do with it? I mean, uh . . . the apartment, and . . . your mother?"

Anya shrugged, looked out the window, at nothing, the violet-white of the security lamp in the middle of the compound silvering her profile.

Save for the chin—the girl's was still tucked tight to her neck—the profile was Galya's. The silver slipped along to her left ear as she turned to look at him, eyes invisible in the now-dark room. He should turn on the lights, should call for dinner, should plug in the spirals. He didn't move.

"It's evening, Papa. . . ." she said softly. "You remember what day it is, today?"

He shook his head, almost certain now that the throbbing in his temples was caused by fingers, huge fingers, holding him gently as they moved him across the board. What he didn't understand, *couldn't* understand was what was the board, and who were the players?

"It's forty days, Papa," the girl said softly.

"Since your mother's death?" Duvakin was genuinely surprised. So little? So much? He felt as if he had been alone forever. Except he wasn't alone now. He had Galya's daughter.

That was a sombering thought, but a stiffening one, too. If he was a pawn, there would be time enough to understand for whom and in what and why.

For now, the main thing was . . . not to be sacrificed.

"Forty days, eh?" he repeated, surprised by his own surge of direction, of purpose. "Well, we should light some candles, shouldn't we? And aren't there prayers?"

"You know the prayers?" Anya sounded surprised, but also relieved, that Duvakin was going to shoulder some of her fears.

Or perhaps that was just what Duvakin wanted to think, because saying he was caring for the girl allowed him to step aside from his own gnawing fears, for the moment at least.

Radiating a confidence that was perhaps exaggerated but that had, nevertheless, a grain of the genuine at its center, he stood up and slapped the light switch on, making both of them squint in the sudden glare. "I'll tell you what. I'll walk over to the main house and ask them for something a little special . . . for a memorial supper," he said, smiling at the girl's look. Gratitude? Release?

He wasn't sure, but whatever it was, it made him feel good enough that he wasn't going to spoil her mood now, by admitting he didn't know the prayers.

He chuckled, shivering in the chilly night. Him, a former professional atheist, wondering about the prayers for the dead . . .

Well, no matter, they would think up *something* that sounded appropriate. Because the one thing that Duvakin was beginning to be certain about, whatever it was he had gotten himself stuck into here in Novii Uzen . . .

A prayer or two would definitely not be superfluous.

C H A P T E R   **T W E L V** E

Papa!" Duvakin heard Anya's sleepy voice from the front room. "There's somebody . . ."

Mother of God, Duvakin thought angrily, if that's Abdulla again . . . Almost every day for a week, the Lezgin had found an excuse to come out to the cottage and admire Anya in her pajamas. Duvakin threw on pants and shirt, came into the front room still buttoning, scowling. *This* time, goddamm it, he was going to tell that smarmy little son-of-a-bitch . . .

Anya was sitting cross-legged on the divan, blanket pulled up to her armpits, a half-annoyed, half-uncertain look on her rumpled, sleep-red face. The television, in front of which the girl had once again fallen asleep, was snowing gray.

And Captain Tansybekov was standing in the doorway, service cap neatly under his left arm. Seeing Duvakin, he grinned, sketched a salute, and said, "Sorry to disturb you, but I have a man wants to see you. From Moscow."

Why would anyone grow a mustache like that? Duvakin wondered again. As if drawn by a pencil, over lips so puffy and moist that they reminded Duvakin of fish just about to spoil. And wearing a leather coat, in the heat of the militia captain's stuffy office?

The man from Moscow was of middling height, but so extravagantly plump that he fit the room like some enormous plum, glistening behind the briefcase he had set ostentatiously on the corner of the Kazakh's desk. Sytykh was the fellow's name, Colonel Sytykh, and it was a good one: "of the replete." He was wheezing, or perhaps purring, looking like an old neutered tom with two mice. The green-eyed smile he gave Duvakin sent ants scurrying all along Duvakin's stomach wall, and something in his look had made Tansybekov flush and begin to rise slowly to his feet, as if conceding the man's unspoken but superior claim on the chair behind the desk.

"No, no, here, sit here!" Duvakin had scrambled up from his chair instead, and even went so far as to touch the fellow lightly on shoulder and elbow, guiding him to the chair, which groaned as it took the investigator's weight.

The captain gave him a glance, eyes dull, like the unwashed windows of an old factory.

"It's all right, I'll . . . stand," Duvakin reassured Tansybekov, who hadn't asked. There were only two chairs, and although standing made Duvakin feel as though this were a reprimand session, it was still better than letting the Moscow investigator take over Tansybekov's chair. "We've inconvenienced the captain enough."

"Perhaps," Sytykh acceded ambiguously after a second, pursing his lips as he pushed first one tab, then the other on his glossy black briefcase. "But that's the service, isn't it, Captain? It's no inconvenience to assist each other where we can."

The Kazakh said nothing, tilted his head in a tiny bow.

"Well, Citizen"—the investigator pulled a file from the case, set the case on his knees as a desk, and then set to untying the ribbons on the file—"you've put us to some considerable trouble as well, you know?"

Duvakin resisted the urge to put his arms behind him like a soldier at parade rest. He fidgeted, finally put one hand in his pocket, leaned against the wall with the other. "I can't see how, I told them everything I knew, about four times. . . ."

"And then left Moscow for . . . here." Sytykh managed with a glance to make plain his opinion of "here." A runnel of sweat had begun in the hollow around his eye, swelling over a cheek, into a dewlap, and back out, to disappear into the man's collar. Imputations hung in the air like ripe bunches of grapes.

Every cell in Duvakin's body begged him to confess, no matter
to what, to *anything*, to throw himself at Sytykh's feet and beat his
head on the floor. Everything about the man—the leather coat, the
cold impatience, the diplomat's briefcase, even the corpulence—all
this spelled AUTHORITY in big letters, which Duvakin had been
trained his entire life to obey. Even Tansybekov seemed to feel it,
for he had gone as hard and smooth as a wind-polished rock, saying
nothing, watching through eyes that now looked like no more than
slashes in a piece of old leather.

Against all this Duvakin had only an animal sense of self-
protection, plus something that Anya had remarked on when he
explained who the visitor from Moscow was, and why he had suddenly gone ashen.

"But isn't that weird," she had asked, "to send a *colonel* all the
way down here, just to ask you a few questions? I mean, why would
they be taking Mama's death so seriously?"

And it wasn't just because this was true—it *was* odd to send so
senior an officer so far—that Duvakin now clutched at her remark
the way villagers might clutch wild garlic as they cut through the
cemetery at night. It was also because he had learned over the week
that Anya knew a lot about the law.

From a practical point of view, so to speak.

It was actually a discussion of narcotics that had brought the
whole thing up. Tortured by the puzzle of who had shot at him in
the desert and why, Duvakin had thought, one evening over supper,
to ask Anya about hemp.

"Papulia"—she had grinned slyly—"you wouldn't be interrogating me, would you? Like the papa in the joke?"

"What papa in what joke?" Duvakin had sniffed severely, to
show that not only wasn't he interrogating her, she could go to the
devil's spotted nurse if she cared to. "Anyway, Dzhimi and those
other fellows you mentioned, they must have used . . . those things?
Substances."

"The papa who asks the daughter why she's coming home so
late, and she says she got raped."

"This is a joke?" Duvakin had asked, almost dropping his fork.

"I didn't finish is why," she said through a chunk of gristle she
was gnawing at, grimacing; then she looked at him again, wiping

her lips. " 'Okay,' the papa says, 'but rape only takes ten minutes, and you've been gone six hours!' "

My God, little daughter, Duvakin had thought sadly, what world is this we've given you? To Duvakin now, being twenty seemed like being in America, a place dimly understood but bathed by golden sunshine and rich with eternal fruit, unreachable through the gray mist of his growing age. There had been a time, though, when, self-consciously adjusting the front of his uniform shirt and setting his cap to an angle that he felt made him look serious, he had strolled past the rude plank bench in front of the kolkhoz office, where the girls in their ginghams sat, swinging their bare feet and spitting sunflower seeds. Coarse braids of sun-bleached hair curled out from kerchiefs stiff with hay dust; the girls' plump arms were freckled and firm from tossing hay shocks onto the wagon.

Sure, the girls had giggled knowingly, shouting suggestively about the nightstick he gripped with such frowning clumsiness. Probably they even knew the word "rape"; after all, it wasn't so long after the war, and anyway, Vasya, the one-legged soldier who usually drove the tractor that pulled the hay wagons, he had a frustrated, leering way about him that turned downright evil when he got into the home brew at all seriously, making him say all sorts of things.

But would any of those girls have such a joke to tell?

Apparently, though, Anya had understood something of his expression, because she surprised him. A soft pat on the left cheek, followed by a dry peck of a kiss on the other, which she leaned across the low table to deliver.

"It's okay, Papa. . . . You're right, *anasha* is everywhere now. What did you want to know?"

Everywhere? Including you? Duvakin couldn't bring himself to ask. Anya wasn't his, after all, and it wasn't as though he had ever been invited to have an opinion about the girl or what she was doing. All that was Galya's affair, or the girl's, and anyway, she was grown-up. An adult, responsible for herself . . .

Then why did he feel this enormous gloom, as if just now aware that he had failed to do something he ought to have done? She couldn't have actually used the drugs, could she? Whenever they showed drug users on television, they were always crumpled-looking people, like something already discarded. And here was Anya, well fed, looking like a tourist from Bonn.

"The money," he had said gruffly, "is there as much money in these narcotics as people say?"

"Phew!" Anya had whistled, eyebrows in the air. "*Money?* Forty rubles for a fifth of an ounce of straw? Two hundred for a gram of tar? You call that money?"

"Tar?"

"These little black bricks, of, like, the pollen or something. It's supposed to be stronger," she had said matter-of-factly, then gone back to the unusually poor pilaf, leaving Duvakin to stare at the top of her head and wonder how she knew.

Colonel Sytykh was from the school of interrogators who let silence do half their work. He continued to scrawl laboriously at a piece of protocol paper, making large round schoolboy letters, with an expression on his face as if he hadn't yet brushed his teeth.

"You have the original report right in front of you!" Duvakin pointed, exasperated, doing his best not to shout. "Why should I keep going over and over the same thing? I was in the militia, you think I don't know what you're doing, trying to catch me forgetting something, or changing something, so you can say I'm lying? It's more than a month now I'm working down here, I would be suspicious if I *didn't* forget something!"

Duvakin fought back the urge to say more, to fill the void; instead, he stared at the top of the man's head, as if somehow he could see through the circle of thinning pomaded hair to the brain below, and so understand why the man had been sent so far. And by whom.

Finally the man from Moscow Criminal Investigation looked up; on his face was the patient weariness of someone surprised by nothing. "Of course, Ivan Palych. But you can appreciate yourself how curious it seems that you would leave so abruptly, so soon after the death of your estranged wife."

"I'm to tell my minister . . . ministry that I'm refusing an assignment because— What do you mean, 'estranged'?"

The purring smile, and a new sheet of paper was plucked from the briefcase. "We have information that relations with your wife were not . . . good?" He raised a mocking eyebrow to indicate how inadequate the adjective was.

"Information from whom?" Duvakin was shaken. "And what does 'not good' mean?"

The man read from the sheet, as if skipping around. "Frequent arguments . . . considerably faster professional advancement than husband . . . drinking . . . evidence of much money being spent, beyond your salary . . ." He looked over the top of the page with a meaningful glance. Then he flourished a translucent brownish receipt, with the faint scribbles of a third carbon on it, which disappeared back into the case. "And she had applied to transfer the registration of the flat into her name."

"She *what*? When?" Duvakin stepped forward, almost as if he were going to grab the briefcase.

Sytykh clutched his case protectively, smiled his tomcat smile. "The day she died."

Duvakin's jaw hung open and his limbs went limp. He would have fallen, but even that required more movement than he was capable of, that second. Jesus in heaven, it was hard to tell who looked worse, him or the girl. She moved out on the day her mother dies, and he . . .

. . . comes home early; they quarrel because he's reassigned; she goes to protect her Moscow registration, comes back . . .

His first reaction—that there had been a mistake, or even that the application was fake, because Galya would *never* have changed her registration without his knowing about it—was slowly devoured by a growing question.

Had they been "estranged"?

The word had a cold formality about it, like "sovereignty" or "profitability" or any score of the other new words that were rattling down on his life. That sense of being a sparrow fledgling sharing a nest with a baby cuckoo, who shoves the other fledglings aside, is that "estrangement"?

The question brought up, like a corpse from the water, something that Duvakin had been struggling to hide from himself, that he had greeted Galya's death with a certain . . . well, relief. In the way that a man who is struggling to quit smoking welcomes disaster, because it gives him reason to relax his willpower and light up, his weakness self-excused, because of stress. Whoever had given Sytykh this information had been correct, in a way. Not that she tormented him, because that wasn't true. If Galya was demanding of anyone, it was of herself. Duvakin she always treated well, even if by the end her attitude was more like affectionate resignation, as if no better could have been expected of him. The sense that conveyed, that for her he never quite got things right, or did them enough, had girdled Duvakin like a belt two notches too tight, knotting up his guts and chafing at him whenever he tried to sit. Because he knew that Galya, somewhere, was still working. At her clinic. Or at some deal. Or on some scheme.

No, Galya had not been easy to live with, because she was never content. Not with Magadan, where she had had a wonderful apartment, not with the first Moscow apartment, and not with the last. Life for her was no calm reeling out of days, so many bus tickets to be cranked from the machine. Life's meaning lay on a mountaintop, the moon, Mars. A goal so high as to be not only unreachable, but unrecognizable, so that Galya wouldn't have known it even if she *were* to reach it. But she would never reach it. Galya always wanted more, and it wearied him.

All right, call that estrangement. Is that cause enough for a man to batter his wife's head with a chair leg, until it resembles ground pork, bristly with little shards of bone?

As he wondered, Duvakin also was remembering the sheepish looks he used to get, back when he was a militiaman in the village, whenever he had to ask why Cross-eyed Sasha had driven the kolkhoz tractor into a pond, or why Olga, the scold, had dragged her ten-year-old Andreiusha across the road by his ear, nearly ripping it off, or why the two truck drivers from Fifty Years on the Path to Communism State Farm had gotten drunk and broken up the beer pavilion out on the main road. The look was always pretty much the same—weathered, tanned faces grinning stupidly or staring in dumb appeal, because what had been absolutely logical at the time was now obviously foolish, even criminal.

Wouldn't he sound about the same if he made any attempt to explain why he didn't think the prickly, exasperating, and utterly familiar relations between him and Galya should be characterized as "estrangement"?

Distracted by such thoughts, Duvakin had apparently put silence to work for him now.

"Well, how *do* you explain it, then?" he heard Sytykh repeat testily.

"Explain what?"

"That the ministry refuses to confirm your alibi for the evening of your wife's death."

Sytykh's smile split a fraction of an inch wider; the tomcat had stunned the mouse again. The Kazakh, too, was watching Duvakin closely. Is he expecting me to throw myself on the floor, Duvakin wondered, or maybe through the window?

Staring at the prosecutor, who was trembling to pounce, Duvakin suddenly understood that this was the critical moment, when the investigator would begin to shift the responsibility of explanation from himself to Duvakin. Until now Duvakin had known one truth—that he had not killed his wife—while the investigator had only questions, theories, and suppositions; if Duvakin now permitted himself to wonder about where the information that Sytykh had just dropped on him had come from, and what it meant, then he would become the one struggling for explanation, and Sytykh would become the one holding truths.

From that seed would grow Duvakin's guilt.

Which made it tremendous good fortune that Sytykh had made a small blunder.

Trying to keep his voice from trembling, Duvakin replied as neutrally as he could, "But I never gave any explanation for where I was. No one ever asked."

The Kazakh looked at Sytykh now, as if at a badminton match.

Sytykh glanced uncertainly at the papers on his briefcase, but recovered, the smile oilier. "It says right here, 'I returned from work and discovered the door was not bolted.' "

"That's true." Duvakin nodded gravely.

"Well"—Sytykh tapped the papers into order and made as if to put them away, as if there could be no more questions—"you work for the Oil Ministry, don't you?"

"I do," Duvakin acknowledged easily, pleased that Tansybekov had not looked back at him; the Kazakh was still studying the man from Moscow.

"Well, then"—Sytykh put the papers back into the case, closed it with a loud click—"we asked your ministry about that, to confirm that you were working that evening . . . and they said no." He folded his hands on top of the horizontal briefcase, with an air that suggested he could wait while Duvakin said his last farewells to freedom.

"Who exactly did you ask?"

"Your superior."

"But who exactly?" Duvakin persisted, because he had a growing hunch that the answer was going to be important.

For the first time Colonel Sytykh's smile disappeared entirely, and a light came on in his eyes, a dull glare of irritation. "I myself didn't ask." His lips pursed petulantly as he clicked the case open again, bent to fish for something. "We have men for jobs like that. . . . Pustobashkin, A. M.," he read from something he had finally found.

"Aleksandr Markovich." Duvakin smiled broadly, relieved. "Did you ask him if *he* was working that night?"

Sytykh shut the case with a shiver of distaste; obviously he would not answer the question, but equally obviously Duvakin's barb had hit a tender spot.

A second later, though, Duvakin's relief withered, in the chill of another question. Why would the militia have asked Pustobashkin, precisely? Kostenko was his real superior, not Aleksandr Markovich. Aleksandr Markovich was the section chief, and always gone, to conferences, and meetings, and conventions. Most of them were overseas, in any of the important oil-producing countries that weren't also hot and dirty; somehow Aleksandr Markovich never found a need to go to Saudia Arabia. So everything but his marital obligations—and who knows, maybe those, too—got delegated to boneheaded Kostenko.

Give Aleksandr Markovich a choice between Duvakin and a dancing bear and he would have needed three tries to guess which of the two worked for him.

So why had anyone asked the section head? By rights they might as well have asked Chistoplotskii himself, because he'd have as little reason to know as Aleksandr Markovich would.

A section head was too high above him to be asked such a question.

Just as a colonel was too high to have been sent so far, for routine questions, even a routine arrest.

They were both too high, too important. Too high to be bothered about a simple break-and-enter that had turned nasty, too high to fuss with a suspected uxoricide.

Sytykh wiped his neck and upper lip with a large linen handkerchief, almost a napkin, then shrugged his shoulders, releasing a horsy smell of sweaty leather into the room. "Look, Duvakin"—he sounded testier now—"jokes are jokes, but these are serious charges, so I suggest—"

"Charges?" His thoughts settling around his neck with the prickly whisper of a noose, Duvakin leaped forward without bothering to work out whether there was another way to save himself. "Now they're *charges*? A few minutes ago they were just *questions*."

"I was speaking in a general way, not a legal one." Sytykh let an irritated ghost of unhappiness flit across his plump face, then glanced at the Kazakh, almost winking. "This one's a difficult number, eh, Captain? But I expect you know him already?"

The Kazakh restricted any answer to a small throat-clearing.

Sytykh now turned sideways in the chair, to face Duvakin squarely. The pine chair registered its complaint loudly. "Look, Ivan Palych." His voice was now weary, a little warmer. "That's one bitch of a journey down here, and I'm tired. I can't imagine you're any buttercup yourself, after hiding out down here for, what is it, six weeks already? This isn't exactly Paris you've made your hideout in, is it? You can't *like* the idea of spending the rest of your days down here, can you? And because of what? Good Christ, we're in the militia, you think we don't know how it can be? You're having a bad day at the office, so you sneak out early, take a couple of quick shots with some of the guys behind a fence someplace, finally get to feeling better, and then you get home, all's you want is some quiet, and maybe a drink or two more, but instead you get nagging about how you don't make enough money to call yourself a man.

She wants you to buy her things, French perfume and a video recorder, might as well be a necklace made of hen's teeth, for all you could afford it or even find it. So a fight gets going, and then maybe she starts hinting around that you're such a chump, you don't even know she's maybe even stuffing somebody else's kielbasa for him when you're not around? A situation like that, a man's temper is going to get the better of him, we understand that. You think it hasn't happened to better men? But the thing of it is, Ivan Palych, why should you let a mistake like that mess up the rest of your life? This isn't America, thank God, our judges are people, just like you. You go in, say it was like this and like that, they give three, maybe four years in a medium-regime camp someplace—maybe less, since you haven't done anything before, and you sure as the devil can't kill your wife again, right? And then you walk away, a free man. No more listening for cars driving up in the middle of the night, no more worrying about some highway inspector asking to see your documents because you walked when the light was red, no more hiding out in these towns you wouldn't send a goat to die in. . . ."

The harder Sytykh worked to convince him to confess, the more horrified Duvakin grew. Not because of the cynicism of the inspector's appeal to confess to a crime he hadn't committed; Duvakin had heard cynicism much worse, and anyway there was no chance that the hypnotic, murmuring appeal would work.

Nor was it how close Sytykh's scenario was to what had really happened, like a bad mirror that makes you look ten kilos heavier than you are, and half again as ugly, but still looks enough like you to make you wonder.

Instead, what made Duvakin feel nauseated, as though someone was running fingertips along the corrugations of his windpipe, was a growing certainty that what Sytykh was sketching was not just some idle guessing that he hoped to get lucky with, so as to add a plus to criminal investigation's generally negative report sheet. The version being laid out was too close to what had happened to be a lucky guess, and too plausible—so plausible that even Duvakin might find himself accepting bits of it, if he weren't careful.

No, the more Sytykh talked the more Duvakin suspected that the scenario had been tailored especially for him. The question then, though, was why, and by what tailor?

Well, Duvakin knew from bitter experience, the first require-
ment for getting that answer would be to make sure he kept out of
the box they were trying to put him in, so he could keep looking.

"Colonel Sytykh," he said firmly, "this isn't 1937, that you can
accuse me of any wild nonsense you want to, and then cart me
away. I know I didn't kill my wife, but if you think I did, then
that's for you to prove, not me to prove I didn't. We're a nation of
laws now, remember?"

The expression that slid across Sytykh's fat face now would
have given a snake the flutters. " 'Nation of laws,' my friend? Laws
are for citizens, not criminals."

"Criminals are citizens, until you prove they are criminals,"
Duvakin shot back.

"And you're saying to yourself, he's going to have the devil's
own time proving it down here, aren't you?" Sytykh laughed, as if
suddenly weary of the whole conversation. He put everything back
in his briefcase, clicked it resoundingly, then said, "Well, we'll just
have to see, eh?" Then, offhandedly, to the Kazakh: "I trust there
is *someplace* in this town where I can wash some of your sand off
me, and maybe get a meal?"

"There is," the Kazakh replied, after a long silence.

Sytykh nodded with satisfaction, hauled himself to his feet,
then gestured to Duvakin. "All right, Mr. Lawyer, let's go."

"Go where?"

"Wherever he says to." Sytykh jerked a fat thumb at the
Kazakh. "He'll be in charge of your accommodations while I wash
some of this damn Kazakhstan off me."

"Accommodations?" both Duvakin and Tansybekov asked, at
almost the same moment, and in almost the same surprised voice.

It was Tansybekov whom Sytykh answered. "A cell, man. A
cell! You've got something like a cell, I take it? A room you can
lock where you won't lose him again, while I get ready to take him
back to Moscow." He was speaking loudly and slowly, as if
Tansybekov were a bit deaf. Or stupid. Then he laughed, and said
in normal tones: "It's been bad enough following him down here; I
surely wouldn't relish going to the *next* place he might find to
hide out in."

Jesus, Anya! was Duvakin's first thought. What would become of Anya? Here she was, in Novii Uzen, alone . . . and if he were just taken off, then . . .

She had thought herself abandoned once already. He backed up, shaking his head. His rear end hit the wall. There was no place for him to go.

Then he realized that Tansybekov had said something, because Sytykh was bellowing in reply. "*Papers?* You want papers, I'll give you papers!" He slammed the briefcase down, rustled furiously in the accordion guts of it. "Judge's order to detain for questioning!" *Bang!* it went on the desk. "Verification of suspect's identity!" *Bang.* "My instructions!" *Bang.* "My identification!" *Bang.* "Papers . . . Have I missed any? Now, do you want to get on with doing what I asked you to, *Captain?*"

The man from Moscow Criminal Investigation even extended a fresh-risen, not-yet-baked roll of a hand, reaching to take Duvakin's arm. Duvakin shrank away, unable to make his brains think of anything more useful. Tansybekov was spreading Sytykh's sheets about on the desk with a ballpoint pen. Then he tilted his head, one eyebrow raised inquiringly. "I don't see a consent to extradition."

"Extradition?" Sytykh's face had gone a clotted color. "*Extradition?*" Then, as suddenly, it cleared, and a light went on in his dirty green eyes. Nodding, he looked back and forth between Duvakin and Tansybekov, then waggled his finger from one to the other. "Ho, ho, I understand. . . . You pay him, and he protects you." Sytykh smiled, amused by their assumption that they could thwart him. "Well, terribly sorry to disappoint you," he said to Duvakin, "but no corrupt little Oriental tricks are going to do you any good this time."

Then he pulled himself up as straight as his paunch permitted. "*Captain* Tansybekov, my orders are to return this murderer to Moscow—"

"And so you may, *Colonel*"—the Kazakh even bobbed his head and clicked his heels softly—"as soon as you have a properly signed consent to extradition that shows the disposition of any local charges pending against him."

"Local charges!" Sytykh's voice moved up an octave, and the liver color returned. "I'm taking this man to Moscow to have him charged with *murder*."

"One moment, please." Tansybekov's voice was almost normal, but he had stood, to get between Sytykh and Duvakin; he had tossed his head back, to look the taller Sytykh in the face, and had crossed his arms, so that they looked about the size of Duvakin's legs. "The new criminal code stipulates, one, that charges shall be cleared in the order brought"—Tansybekov folded pinkie over with thumb—"and two, removal to another republic requires the consent of the procurator, absent a contravening presidential decree. Article Sixty-seven, paragraphs two and five."

Sytykh took a step forward, fists clenched and briefcase rising. "There is no such article," he growled.

The Kazakh raised both eyebrows. "I'm flattered that you have studied our Kazakh laws so closely that you can have an opinion, but I regret to tell you in this case your memory has played you wrong."

"*Kazakh* law?" Sytykh shouted. "*Kazakh* law! I'll show you *Commonwealth* law, you miserable goddamn piece of roast beef, you just see if I don't!" Sytykh slammed Tansybekov's door hard enough to knock out some thumbtacks from the bulletin board beside it.

Papers zigzagged to the floor. Otherwise no one moved, until Duvakin bent numbly, humbly, to gather up the papers. Trembling, he handed these to Tansybekov, unspoken questions in his eyes.

The captain snorted, snatched the papers roughly, went back to his chair. "I hate Ivans," he finally said, when Duvakin continued to stare at him. "*Especially* the ones who think they have to teach us poor benighted sheepfuckers how to breathe and blink our eyes."

Duvakin's mouth was too dry, his palms too wet. "You said . . . other charges? Local . . . What charges?"

Tansybekov pointed at the door with his pen. "Unlawful flight, if you've got any brains, but I'd advise you to take some water with you, if you do run away. Otherwise . . ." The Kazakh studied him a bit longer, then smiled with unexpected warmth. "If I have to, I'll think of something. Just remember, though, do what you have to do, because I won't be able to hold *him* off for more than a few days."

This carnival of a morning, now up, now down, now up, had left Duvakin as limp as after a day at the Turkish baths.

"A few days?" he repeated, stupidly.

Tansybekov was already sorting through papers, speaking to his blotter. "Can't promise you better, Ivan Palych, you saw what kind of a man he is." Then he stopped, looked at Duvakin. His face was serious, but a smile seemed to glint in Tansybekov's inky eyes. "What do you bet that he's out right now, trying to find a telephone?"

CHAPTER THIRTEEN

He might have a week, the captain estimated.

If he was lucky.

And now Anya had disappeared.

"Rosa! Rosa! The girl, you didn't see where the girl went?" The woman was doing something by the back stairs of the big house, sitting with a pan between her knees. She looked up as he rushed over, hot and disheveled. She was picking through rice grains, putting something into another pan at her right side with quick, accustomed movements.

"Ah, Ivan Palych." She nodded, but said nothing more. She didn't smile. A pair of sparrows were quarreling nearby, as if looking for a chance to dart in and steal a few grains.

"Rosa, you don't have any idea where Anya's got to, have you?" He tried to sound casual, but failed.

The Kazakh housekeeper went back to her pan, smoothing the grains out, then picking out what Duvakin could now see were pebbles, bits of straw, and spoiled kernels, black like lice. Sounding grim, she said, in a clipped voice, "Edik came, they talked for a while, and then they went off on his motorcycle."

"Off? Off *where?*"

"For a ride, I guess. She's very pretty, your Anya," Rosa added, as if in explanation, but didn't look up; instead she dumped the cleaned panful into another sack, then took another scoop of kernels from the fuller bag. Something clanged in the bottom of the sorting pan. Rosa inhaled sharply, then held up a pebble the size of a thumbnail. "Look at this!" she complained. "Just *look* at this!" Now she held up the can she had been throwing things into. It was nearly full, mostly with gravel.

Christ and the twelve Apostles, Duvakin thought, panicky, she's gone off with *Edik*. Edik and the rifle, Edik and the chicken fight, Edik and . . . Christ, he had no idea who Edik was, or what he wanted. Why hadn't he warned the girl, why hadn't he said something?

"She didn't . . . Edik didn't . . . say anything? About when they'd . . . might come back?"

"A five-kilo bag of rice." Deeply disgusted, Rosa wasn't even listening, "and I must have half a kilo of this trash already, with the bag not even half empty! Momish will never believe me, that there was that much gravel in there; now he'll say I'm stealing the *rice!*" She turned her head, covering her mouth with her palm. Duvakin was startled to see tears trembling on the lower lids of her deep brown eyes.

"Momish accuses you of stealing?"

Rosa didn't say anything, but after a moment nodded. Then, snatching the hand away from her mouth, she reached imploringly for Duvakin's sleeve. "Ivan Palych, I swear to God, I never steal a thing, you know the sausage that you get, in your eggs? That's *my* sausage, that my cousin makes. In the *aul*."

What sausage? Duvakin couldn't remember, didn't want to remember. He had to find Anya, had to figure out what to do. A week, Tansybekov had said. If he was lucky. Was he lucky? Was a week a long time? He felt he was going frantic.

"Very good it is, too, Rosa. . . . Listen, Edik, you wouldn't know how I could . . . mmm, contact him?"

"It's not like I mind, Ivan Palych, my cousin always keeps a few horses. We're a *bai* family, did you know that?" She glared with fierce pride, then tried a smile, a forced joke. "Besides, how could you tell your friends in Moscow you'd been to Kazakhstan and not eaten our horse sausage?"

"Horse sausage?" A surge of nausea made Duvakin stand.

Rosa, still smiling. "It's a Kazakh custom . . . in the spring."

Duvakin mastered a rising heave with difficulty. "Why . . . why would Momish . . . say you are . . . stealing?"

Rosa's face clouded. "I've worked here twenty-two years, Ivan Palych, and if I had wanted to steal, I would have stolen. And now to assume that just because there's no food I'd be taking *his* food . . ."

The desire to vomit was passing, replaced by an even colder sweat, and a twinge, radiating outward from his stomach. "There's no food?"

Rosa looked as though she wished she could swallow her tongue, and then went back, furiously, to sorting. "There are some shortages," she mumbled, "but no, there's . . ."

Duvakin tried to remember what they had been eating. Rice, he remembered. Pilafs. But the meat? He couldn't remember, save that he had eaten. Not as Galya once fed him, but that had been to the good, probably. His clothes hung on him now, and he constantly had to tug his belt up.

"Rosa," he said sternly, "we're not children, for twenty years people have been complaining there's no food. What do you mean there's no food? Like in the war, there's no food, or just what's in the stores is hard to find?"

The woman's slant-eyed, flattish face, when she looked up, unexpectedly reminded Duvakin of his mother's, when he was small. She would tuck him into bed, singing to him to help him forget the cramps in an empty belly, and then she would go off to ten hours of creosoting railroad ties. Sometimes, when she thought he was asleep, he would peek at her face. The look it had, by the light of their kerosene lamp, was much like this, hard because there was no choice, but soft, too, with hopelessness, because no matter where in the future she looked, she saw only evil.

"Collectivization was when it was bad in Kazakhstan, Ivan Palych," she said tartly, "because Stalin was trying to kill us." But then she softened a bit, nodded. "Not like that, yet, no. But it's bad, Ivan Palych," she finally allowed, "worse than I've ever seen."

How old was she? She *couldn't* remember collectivization, could she? Must be stories she had been told. But she'd never seen worse? She was at least his age, so she would remember the early fifties, just before the start of the Virgin Lands. . . . Those were hungry years, almost as bad as the war.

Duvakin didn't care to be that hungry again.

In the compound the day was still soft, the soil exhaling a cool moistness from where it was worked around the bushes, songbirds squabbling in the newly leafed branches. The sky was a milky blue suffused with gold, and Duvakin could feel only dread, palpable in the sour taste of horse sausage. Christ, what a place to be: hungry among people you didn't know and couldn't trust. . . .

". . . Edik simply won't permit it, that I know for sure."

Duvakin understood that Rosa had been saying something to him.

"Sorry?"

She looked about carefully, then repeated, softly, "I said, that's why I hope Edik wins next Sunday, because he simply won't permit it anymore."

"Permit what?"

"Shipping all our oil off the peninsula. It's our oil, they shouldn't be able to just take it and then give us this trash in exchange!" She held up the can of stones gleaned from the rice. Then, with the furious abandon of someone who has just said aloud what she had not dared even whisper before, she shouted, "Edik will get us our land back! Kazakh land, for Kazakhs! Kazakh oil, for Kazakhs!" The pebbles rattled vehement emphasis.

Startled, Duvakin said, "But he's Russian! Why would—"

"Edik? He's Kazakh!"

"Eduard Andreevich Mordachkin is a Kazakh? And I suppose Mogammed Alioglu Ibragimov is, I don't know, an Estonian! And me, I'm Korean!"

Rosa though had already stood, head thrown back. Eyes bright with the intoxicating smoke of burning bridges, she said haughtily, "Edik's mother is the second cousin of Dinmukhammed Akhmedovich!" Then, after a moment to gather the rest of the rice, she added primly, "And as for what you are, that's for your blood to tell."

"Who's his mother?" Duvakin gaped, out of reflex, but the answer couldn't have mattered. His mother was Kazakh, which made Edik a Kazakh, too.

No, it made him worse, Duvakin understood a second later, it made him neither. Not Russian, not Kazakh. A half-breed.

"Kunaev," Rosa said with a withering glare. "Dinmukhammed Akhmedovich Kunaev. And I suppose you know who *he* is!" She punctuated the scornful sentence by slamming shut the door into the kitchen, leaving Duvakin goggling at the chalky, sun-faded paint.

Kunaev.

Brezhnev's faithful deputy, the tallest man in the old Politburo, always visible there on the podium, a full head and shoulders above the rest. The only Kazakh leader of Kazakhstan since before the czars. Who had been removed, in disgrace, in 1986. Accused of financial corruption, of mismanagement . . .

Of using his influence to help his relatives . . .

And, Duvakin realized with a start, he was still alive. In "retirement." Once Duvakin had seen a ghost, a real ghost. Some errand he didn't remember now had sent him walking through the district behind Kalinin Prospekt. These were the remnants of old Moscow, with the last few graceful mansions still peeking through the cotton-woods and maples, protected from the masses by wrought-iron fences such as no one could make anymore. It was an embassy district, and the more favored trade unions were there, but it was mostly the place where big Bosses preferred to live, because they had made such a muck of the rest of Moscow. And tottering toward him that day, muttering as old men will, had come the ghost.

Lazar Kaganovich.

Once Stalin's right-hand man, now expunged from history.

But not from life.

Standing stunned there that day, Duvakin had tried to imagine what that ghost would be brooding on, spinning out his days, hatch-ing what bloodcurdling plots to take back what had been taken from him; he had failed, but even the effort had been enough to leave Duvakin shivering, for all that the day made the leaves hang down like the tongues of panting dogs, and the pigeons stretch out unmov-ing in the dust.

And Kunaev?

Could *he* be the invisible chessmaster here?

Wandering had brought Duvakin to the end of the path, at the wall that encircled the compound. The fence was high but, as Edik had said, was breached in several places, pieces of the sheet metal ripped back as if by a can opener. There was so much traffic through the holes that a path had been worn, unbraiding to nothing a few meters from the wall. Beyond the fence was just the emptiness of Mangyshlak, the soil of dust, the sparse scrub trembling in the unending wind.

The view, strangely, calmed Duvakin, reassured him that the ghostly conspiracies and plots that had shimmered for a moment in his imagination were no more than that, imagination. Kunaev couldn't be maneuvering for a political return from *here*.

And he wouldn't be using Edik either, Duvakin decided. How favored could such a relative be, if *this* was the only job such influence could gain for him?

Duvakin smiled, at his own fears. He had trouble enough without making Edik into something he wasn't. Edik was just a half-breed, evidence of his mother's disgrace, somebody who would be stuck as far out of the way as he could be stuck.

Christ, Duvakin thought, hanging on the frame of the broken fence, to think that people *fight* over this peninsula! He watched a dust devil hop and twist its way across the empty brown plain before vanishing as suddenly as it had formed. A tumbleweed bounced slowly along, like a man on a moon walk, hit the fence, and stuck, just one more in the tangle of dead weeds that had drifted up against the barrier.

So what was there to fight over? The oil, sure, but even Duvakin knew enough to understand that the fields were tapping out. The easy oil was gone, and no new holes were being drilled. In a couple of years, ten at the most, the pumps wouldn't draw anymore, and then what would you have? A busted-down city full of cutthroats and brigands, that's what. And if Rosa was telling the truth, already there was nothing to feed them.

All right, if there were water. Then maybe this land would blossom.

But then the same thing was probably true of the moon, come to that.

No, Duvakin decided, let them figure out a way to grow something down here, some kind of crop, and then maybe it would be worth fighting over. In the meantime . . .

He was nearing the cottage before he realized what he had said. Crops.

There *was* a crop here. He had seen it.

The hemp.

A whole field, rows of plants, like potatoes or cabbage. That made hemp a product. An agricultural commodity.

He remembered what Anya had told him about prices. Eight rubles a gram for hemp, that made it . . .

Eight thousand rubles a kilo?

Even *oil* isn't worth eight thousand rubles a kilo.

Eight thousand rubles a kilo, Duvakin repeated, now stopped dead in the path, rolling the sum around in his mouth like a stone.

Lord, imagine having a sum like eight thousand rubles in your hands. . . .

Just four bricks, Duvakin remembered. The cockfight. That's all it was, four bricks.

He thought about that close, hot room, the shouting men. And Edik, at his elbow, suddenly, leading him away. Edik, who was smart, who had fought in Afghanistan.

Who had been fired, no doubt, when Kunaev was disgraced.

And who was running for the city Executive Committee.

It was like a snake swallowing an egg, apparently impossible to get down, but still, bit by bit the frightening thought fit into Duvakin's brain. Edik was not a man to sit home and nurse hurt pride. A half-breed in a powerful Kazakh family, he would have grown up prickly anyway, wouldn't he? Never quite *in*, because of his Russian father, but never quite *out*, either, because of the blow it would be to family prestige, to have him living hard. And then, when his family protector was disgraced, he would have become fair game, someone to kick around for everyone who had a grudge against the past but who still feared Kunaev and his more proper relatives, even in disgrace.

And then Duvakin remembered that he had calculated but a single kilogram of hemp. He had no idea how hemp was harvested, but a field had to have more than a kilo's worth in it, didn't it? Otherwise, why go to all that trouble?

So what would you harvest? A hundred kilos? A ton?

Which would be worth over six million rubles.

But what on earth would anyone do with six *million* rubles?

Even chicken fights wouldn't absorb six million rubles.

He watched a moving column of dust for several minutes, like God's finger scratching across the land, before he understood what it was. A vehicle, coming across the flat.

Watching and wondering who it might be, or what, Duvakin suddenly recalled—for no reason he could think of—one of the endlessly tedious sessions at the Moscow Higher Party School. A deep but narrow room, with space enough for a single file of tables; their student collective sat on one side, in flimsy pine chairs that creaked and complained beneath the burden of bureaucratic bottoms, and the instructor, a factory director who had been reassigned for misappropriating funds, sat on the other, lecturing from some unknown person's notes about Marxist economics. The two dead flies along the sill beneath the dirty picture window were suddenly as vivid as yesterday, the view out on a tram yard fifteen stories below, the portrait of Lenin, with his grimace of eternal constipation, in a frame that always tilted, unnoticed, a little to one side. The squeak of the chairs as the well-fed, ambitious thirty- and forty-year-olds carefully adjusted their seats, the buzzing of the fluorescent strips overhead, the drone of the lecturer, a semi-alcoholic who was eternally sobering up and so was unable to take his nose out of the notes he had not written and so couldn't remember.

What Duvakin recalled now, though, was a question: why the Soviet Union had no taxes. The instructor had looked up blearily then riffled through his pages until he found an answer. "Over there they pay them, then make the workers send some of it back. We just pay them what they need, and keep the rest for everybody. It's more efficient and more scientific. After all, it just takes kopeks to buy bread, and millions to buy bakeries."

It was a motorcycle, Duvakin could now see.

"Millions to buy bakeries . . ."

The words set off an association that Duvakin couldn't quite trace, and then he saw that the motorcycle was Edik's.

Thank God, with Anya clutching the young man, her head turned to the side and laid against his back as if she were asleep. She was wearing a black skirt, which might have been a belt, so high did it ride up her legs, astraddle the Jawa.

Acting on some instinct Duvakin didn't understand, he stepped off the path into the oleander bush, to watch Edik wheel the motorcycle through the gate and bring it up to the cottage, where with a jerk and a puff of blue smoke it died. The knifelike leaves obscured his view; he saw a flash of the girl's leg, heard voices as not quite words. Ears straining to hear whether there was a kiss, Duvakin stumbled, braced himself against the bush, missed, almost fell. The shrubs rattled like a tree full of ripe spoons, and some birds flew out, nattering indignantly.

"Who's there?" Edik said sharply, but Anya had already come to look.

"Papulia!" She laughed, hand over mouth. She had on a leather jacket over the short skirt, a black belt with what looked like rifle bullets peeking out beneath it. "What are you doing in the bushes?"

"I was . . ." Duvakin blushed, face crimson. "I was just . . . I thought . . . there was a nest, and I wondered . . ." He extricated himself awkwardly from the shrubbery, picking the leaves and twigs from his clothes.

"You don't want to go fooling about in there, Palych." Edik's irritation was poorly disguised, if disguised at all. "The leaves are poisonous. . . . So"—he turned to the girl—"Sunday?"

Duvakin shouldn't have glared so sharply, suspiciously, but he did it anyway. Anya, though, smiled, took Duvakin's arm, and with a coquettish dip of the knee said, "Thanks, I enjoyed today a lot, but . . . we'll have to see. Sunday is for Papulia."

Edik's face was grave. "I really think you'd find it interesting, and Sunday would be the best time to go. For me to take you."

"Thank you . . . but we'll see, all right?" She hugged Duvakin's arm tighter, making him blush again, conscious of her closeness.

"I don't think you'll want to be out here Sunday, it's going to be . . . very hot. The weather . . ." Edik grinned his insincere grin, waved a gloved hand at the air.

"Sorry," the girl said flatly, in a tone that made it clear she wasn't.

Edik glowered, said nothing, just adjusted his dark glasses and kicked the Jawa to stuttering, belching life. Then, the motorbike sounding somehow contemptuous, he buzzed out of the compound, slewing dust and pebbles at them.

There was a silence, which Duvakin didn't know how to break.

Finally he said, "You should wear more clothes . . . when you mo-torcycle. It's cold. . . ."

Anya let go of his arm—threw it, really—and barked a tense laugh. "And what do *you* know about riding motorcycles, Mr. *Roker?*" she tossed over her shoulder, stalking into the house.

"What do *I* know about—" Duvakin began, but then bit off what he was going to say. He followed the girl into the cottage, blessedly cool still in contrast to outside.

There was a trail of garments. The skirt, the jacket, a T-shirt, other things . . . he heard the water beginning to splash.

"You know where he took me?" she shouted through the door.

"Prison?" Duvakin guessed.

The bathroom door opened a crack, and she stuck her head out. An earring hoop the size of a ruble dangled horizontal above the bare right shoulder, the round knob of faintly tanned clavicle, the tender hollow between collarbone and neck muscle, the hint of hidden breast swelling . . . Duvakin cleared his throat.

"How did you know?" she asked suspiciously.

"Not so many sights in Novii Uzen, are there?" Duvakin was noncommittal.

"So you saw his little project, too, then." She disappeared from the door, but did not shut it entirely. In the crack there was a millimeter of indeterminate flesh, following by a splash, a little gasp. "At least you were *dressed!*" she laughed. "Two or three hundred little droolers with their blue heads and their tough-guy tattoos, no one to give them love but their own right hand for, like, maybe *years* . . . and idiot that I am, I'm wearing everything short and tight . . . Christ in his chair, if looking could put you in the family way, I'd be a Hero Mother four times over by now!" she giggled.

Shocked by her language, having difficulty not thinking about her there on the other side of the door, in the bathtub, splashing, Duvakin cleared his throat, rubbed the bridge of his nose. "You, ah . . . like this Edik?"

No answer came from the bathroom.

It was like being back in Moscow again, Duvakin thought with disgust. She's holed up there, and I'm out here, yelling advice that nobody wants. But Edik was dangerous, wasn't he? He *had* to tell Anya, warn her to stay away from him.

He opened his mouth, closed it again. He could imagine too vividly saying "I think he's raising hemp and he had somebody shoot at me and maybe he killed Ermolov but I don't know how or why and besides he's half Kazakh." Even Duvakin wouldn't have accepted *that* sort of advice.

"I'm sorry, it's none of my business," he said gruffly, "but . . . you don't know him so well. . . ."

"You do?" The tone was simply curious, not antagonistic.

"Well . . . one or two things . . ." he said cautiously, like a pensioner feeding a squirrel that suddenly is *almost* ready to take the bread crumb from his fingers.

The water sloshed; the girl sighed, then said, "See, I can't figure him. . . . He came out this morning, we talked some—that's why I went with him, because I figured he seemed like the perfect type, but then all I got was that damn prison of his, and his stupid workshop—"

"Perfect type?" Duvakin was startled at the constriction in his chest. Good Christ, man! he berated himself. You couldn't have hoped that she'd think *you* are the perfect type?

The water sloshed again; there was the sound of soap squishing, as if she were lathering herself. Duvakin wished he could make himself go away from the door, or go in through the door, or go *anywhere*, just so he wouldn't be standing *here*, his temples throbbing, his fists clenched. . . .

"Sure. I'd swear he's in the business, but I just couldn't get him to talk about the labels, no matter how much I hinted around."

"You were trying to sell him your labels!" Duvakin shouted, as if it were a personal victory.

The girl sounded surprised by his joy. "Yeah, well, I don't want them, but you can't just chuck something like that out, can you? But he just isn't interested."

"So you aren't . . . you weren't . . . interested in him?"

"Does it matter?" Again, the girl's voice made plain the words weren't antagonistically meant.

Duvakin squirmed a little. "Well, I mean, it's not for me to say, he's young and . . . good-looking, but . . . you haven't known him . . . very long, and your backgrounds are . . . different. . . ."

Her laughter was followed by the sound of her getting out of the water, dripping onto the tiles. "That's right!" she shouted above the sound of toweling. "Very different! Like, he's married, and I'm not!"

"Edik is married? He told you that?" Duvakin was startled, then even more startled when the girl burst out of the bathroom, wrapped in one of Momish's thick towels, her hair wrapped in another. He turned his back immediately, but not before he noticed the damp, almost invisible hair on her legs and across her shoulders, turning to descend her spine. Like the strokes of an artist's pencil, modeling her skin. . . .

"No," Anya said seriously. "Rosa did. . . . Warned me, I guess you'd say. That there's . . . problems, between him and his wife." Then she barked a laugh, brushed past him. " 'Scuse me, got to put on something that's not soaked in dust. But I'd *guess* there's problems, if he carries on with everybody like he tried to with me."

"He . . . tried something?" Duvakin choked out, strangled not just by a sense of possessive outrage—paternal? personal?—that he couldn't understand, but also, and perhaps more so, by a flash of wondering. That girl at the cockfight—could *she* be Edik's wife?

And if so, then what had she been doing that evening at the restaurant, talking so familiarly with Momish?

The girl came back out of the bedroom, dressed now in another T-shirt, another short skirt, and not much else; the result was scarcely more modest than the towels, especially as she toweled vigorously at her spiky tufts of blond-brown hair. She came close to Duvakin, smelling of soap and clean skin and something else, not quite flowers, not quite grass. Her eyes were cornflowers—but glistening, too—as she said, "No, Papulia, at least nothing worse than the rest. But thanks." She kissed his cheek gently.

"Thanks?" Duvakin looked at her, amazed. He rubbed his cheek.

"For asking." She smiled, then said, "Christ, you think Rosa can fix us something to eat? That damn prison made me *hungry*."

CHAPTER **FOURTEEN**

Duvakin passed uneasy, restless nights, distracted, edgy days.

Like a man with a bucket full of shards, he kept dumping out all the jagged bits of the past weeks, trying to fit things together, to see whether they made a plate or a teapot.

Galya, Ermolov, Edik, Sytykh, Rosa . . .

Anya . . .

And now it was Saturday night. The election was tomorrow morning. He couldn't sleep. He watched a spider spinning a web across a moonbeam, in the corner of the dusty window. The moonlight, the dust spots on the window, the window frame itself, the plaster on the wall, cracks running along the wall and up to the ceiling—all this combined in complex hieroglyphics, which his eye kept trying to force into meaning. From somewhere drifted up a memory—something he had read? seen on television?—of a fellow in a madhouse, who was convinced that the clouds, the grass, everything around him was specially patterned into an enormous, complex code that he had to break, or else he would die.

Hearing the girl mutter out on the divan, sigh as she rolled over, Duvakin wondered whether his worries weren't like those of that man.

The simplest explanation of the greatest number of facts is likely to be correct. Wasn't that some precept from philosophy, or science?

Or perhaps it was just something Duvakin recalled from a Sherlock Holmes translation; he couldn't remember, now.

He must be mad. Utterly and completely . . .

Could someone be trying to hurt him now?

It was mad to think so, mad as that man . . .

But then what do we do with the mad, such as that man? Throw them into hospitals more filthy than any zoo, inject them with chemicals, leave them at the mercy of sadistic, brutal guards.

Proving that the madman is not mad: The world *does* conspire against him.

And against me? Duvakin tried to imagine that it was his name the wind was whispering, his life that the birds plotted against, that it was warnings that the almond twigs traced out against the evening sky.

All right, Duvakin decided, forcing himself to go methodically, because the answer was already bursting upon him. What were the facts that Edik explained?

Duvakin had no difficulty now in imagining the worst of Edik. Easy as it had been to take Duvakin out into the desert for an "accidental" shooting, it could not have been any harder to get Ermolov to come to that abandoned building at the necessary time. But what would Edik do all this *for*?

Power, presumably. Edik would not be the first proud, intelligent man, burning from insults he was sure he didn't deserve, to want to erase those insults with revenge; and what better revenge than to unseat Momish and usurp his control? To return himself to a power he had never really had but of which he easily might have dreamed.

But why the drugs? Why the killing? Why the money?

Thinking back to that "millions to buy bakeries," Duvakin decided that explanation was inadequate. What would "the bakeries" be in this case? The only thing that might reasonably be a "bakery"—that is, something large enough to cost millions, and worth owning besides—was the oil field, and if Edik managed to unseat Momish, then he didn't *need* the money; the field would fall under his control anyway, or the control of the Executive Committee, which would amount to the same thing.

Duvakin worried at that knot for a long time, because it allowed him to ignore far larger, and far more troubling matters, in which Edik could not have taken part.

Such as that Galya was dead.

Killed by someone, when he wasn't home.

Because he was having this job explained to him.

The job in Novii Uzen, a godforsaken spot where he had been sent in great secret.

Only to have Edik find him immediately.

And now Sytykh, *Colonel* Sytykh, had, too.

To arrest him for Galya's murder.

The simplest explanation for the greatest number of phenomena . . . But what if the only thing that would explain all those facts was that they had been directed by Igor Aleksandrovich Chistoplotskii, minister of energy for the entire Russian Republic? The conclusion was nonsense, as if two plus two equaled a blue bulldog.

Not nonsense, though, because Chistoplotskii wouldn't do such things. Duvakin knew little about the minister, but five decades of life in the Soviet Union had taught him well that all men, any men, were capable of extraordinary evil. Besides, if you swam in deep waters, you had to be either shark bait, or shark.

No, what made that calculation nonsense was the simple arithmetic of the thing. That out of 150 million Russians Chistoplotskii would have chosen Duvakin as a victim, a pawn.

Who would bother, Duvakin had thought, to conspire against *him*? Hurt him, even kill him, as part of the blind onward march of society—absolutely, life was capable of that. Whom in Russia had life *not* chewed up and spat out, like gristle?

But for someone to expend time, thought, and energy specifically to hurt him? That was as unlikely as that anyone would wish to *help* him, or be kind to him. We are all kernels between the millstones of life, he had thought, it's not personal when they pour us down the hopper.

But then Duvakin had made that particular arithmetic error before. With Colonel Polkovnikov.

Polkovnikov twice had conspired to hurt him, to hurt Ivan Pavlovich Duvakin.

"Everything in Russia happens by chance, unless it is by design." Polkovnikov's words echoed around in Duvakin's head, interweaving with the lines of shadow and light on the ceiling and wall.

"The trick is knowing which is which."

All right, so accept, for a moment, that the impossible is possible. Then what?

Galya had once forced him to buy a trip to Leningrad, arranged through the ministry. "The cradle of three revolutions!" she had kept harping at him. "One of the great cities of the world! How can we call ourselves Russians, and know nothing about the former capital?" It was in November, and the people in the office had warned him that the hotels would be dark and cold, and that the bus ride there and back would cripple him. "Cradle of three revolutions, all right," they had said in the office, "but you'll find they didn't change the diapers very often."

They had been right about the city, but had not told him further that Galya would find nothing to buy, and so would carry on like a skinned alley cat for most of the three days, and the entire way back. For all that, though, the city had astonished him, even in its dirty tatters. That people—all right, even only a very, very few people—could ever have lived like *that*!

One place he remembered now, the bedroom ceiling of some palace or estate, which one precisely he didn't recall, part of the jumbled memories of writhing gilded carvings and rich vistas of room opening onto room through doors four meters high. But the ceiling he remembered as clearly as if it were above him now. Painted to look like a sky, in summer, at dawn; the bottoms of the few clouds blushed pink as ripening peaches, the plump wads of fluff cradling chubby naked angels who dangled little bare feet over Duvakin's head and giggled. And above the angels, extending into infinity, a sky so blue and distant and perfect that no one who slept beneath it could fail to awake each morning without a thought for the majesty of the earth, and its endless possibility.

It was something like that rising circle of blue, like standing in a well and seeing the sky, that snatched at Duvakin's breath now.

Let Chistoplotskii explain the events in Moscow; let Edik explain them here. But what possible connection could there be between the two?

The slender reed of what well could have been coincidence—
that Edik had found him so soon upon his arrival—was suddenly
sucked upward in a vortex of surmise, memory, and juxtaposed,
unrelated ideas.

Someone was going to buy the oil field, Edik had intimated.
He had wanted Duvakin to understand that "someone" as Momish,
and now Duvakin had been understanding it to be Edik himself. But
neither would be able to buy so much as the rustiest nut on the
rustiest derrick without the participation of the ministry.

The state economy was being dismantled, and who was inher-
iting the bits? The same people who had run the enterprises into
the ground when they were state-appointed managers.

Red or white, the Bosses had continued to scrub each other's
backs and line each others' pockets.

This produced a sudden, shimmery vista of sense. Chistoplotskii
was simultaneously overseeing the privatization of the oil field and
trying to ensure that the person to whom he sells it is himself. For
which he needed money, and a trustworthy local agent. Such as
Edik, who presumably wouldn't suffer on the exchange, between the
hemp that would generate the money to buy the shares and the
larger obligations that Chistoplotskii would have incurred.

Stunned by that ceiling, Duvakin had lagged behind the group,
until the gnarled old woman in mud-brown clothes, who huddled
in a corner against a dully glowing electric coil, so immobile
Duvakin had not noticed her until she tugged at his sleeve, reminded
him sharply, "It's not permitted to linger."

"But the sky, Granny!" He had tried to gargle out his admiration, even clutching at half-remembered words of poems he had
been forced to memorize at school. "It's . . . the *distance*, the . . .
vault!"

"It's just a ceiling like you must have at home, except with
paint smeared on it, sonny. Now move along, or I'll throw your
whole group out of here!" She had jabbed him out of the room with
a finger such as a fairy-tale witch uses when she checks whether the
captured boy is plump enough to eat yet.

So was this just a ceiling, then, that Duvakin glimpsed now,
smeared with paint so that it gave the illusion of sense? Or had he
somehow glimpsed the inner workings of fate?

And so glimpsed the fingers clasping the top of his little round pawn's head?

Duvakin lay rigid on the bed, thoughts arcing blue between two diverging poles. One pole was that Chistoplotskii had engineered all this, had brought Duvakin to Novii Uzen and was now trying to imprison him, perhaps even kill him.

And the other pole was the only question that that solution left unanswered.

Namely, what in the name of God's round earth could the minister of energy for all of Russia want with a man as small as Duvakin?

"Rosa!"

There was no laundry drying in the sun outside the big house, nothing on Rosa's stove. Duvakin went through the kitchen, into the big dining room, the sitting room beyond, where the chairs had stood covered by sheets even when he arrived.

"Rosa!"

The words echoed up the stairwell to the second floor, where he had never bothered to go. Once, clearly, this compound had handled more visitors, the less favored of whom were sent up these stairs, to rooms instead of to separate cottages. Duvakin went up one stair, two, then halted and came back down.

Rosa wasn't up there. Rosa wasn't anywhere. The house was empty. Abandoned, Duvakin understood now. The sun made cruel pools of light on the highly polished stone floor, dust motes circling crazily above them.

"Rosa!"

Please let her answer, Duvakin prayed, so that I don't have to wake the girl and tell her that there is no food.

Silence. Duvakin stepped over to the sitting area of the first floor and flopped down on a chair, adding another billow of motes to the sunbeam, already scorching though it wasn't yet nine.

It would be hot today, Duvakin remembered Edik having said, when he was trying to convince the girl to join him somewhere. He had been insistent, very insistent. But good Christ, where *wouldn't* it be hot, on this peninsula forgotten by God and cursed by man?

192 / Anthony Olcott

Duvakin sensed a rising fear, like clouds boiling up over Moscow in the heat of a July afternoon, the lightning that would surely come as yet no more than a distant grumbling and a prickling of the neck hairs.

Hot . . .

He bolted from the chair, dogtrotted to the kitchen, cranked the faucet.

There was no water.

Somewhere a mouse scuttered, startling him. He shivered, suddenly conscious of the deserted house surrounded by empty desert.

Empty desert? He remembered the rock through his window, the gun firing at him, the paths wandering away through the holes in the compound's walls. With a sudden choking feeling, Duvakin flung himself outside, through the empty kitchen. Already the sun was hammering the yard, bending the dusty green toward the chalky earth.

It was not quite April; in Moscow the snow must still stand in filthy lumps, and the cold rain would be falling. Here, the sun was already like a physical force, pressing leaves, grass, birds, even Duvakin downward toward the dust, giving him some foretaste of what summer must be on this peninsula.

"It's going to be hot tomorrow" echoed in his head.

Wake the girl? Duvakin wondered, a gnawing in the pit of his stomach. It was nonsense, it couldn't be . . .

The only noise was the wind, keening through the grid of the unattended gate, twanging at the single strand of barbed wire along the top of the wall. Distractedly he headed back for the cottage, wondering what Momish would say if he knew that his guest colony was abandoned.

Momish . . .

He stopped in mid-step.

Could it be *Momish* he had been describing to himself? The winter-melon head, set without neck into the snowman shoulders, the coppery wattle under the iron jaw, the porcine eyes, the fingers like new pickles . . .

The old Boss, the man who was going to lose his job, his position, his prestige. Wasn't *he* the sort of man to stop at nothing to protect himself? Blood, death, misery—what would they mean to him?

"Papulia!" Duvakin heard behind him. Startled, he whirled in a crouch, arms up defensively.

"Whoa!" Anya laughed. "You're doing self-defense now? Karate?" She was wearing a scarf and carrying a wicker basket, held against the hip, arm under the handle, hand clasping the rim. She looked timeless, eternally Russian, despite her tight blue jeans and sweater of nubbled wool. Duvakin fought back a grin of foolish relief.

"What gets you out of bed at this early hour?" he asked, more nastily than he wanted to.

Anya blinked in surprise, her eyes growing guarded. "What devil twisted your tail this morning?" she asked, not wholly pleasantly.

Duvakin forced a smile. "I was . . . wondering. Where you're going."

The girl's look softened, and in concession she rotated the basket forward. "Shopping."

"Shopping? On Sunday? For what? Rosa is supposed to do . . ." Duvakin began, but trailed off. Rosa was gone.

Anya brushed a stray wisp of blond from her face, then pointed in the direction of the main house. "Yes, but last night it was hot, so I was sitting under the trees there. . . . She came up—half scared me to death, I don't mind telling you. She told me about how I should go to the bazaar in the town."

"This morning?"

"No, I said, last night." Anya looked a bit petulant.

"No, no." Duvakin waved his hand urgently. "That you should go this morning?"

"She said it's not held very often and that I really had to go, and that I should go early, because things sell out." She laughed, put her basket back on her hip. "I did the best I could to leave early!"

Urgency rising, Duvakin took her arm. "Listen, this is important. What else did Rosa say? Did she say anything else at all?"

"I told you. I should go to the market."

"How? When? Why?"

"You're hurting my arm!"

"Sorry."

She rubbed the spot, where indeed his thumbprint was mottled white against her muscle. Hearing his urgency, she tried to be precise. "She came, said I should go, and then she even brought me these." She held up the basket, then touched the scarf. "She said I should walk to the end of the road, that a bus would come, and I could go to town."

"Did she say why you should go to town?"

Anya shook her head, mute, her eyes now rounder and bluer than Duvakin remembered as she studied his face. Then she said in a hushed voice, "But she did say I had to be out of here by nine-thirty at the very latest. . . ."

The rabbit sits in the road at night, blinking at the glowing orbs roaring down upon him, and tries to convince himself it is some natural phenomenon approaching, or at worst, some disaster that will turn aside. The wind was rising, strong enough to rattle stinging grains of sand among the oleanders, rasping like thousands of uneasy insects. The wind was hot, as if someone had set a fan in an oven.

Sweet Mother of God, Duvakin thought, I'm mad.

But I'm not going to be dead.

"Come on, girl," he snapped, jerking into motion like a tractor when the clutch is engaged too quickly, "run back and put on some shoes you can walk in."

"Walk?" The girl looked at her boots, then up at him, astonished.

"If we have to." Duvakin was already dogtrotting into the cottage. In passing the sink he flicked the faucet, but the water was off there, too. He yanked opened the little refrigerator. Thank God, no one had stripped this!

He grabbed what there was—four bottles of Cuban grapefruit juice, two of beer, and two of mineral water, and some cheese, so dry that it looked like soap. He dashed into the bedroom, where Anya was irresolutely stepping out of the boots and into tennis shoes. "They'll do, but watch out for the cactus," he said, then grabbed her small bag, dumped everything onto the bed, and ran back to the refrigerator.

"Hey! What in the devil?" she shouted, but Duvakin ignored her. The door of the refrigerator was open, but there was no chug-chug of the compressor. Is the power off, too? he wondered, packing the bottles rapidly. He put all the bottles in, hefted the bag, swore under his breath, took the mineral water out. "Too salty to drink anyway," he muttered, explaining to himself. He hefted the bag again, straightened, and then decided to take the mineral water all the same. The bag clanked against his thigh, and Duvakin knew remotely that his shoulder was going to be painfully sore quite soon, from lugging this awkward load. God grant that that's the worst of my problems today, he thought.

The girl emerged, pale and serious, but ready. She had kept the scarf on and replaced the sweater with her leather jacket. Soundlessly she handed Duvakin his jacket, then patted her right rear pocket. "I brought the money. Who knows, eh?"

"Ready?" he asked Anya, startled to feel a manic gaiety bubbling through him.

"We're traveling, then?" The girl laughed. "Better we sit, then, isn't it? To start our journey?"

Duvakin's hilarity broke through. He laughed. "A journey to God knows where, and God knows for how long! Of course we should sit!"

It was a custom as old as Russia itself, to sit in silence for a moment before embarking on a journey. To make the break between being *here* and moving toward *there*. To pray for return. To think . . .

We are refugees now, Duvakin understood with sudden clarity. In our own nation, with only our clothes and eight bottles, and a cheese you could shave with.

To his own astonishment, though, Duvakin felt no despair. Anya sat quietly across from him, head bowed in thought or prayer. The former Susi, the girl-woman who had mocked and tormented him, she now acceded to his authority, ready to let him take her where he felt he must. He *had* authority now, Duvakin was surprised to recognize. He felt a slender vigor that was like a forgotten friend

from childhood, but instantly remembered, and welcomed, on its
unexpected return.

He stood, and Anya did too. She came up beside him to take
one handle of the bag with bottles.

He had seen no vehicles in the compound, so did not spend
time looking for one now. Nor did he have any idea what lay around
the compound, save the main road, so that was what he went
toward, keeping a prudent distance from the side road into the compound. There was no possibility of hiding in so flat and empty a
landscape, but perhaps distance would make them indistinct. The
wind was continuing to rise, bending the burnt grass nearly double.
The air was hot and dry, rasping with invisible sand. Duvakin was
immediately sweat-soaked in his jacket, but he knew that to remove
it would be worse. As it was, the windblown sand already made his
face feel as if it were being licked insistently by some enormous,
dry-tongued tom.

What looked from the road like an endless tabletop of sand and
scrub proved when they walked on it to be a hellish muddle of
hummocks and runnels, flat sandy stones the shape and color of
oatmeal cookies, some of them loose, others so solidly embedded in
the hard-packed earth that now Duvakin, now Anya stumbled,
nearly falling, the ever-heavier bottles clanking. The knee-high
shrubs were as unyielding as steel wool, forcing them to weave
drunkenly across the plain, roughly cutting the angle toward the
main road.

Everywhere, invisible, was the ground-hugging cactus, the long
translucent spines ready to slice deep through shoes, spearing toes.

"Ow *Christ!*" Duvakin's reflexes snatched his foot away, after a
half hour or so of walking, tumbling him heavily forward to the
dust. He broke the fall and turned, half sitting.

Anya knelt beside him, sweat glistening along her lip and over
her eyebrows, and making dusty channels on the windward side of
her face.

"You all right?" she mouthed above the thrum of wind.

Duvakin plucked the spine from his toe, muttered a curse, then
got ready to haul himself to his feet again. He heaved once, ineffec-
tually, let himself sink back. He glanced at his watch.

"God above, it's just twenty minutes!"

All of Duvakin's confidence, his belief, his urgency trembled, ready to collapse in upon themselves, into an ash pit of acknowledgment that he was demented with crazy fear. Beat a dog long enough, and he will bite you when you try to pet him, and stand numbly frozen while you lash him.

Then Duvakin saw the bus.

He yanked Anya down upon him, and held her, left arm cradling her head against his chest, right arm over her back. For a moment she held the awkward pose, then delicately, almost apologetically, twisted, so that she, too, could look.

It was a small bus, such as kolkhozes keep to ferry workers into neighboring cities. Painted blue at one time, the bus was now faded and seemed badly maintained, to judge by the belch of black smoke that stood out against the ruddy haze of the horizon. There was something tortoiselike about its deliberate approach toward the compound.

The wind was blowing directly in their faces, making it difficult to watch, but Duvakin still huddled, clutching the unresisting Anya. The bus nudged up to the compound and jerked to a stop. There was a split second of eerie stillness, emphasized by the wind keening in the dry shrubs. Then, suddenly, figures—young men, Duvakin guessed—began to tumble from the bus, brandishing what Duvakin thought were picket signs, until he realized that the staffs had no placards; these were simply clubs. Made miniature by the distance, some of the young men bent to scoop up stones, which they flung at the compound. A moment later, tattered by the wind, and wholly divorced from the actions that caused them, the sounds came: shouts, the tinkle of glass, more shouts.

Anya disengaged herself and turned around. Still squatting, she studied his face.

"You knew they were coming?" she asked, her face somber.

"It was something Edik said." Duvakin smiled, doing his best to make it a jest. He stood up. "Come on, don't you think we'd best get on with our walk?"

The first puffs of smoke were just curling above the compound.

CHAPTER **F I F T E E N**

No doubt luckily for Duvakin
and Anya, the only vehicle that had stopped for them—indeed,
almost the only vehicle they had seen, once they reached the main
road—was a roaring Belarus tractor pulling a two-wheeled, long-
bedded cart that Duvakin realized, after they had been nodded into
it by the indifferent Kazakh driver, must at some point have been
a manure spreader. In addition to the unpleasant smell and feel of
the cart, the high-wheeled tractor suffered from hiccups, momentary
stalls that would send the free-coasting wagon hammering against
the drawbar, jerking the passengers forward, then jerking them backward again as the engine fired once more. Too light with its load
of two humans, the cart bounced and danced, forcing them to wedge
themselves into one corner, huddled below the sideboards to avoid
the unceasing abrasion of the hot, rasping wind.

It wasn't Abdulla's air-conditioned Niva, but then the crowds
surging through former Lenin Square in Novii Uzen would certainly
have stopped that little white vehicle, maybe overturned it, or possibly even burned it. Not even pogroms bother with a manure cart,
though. The unshaven, glowering driver simply surged forward,
through the clots of shouting, stone-throwing, club-waving youths, a
good half of whom had bandanas covering their faces, the smoke of
the tractor mingling with the smoke of burning tires, an overturned

police vehicle, and smashed newspaper kiosks, at which Duvakin and Anya peeked through cracks in the stinking sideboards.

Then they pulled into another street, where there were no rioters; with a belch and a jerk the tractor's power was cut, and they coasted into the loading area of a warehouse. Another jerk, and they stopped, the sudden end of the engine's roar replaced by a ringing in Duvakin's ears that seemed nearly as loud.

"Thanks," Duvakin said to the back of the driver's head; the man was already disappearing around the corner of the sheet-metal building.

Duvakin watched for a moment, then, stiffly, helped the girl down from the cart. He had no idea where to go next.

"Well, we make a pretty pair for a day in town," he joked, trembling. Anya was caked in dust, her hair matted and her clothes smeared; a quick glance told Duvakin he wasn't likely to look better. Worse, he had no idea where he and the girl ought to go now. This receiving yard was now empty and shuttered tight, and the houses, the courtyards opposite also looked secured, as before a storm. Panic nibbling at the base of his throat, Duvakin tried to orient himself, but in vain; whatever sense he had of where the militia station might be was far too dangerously vague, for a city roamed by armed packs.

And besides, he suddenly realized, other than that burning car, he had seen no sign of the militia. Could he even *find* Tansybekov?

And if he did . . . what would Tansybekov do? After all, these rioters were Kazakh.

Sent by Edik.

He wasn't sure now exactly when that realization had come. Edik and Rosa and the rock through the window and the attack on Momish's compound . . . Duvakin just knew it, now. Edik, who let Duvakin think he was Russian, but who was half Kazakh. Edik, who had led him into the desert to be shot at.

Edik, who had caused Ermolov's death.

This, too, Duvakin now knew, though he didn't know how precisely it had been done, or even why. What did *that* matter, beside the certainty that it was true, and Ermolov was dead?

Just as Duvakin would have been, and maybe Anya, too, had

it not been for luck, and wit, and Rosa's last-minute kindness to the girl.

That the mob was meant to kill them, or at least him, Duvakin had no doubt. Even now, swift flashes of imagination, immediately suppressed, showed him Anya ravaged, sundered, violated, at the mercy of the slavering, ink-eyed crowd.

It was only now, though, that he wondered: Could Tansybekov be turning a deliberate blind eye?

There was a loud shout from beyond a building across the street, followed by the tinkle of glass and, a moment later, a puff of greasy gray smoke. Duvakin gulped, looked around.

"Come on"—he took Anya's hand roughly, just above the wrist—"we've got to get out of here."

"But where to?" The girl jerked back.

"Away from here, anyway."

"But the whole town is theirs! We'll walk right into them!" The chaotic muffled noises, combined with the unending moan of the wind, made it seem that something even worse was more likely, that any second the mob would surge around the corner and engulf them.

"You're so smart, what in the devil do you suggest?" Duvakin snapped, his breath growing short and his temples throbbing. Christ, she was so young, so pretty, and the mob of crazed young Asians . . .

"Those guys, they're on drugs," Anya said, her grimy face concentrated, as if she was thinking.

"The rioters?" Duvakin looked at her again, distracted by the sounds of the unseen crowd. What did they want? What were they doing? And, most important of all, how in the devil could he keep the girl and himself out of their way? "How can you tell?"

"I can tell, all right?" The girl was going to answer no more questions right now. "Up! Rioters never climb more than a couple of flights!" Anya pointed urgently at the building across from them, then began to run, the bottles clanking heavily.

Up? Confused images of ascending higher, the mob baying at their feet, them trapped on the roof, a gut-wrenching image of being tossed off the roof, falling, falling . . .

Then he understood that Anya knew what she was talking

about. He caught up with her, took the clanking bag, and labored, puffing and blowing, up the seven flights, to a ladder of concrete rungs ending in a hatchway. Anya, monkeylike, scrabbled up, with a grunt shouldered the hatch cover aside, and shoved herself through. Her slender arm reappeared, beckoning urgently to Duvakin. A second's hesitation, then he handed up the bag of bottles and, with difficulty, squeezed through onto the roof.

Anya grunted the cover back into place, then sat on it, with a grin. "The two of us sit on it, *nobody* can shove this open!"

The roof was ribbed metal, slightly sloping, covered with tarred gravel, some pipes, broken bottles and cigarette stubs, evidence that they were not the first to climb through the hatch. There was no railing, no ledge at the end of the roof, making Duvakin's stomach billow up with nausea. Panting and sweaty, he looked back at Anya, who sat, legs akimbo, bits of blond curl clinging to the grit of her forehead. She was grinning broadly.

"Welcome to heaven," she chuckled.

"You've done this before." Duvakin couldn't help laughing, too, so pleased did she look, and so relieved.

"Well, it's not like you exactly threw the apartment open, is it?"

"I never said who you could have to visit, did I?"

Anya thrust her chin up, glowered down her nose. "No, no, very welcome you made us." She did a gruff but recognizable version of his voice. "Come in, wreck my house, eat my food, rape my daughter. . . ."

"I never said any of those things!" Duvakin yelped, taken aback at the warmth he felt near his heart, knowing that she had paid him enough attention to be able to imitate him, and that she had called herself his daughter.

"Doesn't matter, Papulia." She patted the hatch cover, indicating he should sit beside her. "Anyway, the *permission* isn't the thing, you get so damn tired of *permissions* all the time, as if there's nothing you can decide for yourself. Like you don't exist, there's just little bits of you, that different people keep in their desks or pockets or something, and wind you up when they feel like it. So the basements and the roofs, that's *our* world. . . ." She cradled her chin in her right palm. "Of course, that's how I ended up like some damn canary that Dzhimi could keep in a cage. Trying to live my own life, I mean. You don't smoke, do you?"

Duvakin shook his head, feeling muddled from all she had just said. Then he remembered. "You don't either, so why are you asking?"

She shrugged her shoulders, looked to the side, away from him. "I like the taste, after sex. . . ."

Two emotions began at opposite ends of Duvakin, to smash head-on somewhere in the depths of his gut. Was this an offer, from so . . . well, *desired* a woman? His *daughter*? *Sex*? Coupling, smoking . . . discussing it so calmly?

He was staring at her, dry-mouthed and silent, breath a jagged quiver.

Anya turned her head the other way, to look up at him. "Being safe now, doesn't that feel just like after sex?" Then she grinned, impishly. "What I mean, of course—that's how I'd *imagine* it would feel, from what the other girls tell me, Papulia."

"You're dead."

Momish was pale, almost mottled, and his eyes were round, looking even larger because of the blue-black bags sagging beneath them. His cheeks were bristly pouches, unshaved, just like Duvakin's.

"Well, I've felt better, I admit." Duvakin did his best to sound jaunty as he came into the room, Anya at his elbow. "But I think 'dead' is an exaggeration."

The Azerbaijani put down the file folders he had been trying to straighten, ran a hand feebly through the mound of scattered papers on the desk. Someone had sacked the room, ripping the map from the wall, scattering files, throwing the inkwells, breaking the windows. What they had missed, the wind had finished, drifting the papers into dunes, then scattering them with a fine red grit such as might be found on the surface of Mars.

"I got a report . . . the compound . . ."

"You're disappointed?" Duvakin took a chair, indifferent to the slashed seat. It was not easy to sound flippant after two nights and almost three days on that roof, but he did it, because only bravado would keep the girl and him alive now, if he had guessed wrong.

The beginnings of pogroms are never an accident, and the endings are never planned. All through that first night fires had flared, lighting their rooftop island with flickering, menacing glows, which subsided only toward morning. Too stiff with chill to brave going down the ladder, they had sat on the hatch cover, warming in the sun and rising wind, wondering when it would be safe to descend. There had been shots, then shouts, and another day of yelling and sirens and shrill militia whistles. All day the wind blew, scraping backward along their skins like a fork along the bottom of a cooking pot. Something in the wind made them irritable and snappish; no doubt the crowds below felt it, too, because when evening came, it was lit by more flame.

The third morning was quiet, and the wind had subsided, but Duvakin and Anya agreed it was prudent to wait until dusk before coming down.

Momish sat, too, still looking as though he would like to pinch Duvakin. "No, not disappointed," he replied seriously. "Surprised. How did you . . . ? They burned out the compound, did you know that? Ungrateful bastards." He said it almost dispassionately, like a scientific description. Then, an afterthought: "The election was canceled, of course."

Waiting until dusk might have been unnecessary, for the streets were virtually empty, save for young soldiers, standing uncomfortable, diffident guard around the cordoned-off, shattered and burned stores, a few old women or young mothers with infants scuttling through the gathering dark. Still, the dark, and their dirt, made them less obviously Russian—which, Duvakin knew, was to the good. The town had an abashed look to it, like a drunk in the dry-out tank after a spree. Broken glass everywhere; the black tongues of soot licked up the front of stores, or around a few apartment windows—none higher than the third floor, Duvakin noted, acknowledging that Anya had been right. On the way to Momish's they had passed four or five overturned, burned-out vehicles. One was the militia vehicle, still showing some yellow-and-blue paint. The oil headquarters itself was under guard, but Duvakin's identity card got them past the fellow in charge, Russian by look and speech, for all that his uniform was that of the Kazakh National Guard. The Kalashnikov that the even younger guard behind him was nervously holding made Duvakin stand still and calm, until a jerk of the lieutenant's head indicated they could go in.

"Were there many casualties?" Anya asked, over Duvakin's shoulder.

Momish waved, beyond caring. "What is many? The young woman, her womb ripped open and her unborn child stuffed down her throat, is that many? The three schoolchildren tied up in grain sacks and soaked in kerosene, set alight, are they many? The old man forced to eat his own ears, before they beat him to death with sticks—these people died in our town. These and more. Are these 'too many,' or are such casualties permissible, to be expected?"

Duvakin felt a greasy nausea doing what it could with three days of nothing but Cuban grapefruit juice and a quarter kilo of rock-hard cheese. They would have to eat soon, he and Anya.

"The army seemed slow to respond," Duvakin said, neither question nor statement. Accusation, almost. "I assume there is a curfew."

The Azerbaijani shrugged again, then ran a dirty hand through his ragged hair. "Dusk to dawn, but I can't say it's much enforced, just going through the motions," he finally said, in a voice that sounded much like someone shouting from deep within an abandoned house. "They were here two years ago, remember. Different name, same army. We aren't Kazakhs, so what's the hurry?" He tried a sarcastic smile, but was apparently too weary, too soul-sick. After a moment of staring numbly ahead, the Azerbaijani said softly, "This will be my responsibility, of course. I will be replaced, without an election."

"Of course," Duvakin agreed, as casually as if Momish had remarked on the weather. "The minister will fire you personally, as soon as he looks the town over."

Momish shoved himself deep into his chair, from where he studied Duvakin with intent, frightened eyes, like some creature caught too far from its burrow, bracing for a fight. "The minister? What has the minister to do with this? I was speaking of the president, in Alma-Ata."

Now Duvakin sat up, worried. "You mean there has been no

word that Chistoplotskii is coming?" A jagged bolt of light-headed doubt shot through him, rattling from bone to bone; could he have been wrong after all?

But Momish's cautious, watchful reply reassured him, for the man was now definitely afraid. Of me! Duvakin thought giddily, and held the edge of the table, to be safe.

"His party has been delayed . . . in Alma-Ata. By snow."

"Snow?" Duvakin asked, surprised, because he felt as if he had spent three days in an oven.

Momish answered mechanically, like a man not listening to what is coming out of his own mouth. "The other side of our yellow wind . . . the cyclone blows the hot desert air onto us, and pulls the mountain air down onto them. We have sand, they have snow."

"Yellow wind?"

"This, our storm . . . This one has come early, very early, but perhaps that is why it was so short. A fortunate thing, because the yellow wind makes men crazy, makes them fight. Three days, and they have burned out much of the town. What would have happened if it had lasted a week, as it can, I don't know. . . ."

Momish ran down, his eyes so intent on Duvakin that it seemed he was simply forgetting to speak. Who *are* you, the dully glowing black eyes begged, and what the devil do you want of me? Duvakin glanced over his shoulder at Anya, who was still leaning lightly against the back of his chair, watching the Azeri with her incredible summer-sky eyes. She was scruffy and matted, but still pretty enough to distract. She caught Duvakin's eye, and didn't so much smile as rearrange her face, just for a second, to let him know she would have smiled had the occasion not required solemnity. Duvakin had trouble not smiling himself; this was crazy, but they were going to do it!

"All right, then," Duvakin ordered Momish crisply, with a look that underscored that the social portion of the evening was at an end. "Arrange a telephone patch-through for the girl—she'll give you the number, in Moscow—and then get us something to eat and a place to clean up."

Momish had instinctively pulled himself forward, ready to haul himself from the chair to obey; he paused to look from one to the other uncertainly.

"Mogammed Alioglu"—Duvakin did his best to imitate that

silky voice he remembered from Chistoplotskii—"we have so little time. . . . Or perhaps I am wrong, and you are relishing the thought of retirement?"

Without a word the heavyset man heaved himself from his chair and went out to make arrangements.

Duvakin stopped him, calling over his shoulder. "Remember, Momish, we are dead. Perhaps it would be best if things remained that way, all right?"

Duvakin walked from corner to corner, flexing muscles, sometimes bouncing on his toes, like a boxer. Well, an older boxer, maybe. But his clothes hung loosely on him, and he felt lean. Well, perhaps not precisely lean, but without the sensation he had arrived in Novii Uzen with, of being wrapped in lard.

"You're a *kombinator*," the girl had teased him, when he explained to her what she must do, and why.

Duvakin had smiled, shrugged it away. "Your mother taught me."

Then they both grew somber, and went back to waiting.

The telephone patch-through had taken much longer to arrange than they had expected, and then Dzhimi had not been where Anya had expected. It was well after midnight in Moscow, and after two for them, when finally she remembered a telephone number for someplace where Dzhimi in fact proved to be—another girl's, Anya said with a grimace—and the radio-to-telephone connection was so miserable that the kittenish voice of stupidity she had first tried with him proved useless. She bellowed down the line, *"Novii Uzen, in Kazakhstan . . . a map, get a map! . . . Money, dear heart, more money than we ever dreamed of! . . . I'm waiting, my love!"*

"He'll come?" Duvakin had asked, weary and nervous, when the girl released her thumb from the radio speaker for the last time, her face ashen and haunted.

"I owe him money, don't I?" she answered bitterly, then spat. *"My love,"* she repeated; her face looked as if a gnat had just flown into her mouth.

If they were to stay dead, where could they wait? Momish pondered the question in stony silence, then, with a bent finger, indicated they should follow. Duvakin had assumed they were being led to the white Niva; instead they spent a harrowing few minutes slipping through the shadows of empty courtyards, knowing that if they were discovered in violation of curfew they might be shot.

Fortunately, where they were led was only a few houses away, a door leading into a basement. Momish knocked, quietly, looking about. After a time almost long enough to turn Duvakin's hair white from nerves, it opened a crack. Momish muttered something, and they were pushed through, the door closed.

It was filthy, as only a combination of many people and long neglect can make a place.

Was it an apartment? A warehouse? A shop? Duvakin couldn't tell. It was too big, and too dark. And too filled with people.

When he had realized that the mutterings and the murmurings coming from the dark, cell-like rooms were other people, he had yanked on Anya's arm, in panic. They should leave. Who were these people, and how could they hide among them?

"Don't worry, Papulia," she had whispered over her shoulder at him. "It's a smoke house. We'll be perfectly safe."

The wizened old woman in a dirty housecoat who was leading them along the narrow, cluttered corridor stopped, gestured with a sticklike hand that they should enter. It was a cell, no more than three square meters, stinking of burning rope; the outer walls were plywood, with one of stone, flaky with some white crystalline growth that turned to powder when Duvakin touched it.

When he turned around, Anya was already stretched out on the bare, dirty mattress on the floor, her bag wadded up as a pillow.

"Smoke house?" he asked softly, meaning both What is it? and Why in the devil do you know?

"Where people come to use stuff." She yawned luxuriously. "Nobody will bother us . . . as long as you keep paying."

Duvakin had still been staring at her, curled up on the floor, when the crone returned with two glasses of steaming, inky tea.

Christ, Duvakin thought bitterly, at least there's service, even if the place does look like the split in the devil's hind hoof. He was already feeling the welcome warmth in his fingers when Anya warned drowsily, "Don't drink it, it's poppy heads. . . ."

*   *   *

How did Anya know the sordid things she did?

"I ran away, remember?" she explained simply the next morn-ing, as if they were just chatting. "I was twelve, I think, or thirteen. Mama was angry, because I was getting just twos and threes in school, and wouldn't come home on time. Because of the sirens of the stairwell." She grimaced sardonically. "And Mama insisted I could do better, that I *had* to do better, if I was ever to get out of Magadan. So I started threatening to move in with my father. Non-sense, naturally, since I didn't even know where he was, but I could see how it got Mama upset, so . . ." She shrugged, grimaced. "You know how kids are."

Duvakin nodded, not wanting to point out that the only child he had ever known was her, and that of her he was only learning.

Anya was sitting cross-legged on the mattress, doing what she could to clean her hair; she tossed her head back, studying her past thoughtfully. "There's no place to run to, in Magadan. You know that. . . . So I stowed away on a ship. When they caught me, I lied, and told them I was an orphan, that my parents had died in a fire. The captain didn't want to bother, so they just dumped me in an *internat* in Khabarovsk. You learn a lot in an *internat*." She laughed at her own rhyme. "When I was old enough that they had to let me leave there, Mama had moved. It took a while to find her," she added simply.

Duvakin couldn't imagine what the girl had gone through, didn't wish even to try. It wasn't hard, though, to understand Galya's joy when, after years in which she must have thought her daughter dead, the girl suddenly returned.

It explained a great deal: Galya's fierce devotion to the girl, and her new indifference to him.

"Even so," Anya had gone on, "she never let up, did she? 'Take English, take extra math, make up in this, do extra that.' . . . It wasn't precisely *studying* that they taught me in that *internat*." She studied her foot now, picking at something invisible on the sole of her shoe. "That's why I ran away again." She looked up, defying him to criticize. "With Dzhimi."

Dzhimi . . .

Duvakin gave up worrying about the girl and her past. Of far more moment right now was whether that phone call had been enough to get Dzhimi to come.

Dzhimi had to come, he *had* to . . .

The curse of Duvakin's life was his feebleminded inability to ignore injustice. Injustice bothered him, the way some people can't let a picture hang crooked in someone else's house. Except what Duvakin had gotten into because of this trait of his wasn't just straightening someone else's picture. In fact, it was probably just plain luck that he was even still alive.

The whole three days on the roof it had itched at him, like eczema, that a minister, *a Russian minister*, might be involved in the distribution of hemp, and perhaps even in murder. What could such a man *want*, that made such crimes worth committing? How much can one man eat; how much can one man wear?

The three days had also given him lots of time to think about something else, too.

What Galya would have said. Such as: "What's the matter with you, Vanya? You haven't spent long enough in Magadan yet?"

In all the years he knew her, Duvakin had never seen Galya waste time looking for what couldn't be had. For the difficult she had endless energy, for the impossible not a single wasted second.

Report a corrupt minister? To whom? His superiors. Who are his superiors? The people who appointed him in the first place. Are they unaware of what kind of man he is? That is not to be believed. And besides, what are those who appointed him, anyway?

This was no question of right and wrong, or good and bad. This was just the snapping and gnashing of wolves, tearing at the carcass of a dead horse. Will that be justice if I yank one wolf away from the meaty haunches so that another can sink his own fangs in the deeper?

Galya wouldn't have looked for justice.

Galya would have gotten revenge.

That was what Duvakin was going to get for her now—his last present, which would let her lie in peace.

For revenge, though, he would need Dzhimi, and luck.

As much luck as he'd ever had in his life, Duvakin thought, resting his head against the powdery stone of the wall.

CHAPTER SIXTEEN

T hey don't take much care of you here, do they, Pops?"

Duvakin frowned as he shut the door, remembering now the easy grin of the tall blond boy who, among other things, gave English lessons, his obvious assumption that Duvakin was both harmless and amusing. Duvakin ran a hand over his chin, which scraped against his neck like a hedgehog preparing for winter. Lord God, as soon as this is well over, me for a bath, Duvakin thought, deliberately trying to keep his mind clear and calm; still, he couldn't entirely silence the voice that insisted on pointing out that well over or badly, he would get his bath, because they don't send you to the gulag filthy. Not nowadays.

"You took your time getting down here," he said accusingly, taking a seat opposite the rangy boy, who slouched, arms crossed, against a desk. "I thought this was of some importance to you."

"You hate to hurry when you're seeing the sights." Dzhimi scratched thoughtfully at his ear. Then he glanced at his companions, one of whom was dark, with a shaved head, so short that he had to wear spike-heeled boots just to come even with Dzhimi's breast pocket. The other was taller, and fair, but sloppy plump, so that he looked sticky, like a piece of Turkish delight left in the sun. "Besides, this isn't like getting out to Peredelkino, hop on the train and you're there. So where's our hostess? Susi?"

The pair would be Wolf and Kostya, Duvakin guessed, recalling Anya's descriptions; he remembered, too, that Kostya was the one she particularly warned against, as a sadistic brute. The only problem was, which was which?

No, Duvakin pulled himself together, that was not the only problem.

"Susi?" he repeated automatically, then smiled. "The girl, you mean. She's fine. But we call her Anya now. It's her name."

Dzhimi rose, slapped his arms demonstratively, raising small poofs of dust. Duvakin noticed that he had a ring tattooed around the third finger of his right hand, and a rising sun in the space between thumb and forefinger. Crude work, such as they do in prisons. "That's wonderful news, Pops, since I've just walked through seven times seven kingdoms to get to your little hideaway here, looking for her. I'm perfectly happy to let her stay fine, too, provided she gives me back . . . what she stole."

Christ, Duvakin wondered, does he *inflate*, that he looks so tall now? Half conscious he was doing so, Duvakin tensed his shoulders, trying to look more bull-like. "Your labels, you mean?"

Dzhimi pursed his lips, screwed up his eyes as he studied Duvakin. "My labels," he agreed after a moment. "That that little bitch stole."

"Here, here, no need for that kind of talk," he scolded automatically, but barely noticing the boy and his tense anger. He was thinking instead of his first card, which he was ready to put on the table, even though he half believed it would prove to be a queen of some kind, and not the ace he needed. And what then of the rest of his plan?

"The l-l-labels . . ." Duvakin cleared his throat, tried again. "The labels have been destroyed."

Dzhimi studied him, head slightly turned to the right, as if the left ear worked better than the right. The two other young men came up on either side, the dark one blank-faced, the other one grinning.

"Let's have that one more time, old fellow." Dzhimi was doing his best to sound cool and jesting, but the stress was plain. "You're telling me that we've spent three days getting down to this . . . tropical paradise, just so's you can tell us personally that labels worth *sixty-five thousand rubles . . .*" His voice gave him away entirely when it reached the money.

Duvakin nodded cheerfully, confident now that his card was a winner. "Destroyed, burned to ashes."

"Well, Jesus *Christ* what did that slut phone us . . ." the dark one growled, to fall silent when Dzhimi touched his arm.

"Those labels were a work of art." Dzhimi was doing his best to look relaxed, but the habit he had, of jerking his head to clear the hair from his eyes, was turning into a tic. "It's like she destroyed a Rembrandt, or something."

"You hadn't paid for them yet, had you?" Duvakin understood that with a rush of elation. He hadn't planned on this, but it didn't hurt! "You still owe for them!"

The last of his cool deserted Dzhimi; arm raised, the boy took a step forward, then stopped, mastering himself, though his blue eyes crackled and glowed. "Susi tell you that, too? You helped her destroy them, did you?"

"I told you, she calls herself Anya now, and what she told me or didn't isn't what we're here to discuss," Duvakin said briskly. The room was warm and still, the heat of the sun penetrating even into this half-subterranean world. "You're in a bad spot, Dzhimi."

The other two boys took another step forward, putting them slightly in front of their leader, like sheepdogs facing down a wolf. Dzhimi smiled. "You brought me all this way just to tell me something I know already? My spot couldn't be worse, Papasha. It's Vakhtang Beria I owe for those labels, not just Auntie Masha. . . . In fact"—he took a step closer, as did the rest of the pack—"that makes my spot so big and so bad that there's plenty of room in it for Susi, and for you, too, Papasha."

The name meant nothing to Duvakin, but it seemed a pretty sound rule of life never to owe money to a man named Vakhtang Beria.

"Does this Vakhtang of yours like stories? Most of the Vakhtangs I've run across in my day don't, you know? Guys like them, their interests tend to be real limited. Practical. Labels or money, that's what these kind of Vakhtangs generally expect. Not tales of some runaway Susi and a trip beyond thirty-three seas."

Dzhimi answered slowly, very much a young man making brave noises while thinking desperately what to do. "You can leave Vakhtang to me, Papasha, never fear. But Susi, now—or Anya, or whatever she's calling herself—you going to let me see her?"

"The labels are gone, Dzhimi," Duvakin said the words like hammer taps. "Burned, if you want to be precise. Scattered to the wind." With his hands he mimed dispersal to the four corners of the room, then refolded them and put them in his lap.

Dzhimi nodded thoughtfully, then leered. "But she's my wife, Papasha. You wouldn't deny a fellow his own wife, would you?"

Surprised at his own stiff resentment, Duvakin managed to say, "Wives are generally registered legally."

Even in his anger, Duvakin could appreciate how quick the boy had been to spot his weakness. "What's a paper, old man"—Dzhimi smiled lubriciously—"so long as you've got the warm and wet between the sheets, eh?"

Duvakin fought back an urge to hit the leering pup, and simply shrugged, as if he had forgotten more about that side of life than this curly-headed thug would ever learn. "Funny place, this Novii Uzen," he said softly instead. "Not a place that takes well to *newcomers*."

He let that work its way in, knowing from experience how disorienting it was to arrive in Novii Uzen. Abdulla was in the hospital in Ak Tau, badly burned, and Momish's empire lay about him in shards, but still the old man had retained control enough in the town to have three Russian youths picked up as soon as they appeared, and brought immediately to Duvakin, in his smoke house.

"Especially now that there's no food," Duvakin added, in the continuing silence.

"You think maybe the gutters are running sour cream up in Moscow?" Dzhimi asked with aggressive flippancy; but he stepped back again, toward the wall.

Duvakin gave the message another tap, to make sure Dzhimi got it. "Up there, though, you've got your connections, don't you, you've got your ration cards." Duvakin smiled thinly. "But down here? Know what you are down here? An Ivan. A poor stupid Ivan."

"You too, old man." Dzhimi seemed to be hugging himself, but his smile was broad enough, a gold canine tooth glinting. The message had gotten through. "All Ivans together, aren't we? So what's your offer? What do you want?"

Bless the boy, Duvakin thought, rubbing his nose to conceal a grin of excitement, he's got a full set of switches after all! Although the thought of Anya and this one doing . . . being that . . . together . . . was so hard to bear that it flicked out of his mind as quickly as it came in, Duvakin at least permitted himself an oblique admiration for the girl's choice. Say what you will, Dzhimi was quick!

"You haven't asked who destroyed your labels, have you?" He grinned. "Nor how you're going to get your money back?"

Now Dzhimi's grin, too, was less artificial, more relieved. "So that wasn't just bait, to get us down here?"

"What?"

"Susi . . . Anya mentioned money."

"Oh, there's money all right." Duvakin nodded vigorously and sat forward. "Money's the least of our problems."

"I've heard rumors about this, but I wouldn't have believed it, if I didn't have to go through—" Momish's voice choked, so he shrugged, shaking his head with mournful amazement.

"You look nice. Impressive," Anya said softly, smoothing an imaginary piece of lint from the Azerbaijani's broad shoulder, which was encased in a dark suit of some material so heavy that Duvakin could feel his own thighs prickling with sympathetic sweat. She was in the gray acetate dress of a bus-girl.

"They always wash the lamb before they cut his throat," Momish said gloomily, then stood. "A life of work, and it comes to this. . . ." He held his hands out briefly, sketching the vast volume of the empty nothing he felt.

Duvakin was too jittery to trust his voice, so he simply clapped the man on the shoulder, then stood back from the door as Momish left, trudging his own slope to Golgotha.

People assumed that it was an American custom, or maybe a Canadian one, that the minister had imported as something to boast about from his trip abroad, the way a normal person would bring back a video recorder, or one of those telephones you can carry from room to room. Watching the way the proud Azeri's resilience bent beneath this humiliation, oaken fibers crackling and popping, Duvakin found it easier to believe, though, that Chistoplotskii had invented the practice himself, as a way to increase his own pleasure and the torments of his victims.

A "testimonial dinner," Momish said it was called, adding that it had become the hallmark of Chistoplotskii's ministry. In the old days, when a man was "released from duty by reason of health, at his own request"—fired, in plain Russian—it took place behind the big double doors of the Boss's office, so that no matter what kind of idiot and fool they called you, your disgrace remained private. Secret, even, because once those doors closed on you, the authorities could never admit they had made the mistake of appointing you in the first place, so your name simply never came up again. As much as it might irk you to be treated as if you had never existed, at least you could retire to the sunny bench in front of your dacha secure in the consolation that since the rest of the country was pretending you had never held your job, you could not be said to have failed at it.

Not Chistoplotskii. He made a public banquet of a firing, with you as the victim of honor. Food, drink, even toasts, a style of feasting that had gone out of official favor years ago, to which were invited all the colleagues with whom you had jostled and jabbed all those years for position, and your immediate underlings, who could gloat and wallow in the sweet spectacle of your debasement. Even your family, sometimes, to make the disgrace domestic. And in case any of the guests were so dense as still to miss the point, Chistoplotskii finished the evening with a long speech "thanking" you for your service, and sometimes even gave you a "gift." A coffee service, maybe, or a chess set with carved stone men. Something useless, but too expensive and large to throw away, so he could be certain you would keep it around, as an eternal reminder of your humiliation.

"What they did to Bekobosynov, when he got his 'dinner' . . . it gave me nightmares for a month." Momish shivered, then nodded, a rueful look on his sad and sleepless face. "And I swore to myself I would do anything to prevent it happening to me." Then he sighed heavily. "I would rather die than be retired in this way."

However, after the riots it could not have been a surprise to Momish that his turn for a testimonial had now come; in fact, the Azeri had made the formal request for pension as soon as Chistoplotskii reached the city, to forestall the obvious, in the hopes of avoiding this humiliation. In vain. The "testimonial" was swiftly arranged for the next evening, in the Tumbleweed Restaurant.

With the sad dignity of a former aristocrat numbly trading away her last golden earrings, Momish used what remained of his influence to make the arrangements Duvakin requested, the Russian almost imperious in his nervy curtness. Waiters' jackets for the three boys, a waitress's dress for Anya, and a room, with a door, where they could all wait.

It must have been the manager's office they were led to, a cubicle separated from the mirrors and smoke of the café by the steaming vats and dirty tiles of the kitchen, but reachable, too, by a back door that let out onto a closed courtyard, where deliveries and other arrangements could be made discreetly. The little room had a small desk, three chairs, and, incongruously, a calendar from Japan, two years old but with an absolutely marvel of a girl on it, hand-supporting her bared breasts, which needed it. The window had been painted over, the brushstrokes like slashes in the dried-blood red. A battered air conditioner, not turned on, made plain the window was never opened, and the faint but stomach-churning tendril of old-grease-and-coffee-grounds smell that curled in from the battered trash vats outside explained why. The clatter in the kitchen was as loud as if there had been no door between them and it, and above that Duvakin thought he could even make out the scrape and squeak of chairs, the shouts of greeting, all the noise that tense guests make on arrival to show each other how carefree and relaxed they are. Momish had not known who was invited, nor did he care.

"Give them an hour," Duvakin growled at Anya. She smiled and winked, then blew a kiss at him, the O of her crimson lips reminding him of a life preserver. The borrowed uniform looked snug on her as she walked out, especially on the hips and bust, but . . .

Well, that wouldn't hurt, either, would it?

The room was too small to pace. Besides, why pace? His plan was going to work, damn it; it had to.

And if it didn't . . .

Well, Anya's bottom wouldn't help him then, no matter how tight her dress.

The minutes passed. The roar from the restaurant grew louder, the scuffle of the waiters' shoes more hurried. Some of the food and drink had come from Moscow, Momish had said, with the morbid pride of someone who was to be given the honor of crucifixion with real nails, instead of just being tied up with rope.

Then there were voices at the window, the screech of the back door opening, the click of high heels, a knock, his door pushed open.

It was the boys, with Sytykh.

"You're late," Duvakin snarled, nervous. "Was there a problem?" he asked Dzhimi, glancing at the colonel as if he were a ham, not a senior inspector of Moscow's criminal division. The stay in Novii Uzen had not been kind to Sytykh. His clothes were sweat-stained, and he looked as haggard as it is possible for someone so plump to look. It was the mustache, Duvakin understood after a moment. That silly line of hair was a victim of Novii Uzen's shortage of razor blades, and what had been an eyebrow for his mouth was now sinking into a week's worth of unshaved mug.

"No problem, except that we practically had to tie him up and sling him on a pole, he was that afraid to leave the hotel." Dzhimi laughed, indicating with a flick of his hand that Kostya and Wolf should wait outside. Duvakin was glad when the pair closed the door behind them; between Dzhimi's height and Sytykh's girth the room was as full as a tin of sprats.

"Evening, Sytykh. Forgive me if I've forgotten your name and patronymic, will you?" Duvakin did the best imitation of Sytykh's own manner that he could manage.

Even outnumbered and off balance, though, the inspector pulled himself together. "Ivan Palych." He smiled like a man fighting off a bad meal, "A pleasure I no longer expected to have." Sytykh glanced at Dzhimi, then said, "Actually . . . they told me you were dead. In the pogrom."

"I'm recovering, wouldn't you say? Anyway, I wouldn't say that's a pogrom. . . . Here in Novii Uzen, that's just boys having a little fun."

Duvakin knew, though, that he couldn't permit himself the pleasure of baiting this dumpling from Moscow. He had to concentrate on the next hour if the pawn were to succeed at kicking over the board and putting the chess master in check.

"I have put in an order for a flight to Moscow . . . special evacuation," Sytykh hinted weightily, looking around for someplace to sit. Finding none, he smiled at Duvakin. "I could take you with me."

Moscow, his apartment . . . the lime-tree buds would be starting to open on Fotieva, and the earth would smell of melting snow and moldy leaves and spring . . . And safety, in a place where none of this had ever happened. For the briefest of moments the temptation was so strong that Duvakin felt himself turning to wax. Then he remembered his first meeting with the investigator, luxuriously squeaked his chair, the only one in the room, and smiled. "You can stand, we won't be long . . . and no, thank you, when I want to go to Moscow I'll be making my own arrangements. Dzhimi, wait outside, will you?"

The boy looked surprised, then pouty, but he went, shutting the door too loudly. When they were alone, Duvakin spoke sternly to Sytykh. "Enough jokes now, Sytykh. It's time to do your job, and I'm going to help you. There was a murder, and you've been ordered to bring the murderer in, correct?"

"Unless what you're offering is to walk out that door with me, the chances of my doing that don't look so bright, wouldn't you agree?" Sytykh's black-ringed eyes belied his light tone.

"I said, enough cleverness," Duvakin snapped. "Pay attention. This is important. There is a man out there who tried to kill me, and who has killed at least one other man. He did so, or so I think, on the orders of another man, who is also there."

There was an awkwardness, as when two strangers tell each other anecdotes, and one does not realize he has missed a punch line. Sytykh licked his lips, waited. "So?"

Duvakin sniffed, scornful. "Meaning it isn't the crime that interests you, it's just arresting me? Why the make-believe, then? Just knock on my door some midnight and send me off to some Arctic labor camp, like in the good old days. It's Duvakin who's got to go, and murderers can walk around free? Fine, put on your cuffs, then!"

Astonished at his own anger, and at what he was doing, Duvakin thrust his wrists out, like sacrifices proffered to be bound.

"No, of course it's the crime that's— But . . . you're the only one that I've got orders for." Sytykh was obviously unsettled by Duvakin's odd gesture. He glanced from Duvakin to the door and back, licking his lips. "And besides, my case is the death of your wife . . . in Moscow. How could anyone here have . . . ? I mean, whatever some local has done, I can't— I mean, it's not my jurisdiction, is it? This is another republic, you heard that militia captain."

"It's my wife I'm talking about." Duvakin still had his wrists out, as if he had forgotten them. Sytykh didn't move, but kept his gaze nailed to Duvakin, lips chewing tensely.

Finally dropping his arms, Duvakin spoke, firmness exaggerated by the softness of his voice.

"I am going to prove something to you this evening. What you do with the information, that is for you to decide. I warn you, though, I won't be jailed for another man's crime. Because whoever actually killed my wife . . . I believe it was this man's fault."

Sytykh spoke now with the false heartiness of someone who had plainly decided Duvakin was mad. "Very good job, Ivan Palych . . . Someone here in Novii Uzen killed your wife? And you have found him? Excellent, well done, Ivan Palych."

Duvakin smiled, mirthless. "You are thinking, it is a long way from Moscow. I've been here three months; how far it is, I know better than you, Comrade Investigator." Duvakin paused, savoring the sarcasm of the title. Then, more forcefully: "The man you will see is from Moscow. In fact, I think perhaps you have spoken with him before."

Sytykh's eyes told Duvakin the inspector wasn't humoring him now; he held his head erect, twisted a little to the side, like a man watching a snake. Duvakin studied the rolls over the investigator's collar, which made him think with pleasure of the new looseness inside his own collar, the way his Moscow clothes hung on him now, as if on . . . well, not quite a scarecrow, perhaps, but on a younger and more vigorous Duvakin. He hitched up his own sagging trousers, feeling bold.

"There is someone I know out there?" the criminal-investigation man from the center asked carefully.

Duvakin wondered for a moment whether to imperil this first crack in Sytykh's adamantine disbelief by making what was, after all, just a wild guess. Then he shrugged—if you're going to spit in the devil's face, go for the eye.

"The man who told you I am in Novii Uzen."

After a half beat Sytykh's porcine eyes widened, and his round unshaven cheeks went the green of giant gooseberries. Bull's-eye! Duvakin exulted, but had no opportunity to savor the sensation, for the door opened.

"I think maybe now, Papulia," Anya leaned in to say. "The speech has begun."

Duvakin nodded and stood, his heart suddenly hammering. He looked at Sytykh, eyes narrowed. "He thinks I am safely dead. When he understands that I am not . . . I will ask him a question."

There was a strained silence, until Sytykh asked, "That's all?"

How do you define revenge? It was a question Duvakin had asked himself often enough on that roof. The first reaction had been the obvious one: Blood washes blood, as Momish had said. Fantasies of Chistoplotskii collapsing before a stream of bullets, Chistoplotskii evaporating in a bomb explosion, Chistoplotskii beaten slowly to goulash, as had been done with Galya . . .

By degrees, though, waiting in that skin-stripping hot wind for the swirling riots below to end, Duvakin had begun to understand that one thing of which Russia had no shortage was blood. Rivers of it, tides of it, bodies piled on bodies.

"That's all." Duvakin nodded firmly. "His answer will show others what he is, and they will understand that he is not what he wishes to seem. For me, that will be enough. As for you . . ." Duvakin managed a crooked smile. "Well, what you do about what he is . . . that depends upon what kind of a man *you* are, doesn't it?"

Duvakin felt unexpectedly light-headed as he pushed past the Moscow investigator and stepped out into the hall. As if this were still what he had imagined, and not, at last, the real thing. No, he convinced himself again, passing the stacks of soiled dishes that sweaty, narrow-eyed Asians were halfheartedly washing, the cooks who looked like doctors in their greasy aprons and high paper hats: Death is simply blood.

So what would be revenge?

Truth was revenge, and Duvakin, for the first time in his life, was going to get it.

The main dining room of the restaurant had been rearranged to make a horseshoe of tables, with men sitting down all four sides, and a head table, empty save for Momish, Chistoplotskii, and a young woman pretty enough to make Duvakin break stride, stumble for a second. Tall and long-legged, with high Tartar cheekbones but silky blond hair and eyes that glinted blue when they caught the overhead lights. Chistoplotskii's secretary? Duvakin wondered, for a moment wondering, too, whether she was prettier than Anya, who was fussing with dishes in the corner. The hall was much more crowded than Duvakin had supposed it would be; he tried to pick out faces, but they all were pale, blurry smudges, like stones on the bottom of a pond. The dirty mirrors on the wall multiplied the room, making Duvakin suddenly giddy.

To reassure himself, he looked for the boys. Dzhimi, idling by the door. The thick dark one, scraping plates in the rear. The plump one . . . nowhere to be seen.

Chistoplotskii was standing, surveying the hall through his squarish, slightly tinted glasses, his wineglass raised. Duvakin turned aside as the man looked his way, even though he was sure the darkness of the serving area would preserve his advantage of surprise.

"Mogammed Alioglu . . . Momish." Chistoplotskii nodded sideways at the guest of honor. "I may not have been minister long, but it's time enough for mistakes aplenty. . . ." Nervous titters in the room, people uncertain whether to object or agree, but Chistoplotskii swept on. "However, your friends and colleagues who have gathered here are doing their best to convince me that letting you retire is my worst mistake."

The new minister waited a second, for the rumble of inaudible comment to pass, then smiled. "In vain. I *know* it is a mistake, gentleman!"

The laughter was too large, forced by relief and the novelty of being addressed by that antique "gentlemen." Chistoplotskii caught the receding wave of laughter perfectly.

"In many ways, for Mangyshlak, Momish *was* the ministry, he has watched over the ministry here, nursing it and protecting it, just like the trees he has planted for the city to enjoy. First assistant head of Mingaz, for many years, and then head, first secretary of the trade union committee, first secretary of the oblast party committee, first secretary of the city Executive Committee, then first mayor of Novii Uzen—the list of what Momish has meant for Novii Uzen is almost endless. Momish has poured energy like a gusher, a flowing fountain of labor, of selfless work." At each compliment the minister bowed slightly in the direction of the Azerbaijani, whose only acknowledgment was a deepening scowl and an angry glare at this public catalogue of all that was being taken from him. "However, you are all oil men, one way or another"—the new minister's voice changed gears silkily—"and you know that gushers run their course. The first oil is easy; the next is hard. So it was with Mingaz, the kingdom of heaven be its; the country told men like Momish to get oil, and they got the country oil—oil first, oil last, nothing but oil. Our Momish is an *oil man*; what we must have today, though, is . . . *managers. Efficiency* of production, that's what we must have"—he enunciated the foreign word lovingly—"that is what the country demands now, and we must give it to her. We must learn from the Americans, who can sell fifteen-dollar oil and *make money!*" Chistoplotskii smoothed his cuffs, as if restraining himself. "However, gentlemen"—his voice was less unctuous now—"however, the time to talk of this will come. . . . Still, it may be well to remember that with Momish will go many of the familiar ways we have done business. New times demand new work, and I would like to take part of this evening to speak to you of some of the changes."

Duvakin had a sudden fit of indecision; he could feel Sytykh at his elbow, shifting from foot to foot. The men at the tables were hunching forward to show that they were concentrating, that they knew this was the important part of the evening. For the first time, Duvakin noticed that the tables were covered with boxes of videocassettes, two per setting; some of the men toyed with theirs, but most simply held them, not willing to risk damaging anything so valuable.

Moscow goods, Duvakin thought bitterly. The bait, which would ensure no one would be ill, unable to come.

Christ, was this a mistake? He had spent too long alone in Novii Uzen; he had forgotten the crafty, greedy faces of the successful, the smiles with which they would exchange their own mothers for two bars of French soap and a bottle of Hungarian brandy. "The revenge of truth"; he derided himself, an innocent fool. The only truth these men would bother about was that it was Momish whom they were seeing off, and not the other way about.

". . . greater horizontal integration of republic economies with the commonwealth expectations of the major enterprises, in a context of reduced vertical integration of the decision-making process." Chistoplotskii was rolling out the large fat words like yards of sausage, glistening and plump, but filled with indigestible bone, sawdust, and mouse shit. Chistoplotskii's speech was like all the new words, Duvakin seethed, all speeches, discussion, and talk. . . .

"But!" Chistoplotskii suddenly brought himself up short, as Duvakin had seen him do back in Moscow, when his passions carried him away. He lifted his glass again. "Now, I know that we have all grown unaccustomed to our friend the green snake"—he pointed with his left hand at the wineglass he held in his right—drawing another nervous chuckle from the room, "but I would ask you to join me as I lift my cup to toast Momish . . . Mogammed Alioglu . . . to express my thanks, the thanks of the Ministry of Energy, for his long years of selfless service, and to wish him well in his retirement. Let us envy him, a man who had the wisdom to do his loving before AIDS, to have his children before rock and roll, to do his drinking before the dry law, and to retire before perestroika!"

The minister tipped his head back to drain the small glass, as did most of the men in the room; Chistoplotskii finished the glass with a flourish, and a smile so self-satisfied that Duvakin could endure it no longer.

"Why did you have my wife killed?"

Startled, the entire hall turned to look at him, although he had spoken softly. Chistoplotskii squinted against the overhead light, his eyes glinting rapaciously.

Duvakin's heart stalled. He stepped forward, knowing he must do something now, not knowing what.

He had reached the open end of the horseshoe, where the light would show his face. Unable to think of a better shaft than he had already loosed, Duvakin simply repeated it.

"Why did you have my wife killed?"

"Duvakin!" Chistoplotskii's jaw sagged in surprise. "I had nothing to do with your wife's death."

No actor could have sounded so sure, and so startled. Duvakin's stomach flooded with ice, with terror. This must be what a man being hanged feels, as the floor drops away below, and all that remains to him is half a yard of rope, the end of which will break his neck.

"*He* kill your wife?" a familiar voice suddenly barked, to Duvakin's left. "When it's *you* killed your own *daughter?*" The sneer in the last word rose with Edik, who had been seated to Chistoplotskii's right. He glared at Duvakin, before shouting something in Kazakh at someone else. Then Edik said to the minister, "I'm sorry, Minister, I was misled about his death . . . as I suppose I was meant to be." He looked back at Duvakin now, lip curled. "The fire at the compound, it was all just a cover, wasn't it? Meant to fool us . . . And now we learn that the girl wasn't your first victim, Ivan Palych."

Duvakin felt a hand grip his elbow; he whirled. Sytykh. Smiling. "One of your kinks, is it?" The detective squeezed unpleasantly. "Like to hear them scream, I suppose?"

Duvakin was still numb. Chistoplotskii hadn't had his wife killed? The entire string of events that he had so laboriously teased from the weavings of fate . . . was simply chance?

And he was wrong?

Not about Edik, though, Duvakin understood. Edik had wanted him dead, Edik had *thought* he was dead, and Anya too. . . .

Angry, Duvakin turned to make the point even though the hands now grasping at him said that it was irrelevant.

"I didn't kill my daughter, my daughter—"

But Anya had now stepped forward, too, so that the light shone directly down on her forehead, making black caverns of her eyes and a triangle shadow beneath her nose. She flung her arms around

the minister, said clearly, "Hello, Igor, sweetie . . ." Then, squint-
ing against the blackness she couldn't see into, Anya said, louder,
"Dzhimi? This is the guy that gave me the two kilos, the ones that
were just parsley."

The minister looked down at Anya, stepped back with a look
of confusion changing to fright. He looked out into the hall, where
Kostya and Wolf were making their purposeful way toward the head
table.

And then, incredibly, Chistoplotskii turned and bolted toward
the private dining room and its door.

CHAPTER SEVENTEEN

L ate night again, the brilliance of the three bare bulbs overhead multiplied to the point of pain by the mirroring windows. Duvakin stared at the little galaxy of burning reflections until tears came. He should look away, but he needed that pain, just as he did the pain of his body—which had sat unshifting—how many hours?—on this chair. The pain was punishment; the pain reminded him this was no dream. And the pain was a welcome distraction; without it the only company he would have had was his heart. Which was bound round with barbed wire, rolled through ground glass.

He cradled his head in his hands.

Someone came in behind him, but he didn't look up, even as the person came around, took the seat opposite him.

"Tired, Ivan Palych? I don't blame you. . . . When the battle is over, the soldier can rest, eh? Some tea?"

Duvakin looked up, shook his head, even as he could imagine the blessed soothing warmth of tea sliding down his throat. Weren't his own thoughts punishment enough, without having to endure Tansybekov's praise and admiration as well?

The Kazakh looked weary, too, his eyes baggy and scratchy-looking, his beard now a stubble like that on his head. His uniform was rumpled and sweaty, and his hands shook slightly as he poured himself a small cup from the teapot he had brought in, but for all that, he was beaming.

"I hope you won't be offended, Ivan Palych," Tansybekov began cautiously, after much lip-smacking and throat-clearing that said how good the tea was, and how much the captain was stalling, "that I was so . . . well, unhelpful, I suppose, is the word. You see, ever since the declaration of sovereignty, MVD coming from outside . . ." He rearranged his pencils while he thought, then took another sip of tea. "What I'm saying is, in the first place, it's illegal, since we are a separate country, and in the second place, Sytykh is typical, if you know what I mean. So when you first showed up here, poking around . . . I guess what I'm trying to say is, I could kick myself, that we didn't . . ." Again the Kazakh faded off, then shrugged, raised his teacup high, in a salute. "A brilliant piece of criminal investigation, Comrade! Simply brilliant!"

"The minister confessed, then?" Duvakin asked, his voice as ashen as his face.

The captain put his cup down, twisting it slightly, as if undoing a combination lock. "Not in so many words, but the girl is very precise. . . ."

"A *girl*, against the word of a *minister*?" Even in his own crushed mood, Duvakin found that amusing enough to snort at.

The captain now smiled, pleased with himself. "It is not just her word. . . ."

Duvakin wasn't listening; instead he berated himself—again—for the fact that it had never occurred to him to inquire why it was Anya had known so well the price of narcotics. He understood now, of course. The merchant always knows the value of her goods.

When Duvakin failed to rise to his hint, the Kazakh's face showed a certain irritation, but let it pass, an allowance for Duvakin's mood. Like a fan returning from a close soccer match, though, he couldn't keep quiet for long. "Incredible, isn't it, that he would have done something so stupid, giving that girl the narcotics—"

"She didn't know he was a minister," Duvakin defended Anya hotly, before realizing the defense was nonsensical and subsiding back into himself once more, crushed by things more incredible than the fact that Chistoplotskii had given Anya two kilos of parsley, more incredible even than that what the girl had *asked* for was two kilos of hemp.

No, to Duvakin these paled beside the biggest shock of all: that Chistoplotskii and Anya had met through Galya.

So what had Chistoploskii given Galya? And in exchange for what?

Galya's evening trips in search for goods, her Sunday afternoons spent at a girlfriend's, her trips to the theater . . . Duvakin's brain flung up each memory like an accusation in court, like a stab in the heart.

Had some of those explanations been false?

Worse, had *any* of those explanations been true?

And the goods, the scarce goods that she never explained where she got. The rug, the television, the refrigerator. Lord, his own clothes . . . So had he been wearing the evidence of his own horns?

Horns? Mother of God, Duvakin berated himself angrily, for the seven hundredth or eight hundredth time, to wear *horns* didn't you have to . . . Well, it wasn't as though he and Galya had been terribly intimate in those last years, and even in the beginning she had never been . . . shy. He remembered how they had met in Magadan, when she had offered herself to him there in the clinic, almost on the examining table. Like a medical procedure, you could have thought . . . And all that was *before* she had conquered Moscow.

Duvakin made an unsatisfactory partner for the captain's elated postmortem, but Tansybekov had no one else and was too inspired still to submit to Duvakin's much gloomier mood. He tried again. "It's Mordachkin that's really the key, though. He doesn't have a chance now."

Duvakin pulled his mind away from its endless shuffling through the past, the dredging up of years of absences, comments, looks . . . Just discovering as false one of the major assumptions of his life, he had now to reexamine every knot, every fiber of that life, to see whether any still held. When had they met, his wife and the minister? Surely not before she and Duvakin had? So he hadn't been wrong in trusting Galya when they first came to Moscow, had he? But . . .

"To do what?" He did his best to be a weary hero.

"Keep control of his farm."

"His farm?" Duvakin blinked dumbly, aware that Tansybekov expected him to understand what he meant, painfully aware that he didn't.

"His supposed private *farm*." Tansybekov was scornful and mocking, but his eyes studied Duvakin, wondering. "Out at Tenga . . ."

"So it was his . . ." Duvakin nodded, mumbled to himself. "The hemp, I mean. That he was growing." He tried to give the impression he cared, but Duvakin knew he didn't.

But Tansybekov was now looking at him as if he had two heads. "There was no hemp—you knew that. That was what got Ermolov . . . what it got him. Ermolov wanted to do a deal with Edik, but then he found out it wasn't hemp they were growing, and so Edik—" Tansybekov laughed, ran his hand over his head with a noise like sandpaper. "Did a deal on him!"

Duvakin stared uncomprehending at Tansybekov, as if the man had just addressed him in Kazakh.

Seriously discomfited, the captain looked away, moved his pencils into precise forms. A square, a rhombus, part of a star. "I thought you knew that. Edik's people were spreading the hemp story around just to encourage people to stay away."

Somewhere in Duvakin's tired and distracted head it registered: How odd to put about false stories of growing narcotics illegally, to protect . . .

What?

Now Tansybekov was fully confused. "You are tired, of course, Ivan Palych . . ." he began hesitantly. "I am referring to the new oil field, out at Tenga, where Edik was renting the land. Through a number of people, of course. He controlled almost fifty square *kilometers* in all."

"A lot of land," Duvakin said, because he must say something. Then he recrossed his legs, then bent over them again, almost huddling, too miserable to pretend that he understood what the militia commander was talking about. Or cared.

"Ivan Palych," Tansybekov said intently, as if Duvakin's behavior was beginning to border on insulting. "You're from Moscow; perhaps you don't appreciate what this *means*. That Tenga field is the biggest new oil deposit that geologists have turned up

since the sixties. And more secret than the space center at Baiko-
nur. The Americans want to develop the field and will pay millions to do so. *Dollars*. Millions and millions of *dollars*. Everyone
was trying to control that field—Moscow, Alma-Ata, the Russian
parliament, the council . . . Edik got wind of it, though, and
managed to beat most of them to get control. We knew about
Edik and his people, of course." Tansybekov tried to suppress his
pleased grin with a businesslike scowl. "Taking out all those
leases, for 'private agriculture.' Ha! Most of those boys wouldn't
know what end of the sheep you put the hay into . . . so I always
wondered."

"You never thought to see what they were *growing* out there?"
Duvakin looked up, his voice dripping acid. He recalled the windy
hill on which they had stood, the scratched rows down below, the
huge expanse beyond.

The captain turned from the window, a glaze of chill in his
eyes now. "It is not our Kazakhs who wanted to buy hemp," Tansybekov said softly, then smiled, with a bit of an effort. "But I know
what you mean. . . . Of course we wondered about *anasha*. For almost a decade now, every fall, suddenly hundreds of teenagers decide
to go 'hiking,' even out in these steppes. So yes, I had thought
about it, but it isn't such an easy thing anymore, you know, to just
check. . . . We are a nation of laws now." Then he smiled. "But I
managed, here and there. Nothing more dangerous than a few
scrawny sheep. Grazing on top of a sea of oil."

Which Edik would have controlled, Duvakin realized dimly,
still indifferent to anything but his own misery. It was an idea that
he couldn't quite grasp—that all that oil, all that money, would
have *belonged* to Edik.

Except it wouldn't, really, because behind Edik stood Chistoplotskii.

Who was an oil geologist and would have known the oil was
there. Perhaps he had even discovered it himself, on expedition, in
his earlier days? And ever since he had waited, begging fate for the
chance to make that field his.

Not *wholly* his, of course. He would have needed a trusted
lieutenant. Someone local. Like Edik. Who could begin leasing the
land. "For agricultural purposes."

And Edik would have needed him. Someone influential, who could argue that the huge new oil field should be developed in a new and more profitable way. Privately, by foreigners. New thinking, new ways of working.

Which would make Chistoplotskii a very wealthy man.

Not in rubles, either.

In dollars.

Chistoplotskii would have become one of the wealthiest men in the world, Duvakin supposed. The idea was as remote to him as Africa.

"I must sleep, Captain," he murmured, his lips wooden.

"Of course, of course." The captain came around his desk hastily. "I will call for a driver; there is room at the ministry hotel." He already had the receiver in hand, then smiled. "Poor Colonel Sytykh had to change rooms rather suddenly. I put him in next to those boys. . . . Let them talk, eh?"

Duvakin looked at the windows, where a faint thread of dawn was inserting itself between night and the empty land. He fancied he could see the eternal iron birds of the pumps, endlessly dipping their beaks. Sytykh, and Dzhimi, and Wolf . . .

The dinner had become a melee, of course.

Kostya and Wolf had launched themselves over the table after Dzhimi, who had leaped on the table, running along it after Chistoplotskii. Surprisingly, it was the puffy boy who had proven fastest, maybe because the dark boy had broken the heel off his boot when he stopped to punch somebody who had been sitting next to Edik. Dzhimi had gotten a piece of the minister's jacket, but was then knocked down by Momish, who had stood to shout something at people on the other side of the horseshoe. These had leaped forward, too, knocking over their table and sending food, dishes, and bottles crashing into the middle of the room. Duvakin was surprised to see that the Azerbaijani still had so many supporters, but then understood from their wild grins as they flung themselves upon Edik's men that this quarrel must be ancient and familiar. Sytykh was yanking at Duvakin's arm as if wishing to remove it, not him, but then had stopped when a waiter suddenly brought his tray down on the Muscovite's head, before taking a swipe with it at

Duvakin. Duvakin gave the man a look of puzzled exasperation: Which damn side are you on? The man's happy smile, though, made clear it didn't matter; he was simply enjoying a good fight.

Duvakin could see Anya across the room, backed against the wall, making herself as small as possible in the flurry of flailing bodies, crashing plates. She looked so young, so vulnerable. . . .

Duvakin had reached her. Somehow.

"Come on, we've got to get out of here," he panted, pulling her toward where the minister had disappeared. There would be some sort of exit there. "That was clever, about the parsley," he panted.

"It was true," Anya had said grimly, though following readily enough, "and Dzhimi beat me black-and-blue for it, the son of a bitch."

"He gave you narcotics?" Duvakin had stopped dead, as if a glass wall had sprouted before him. "For *what?*"

"What do you think? For the usual!" she had spat angrily as they squeezed out the door and into the arms of an oversize Kazakh militiaman, knocking his cap awry. Grinning, the militiaman had carried Anya off to a waiting bus that had wire instead of windows, squeezing her in all sorts of unnecessary ways.

She soon had company enough.

Why the militia had been outside, Duvakin couldn't even wonder because he stood stunned by Anya's confession. Confession? How can you call it a confession? A confession means you know you did something wrong; Anya was just cursing a bad bargain.

In which she had tried to trade *narcotics* . . . for *the usual.*

Anya was a *putana.* A whore.

Duvakin's heart was as empty and ugly as the Novii Uzen landscape. He stood.

In the middle of his sixth decade, he had nothing. His wife was dead, and tonight her memory had become vile to him, a lie. The girl whom he had come to think of as a daughter was a common prostitute, a dealer in narcotics. And as for his faith in his country . . .

Suddenly a bright, steady flame of anger burst in Duvakin's chest.

"Captain, before I go . . ."

"You wish to speak to the girl?" The captain spoke with unexpected softness, prompting Duvakin to ask.

"She wants me to?"

"She's wondered . . ."

"Dearest Papulia." Duvakin recalled her letter bitterly. And "Why have you left me like an orphan?"

Mother of God, she'd played him like a *dudka*, a shepherd's pipe! Let her rot in her Kazakh cell!

"No, the minister. I want to ask Chistoplotskii something."

Chistoplotskii was important enough to have a cell to himself. On the other hand, it was without question a cell. Limestone walls, with black blossoms of mildew along the corners. A bucket in the corner, a light bulb in a wire cage on the ceiling, and an iron bed, bolted to the wall. The cell was, Duvakin noted, a little bigger than the room in the smoke house where he had passed nearly a week.

The minister sat, legs crossed, on the bed, his American shirt rolled up over finely chiseled wrists, the jacket of his American suit folded carefully, draped over the end of the bed.

"Moscow has informed you that you have made a mistake even your grandchildren are going to regret?" Chistoplotskii spoke to Tansybekov, not even bothering to so much as glance at Duvakin. His manner was the amused contempt of a caged tiger, aware of the bars but secure in the knowledge that given the slightest of opportunities, he will rip the man who cages him into bloody chunks of stew meat.

"Of course, Minister," Tansybekov said, in noticeably poorer Russian than he had just been speaking in his office. "Moscow is trying to be notified. But some very serious charges has been made, they must to be answer."

"By *him*?" Chistoplotskii unfurled an incredibly long arm to point a finger at Duvakin, flaunting the foreign wristwatch he had been allowed to keep, no doubt because all the militiamen were afraid that someone among them might steal it. "The man is a felon! And you believe *him* over a *minister*?" Chistoplotskii inquired, smiling, as one might ask a child if he still believed in Father Frost.

That assurance made Duvakin's angry flame flare brighter.

"Listen, *Minister*"—he tried to match Chistoplotskii's chill aplomb—"I want to know something—"

"No, Duvakin," the minister cut in, "let me ask first. How are you going to like Magadan again, eh?" He smiled. "Or maybe some-place even more remote?"

Duvakin couldn't help the slush of fear that washed along the inside of his gut, but he could hate himself for it. Let them send him anywhere, damn it! Wherever it was, it would still be *here*, inside this pus-drenched whore of a syphilitic empire.

"You shut up, *American*." He made the word sound as much like a slap in the face as he could. "Just tell me—sending me down here in the first place, what was the point? To get me out of the way so that you . . . and my wife . . . could be together?"

There it was, his shame laid out before the two men as if it were his member, withered, ineffectual, laughable. . . .

"Your *wife*!" The minister gaped. "Your *wife*? What would I want with your wife?" He laughed, leaning back on the bunk, not mindful of the flakes of old plaster, paint, and mildew that fluttered to his shoulders, stuck to his hair. "Christ, man, she was . . . Your wife? Ha!"

Duvakin felt a wash of relief, which he tried for a moment to resist, but then let pour over him. "Well, why did you send me down here, then?"

The minister was still laughing, his own anger, fear, exhaustion apparently now draining through what to him must seem an absur-dity of colossal proportion. "Because," he choked out, "because you're so damn . . . *lucky*!"

"I'm lucky?" Duvakin repeated, as stupidly as if the minister had said he was a Hottentot.

"As I've learned." The minister stopped laughing, rubbed his wrists as if the shadow of handcuffs had passed across them. Then he shrugged. "I always thought I was too, but . . ."

"Because I'm *lucky* you send me *here*? You put me in— There was a *building* fell on a man, they *shot* at me, there are *riots*— The man from Moscow, who you tried to have put me under arrest— This is *lucky*?" Duvakin was stunned.

The minister smiled, thinly. "Which of us is on what side of the bars?"

Duvakin understood the point, and understood, too, at that moment, that his file would say the same, only more so. He had survived the Red October business in Moscow, and then he had survived Magadan. And now he was surviving Novii Uzen. . . .

"I'm so lucky I'm the only lucky person in the entire ministry?" he asked bitterly. "You went through every file and you picked lucky me?"

"It was your wife." Chistoplotskii turned away, no longer interested in the conversation and unwilling to sully himself by speaking with people who dared, even for the moment, to be his jailers. "She talked about you, and the idea occurred to me: Maybe I can use that luck."

"When did she talk about me?" Duvakin asked, then, not thinking, took the minister's shoulder, shook it. "*When*, damn it?"

"At her clinic." He snatched the shoulder away, and turned with eyes blazing. Even angry, Duvakin knew enough to step back.

But he refused not to ask: "You went to a clinic for women's complaints?"

For the first time since they had entered the cell, the minister looked uncomfortable. He hunched in on himself, looked at his knee, then shrugged. "I have a lot of women friends."

"And you go with them to the gynecologist?" Duvakin shuddered, appalled. He used to leave the room whenever Galya happened to mention her work, or anything connected with it.

"Ha!" Tansybekov cut in unexpectedly, "Careful man! Probably *make* girls go, check no dirty! Smart!" He tapped his head sagely, still playing Stupid Kazakh for reasons that Duvakin couldn't make out.

The minister drew himself haughtily, betrayed by a blush on his pallid and now prickly cheeks. "You spend as much time overseas as I have, see some of the diseases I've seen, and *then* you laugh at a little elementary caution! You think AIDS is the worst thing you can get?"

"Probably peels apple before eat, too." The captain elbowed Duvakin, who somehow understood that the enigmatic Asian was struggling mightily to avoid laughing.

"Shakes hands with his gloves on!" Duvakin elbowed him back, getting a huge snort from the militia captain, who then grinned, catching Duvakin's eye.

"Does it with his fly still buttoned!" they shouted more or less together, then bent over laughing.

The minister's only answer was to pick up his suit jacket and throw it over his shoulders, like a shawl. The left coattail was partially ripped away.

What would Galya have said?

Duvakin just then understood that the barbed-wire noose about his heart had gone slack, the glistening shards of glass had been swept up. His mood rose, not quite soaring, but heading up. Definitely up. Because while he could imagine Galya and Chistoplottskii . . . in bed, and Chistoplotskii and Anya, too—too damn easy to imagine *that!*—what he could not imagine, though . . .

. . . was Galya with her own daughter in the stirrups, checking whether Anya was clean enough for Chistoplotskii's attentions.

"The girl!" he hooted. "She wouldn't do it, would she? Go to bed with you?"

"Bitch," the minister couldn't forbear muttering, after a moment's silence. Then he glared at Duvakin, at the captain. "Happy enough to take hemp for it, though, wasn't she?"

Tansybekov squared his shoulders, tilted his head back a bit, so that he looked implacable, stern. "I will remember what you say . . . in case there are any difficulties with the Tenga field."

The minister pulled the coat closer about himself. "Not likely, eh? Now that that venomous half-breed has sold *me* out."

The captain touched Duvakin's sleeve, tipped his head toward the door. Time to go. Duvakin nodded, turned, went toward the bolt-studded slab of crudely welded steel, the dark green paint bubbly with rust. For a second, Duvakin could imagine all too well what that door would sound like when it shut, and how it would feel from where Chistoplotskii sat.

And he was glad.

Then he remembered another question. "But who's going to take Momish's place?"

The Kazakh didn't let him finish the sentence, pushed him out, shut the door. Which clanged, just as Duvakin had imagined.

"Mordachkin," the captain said, softly for some reason, as he turned the key in the lock.

"Edik?" Duvakin was surprised. "But he's—"

"A venomous little half-breed?" The captain nodded. "I have to agree there. Your Russian comrade has a way with a phrase." He stepped off along the corridor, which was heavy with predawn silence.

Duvakin stayed where he was. "No, what I was going to say is, didn't Edik kill—"

With a speed that startled Duvakin, the captain was back in front of his face, glowering, his hand held up, almost touching Duvakin's lips. He cocked his head back.

"Exactly," Tansybekov said softly, then looked at the door of the cell they had just left. "And *he* still hasn't signed the letter of request to Alma-Ata that we drew up, so . . ." Tansybekov actually tapped Duvakin's lips now, and winked.

Duvakin followed numbly, trying to digest the fact that the Kazakh not only knew that Edik had killed Ermolov, but was worried that Mordachkin *wouldn't* be named Momish's replacement.

They passed through the bars set at the end of the corridor, the captain nodding at the guard, who unlocked before them, locked after. The guard was a Kazakh, too, as were the duty man upstairs, the few militiamen still around the station, the ones who would be coming on duty in a few hours. . . .

"Jesus Christ." Duvakin stopped again, disgusted. "The man is a murderer, and just because he's *half Kazakh* you are willing to have him replace . . . ?"

Weariness seemed to have overcome the captain, too. He rubbed his head, the stiff black hairs rasping. His eyes, when he met Duvakin's gaze, were no longer so friendly. "Yes, because he is half Kazakh, and a murderer. Because they take our oil and give us *this*." The captain spread his hands, embracing the dirty, run-down hallway, the cracked floor tiles, the plaster-flaking, damp-stained ceiling. And Duvakin somehow understood that he meant, as well, the windowless houses, the open settling ponds, the crowded apartments, the swirling dust, the empty stores, the dying children beyond. Then the captain smiled, weary and sad, like a man despairing of making himself understood in a foreign language. "Because Edik knows that he is also half Russian, and that *we* know he is a murderer. *This* administrator will do as the people of Novii Uzen ask him to, don't you think? *This* time the oil money will stay here, don't you agree?"

The question was plainly rhetorical, but as illumination seeped gently through his tired brain, Duvakin had to nod. Even smile. "I'd say Edik will make an ideal bureaucrat." Then, unexpectedly even to himself, Duvakin asked: "Listen . . . the girl. Could I . . . see her, too?" After a moment, he added, "Alone?"

CHAPTER **EIGHTEEN**

S, with the minister, you didn't . . . ?"

"I didn't know he was a minister, he was just some guy. . . . Mama liked him."

"Liked him?"

"*Jee-zuz, liked* him—he got things for her. Arranged things. And she was always willing to check for him . . . even late, I mean."

"*Check?*"

"His girls."

A long silence. "And you were never . . . ?"

Answering long silence. "Suppose I was? If I say no, you get me out of here? Yes, and I can rot? Okay, no, my God, such a thing would be unthinkable, for a nice girl like me, a virgin since the age of twelve! You happy now?"

"So you did . . ." Duvakin felt depression tumbling back on him, like a mountain of stale laundry.

Anya turned away from the window; the captain had given them his office.

"As it happens, I can't stand old men who are always pawing and drooling, and I can't stand men who think that everybody's a whore, you just have to find the right price! But what business is it of yours who I—"

"You don't have to tell me!" Duvakin leaped up, not wishing to hear the verb. "You're right!"

The girl stalked over angrily from the window, to grab him by both ears, forcing his face to center on hers. "You listen to me now, because this is important," she said, tugging hard enough to bring tears to his eyes. "You can leave me here, just like you did back in Moscow, or you can take me with you, wherever you're going to go after this. You do what you think is right. But whatever you do, you *don't* do it on account of who I let in between my sheets. You didn't ask *me* before you got in between Mama's sheets, I'm not going to ask *you* before I let someone in between mine. Understood?" She gave a final yank, then pushed him away.

Duvakin's ears flamed, and his eyes were liquid with the tears the pain had brought, but he kept his hands at his sides, staring at the girl's back, which she had turned toward him. She was still in waitress's uniform, now crumpled and sweat-spotted by the events of the evening. The increasingly pale electrical light, the gathering dawn picked out the smudge of dirt on her neck, the thin tendons that fastened the close-cropped head to the thin, square shoulders. The blond part of her hair looked almost gray in this light, and the dark roots showed clearly, emphasized by the fuzz trailing down her cheeks, just a little too far and too dark to be proper, for a woman.

To be proper . . . People cared somehow that her skirt ended *here*, and not *here*, that her cheeks had hair to *there*, instead of stopping *there*. And nobody gave a blind man's blink that this girl, this *child*, had been pitched out into a world that had no history, no order, no shape. Who had helped her? Who had guided her? Not Galya: She was busy with her desires, her acquisitions. Not him: He was too angry, too diffident. Too . . . well, attracted . . .

Schools? An *internat* would teach her that the weak get eaten. The television? It would look her in the face and tell her black was white and day was night. Youth organizations? Other adults?

So what was left to shape her? The street, the courtyard, that god-awful music. Other kids born of a world as formless and empty as hers.

He thought of their three days on the roof, her quiet courage, her levelheadedness. Her willingness to smile and be cheerful even though she understood the world so well. Her love for her mother, though she knew all Galya's faults.

And, he now understood it—her attachment to him. Trying to make him be her father.

With difficulty he beat back a desire to hug her, understanding with an instinct he didn't realize he possessed that the hug would diminish and dull the respect for her that was growing within him. Christ, even if she hadn't started from nothing, the girl had done well. Better than he had!

But . . .

"The drugs . . ." he croaked. "Why . . . ?"

Anya turned partway around. "From him? Or in general?"

"From him. And in general. You were *selling* drugs."

"He forced them on me, said it was hemp. Trying to impress me, I suppose," she said wearily, "and I gave them to Dzhimi." She smiled crookedly. "Trying to impress *him*."

"*He* sold drugs."

"I thought I was in love with him. I wanted him to love me. I wanted . . . someone to love me. To be somebody that somebody loves." The words cut the deeper, for being said so matter-of-factly. Then, rummaging in the pockets of the uniform for cigarettes she didn't have, Anya asked, "Did you notice Kostya's boots?"

"I never knew for sure which was Kostya."

"The little dark one . . . Those are Mama's boots." Suddenly, with no movement from her, and no sound, tears were running down her cheeks, like water running over the edge of a tub too full.

It was the last piece, and it added up to nothing. Anya had chosen the wrong night to run away, to the wrong knight in armor, on the wrong white horse. Kostya and Wolf had seen the flat when they helped her move, and had come back to burgle it. Galya had come in, and been made meat. Chance. Formless, meaningless chance. Like everything else in Duvakin's life, like a piece of meaningless scum floating at the edge of some dead lake. Things bob up against him and then bob away, and he had no more control or direction than a rotting fish carcass, borne along by the indifferent waves.

The weight of fifty-three years, of an absent father and a dead mother, a lost love, a murdered wife, a war, a peace, a country that had made his life meaningless, all this drove him to a chair, where he collapsed. Had he had, at that moment, to ask himself why he was inhaling, he would have choked, because he could not have answered. Why live? His life had been nothing . . . nothing lay before him.

"Where do I go now, Papulia?" Anya's eyes were still weeping, but now her body was beginning to join in, a tremble in her arms, a quivering in her shoulders. "I made a mess of all this. . . . What do I do? Where do I go?"

What do any of us do? Duvakin looked at her, thinking this with a remote astonishment bordering on bitterness. Christ, you're twenty, you've got your whole life ahead of you, you've *made* your mistakes, you've learned, and now . . .

And you? Duvakin suddenly realized. What's holding *you* here?

Familiar voices of caution, of hesitancy, whispered, spoke, finally shrieked as he stood, crossed the captain's office. Don't do it! It will never work! They won't let you!

He touched the girl's arm, felt the warmth of her skin, the soft hair on her forearm.

"Come on . . ."

She looked up, eyes puddles. "Come on where?"

"Out of here. Back to Moscow."

"Just like that? The case against me? The guards?"

"Walk," Duvakin said, "just walk."

"Out of here, fine, but to Moscow?"

Duvakin grinned, feeling his blood pulsing freer and freer. "We'll take Momish's car. We'll drive."

The girl followed, hesitant and mistrustful—but, Duvakin could tell, wanting to trust. "Across the desert?"

"Across the desert, across the world if need be." Duvakin's pace was faster now. They were out the door, down the corridor. The few militiamen on duty looked up, indifferent.

"To do what?" The girl was beginning to smile, catching his mood.

"Live. Not wait anymore. Make this life . . . make it . . . ours. I don't know. I can't explain." He pushed open the door to the outside. With dawn the wind was rising, carrying the eternal grit of the Mangyshlak peninsula in the same swirls it had since time began. It was a world not yet formed, on a day not yet begun. He looked back at the girl. "I don't know what it is, but I know that I have to make it. Not be given it, not force someone else to make it for me. . . . Me, I have to do it. And I better start now."

The girl stepped outside, shivering in the predawn chill. "Want help?" she smiled.

He nodded. "Very much."

ABOUT THE AUTHOR

Soviet newspapers once insisted that Anthony
Olcott was a CIA agent whose mission was
to destroy the USSR with his fiction. In fact,
though, Olcott is simply a professor of Russian
whose idea of fun is to travel around the shards
of the Soviet empire. *Rough Beast* is his third
novel about Ivan Duvakin.